THE BLOOD OF THE BULL

BEING THE THIRD PART OF THE MEMOIRS OF THE BORGIA SIBYL

JO GRAHAM

PRAISE FOR JO GRAHAM

Praise for *The Blood of the Bull*

I love Jo Graham's Giulia Farnese and this is my favourite of the series yet! Graham's meticulous research not only sets the stage but shapes the story of a woman overlooked or reduced to a pope's bit of fluff in most historical accounts, despite the compelling contemporary evidence of her intellectual attainments and prominent role in the political world of early Renaissance Italy. Giulia's vivid personality, combined with Graham's blending of history and Renaissance magic, makes for a compelling story as the French king asserts his claim to Naples, bringing war to the Papal States on his march south. Giulia herself is in the thick of things, as historically she was, not merely reacting to events to survive but seizing control and shaping them, her dedication to the humanist side of the conflict with the Catholic hierarchy never wavering. Throughout this phase of her story we see her maturing, reassessing her choices and considering them from new angles, while finding a way to shape not only her own fate, but the course Rome will follow. I'm already impatient for the next install-ment in Giulia's saga. —K. V. Johansen, author of the *Gods of the Caravan Road* series and *The Wolf and the Wild King*

Exquisitely timely, Jo Graham's *The Blood of the Bull* continues this three-book historical fantasy centered around one of the most colorful and controversial popes in Renaissance history, as seen through the eyes of Giulia Farnese, concubine, and some say witch. This unputdownable novel is graceful, vivid, and passionate, infused with a kerygmatic hint of the numinous. —Sherwood Smith

Praise for *The Borgia Dove*

An insightful meditation on the rare alignment of true love and pure ambition—no one writes the Borgias like Jo Graham. —E. K. Johnston

The Borgia Dove is a very sensual and sensuous book, and readers of Graham before are not going to be surprised by this. Not just sexual and carnal pleasures, mind you, but the entire world is brought alive with all the senses in mind. We get to feel, to smell, to taste, to see and to touch the late 15th century Rome that Giulia Farnese inhabits. The charm of having breakfast with a friend, spreading soft cheese over bread. The deadly darkness of the streets of Rome at night. The elegant seductiveness of a dance and a party. And much more. Graham's *The Borgia Dove* brings us into Giulia's world, life, passions and desires in a fully immersive way. —Paul Weimer

The Borgia Dove is an intelligent, action-packed fantasy of vivid characters and well-researched history, filled with so much life. I know I won't be able to read about Rome in this era now without hearing Giulia's voice and seeing it through her eyes; Graham's character has become the real Giulia Farnese for me. I'm looking forward to the next in the series. —K.V. Johansen

I relished every word of *Borgia Dove*. Jo Graham paints these larger-than-life characters in a gloriously dynamic mural with grace and wit. —Sherwood Smith

Passion, intrigue, politics, and a papal election, all portrayed with Graham's trademark historical flair. I was planning to read this one slowly to savor every beautifully-chosen detail, but ended up finishing it in two days - I couldn't put it down.   Melissa Scott

Praise for *A Blackened Mirror*

Ancient Greek and Roman rituals lie like a palimpsest beneath the streets of a Rome resplendent in full Catholic regalia in this tale of ambition, desire, intrigue and enchantment. La Bella Farnese is a compelling heroine, and author Jo Graham casts her Renaissance spell with a deft hand. —Jacqueline Carey

Jo Graham's *A Blackened Mirror* showcases the breadth of her writing talents, taking her from her usual outer space writing haunts as of late to a quite different setting. The setting is a secret history of late 15th century Italy, and her heroine, La Belle Farnese herself, Giulia. In Graham's richly imagined secret history, Giulia's slow rise to the attention of her (eventual) most famous lover, the infamous Rodrigo Borgia, comes because of her abilities as a seer. Graham gives us a fresh and underappreciated perspective on the life and times of late 15th century Rome, with a strong heroine, rich worldbuilding and language clever, refined and immersibly readable. —Paul Weimer

A lush, addictive, and utterly compulsive read. —Stephanie Burgis

Once again, Graham proves herself a master of historical fantasy—this time, the Italian Renaissance, portrayed in all its glorious complexity. Giulia Farnese is the ideal protagonist, ardent, ambitious, sharp of wit and tongue, willing to risk everything. I devoured the book, and cannot wait for the rest of the series. —Melissa Scott

Jo Graham returns to magical history with a fresh take on some of Rome's most notorious. Witty and loving, with sharp edges in all the right places. —EK Johnston

Jo Graham skillfully brings life in Renaissance Rome and Italy to life, her sense of world-building and character development allows us to sit on the shoulders of the Borgias and their contemporaries and to delve into the complexities and struggles of the Renaissance. It is a highly enjoyable read, perfect for those who want to get to grips with the skullduggery of life in Renaissance Rome and the Curia. —Dr. Katharine Fellows, Oxford University

Vivid characters, especially the charming and indomitable young Giulia Farnese herself, bring to life a story of conspiracy, intrigue, and Renaissance magic—Jo Graham's *A Blackened Mirror* is a wonderful adventure. —K.V. Johansen

First edition published 2025
Copyright © 2025 by Jo Graham

For information, address
Candlemark & Gleam LLC,
2523 Solstice Trail, Chapel Hill, NC 27516
mes@candlemarkandgleam.com

Library of Congress Cataloguing-in-Publication Data
In Progress

ISBNs: print 978-1-952456-29-9,
ebook 978-1-952456-30-5

Cover art by Alexandra Torres Ferrer

Editors: Athena Andreadis, Melissa Scott

Proofreader: Patti Exster

www.candlemarkandgleam.com

CONTENTS

The bull is wreathed for the sacrifice, and the slayer too is ready.
-the Oracle at Delphi to Philip of Macedon

THE CHURCH HOURS

AS RECOGNIZED IN ROME IN THE 15TH CENTURY

In the Renaissance, timekeeping for people in cities depended on church bells which were rung at specific hours of the day. A day began at sunset and went around until sunset the next day. Here are the hours as referenced in *The Blood of the Bull*.

Vespers – the Vespers bells rang at sunset, whatever time that was. In other words, what time Vespers is varied depending on the season. In Rome that's as early as 4:41 at midwinter. On June 22, the midsummer's eve of the last chapter of the book, sunset is not until 8:49 pm.

Compline – an hour after Vespers. Thus, "dinner after Compline" means anything from 6:00 to 10:00!

Vigil – two hours after midnight, so approximately 2:00 am.

Lauds – at dawn, which again means that it moves around. At midwinter, that's 7:02 am. At midsummer, it's 5:01 am. Thus, on June 22 if you come home at Vigil and are up for Lauds, you get three hours sleep!

Prime – an hour after dawn, generally the beginning of the working day

Terce – the third our, or two hours after Prime

Sext – three hours later, so at midwinter it's about 1:00 pm and at midsummer at about 11:00 am, so noonish

PEOPLE, PLACES AND THINGS

Alfonzo, Prince of Naples – he is the heir apparent to the throne of Naples, son of King Ferrante and father of Prince Ferrandino and Sancia. He is a scholar and known as a kindly, bookish man.

Borgia, Cesare – the oldest son of Rodrigo Borgia and Vannozza dei Cattanei. Though only twenty-one, he was made a Cardinal a year after his father's accession. While he's always been intended for a career in the Church, he is a fine swordsman and soldier and would much prefer a different life.

Borgia, Gioffre – the youngest son of Rodrigo Borgia and Vannozza dei Cattanei. He is twelve years old and is about to make a marriage of state to Sancia of the Neapolitan royal family.

Borgia, Juan – the middle son of Rodrigo Borgia and Vannozza dei Cattanei. He is eighteen years old and engaged to a Spanish noblewoman who is a cousin of the queen. He is expected to take up family lands in Spain and serve the crown.

Borgia, Lucrezia – the daughter of Rodrigo Borgia and Vannozza dei Cattanei. At the beginning of The Blood of the Bull she is not quite fourteen years old and lives with Giulia Farnese and Adriana de Mila at Palazzo Santa Maria in Portico. While technically married to

Giovanni Sforza, the marriage is in name only and will not be consummated until later.

Borgia, Pedro Luis – Rodrigo Borgia's oldest son by a relationship before Vannozza, he was killed in service to the Spanish crown.

Borgia, Rodrigo (Pope Alexander VI) – Now crowned as pope, he is a longtime leader of the Humanist faction in the Vatican despite being Spanish and a foreigner. His election was a triumph for the Humanists, and he immediately took controversial actions, including allowing asylum to Jews from Spain fleeing the Inquisition, pardoning or acquitting humanist authors accused of heresy, and allowing women to plead cases before the papal law courts. He is hated by the Traditionalist faction led by Cardinal della Rovere, who lost the election and says it was invalid. He is the father of Cesare, Lucrezia and Juan Borgia. He is also the lover of Giulia Farnese and the father of her baby daughter Laura.

Bracciano – a major fortress a day's ride from Rome held by the powerful Orsini family as the personal property of the head of the family, Virginio Orsini, known as Lord Bracciano.

Burchard, Johann – chronicler of the papal court

Caetani, Giovanna – Now holding the castle of Montalto, she is the widow of Pier Luigi Farnese and the mother of Giulia and her brothers and sister.

Canale, Carlo – Vannozza dei Cattanei's husband

Carafa, Cardinal Oliviero – One of the leaders of the Humanist Faction in the College of Cardinals, he is a Neapolitan nobleman who has served for decades. He is regarded as a leading intellectual with one of the finest personal libraries in Rome.

Cardinal – the highest officials of the Catholic Church besides the pope, they are appointed for life to the College of Cardinals. It is their vote that elects one of their peers to be pope.

Charles VIII, King of France – age twenty-three, he has outgrown the regency that ruled in his name until he was twenty-one and now wishes to make a name for himself as a warrior king. He intends to press his claim to the Kingdom of Naples when King Ferrante dies.

Colonna – one of the great families of Rome

Conclave – the mechanism by which a new pope is elected. When a pope dies, the cardinals go into conclave and vote on his successor. A 2/3 majority of the present and voting cardinals is required to win the election.

Condottiero – a mercenary soldier of purportedly noble birth who sells his sword and supposed military acumen to the highest bidder.

Cybo, Franchesetto – a Roman nobleman, the illegitimate son of Pope Innocent VIII

D'Allegre, Captain Yves – a French cavalry commander in the service of King Charles VIII

De Bastian, Giani – a young Venetian nobleman on the staff of the Venetian ambassador

De Michelis, Fiammetta – currently the foremost courtesan of Rome, and something of a celebrity in her own right. She became the concubine of Cardinal Piccolomini when she was thirteen, and he died two years later leaving her a fortune. She has an elegant house in town where she entertains fashionably and lavishly and chooses her patrons according to her own tastes. She has befriended Giulia at Rodrigo's request. She has now begun a relationship with Cesare Borgia.

De Mila, Adriana – Rodrigo Borgia's cousin, widow of Ludovico Orsini and stepmother to Orsino Orsini. She currently lives with Giulia and Lucrezia at Palazzo Santa Maria in Portico to chaperone Lucrezia.

Dei Cattanei, Vannozza – once the foremost courtesan of Rome, she became the concubine of Rodrigo Borgia more than twenty years ago. They had four children together before they parted. She is now happily married to Carlo Canale and has a considerable business as a real estate manager and owner of a working vineyard.

Della Rovere, Cardinal Giuliano – Papal Legate to France, staunch Traditionalist, and one of the most powerful cardinals, he was considered a leading contender for the papacy when Pope Innocent died. However, he did not win the election and has since said that it was illegitimate and tainted by scandal. He has gone to France to persuade the King of France to intervene.

Erythrean Sibyl – one of the sibyls of the ancient world, she was a series of women who served as an oracle in Asia Minor "from before the Trojan War" who foresaw both Alexander the Great and Jesus Christ. In *Black Ships*, this is the shrine of the Lady of the Dead that Gull would have been pledged to if she had not been born in exile.

Farnese, Alessandro – the oldest son of Pier Luigi Farnese and Giovanna Caetani, now twenty-four. His parents managed to afford a good education for him at the University of Pisa so that he could have a career in the Church. A year ago he was one of the first group of cardinals elevated by Rodrigo Borgia.

Farnese, Amadeo – the youngest son of Pier Luigi Farnese and Giovanna Caetani, he died in 1487 at the age of not quite two.

Farnese, Angelo – the third son of Pier Luigi Farnese and Giovanna Caetani, he is twelve years old.

Farnese, Bartolemeo – the second son of Pier Luigi Farnese and Giovanna Caetani, he is fifteen years old.

Farnese, Giulia – a natural seer, a young woman born with the gifts of the ancient sibyls, she is the mistress of Pope Alexander VI, Rodrigo Borgia, and uncrowned queen of a city state. She is the oldest daughter of Pier Luigi Farnese and Giovanna Caetani and was married to Orsino Orsini in an arranged marriage five years ago. It was kept unconsummated to preserve her abilities as a virgin Dove for his kinsman, Lord Bracciano. Giulia thwarted Bracciano's plans and become the mistress of Cardinal Rodrigo Borgia. A year ago their daughter, Laura, was born.

Farnese, Girolama – the youngest daughter of Pier Luigi Farnese and Giovanna Caetani, she is not quite seven years old.

Farnese, Pier Luigi – the former Lord of Montalto, father of Giulia and her brothers and sister. He had been a condottiero for many years before he inherited Montalto unexpectedly at the age of 39. He died of the summer sickness in 1487.

Ferrandino, Prince of Naples – He is the twenty-four year old grandson of King Ferrante and is known as a chivalrous young knight. He is the half-brother of Sancia. His mother was the late Hippolyta Sforza, so he is also the nephew of Cardinal Ascanio Sforza and the Duke of Milan.

Ferrante, King of Naples – the ruthless and cruel king of Naples who has ruled for more than thirty years, he is now an elderly man suffering from cancer and is not expected to live long. His son and heir apparent is Prince Alfonzo, who is in his forties and a scholar who is much his father's opposite.

Ficino, Marsilio – a leading humanist writer, founder of the Neoplatonist movement. He was the tutor of Lorenzo de Medici and now leads an academy of young writers and artists in Florence. Among other things, he has translated and introduced the writings of Hermes Trismegistus, and as such is the father of Hermetic magic in the western magical tradition.

Gonfaloniere – the title of the general in charge of the Papal Armies

Humanist faction – a faction in the College of Cardinals that favors the expansion of Renaissance thought, including the translation of ancient pagan writers like Plato and Pliny and their inclusion in the curriculum of the universities. The Humanists support the spread of printing and literacy.

Medici – the ruling family of Florence, merchant bankers and patrons of the arts

Medici, Cardinal Giovanni de – a son of Lorenzo the Magnificent of Florence, he was made a cardinal at a young age because of his family's great wealth. He is the younger brother of Piero de Medici, the head of the family and the de facto ruler of Florence.

Medici, Giulio de – the illegitimate son of Lorenzo's brother, he is the sixteen year old cousin of Cardinal de Medici, who has promised to get him a position as a Vatican clerk.

Medici, Piero de – the oldest son of Lorenzo the Magnificent, he has inherited the Medici wealth and position in Florence. However, he is ineffectual and is failing to respond well to either the challenge posed by the French or by the street preacher Savonarola.

Miglio (plural = miglia) – a measure of distance, about a mile

Montalto – a small fortress north of Rome along the ancient Via Aurelia near the seashore

Nepi – a fortress belonging to Rodrigo Borgia as his personal holding

Osteria – a restaurant or tavern

Orsini – one of the great families of Rome

Orsini, Laura – Giulia and Rodrigo's baby daughter, theoretically the child of Guilia's husband Orsino.

Orsini, Cardinal Giovanni – one of the leading members of the powerful Orsini family and a Cardinal of the Catholic Church

Orsini, Orsino – a young man of the Orsini family, son of the late Ludovico Orsini and stepson of Adriana de Mila. He was married to Giulia Farnese in an arranged marriage five years ago, but for the last four years has lived at the estate of Vasanello, a great country property that was deeded to him by Cardinal Borgia.

Orsini, Virginio (Lord Bracciano) – head of the powerful Orsini family, he is the Lord of Bracciano, a substantial castle, and a wealthy landowner. He is also the Gonfaloniere of the Papal Armies, first appointed by Pope Innocent as his military commander.

Pico della Mirandola, Giovanni – a Florentine philosopher and thinker, student of Marsilio Ficino, and the teacher of Dionisio Treschi. He is considered one of the fathers of the western magical tradition due to his expansion of the teachings of Hermes Trismegistus into operative magic. Though charged with heresy, he was acquitted by Rodrigo Borgia. However, he has now become a follower of Savonarola.

Pluto – the Roman god of the underworld, the equivalent of the Greek Hades. He is also called Father Dis.

Pope Innocent VIII – born Giovanni Cybo, he was elected pope five years before the events of *A Blackened Mirror* and was in ill health for much of his reign. Part of the Traditionalist faction, he published the *Malleus Mallificarum*, which authorized the investigation and persecution of witchcraft, and encouraged the founding of the Spanish Inquisition. He died in July 1492 and the election that followed elected Cardinal Rodrigo Borgia as pope.

Proserpina – the Roman goddess of the underworld, the equivalent of the Greek Persephone. She is the spring maiden who descends to the underworld and then returns over and over, thus creating the cycle of the seasons.

Riario, Cardinal Raffaele – one of the youngest cardinals, he had been made a cardinal at the age of 16 by his uncle, the pope before Innocent VIII. Now thirty-two, he's a patron of the arts and a solid member of the Humanist Faction.

Sancia of Naples – age sixteen, she is the illegitimate daughter of Alfonzo, the prince and heir apparent to the throne of Naples. Her father has arranged for her to marry Gioffre Borgia to cement an alliance, though the marriage will not be consummated immediately because the groom is too young. Sancia is spirited and intelligent.

Sarfati, Chaya – a seventeen-year-old Jewish girl from Grenada, she has fled the Spanish Inquisition with her older brother and younger sister and now lives in Rome. She had hoped to be a teacher.

Sarfati, Mois – a young Jewish scholar from Grenada. Fleeing the Spanish Inquisition, he is now a refugee in Rome with his two younger sisters and has set up shop as a bookbinder.

Sarfati, Sincha – a fourteen-year-old Jewish girl from Grenada, she has fled the Spanish Inquisition with her older brother and sister. She loves fashion and wishes she could be a designer and seamstress of fine clothes.

Savonarola, Friar – Florentine monk and preacher who is a force in Florentine politics. He is extremely conservative and opposes the humanism of the Medici.

Sforza – one of the most powerful families of Italy

Sforza, Cardinal Ascanio – a member of the College of Cardinals from the powerful Sforza family, he is the brother of the Duke of Milan and the uncle of Prince Ferrandino of Naples, the King of Naples' grandson and heir.

Sforza, Giovanni – Lord of Pesaro, a town and castle on Italy's Adriatic coast, he is a member of the powerful Sforza family. Though he is illegitimate, he is the cousin of Cardinal Sforza and the Duke of Milan. He is twenty-five and known as an athlete and hunter. He is married in name only to Lucrezia Borgia, though the marriage has not been consummated.

Sforza, Duke Ludovico – Duke of Milan, he is the head of the powerful Sforza family. He is the older brother of Cardinal Ascanio Sforza. His younger sister, Hippolyta, was married to the prince and heir apparent of Naples, however she died two years ago.

Summer sickness – an endemic and serious disease, probably malaria

Tarocchi – a card game with four players that is the ancestor of bridge, but also the deck itself which is the precursor of the modern tarot deck

Traditionalist faction – a faction in the College of Cardinals which seeks to limit the spread of non-Christian ideas, including ancient pagan books and art. They oppose the translation of ancient works and the expansion of printing and literacy.

Treschi, Dionisio – a Florentine scholar and magician, now the client of Giulia Farnese in the official position of her secretary

Valencia – a city on the Mediterranean coast of Spain, part of the Kingdom of Aragon, Rodrigo Borgia's home city. He held the Archbishopric of Valencia for many years until he ceded it to his son, Cesare.

Vasanello – an estate north of Rome belonging to Orsino Orsini, Giulia's husband

Via Aurelia – the ancient Roman road going northward from Rome passing through Montalto on the way to Pisa

Xatavia – the small town outside Valencia where Rodrigo Borgia was born.

CHAPTER 1

Stories tell us that while Proserpina reigned below as Death's Bride, her mother sought her through the withering world above, and at last pled with the king of the gods for her return. Thus Proserpina was restored to sun and sky, emerging as the spring maiden wreathed in flowers to live in bower and field. The poets speak as though this was a good thing. But then, I doubt they asked Proserpina.

I have walked her path, and my choices are my own. For good or ill I have made my life, and if it is the processional path of the great mysteries, I did not know it at the time. This story begins as it should, with a wedding.

The bride, of course, was Lucrezia. Suffice it to say that as soon as Rodrigo was elevated as His Holiness Pope Alexander VI, Lucrezia did not lack for noble suitors. Rodrigo decided on Giovanni Sforza, Lord of Pesaro. He was twenty-four, the age of my brother Alessandro, and cut a fine figure at the hunt, tall and dark haired and hairy and muscular. He was Cardinal Ascanio Sforza's cousin. Originally illegitimate, he had been legitimized and inherited the town and estate of Pesaro when his father had no other living issue. They were married by proxy, then in person in a grand ceremony that lacked for no pomp or fine clothes, though because Lucrezia was just turning thirteen, Rodrigo stipulated in the contract that the marriage was not to be consummated until after her fourteenth birthday. In the meantime, Lucrezia would live with me, a respectable Orsini wife. Thus, there was a grand wedding and then Giovanni Sforza was sent back to Pesaro with the promise that he could collect his bride next year!

Of course I was not a respectable Orsini wife. I was the Pope's mistress. Our baby daughter, Laura, had never been seen by her purported father, my husband. And yet Laura never lacked for love or anything else. She knew her Papa. The house he had bought for us, Palazzo Santa Maria in Portico, backed up on the Vatican itself, accessible by an actual secret passage so that Rodrigo did not have to parade through the streets to visit us. Several times a week he would attend Vespers in St. Peter's Basilica and then excuse himself at the end of the service to the Choir Chapel, where he would slip into the robing room and through the hidden door. Divested of his grand vestments, he would take dinner in the pretty little sala with me, Lucrezia, and Donna Adriana, my mother-in-law and his cousin. As the months passed, Laura would often join us to her nurse's consternation, sitting up on Rodrigo's lap so that he could bounce her while we talked, or sitting on mine gnawing on a piece of bread from my plate. Lucrezia would attempt to shock us with some adventure she planned. I would bring up what I had learned from my various tutors, or the work of artists and writers that I stood as patron to, and Rodrigo would tell amusing stories of the foibles of various cardinals or the life of the Vatican. More serious conversations were saved for later, by the fire in my camera. They were not for Adriana's ears, and Lucrezia had no discretion.

We would lie in my big, curtained bed, my head on his left shoulder, while he sketched visions in the air above us, talking and talking and talking. Politics, gossip, art, history, ribald tales, theology, news from the cities of Italy and of the strange discoveries of Spanish explorers beyond the Ocean Sea – there were no boundaries to our conversations. Worlds were endless between us. We could be anyone for each other in the vessel of my bed. Merlin and Viviane, priest and succubus, Pluto and Proserpina, divine or filthy – all doors open to endless invention. He was God's before he was mine, but he was mine quite a lot.

People said I profited handsomely, and it was true that there was a red hat for my brother. In the summer of 1493, a year after his election, Rodrigo raised his first group of cardinals to the College. To no one's surprise, one was his eldest son, Cesare, the Bishop of Valencia, to his own old seat in consistory. Another was my brother, Alessandro. The new Cardinal Farnese had been a very competent Vatican clerk the last three years, and he was certainly not the youngest cardinal, but it was undeniable that he would not have been elevated at this point if he were not my brother. It wasn't worth telling anyone that I hadn't begged Rodrigo for it in some intimate circumstance, but that Alessandro was a useful and loyal follower, and factions are built on members. Rodrigo needed votes he could count on in the College.

And yet Lucrezia's was not the only wedding. Her youngest brother, Gioffre, had been betrothed to King Ferrante of Naples's illegitimate granddaughter, Sancia, and a proxy wedding done in the fall. The entire business was rendered slightly ridiculous by the fact that while Sancia was a young woman of sixteen, Gioffre was only eleven and looked about eight! The idea that he would bed her, much less rule over her, was simply silly.

Of course there was nothing to do about it. I did bring it up to Rodrigo in the confines of our bed. "What in the world were you thinking?" I asked. "She'll run circles around him and she'll have a lover long before he's ready. Surely this could have waited a year or two."

"We don't have a year or two, my sweet," he said, flopping on his back amid the pillows. I came to his side, curling up against him. "King Ferrante is very sick. Tumors, I understand. He's ruled nearly forty years and been a holy terror the entire time, but I'd be shocked if he lived another year. He needs this alliance for his son."

"But Prince Alfonso is a grown man and a reasonable scholar," I said. "Surely there's no doubt he's the heir or that he's fit to rule. And

Sancia's half-brother, Prince Ferrandino, is twenty-five and quite the swordsman. Ferrante has a son and grandson in the wings."

Rodrigo played with a strand of my long hair. "True. But the French have made a claim to Naples for a long time. In Ferrante's day they have hesitated to press it. Ferrante is both canny and cruel, and the King of France was a child when he came to the throne. But now King Charles is a young man and fancies himself a warrior king. He'll press his claim to Naples the moment Ferrante dies. The more ties Prince Alfonso has, the more likely he is to keep his throne. Marrying his daughter to Gioffre is advantageous, especially now that he's a widower." He twined the strand around his finger. "His late wife was Ascanio and Ludovico's sister, but she's dead and he can't count on Sforza support."

"So a papal alliance, even illegitimate child to illegitimate child, is worth a great deal."

"Just so," he said. "She's a beautiful girl and seems clever and well-spoken. She'll make Gioffre a good wife when he's grown up a bit. And he will grow, my dear."

"Without a doubt," I said.

"And now that Juan is settled...." Rodrigo's second son, Juan, had just left for Spain to take up the dukedom that Queen Isabella had given his elder half-brother, Pedro Luis, who had died in her service. She had also arranged a marriage for him with a noblewoman who was her cousin – triply blessed with youth, beauty, and being related to a sovereign queen! One could hope that Juan would make the most of extraordinary good fortune.

"And perhaps he will give you grandchildren soon," I said. He certainly wouldn't be getting them from Lucrezia or Gioffre in the near future.

"All of my sons are extraordinarily virile," he said smugly.

"They take after the old bull," I said.

In August the summer sickness came to Rome. Rodrigo was worried about Lucrezia and Laura, and so he decided the entire papal court would go to the country, accompanying us to his estate at Nepi. The castle of Nepi was an older castle, perhaps as old as Montalto where I had been born, but it was larger and much more well-constructed, a fine and sturdy fortress. It had been Rodrigo's personal property for some years, and everything showed a good master's hand. The stables were airy and well-kept, and so too were the chambers, with furniture that was comfortable rather than grand. My chamber was on an upper floor with a small window that looked out on the countryside, designed for defense rather than beauty, but the appointments of the room were new and as lovely as anyone might wish, the bed draped in velvet curtains that happened to be Farnese blue. One would suspect it had been made ready for me. I laughed with delight when I saw it the first day, the big fireplace and standing candlestands, the blue velvet and the walls washed in pale gold.

A door gave onto a small private room, a toilet chair and a copper bathing tub put neatly away to bring out before the fire when it was called for, shelves holding bathing sheets with lavender sachets. There was a second door, and I opened it.

The room beyond was the mirror of mine, the fireplace on the opposite wall with a pair of carved chairs with scarlet cushions before it, window and bed curtains in the same scarlet velvet, the bed itself monstrous dark wood piled high with pillows. Rodrigo's room. Nepi followed the old style of having the lord and lady's room adjoining rather than in different wings. He had put me in the lady's chamber. Well, I thought, going back into my room and closing the door, that was clear enough. Here I would live as though I were his lady.

The first morning he wakened me with a kiss at the lightening of the sky. "Get up, little dove!" he said. "We have places to be!"

I groaned and put a pillow over my head. "It's dawn, Rodrigo." Surely on the first day in the country one could sleep past dawn!

"Up!" He took the pillow away, and I opened my eyes to see him grinning like a boy, unshaven and cheerful. "Come on, sweetness. I thought you were a country girl."

"I am," I said, and sat up. He looked as though he had some treat planned, that infectious smile that no woman was immune to. "What am I dressing for?"

"Riding," he said, and helped me dress, doing up my hair in a snood as though he were my maid. I leaned back a moment against him. He was all but bursting with energy.

We rode the bounds of the estate, watching the sun rise from a copse on a hill that looked back toward the castle, the walls turning to gold in the new light as though the entire fortress had been dipped in gilt. Surrounded by fields and woods still in the deep, overripe colors of very late summer, it was the most beautiful thing imaginable. High above a hawk called. I glanced up, watching it dart through the light which did not touch us yet on the ground.

"I thought you would like to see this," Rodrigo said quietly.

"Yes," I said. We had paused stirrup to stirrup, and I reached across and took his hand.

We went back to his chamber, locked the door, and made love as the first light came in the windows. I dozed off after, barely aware that he got up and went about the day's business. When I woke again the sun was high and I reflected that it was an ideal beginning to a visit to the country.

Rodrigo unbent at Nepi. Of course the business of the Vatican followed him, and half of each day was given over to work, cloistered with secretary and clerk, various couriers coming and going twice daily to Rome. However, there was no need for vestments and miter in his own study, and certainly not about the grounds of Nepi. In a short coat over hose and doublet, velvet hat ornamented with a ruby brooch, he looked like a gentleman, not a cleric.

At nine months old, Laura had never been to the country before, but she was old enough to appreciate its beauties, at least garden and barns. She was fascinated by a calf who nosed at her curiously while she pulled up, holding onto my skirts. "It's a baby cow," I explained. "That's her mother, there. I'll wager she's the one who gives your milk every morning." The cow looked at me placidly, as though to say our babies could be friends.

I picked Laura up, and she leaned out of my arms to try to pat the calf on the head. "Baaa!" she chortled.

"That's a sheep," I said. "Cows say moo, not baa." She looked at me like I'd taken leave of my senses. "Cows say moo, sheep say baa, ducks say quack," I elaborated.

"And what does the bull say?" Rodrigo asked from the barn door.

"Usually that he has a lot of work to do," I said. He was smiling as though we were the most beautiful thing he'd ever seen.

"It's not easy being a bull," he said. He caught Laura out of my arms. "All that stomping around and snorting." He snorted for good measure, and Laura made a grab for his nose, giggling. She was a very wiggly baby.

"I can see it would be taxing," I said. He whispered something in Laura's ear and she giggled again. "What secrets are you telling her?"

"Asking if she's told you about the surprise," he said.

"She can't talk," I said.

"And therefore is ideal to keep secrets." He held her on his shoulder. "Come on, darling. Let's show your mama her surprise."

"I don't need a surprise," I said. Truly, the lovely rooms had been a lavish gift. I followed him and Laura out of the barn and around the corner to the stables.

"You need this one," he said. "You've been saying you wanted to hunt, so...."

I caught my breath. He'd stopped in front of a stall from which a head popped out, ears pricked forward curiously. It was a fine head, high crested, a light dapple-gray mare with intelligent eyes. She nickered a welcome. "Oh my goodness," I said. She was utterly lovely.

"Her name is Lilas," Rodrigo said. "She's a purebred Andalusian, acquired by my sister in Valencia just for you." He looked smug. "The hunting is excellent here. Your palfrey can't keep up with Memnon, but Lilas will."

"How utterly beautiful, Rodrigo!" I said, presenting my hand to Lilas for her to nose. "You are much too generous."

"It gives me pleasure to give you things," he shrugged. "And I can." Laura giggled again, reaching for Lilas. "No, Laura. Not a horse that doesn't know us yet. She's your mother's horse. When you are bigger, you will have one of your own."

Like Lucrezia, I thought. But Lucrezia professed that she hated hunting, so I did not imagine she would accompany us. "Welcome, Lilas." She lipped my palm. "You are a lovely lady."

Needless to say, Laura stayed with her nurse while we tore around the hills. I had not hunted in several years, and Rodrigo was not as young as he thought he was, so both of us overdid it and moaned a great deal later in pain rather than passion, but we laughed about it together, tangled in my blue bed.

AUTUMN CAME IN TRUTH, cooler days and a soft rain that drifted into peaceful nights. While the pace of entertaining at Nepi was calmer than in Rome, Rodrigo had planned a revel for the tenth day of October to celebrate the vendemmia, the grape harvest. Of course the theme was the Bacchanalia.

Cesare came out from Rome and brought Fiammetta, who I was delighted to spend time with, as I counted her a true friend. I hadn't expected that they would still be going a year later, but it seemed that they suited one another. I couldn't see it and neither could Rodrigo, though his reason was rich. "Don't you think she's a bit old for him?" he'd commented to me once.

I had simply stared at him. "Cesare and I are the same age," I said, "And you have decades on Fiammetta."

"It's not the same thing," he'd said, but not really crossly. Perhaps he just couldn't imagine being with Fiammetta anymore than I could imagine Cesare!

Now that Lucrezia was theoretically a married woman, though not actually one, she was allowed to attend provided Adriana kept a close watch on her and she retired early. I was relieved that Adriana was doing it rather than me; I had not really been able to unbend at a party since well before Laura was born, and I was looking forward to a bit of wildness. I had a maenad costume made, a sleeveless camisa with a ragged hem as though I had run through the woods, long ribbons to adorn my unbound hair which fell to my knees, and a little rod with a gilded pinecone on the end. It was quite racy. But then this was a party with friends, and it was not anywhere near the Vatican.

Rodrigo was Silenus, the tutor of Dionysos, to rule over prophetic ecstasy and drunken joy. He had a wreath of vine and a purple robe, a golden cup in his hand which he proclaimed must never be allowed to be empty. It was probably a good thing that Lucrezia was supposed to leave early. Cesare, in his leopardskin, certainly did not intend to. With his dark hair tangled and wild, he did look quite the Dionysos.

The gardens at Nepi were outside the curtain walls, and therefore were extensive. There were nooks and corners, bits of wall that enclosed kitchen gardens, an arbor and a fountain in a clipped herb knot, cedars that screened the gardens from fields and woods beyond, and a low ornamental wall to keep the livestock out of the gardens. The main refreshments and the musicians were set up in the French garden near the castle, but the party could wander about as it liked. I had no doubt that there would be plenty of wandering, even if the gardens were hardly a Thracian wilderness!

Rodrigo had invited so many people. I had expected thirty or so, but it seemed more like fifty as I greeted them. The steward would be frantic to make certain that important guests were appropriately housed. Or perhaps the costumes made it seem like more – there were satyrs everywhere and at least a dozen other maenads, including Fiammetta, in a daring tattered gown of blush-colored silk that seemed like she was wearing nothing at all at first glance, so transparent and clinging that her nipples showed dark beneath the drapery. I wouldn't have worn anything quite that sheer, though I did now wonder if the white linen showed more than I expected.

Well, if it did, it was too late, I thought, greeting Cardinal Riario and his Emanuela with a kiss. Riario was very much in favor with Rodrigo just now, having voted for him last year despite his cousin's objections. Emanuela had a daughter just two months younger than Laura, and she was very congenial company, though they had not brought little Isabella but left her in Rome with her nurse. Emanuela dragged me off immediately to tell me how worried she was, as she hadn't been away from her overnight before, but Raffaele had said that she'd be fine and she'd hardly know they were gone and....

We were interrupted by some question about refreshments that the cook did not want to interrupt Rodrigo about. After six weeks, the servants deferred to me as the lady of the house. Was there supposed to be a meal for the grooms and ostlers who were staying in tents along the picket lines? Between riding horses and carriages, there were nearly a hundred horses in addition to approximately a hundred and fifty servants that came with number of guests, and even a great estate like Nepi could not add a hundred horses to the stables. Only the finest riding horses were accommodated. The rest were on picket lines in the field, attended to by their own grooms. It was a pleasant, dry autumn evening and they would take no harm. Yes, I replied, the grooms and ostlers should be fed a good plain dinner if they wished, though many of them had already made campfires and were planning to cook their own, but tomorrow's meals were their own responsibility. We were not planning to keep the entire crowd for a week!

By the time I was finished with the question, Emanuela had disappeared. Lit only by torches and lanterns, what was by day a pretty but ordinary place became mysterious. Shadows leaped in the garden, tall shapely cedars standing like spades, a serrated border behind which laughter and music welled. I went to the gap in the trees and paused a moment. It was an enchantment. Some danced on the lawn, figures turning in the firelight. Bright colors glowed like jewels. Fire glanced off gold – a ring on a man's hand, the net in a woman's hair, the goblet Rodrigo held. He looked up as though I had called his name, eyes meeting mine across the crowd, dark as the night between stars. His mouth quirked a little, not quite a smile. There was that strangeness in him, Rodrigo and something else, like shadows moving underwater. I answered to it like a child to her father's voice or a dog to his master's hand.

I lifted my head, lips parting in a smile that showed teeth, and his expression changed. Well I could believe he could woo one away from civilized places to revel on the mountain! He did not fear the dark. I did not either.

I made my way among the revelers to his side, his left arm going around my waist as he talked to a young man I did not know. "My dear, this is Giulio de Medici. He has recently come from the university at Pisa and hopes for a career in the Church."

"The pleasure is mine," he said, bending over my hand. "I have seen Madonna Giulia at a distance, but never stepped within the sphere of her light."

I let him kiss my hand. "He has come with his cousin, Cardinal de Medici," Rodrigo said, which meant he hadn't been invited but had to be welcomed. No wonder the guest list had swelled!

"I hope you will enjoy our little festival," I said.

"I was present on the happy event of His Holiness's coronation," de Medici said. "I profess myself an admirer of his reforms."

Very wise to profess oneself an admirer of the Pope when one wished to begin a career in the Church, I thought. Still, factions are built on followers. "Have you met my brother, Cardinal Farnese?" I asked. "He attended the university at Pisa as well, though he completed his studies several years ago."

"I have not had the honor, Madonna," he said prettily. He was a chubby youth probably no more than sixteen, but he had good manners and wasn't quaking in his shoes at talking to Rodrigo, so that was a score.

"I will have to introduce you." I glanced around. "I know Alessandro is here somewhere as I saw his party arrive, but I confess I have not yet spoken to him."

"Er," de Medici said, and I wondered if he thought I meant to recommend him to my brother in more ways than one. Medici was Florentine, and Alessandro was particular in his friendships but not overly discreet. The thought would occur to him. "I would be delighted," he said gamely if not enthusiastically. I could hardly say that wasn't what I'd meant! Alessandro would have to straighten that out himself.

Rodrigo was smirking at my dilemma. He handed me a glass of wine from a passing servant. "Drink, darling. It can only improve matters," he said as Medici vanished into the crowd.

I took a deep drink. It was sweet and cool, only watered by half if that, with no spices added. One does not need to gild the lily. Rodrigo served good wine that needed no embellishment. It was my second glass. "I've made a muddle," I said.

"Nonsense, sweet," he said, leaning close to my ear, his body along mine. "The children will have to work out their own arrangements."

"Aren't you supposed to remember that sodomy is a sin?" I murmured, taking another sip.

"So is fornication." He nuzzled my temple. "But we are not counting sins tonight."

"Ah," I said. There was that burr in his voice that made a thrill run through me, like answering to like. If he dreamed of ecstasy in its dangerous forms, I was a willing maenad waiting for the drums.

We danced a turn or two, though the golden goblet never left his hand, and I took my shoes off to dance on the grass, then stood under the trees to cool off. The nights were not chilly yet. I had another glass, feeling the world take on a bright haze of delight. So beautiful, so bright, my dear friends and family, everyone joyful and light. Dionysos's magic touched us all. I leaned on Silenus's arm, Rodrigo telling a story expansively, the wreath of vine a little askew on his head. I had not truly indulged at a party since months before Laura was born, and it was good to let go. I had been so conscious of appearances, so careful. People said enough as it was, calling me the Bride of Christ if they were being vicious and the Whore of Babylon if they were being worse. Well, let them! I twined my arm around Rodrigo's, my arms bare in the thin costume, and watched him smile.

Now it was Cesare and Fiammetta talking with us. Cesare had a few days' growth of beard which definitely went with his costume. The freckles on Fiammetta's neck looked like gold dust.

"What a lovely pair of maenads," Rodrigo said. There was a glint in his eye.

"Maybe you should have Pinturicchio paint them," Cesare said. "You've had him do Giulia as the Madonna. How about a maenad next?"

"Or a succubus," Fiammetta said wickedly, licking her lower lip. "They run in packs too."

"Succubi on the walls of the Vatican?" Rodrigo looked as though he took it as a challenge. I felt myself blushing. I had certainly not ever mentioned anything to Fiammetta about our game of the little succubus. And yet the idea of a pack of succubi was enticing.

"If anyone would, it's you, Papa," Cesare said.

"A group of them, perhaps. Being friendly," Rodrigo said.

"How friendly?" Fiammetta asked. Her eyes met mine. There was a dare in them.

"Quite friendly," I said. "After all, they're succubi." I reached for Fiammetta with my other arm, hand on her bare shoulder, and she leaned in, smelling of orange flower water and smoke. Her lips, when I kissed them, tasted of new wine. I just brushed them with mine, feeling her smile, and then deepened it, Rodrigo's arm tightening around my waist.

"Oh my," he said.

Fiammetta's lips opened, the tip of her tongue teasing mine, a pulse suddenly throbbing between my legs. Kissing her, Rodrigo's arm around me, Cesare watching, where anyone could see…. She lifted her head, eyes bright with laughter. "Double treat?" she said to Cesare teasingly.

He looked at her smolderingly. "I'm not sure I'm sharing." He glanced at Rodrigo. "Not with Papa."

"I won't steal her away," Rodrigo said expansively. "But Giulia might. If she wants to."

I'm not sure what I would have said. Would I have gone aside with Fiammetta? Probably not with Cesare, as that would have been strange, but Rodrigo and Fiammetta or Fiammetta alone? In another heartbeat or two, almost certainly.

There was a crash, a sudden murmur of voices, and a man came pushing through the revelers. "Beast! Anti-pope!" he shouted, shoving Fiammetta, who stumbled into Cesare. He was brandishing a dagger with which he flew at Rodrigo.

Rodrigo threw up a defensive hand instinctively, catching the dagger on the golden cup, wine flying everywhere. The man shouted again, overbalancing and recovering for another thrust. I screamed, trying to get between them and instead catching an elbow in the ribs.

Cesare threw Fiammetta off and drew a knife. Of course he had one at a revel. Was Cesare ever unarmed? And yet he wasn't close enough. The man stabbed again for Rodrigo's chest.

Something hit him hard in the back of the knees and he fell forward, Rodrigo getting out of the way in an undignified scramble. Giulio de Medici had tackled him. They rolled on the ground. The man was armed, but Giulio was a big boy and a dogged wrestler. He got him down and Cesare stomped on the man's fingers, the dagger falling from his hand as he shrieked. In a moment they had him, a guard and two manservants running up belatedly.

The assassin was still yelling. "Beast! He is coming like the wind on the mountain! You will feel the wrath of the Lord!" They dragged him to his feet, an ordinary looking man in clothes that wouldn't be out of place on a servant. "The Hand of the Lord hangs over you! It hangs over us all. It will purify us with fire, and like the kings of Babylon you will fall before His wrath!"

Rodrigo had regained his composure and lost his vine wreath in the scuffle. "Who sent you?" he demanded.

"The Lord your God!" the man replied. "God sees you!" Another guard arrived, two of them holding his arms while Cesare stood by with knife in hand, Giulio de Medici getting to his feet and brushing himself off.

"What kind of assassin screams before he stabs?" Cesare asked. "You'd have had him if you'd come on quietly."

The man's eyes focused on Cesare. "Creature of darkness," he said. "Bastard demon son of the great beast."

"He's mad," Fiammetta said.

"Who sent you?" Rodrigo asked again.

The man's eyes fixed on me, staring as though he could look into my soul. Hazel eyes, wild and desperate. His voice was suddenly even. "The darkness is real."

I took a step closer, my feet bare on the grass. "So is the light," I said gently.

He spat at me, spittle landing on my skirts. "You will all burn and the sword of Cyrus will cleanse the land."

"Take him away," Rodrigo said to the guards, "and put him to the question." There was no Silenus, no lover limned with gold. He was a jowly middle-aged man in a preposterous costume stained with spilled wine, lines of cruelty around his mouth. "I'll know who sent him."

"I'll make sure of it," Cesare said, dark and lithe as a panther, the knife still in his hand, an unpleasant little smile on his face.

Around us the party had swirled to a stop, people staring and milling around, glasses in hand. The shifting shadows made them into goblins. We were all creatures of darkness, an unholy court. I closed my eyes, suddenly unsteady on my feet.

CHAPTER 2

I remember little of the rest of the party. I talked to a great many people. Alessandro wanted to know if I was well, and I assured him I'd taken no worse hurt than a push. It was hours before everyone settled down and I went up to check on Laura out of a sudden fear that made me run up the stairs like a ghost, a spirit in a torn camisa haunting a castle falling into ruins around me. Laura slept, her nurse in the bed beside the cradle, and I did not wake them.

I went instead to my room, still trying to shake the strangeness that enveloped me. I took off the costume, changing it for a clean camisa and the full, gold robe of figured velvet Rodrigo had given me three years ago. I stood before the mirror looking at my face, dark eyes and winged eyebrows like a hunting bird, soft ivory skin, full lips tinted with wine. Was this what a succubus looked like? Beautiful, treacherous, evil....

When I looked in the mirror, I saw fire.

The door opened and Rodrigo came in. He'd changed too, a doublet of Borgia red. He came to stand behind me, his arm around my waist, and his reflection in the mirror beside mine was ugly, a paunchy, swarthy face with a big nose and a shadow of dark beard, the banal face of the villain. I caught my breath. "What's wrong?" he asked.

"I don't know," I said. Was I caught in some illusion, or was this all illusions stripped away? "The assassin...."

"He's a lunatic," Rodrigo said bluntly. "A raving madman. He says voices told him to kill the Pope."

"Is he dead?" I asked. Nepi had a dungeon. It was a castle. It had a dungeon.

"No." Rodrigo shook his head. "But he'll have to be, won't he? Attempted assassination in front of dozens of witnesses." He dipped his face against my shoulder. "Ah, sweet."

"If he's a madman, you will seem to make too much of it if you hang him," I said. "Send him to the care of some remote monastery. It will not do for you to appear frightened of a man who has taken leave of his senses." In the mirror we were a disturbing picture, myself in gold, young and beautiful and coldly dangerous, Rodrigo in red, his jeweled hand around me resting on my breast possessively.

"I suppose I could do that," he said. He did not look up, just leaned his forehead on my shoulder. There was something tender in that touch. "He's Florentine. He's been listening to Friar Savonarola."

"Ah," I said. I had heard about him before, from my friend Dionisio Treschi particularly. "I thought he hated ancient books."

"He does. He hates a lot of things. Ancient books. Paintings. Comfortable furniture. Sodomites. Philosophy. Silk and velvet. Sex and procreation. And me, apparently." Rodrigo lifted his head, eyes meeting mine in the mirror. He looked more like himself. Or I saw more like myself. "He says that a new Cyrus the Great is coming to cleanse Babylon and that the people of Italy will burn in the fires of hell unless they repent and burn instead those things that tempt them to sin."

"Like loose women?" I asked.

He twined a strand of my hair around his finger. "Beauty is temptation. If there were no beauty, there would be no sin."

"And no joy," I said. I felt something stiffen within me, something knitting whole again. I had been open, receptive, vulnerable to what-ever hatred animated this poor madman. It had torn me like a knife though I took no physical wound.

"Does God desire happiness or suffering?" Rodrigo asked. "If one believes that He joys in pain, and that union can only be achieved by the transport of pain beyond pain…." He shook his head. "By that rationale, one can only know God at the moment of martyrdom."

"You are the Pope," I said. "Don't you know?"

"I don't pretend to know the mind of God," Rodrigo said. "And I think those who claim that God reveals His secret plans to them are deluded. If Friar Savonarola claims divine inspiration and sees demons everywhere, it is he who is led astray, either by pride or greed."

I took a deep breath. This was my Rodrigo. I was myself. I knew who I was and what I was doing. This was my life, my friends and my family who I loved, not some grotesque scene from hell. I could not be bent or turned by whatever power this was. I had a choice.

Rodrigo shrugged, still meeting my eyes over my shoulder in the mirror. "This wasn't how I wanted this evening to end."

"Well," I said, "we are together." I smiled at him. My own smile still had too many teeth, but his face was my own beloved again. I turned my back on the mirror, turned to him, and rested my forehead against his. "That is enough." And it was.

We slept. It was late when we retired, and it had been a long night. Nevertheless, I woke before dawn to Rodrigo moving around in the dark. "Lauds," he said. We were not close enough to hear any bell, but he was long accustomed to the hours. Yet instead of getting up, he settled back around me, holding me close with his chest against my back. No light came in through the drawn blue velvet bedcurtains.

Sober, I thought. And now I vibrated like a broken lute string, on edge and discordant, as though all the notes were still wrong. I lay with my eyes open in the dark. It wasn't that I hated the poor madman. The mad are not responsible for their deeds and believing that he heard voices telling him to kill the Pope was certainly madness. No, I felt no anger toward him. And yet....

"What are you thinking?" Rodrigo asked quietly.

"It's hard to put into words," I said. He waited, and I went on hesitantly. "You know how sometimes you're in a busy street and you see an old person who shivers in the heat of the day? And you wonder, is it just that they're old and ill, or does the summer sickness come and it takes the vulnerable first?"

"I suppose," he said, a neutral answer that could have been that he had no idea what I meant or that he hesitated lest I stray into things we had agreed not to discuss. But he had asked what I was thinking, and I would tell him unless he stopped me.

"It's like a sickness. A malaise. They say the eyes of love see no flaws, but what do the eyes of hate see?"

I felt him swallow, his arm tightening around me. "I don't know," he said.

"All turned to monsters. All twisted into darkness. And for a moment I wondered...." I stopped, then made myself go on, to look it in the face. "Was it that it stripped my illusions away so that at last I saw the truth? That I had been deluded and now I waked?"

"My darling, sometimes nightmares are just nightmares." His voice caught a little. "When people are afraid, they imagine monsters where there are only other people."

I closed my eyes. I had wanted him to say there were no monsters, even though I was old enough to know that there were. "Rodrigo."

"There is always someone trying to kill me. It's a fact of my life. I told you that years ago," he said. "That you would never know safety or peace with me."

"That is what it is to be a Borgia," I quoted. "I remember. And I agreed to it."

"I'm unreasonably crosswise because it spoiled this lovely thing," he said, a falsely light note in his voice. "It was a wonderful party."

And more besides. A masque, a performance, a rite, something riding like a boat on deeper currents. It was always thus with Rodrigo, whether he planned a Bacchanal or a solemn Mass. It reached. It touched. It made the unseen visible, or at least experienceable. Whether it was a hundred people or just us two, doors opened at his touch.

"How do you do it?" I asked quietly. "How do you make that happen?"

I hadn't expected him to answer. He never did. "I don't entirely know," Rodrigo said.

"Have you always been able to do it?" Was it part of his priesthood, I wondered? Or something fundamental that he brought to it? I had known many priests, but none who resonated as Rodrigo did, as though the world were the sounding box of an instrument he played.

"I suppose." He sounded thoughtful.

I ventured another question. "Have you ever known anyone like me?"

I felt him smile against my shoulder. "No. Not who could see what I'm doing the way you do, and who wanted to put words to it." As though I sang to a lute he played. His hand moved from my waist, sketching out forms in the air. "Reaching through, opening doors, yes. I've seen that often enough. But drawing in, encompassing...." He stopped, then went on. "A priest I knew when I was young. A troubadour I saw once. A lady who welcomed all into her house and who forged the most unlikely alliances. But this...."

Another player on the stage, another performer who picked up the line of the melody, echoing it back, embroidering it in a soprano line, weaving her voice around it.... "I would be your Viviane," I said. "Following after you with mask and mirror."

He kissed my shoulder lightly. "Are you a deadly trap then?"

"I don't know what I am," I said. "Am I your mask or your mirror?"

"Both."

I turned into his arms, sliding my arm under his, my hand against his back, the loose neck of his shirt letting me rest my hand on flesh. "It hurt when it broke. And now I feel it like ragged shards of glass, like pieces of broken wire worrying themselves against my flesh. I don't know how to fix it." It was strange to put words to what I felt. And yet I could still feel the wrongness, like a discordant note hanging in the air. I wondered if it affected everyone who had been there, to one degree or another, even if they didn't quite know why.

I couldn't see his face in the dark, only feel his movements. He tilted my head back, hand where the pulse welled, as though he bared my throat for the blade. "This, perhaps." Slow pressure, shifting against me, heavy and solid, pinning me beneath his weight, gathering my long hair in one hand. It was as though he picked up one strand, one shattered string, and plucked it, sounding it, sounding me. I rang like crystal, the note of desire running through me.

We were rarely rough. Inventive, often, but never coarse and rarely cruel, pushing one another into darker realms. And yet this called for that edge. A Bacchanalia isn't safe. It can't be and be true to the thing it is. Even between us, even in this room and the square of the bedcurtains, there had to be a frisson of jeopardy. It had to be that it could go wrong.

We struggled in the darkness among the bedcovers, but did I struggle to get away or to master him first? Raking him with my nails, grasping him by the organ – and then tables turned, scrambling to crawl away while he caught me, a finger sliding inside me as he held me by my pubic hair, sweating and straining wordlessly. Wet, open, legs around his waist, thumb on my sensitive flesh pushing me to the edge, every muscle clenching. I might have screamed. He might have bellowed like a bull, and even in this wildness I felt the warp and weft coming right, tattered edges knitting together. Utter darkness. I pushed him to the end, nails in the small of his back, tiny circles of welling blood under my fingers, a thrust that was almost pain. And then there was oblivion, lying nearly senseless, feeling the pounding of our hearts. His hair was wet with sweat.

"There, my dear," I said, and he laid his face against my breasts, heavy and rough with yesterday's beard, and I twined my fingers in his damp hair.

"Sweet angel," he said.

"Now I am an angel again," I said, closing my eyes.

"You are everything," he said, and I slept before he said anything else.

In the day we were kind to one another. We were gentle and generous. There was a lavish First Meal for our guests in the hall since the servants were still cleaning up in the garden. Between us we spoke to everyone. I saw their faces ease of tension they didn't realize they held, and by afternoon people were merrily preparing to leave or hoping to stay to dinner one more night.

"It's a good feed," I heard Giulio de Medici telling another young man as he prepared to settle in until the next day. Surely a Medici didn't need to sponge dinners! On the other hand, he was the illegitimate son of Lorenzo's dead brother rather than mainline family, so perhaps his allowance had ended when his uncle died the year before. Many men would have tossed such a child out, but Lorenzo had been known as the Magnificent for a reason. Whether anyone was supporting him now was a question. Well, Cardinal de Medici, obviously, who had brought him along in hopes of getting him a job in the Vatican. We owed him that much at least. I resolved to speak to Rodrigo about it if he hadn't done it already.

We did not speak of the other, of the masque gone wrong or anything we had said in the night. The flesh of our world had been sewn like a wound, and now we must let it heal. We had nothing to apologize to one another for.

Lucrezia was disappointed to have missed the entire business because she had been sent to bed early and complained to anyone who would hear. I told her of Giulio's heroism and suggested she should get the story from him. I saw them a bit later, sitting in the garden on a bench. He looked a bit gobsmacked to have a beautiful young woman not far off his age listening attentively to the tale of how he saved her father from a dire fate. I smiled and turned away. It was a harmless flirtation.

· · ·

WE DID NOT RETURN to Rome until the week before Advent, nearly upon Laura's first birthday. Her presents were lavish, if not always appropriate. Cesare gave her a pair of pearl earrings that would have looked nice on Lucrezia. I supposed someday they'd come in handy. The best, in Laura's opinion, was a large black bull made of stitched leather that was set upon a platform with wheels and a string so that she could ride the bull about while someone pulled it. The possible off-color jokes were legion, beginning with taking after her mother, but Laura adored it. She chortled and screamed while Lucrezia towed her about on the tiled floor. Needless to say, it was Rodrigo's gift.

In the year since Rodrigo had bought Palazzo Santa Maria in Portico I had made it into a haven. It was small, a little gem of a palazzo that had graceful rooms and was also extremely secure. He had given me free rein and a large sum of money to decorate it, and it was quite clear that while Adriana lived there as chaperone to Lucrezia and theoretically me, I was the mistress of the house. Adriana brought some of her things from her house to furnish her own suite, but I chose the furnishings for the rest of it, though there were a few things of Rodrigo's that came from the Vice-Chancellor's palazzo where he had lived before his election. I like to think I had good taste. Rodrigo liked the maximum in everything, but my tastes were somewhat more subdued, preferring lush comfort and expensive things that spoke for their own quality. A little Borgia red goes a long way. I decorated mainly in blue and green and a pale gold which set off the other colors admirably. In summer it seemed cool and comforting, while in winter it was a whisper of brighter days, sun and sky and the velvet green of deep woodlands or the pale, bluish green of the salt marshes near Montalto. In short, it was a respite from the Vatican's gilded everything, and Rodrigo proclaimed it a perfect sanctuary.

He needed one. On most days his schedule began at dawn, and if he was fortunate, finished after Compline services, which began an hour after sunset, meaning the day was some sixteen hours in summer. His enemies said he enjoyed himself too much. Well, it was fortunate he enjoyed the business of the Vatican, because he spent most of his time at it. It was rare for him to not hear Mass every day, and he celebrated it himself more often than most of his predecessors, but then that too was a pleasure to him. If, when all was done, he slipped off to have dinner with his family, what of it?

Of course I also had work to do. In Rome I did not spend my days in idleness waiting on his pleasure. In addition to Laura, I had my clients – writers, artists, craftsmen and women of all sorts, scholars and priests. Chief among them was Dr. Dionisio Treschi, natural philosopher, astrologer, and sometime magus. Carefully, for I thought him more daring than even I could countenance, I experimented with controlling what seemed to be my natural abilities as a sibyl. Could a woman learn magic? It seemed that one could.

I also arranged a great deal of unofficial access to His Holiness. Ambassadors and prelates went through official channels for the most part, but there were always reasons to wish a more private audience. Additionally, there were others who ought to come to his attention – artists in need of patronage, those who had recovered some ancient statue or simple drinking vessel that he would like to collect, parents who wanted their son recommended for a job or printers who sought approval for some written work. Those sorts of favors went through me. The world may run on patronage, but there were far too many demands for Rodrigo to even begin to hear them unless someone weeded them for him.

There was also a vast amount of entertaining and all the spectacles expected of a great court. While the official Vatican functions were overseen by Papal staff, including the redoubtable Burchard, masques and dinners were not technically on the Pope's schedule. Nor were all the arrangements for Lucrezia's marriage, or anything else touching on Lucrezia. At fourteen, she required more supervision than Laura! Laura, at least, stayed where she was put. Attempting to keep Lucrezia out of trouble was a good deal more work, and Rodrigo did not put his foot down unless it was truly egregious.

On one occasion during Carnival I returned home after attending a dinner with Rodrigo to find Lucrezia gone. It was midnight and Adriana was wringing her hands. "I have no idea! Cesare called for her and the next thing I knew, she'd left with him! What was I to do? It's not as though her brother's not allowed to call for her!"

"Of course not," I said. "She is not a prisoner." Cesare and Lucrezia had always been close as Alessandro and I were. Naturally he could visit her when he wished. "Cesare will let her come to no harm," I said soothingly. "It isn't as though she's abroad in the city at midnight by herself."

"I had no idea she'd left with him!" Adriana expostulated. "I don't know what Rodrigo will say."

"Probably nothing," I said. "It's true that the city is dangerous, but she's with Cesare." I had a sneaking suspicion that they might be at Fiammetta's house and that she might be having some kind of Carnival party. It hadn't escaped my notice that Rodrigo and I were invited to the wilder parties less often since Fiammetta and Cesare were together. Perhaps he found his father's presence discouraging.

"It's after midnight!"

"I'm sure Cesare will bring her home soon," I said, and settled down to wait, deeply annoyed that I couldn't go to bed.

The bells of St. Peter's were ringing Vigil when they arrived, Lucrezia looking flushed and smelling of smoke and wine. I left Adriana attempting to lecture Cesare, who wore leather and sword, while I took Lucrezia up to her rooms. "Where have you been?" I demanded. "Were you at Fiammetta's house? You know that you're not supposed to be there!"

"I was not at Fiammetta's house," Lucrezia said with a toss of her head. "And I don't see why I shouldn't be."

That was another topic. "Where were you?"

Lucrezia started unfastening her sleeves. "At a taverna with Cesare and his friends."

"Lucrezia!"

She raised her chin. "It was perfectly safe. Cesare and his friend Micheletto were with me the entire time. I was in the company of five of the finest swordsmen in Rome."

I put my fingers to my temples. "And what did you do in this taverna?"

"Drank wine. Sang songs. Listened to bawdy jests." She smirked. "Cesare even told them to mind their language around me. Gambled."

"Did you have any money?" I didn't think Lucrezia had anything left over from her cash allowance this month. She always spent it all in the first few days.

"A few soldi," she said. "And then they let me play for forfeits."

"What kind of forfeits?"

"I had to sit in Luca's lap when I lost to him. That's Luca di Aldi. He's eighteen and very, very strong. Such a nice little beard and blue eyes." Lucrezia blinked her own blue eyes at me. "Giulia, when you're sitting in a man's lap and he gets hard, does that mean you're attracting him?"

"Lucrezia!" I felt a furious blush rising. I often sat in Rodrigo's lap. "You are not supposed to be in tavernas sitting in soldier's laps! You are a virgin bride. At least I hope you are."

"Of course I am." She pursed her lips. "Cesare wouldn't even let me kiss Luca. He's such a spoilsport. Other girls get to kiss."

"Other girls are not the pope's daughter."

"Well I know it," Lucrezia said tartly. "I'm always different. The girls I go to school with are all noble born and some of them are nice and some of them are my friends, but nobody ever forgets that my mother is a courtesan and my father a priest. And then the girls Cesare knows are courtesans and they can do what they want and don't have marriages arranged for them with men who aren't even in Rome!" She threw her sleeves on the bed, and I went around behind her to unlace her dress. "I wish I were a courtesan like my mother."

I started unlacing. "My dear, your parents wanted a better life for you."

"I don't see what's wrong with my mother's life," Lucrezia said. "She did as she pleased until she was more than forty and then married Carlo who loves her. She owns her house and three rental properties and a vineyard in the country and she manages her businesses herself. Carlo doesn't tell her what to do. Papa never did." She turned to face me. "But Mama wants me to marry for 'financial security' and Papa wants me to marry for the good of the family. Maybe

I'd rather not! Maybe I'd rather take up with whoever I wanted. I'm pretty. I could find a protector easily enough. All of Cesare's friends except Micheletto were at my feet. Luca even said he'd be my slave and that he was chained by my eyes!"

I took a deep breath. She had not heard the worse talk among the courtesans. I was certain that Fiammetta didn't share those things with her. Fiammetta had been thirteen when she'd taken up with Cardinal Piccolomini, who hadn't ill-used her but she had a great deal to say in the company of women older than Lucrezia about his drooling and flabby stomach and endless fellatio to rouse his flagging appetite. And yes, she'd gotten a generous bequest and been her own woman before she was fifteen, but she'd paid for it. I heard a great deal of talk among Fiammetta's sisterhood, and I thanked the Virgin that I had found Rodrigo rather than a man like Simona's, who had broken her jaw in a rage.

"Men say a lot of things when they want you," I said. "But whether they mean them or not is entirely different."

"So you got my father under contract before you bedded him," Lucrezia said. "He was so desperate for you he'd have given you anything you wanted. I remember. I was there."

I had not been so calculating. I would have bedded him as precipitously as Lucrezia, had he not insisted that I consider him coldly and made a fair offer of concubinage. He had been the one thinking of financial security. Well, how should I expect Lucrezia to make any more sense than I had? She was much younger than I had been. "I am a concubine, not a courtesan," I said. "And you understand there is a legal difference?" She rolled her eyes and I went on. "I have the full financial support of one man to whom I am faithful. He provides my home, is the father of my child, and lives here as much as he may. I am not a prostitute, Lucrezia. I do not go with soldiers or sell my favors. Nor did your mother. You know well that your father bought her that lovely house and lived with her in it for fifteen years! When they ended, she kept it and all of the properties she'd bought as investments, and they agreed upon your education and your brothers'. But I am sure your mother knows well how uncertain it is to embark upon a career as a courtesan. She wants you married respectably to someone who will provide financial security."

"Just like a concubine!" Lucrezia said. "What's the difference between a wife and a concubine then? I am given to one man under contract as a virgin and then can hope I like him."

"The difference is that a wife is married in the eyes of God and in the Church, and her children are legitimate," I said. "And he cannot simply leave her and refuse to pay her support. A concubine can be deserted, and perhaps a court will rule in her favor or not. A wife has rights."

"To money," Lucrezia countered. "But not the right to leave him if she wants."

"No," I said. "They are yoked together whether they wish it or not."

"Orsino," she said. She knew my husband well.

"Yes." I pursed my lips. "He can't get rid of me or me of him, not now. But I have not seen him in four years, and that he exists is convenient. He makes me respectable, and your father gave a great estate into his ownership in exchange for me, so he has profited handsomely by it as well." I refrained from mentioning how much I had wished to be rid of Orsino. Lucrezia had known that. She'd lived in the house with us both during our year and a bit of unconsummated misery, and while she had been a child, she had certainly known how we had come to dislike one another. "And besides," I said, "you are already married. You and Giovanni Sforza had the wedding last year."

"It's unconsummated." Lucrezia tossed her head. "It could be annulled."

"Not if you are pregnant by some friend of Cesare's!" I exclaimed. "Lucrezia, you have to go to your husband's bed a virgin. That won't be so long. It's February. That will be the beginning of May. You need to wait two and a half months! When I think of the time I spent chewing on my fingers in frustrated virginity for more than a year...."

Lucrezia started giggling. "You were so frustrated that Papa looked good!"

"That is not what happened," I said.

"You've got to admit he's not young and dashing," Lucrezia said.

"And he's got a tummy, doesn't he? And it's been decades since he had a duel."

"Your father is very handsome and entirely to my taste," I said. "Now stop trying to embarrass me and change the subject! You cannot be a courtesan or a *condottiere* or anything else. You are a respectable married woman. Once the marriage is consummated and you have had a baby, then perhaps you and your husband can come to some friendly arrangement about lovers." She snorted. I decided to try a different tack. "Chances are he's no more excited about you than you are about him. You can be respectful partners."

"And he can sleep with whoever he wants." She grimaced. "Men can and I can't. All I want is to live! I want to go to parties and do what I want! I'm thirteen!"

I was losing my temper. "Well, you can't! You must behave yourself for two and a half months. If I have to forbid you to leave the house without a chaperone, I will."

"You're such a hypocrite!" Lucrezia yelled. "I hate you!"

"Good," I said, and stalked out, slamming the door behind me.

I stood in the hallway catching my breath. I should not have gotten angry. It was quiet in the hall below. I presumed Adriana had finished lecturing Cesare and sent him off. I went into my sala and shut the door, then through to my camera. I had let my maid, Tina, go to bed hours before, so I worked my way out of my gown myself. Lucrezia frustrated me, I thought, for all the same reasons that I loved her. She had never known cruelty. Yes, her parents had separated when she was six, but she had always had them both, and they were good parents who loved her. Vannozza was strict and Rodrigo lax, but both wanted the best for her. She had good tutors and a good school. She had friends and trips to the country and Adriana had cared for her as tenderly as if she had been her own mother. She had me and Laura. No one had ever beaten her or mistreated her. No tragedy had ever befallen her.

I put my gown over the chair for Tina to air in the morning, stopping to look at my face in the mirror. When I was Lucrezia's age, the summer sickness had come to Montalto. I had been one of the first sick, me and my grandmother. She had died while I was ill. My father had followed her a day and a half later. Then it was our steward, then the old priest, and seventeen other people in the village. And it was my baby brother Amadeo, twenty months old when he died in my arms. I had washed him and dressed him for the grave. My mother was too sick to, eight months gone in pregnancy. I thought I would lose her, going from the funeral to her room, watching her toss and turn in delirium in my parents' bed, her stomach moving with the flailing of the child within. I stood there, thirteen years old, wondering if I had the courage to try to take the baby if she died, and who would help me do it.

I didn't have to. She got better. Alessandro arrived from the university. He was just turned seventeen. We managed together. My baby sister was born. My mother was too weak and had no milk. I cut the little finger from one of my leather gloves, poked three holes in it, and fed Girolama goat's milk from it as a pap. The fevers waned. Autumn came, and we went on. I cooked and cleaned and took care of my brothers who were nine and six, and Alessandro and I leaned on each other. I tried not to think about the dead. I gave myself to the living.

I reached up, touching my face and looking at it in the mirror. I had been a virgin and had never been ill-used, but I had not come to Rodrigo unscarred. My scars were not in bed. Love was a joy and a consolation, giving wings to a girl too responsible and too old for her age. And I had been seventeen, not thirteen, when I said yes to his offer of concubinage. Well, a month short of seventeen, but all the same he was a man I had known more than a year who made an honest offer, not a soldier of eighteen with no means of caring for me who I'd met two hours before!

I took a deep breath. I should not be angry with Lucrezia. She didn't understand. She had been protected and now yearned to try her wings. I had tried mine with her father. Rodrigo gave me the means to soar. Education, love, art, power – he had promised those fruits – that I could become all I wanted to be. He did not even forbid me magic.

Or vocation. Or whatever these gifts were. He encouraged me. We explored together.

Of course Lucrezia wanted such a partnership. She was unlikely to find one at thirteen in an arranged marriage, but marriage was not the end, only the beginning. She had to be patient. And in the meantime, I had to watch her like a hawk.

CHAPTER 3

Needless to say, Rodrigo was not amused when he heard of these events. He put his foot down and told Lucrezia she would not leave the house except for school and then relented when she cried. I was annoyed. "How is she to take a punishment seriously if you do not stand by it so much as a day?" I said when we were alone in my rooms. "I am the one who is living with her! She has to obey some rules which are there for her protection."

"Oh, she's my baby," he said, putting his hands on my shoulders. "My little girl. And in three months she'll be gone to her new home with her husband. I will miss her."

I sighed. The things I loved about him most were also his worst flaws. He was indulgent to the point of folly. "This Luca di Aldi is the illegitimate son of a dead Colonna and is one of Cesare's bravos. Apparently, that's his employment."

"Spending time in taverns with Cesare is not a job," Rodrigo said. "He may have his wolf pack, but that's not a future for any woman, much less Lucrezia."

"She liked Giulio de Medici," I said.

"A Vatican clerk." Rodrigo had indeed come through with that.

"Alessandro says he's better at finance than Alessandro ever was," I said.

"He's a penniless Medici. The whole point of the Medici is that they're rich. He's for the Church. He can't marry her." Rodrigo kissed my forehead. "Besides, what's wrong with Giovanni Sforza? He's young, handsome, intelligent, rich and well-connected. What else does she want? It's not as though I can choose just any man. Most of the men who are all of those things are married!"

"I know," I said.

"I can hardly go around knocking off wives to make them eligible. I doubt God would pardon that even as excessive paternal affection." There was a quirk at the corner of his mouth.

"Well, no." I kissed the quirk. "I am fortunate I was able to choose."

"She can too. After she's married." He let go, pacing over beside the fire. It burned comfortingly, the February night being cold. "And there's Gioffre's wedding to get through as well. We've set the date in May."

"So soon?" I had thought he intended the betrothal to go on for some time. Gioffre had just turned twelve. There were not quite two years between him and Lucrezia. Sancia of Naples, his bride, was sixteen.

Rodrigo leaned against the mantel, his back to me, his red knee length robe trimmed with gray fur. "My sweet, Ferrante of Naples has died. King Alfonso wants this wedding as soon as possible. He needs the alliance."

I went to the table and poured myself a glass of wine. "King Charles intends to press his claim?"

I poured a second glass for him. "Why would he do that? It's a big risk. Doesn't he have problems with England? Why would he tie up his army in Italy?"

Rodrigo shrugged. "He thinks he can keep Henry of England busy by surreptitiously backing a rival claimant, a young man who says he's old King Edward's son Richard. He's got a reasonable claim – the Holy Roman Emperor has recognized him as Richard IV. Charles received him and if he's not giving him money, I'll eat my horse's crupper." I handed him the glass and he took it but didn't drink. "Which means Charles is free to pursue an Italian adventure." He looked into the depths of the cup. "And he has Cardinal della Rovere in Paris urging him on for his own reasons."

"Della Rovere again," I said. He had failed to whip up support for overturning the papal election which had chosen Rodrigo instead of him a year and a half ago. Neither Florence nor Venice saw sufficient advantage in something so risky.

"If Charles wants to press his claim to Naples, he has to pass through the Papal States on his way south. If he stopped off and deposed me on the way…." Rodrigo shrugged again. "…and installed a pope who would recognize his sovereign claim to Naples…."

"Which of course you won't," I said.

"How could I do that?" he said. "It would throw all of Italy into chaos. Alfonso is the clear heir, backed by Spain and the Holy Roman Emperor. If I begin delegitimizing kings, where does that end? That's a question every sovereign will ask. None of them would be able to trust the pope. It would damage the papacy irrevocably. Since the Avignon Captivity, we've rebuilt the reputation that we stand apart and above any secular government. Our power rests on integrity, strange as that is coupled with me." Rodrigo smiled.

"An honest scoundrel," I said.

"We can't possibly let France tell us to depose a king for them. Of course Alfonso is nervous and wants to be sure of us. Consequently, the wedding." He did take a drink. "So we must make it lovely, my darling. A play. A banquet. Perhaps a bullfight. We haven't done a bullfight lately. Alfonso must not think we are stinting Sancia in any way."

Clothes. Banquets. Plays. What an awful lot of work right on top of Lucrezia's business! I took a deep breath. "Well, which pieces do you need me to do?"

IN THE END, I got the wedding dinner and the play and Cesare got the bullfight, which was as well because I knew nothing about them.

Burchard, grumbling mightily, got the ceremony itself. Vannozza, equally thrilled, had the groom's clothing and the wedding procession. She utterly hated this kind of thing, but Gioffre was her son. Rodrigo had his fingers in everything.

It didn't help that this was two weeks after Giovanni Sforza was collecting his bride. It was almost like a second wedding for Lucrezia, feast and a masque and the bride seen to bed in the Vice-Chancellor's palazzo, the grand house now belonging to Cardinal Sforza where Rodrigo had lived when I had first known him. I thought with only a small sigh that Lucrezia's wedding night would be celebrated in the same room where mine had been. My marriage to Orsino had never been consummated. I counted my first night with Rodrigo as my true wedding. It was that in my heart even if it would never be such in the eyes of God or man.

A few days later Prince Ferrandino of Naples arrived with his half-sister, Sancia. The Neapolitans made a fine and martial entrance, horses with bright caparisons, knights with lances bedecked with noble pennants, and Ferrandino himself on a white horse, young and dark haired and handsome, all of twenty-five years old. His half-sister rode beside him rather than in a litter. She was as beautiful as I had heard, with black hair smooth as silk and a slender, athletic figure. She rode effortlessly, looking about her with curiosity. Her eyes lit when they fell on Cesare, who came out to make the official greeting. He did cut a fine figure in Borgia red and gold, the bull standard flying above him. Once again he wasn't wearing his cardinal's robes, but I supposed he was doing the honors as brother, not cardinal.

The prospect of essentially an entire month of bridal festivities involving the royal family of Naples and the Sforza attracted every noble house in Italy, it seemed. Every palazzo in town was open, and each night there were parties, revelries, plays, masques, dancing, and dinners. In the back streets there were revels of a lower kind, and the gambling houses and brothels were doing a fine business. I had never seen Rome more filled with light! Not even after the papal election had I seen such celebration.

Like a frantic dance before the dark, something whispered inside me, but I shoved it aside. It was not that I had abandoned my studies with Dionisio, but that there had been no time for them in weeks. Every moment was filled with something.

Rodrigo was so busy with audiences and noble guests and this deepening diplomatic crisis with France that I did not even see him for six days. When I did, he came to my bed late and fell asleep after a few drowsy caresses. I lay awake frustrated, listening to him snore. Well, he was tired, and how not? In the morning he had to be in consistory in the second hour, so he was gone just after dawn, seven hours in my house from start to finish. It was not conducive to carnal relations.

Not that I had much time either. Between Laura and all the rest of it, I ran from very early to very late. The play was the night before the wedding. Fortunately, I hired an experienced theater troupe for the play, which was Terence's *The Two Brothers*. It was a comedy that would appeal to all, with wild misunderstandings and a happy ending for everyone. The message that children are best reared with kindness rather than strictness would appeal to Rodrigo, and the idea of Pope as loving father rather than punisher was in keeping with his theological positions, which would surely be read into any production chosen. I was very careful that everything with his imprimatur consistently said what he wanted to say.

The wedding came off beautifully. I was present halfway back, behind royalty, ambassadors, cardinals, notables, and the Sforza, who had prominent places, including Lucrezia, who looked utterly lovely. I hadn't had a chance to talk to her privately since the bedding, but she seemed well satisfied. *Thank God*, I thought. If she were pleased in her husband, I could not be happier for her.

Needless to say, Gioffre's bedding was a farce. The procession went nicely. I was one of the ladies deputized to see the bride to her chamber in the middle of the afternoon. Sancia stripped off neatly with a little smirk – she was beautiful and she knew it, standing nude in the lavish bedroom, full breasted and slender, her hair unbound down her back. We tucked her between the sheets, the embroidered top hem around her waist, and she gave us all cheerful smiles. If she was virgin, I'd be surprised, but it wasn't as though Gioffre was actually expected to do her.

He came in trepidatiously, still wearing drawers but no shirt, escorted by the gentlemen, and was tucked into bed beside her. Cesare, for once in his red robes, blessed the happy couple. If his eyes seemed to linger a bit too long on Sancia's breasts, it was only to be expected. She smiled back at him guilelessly, clearly enjoying discomfiting a cardinal. Who could blame a young woman married to a child if she found his twenty-year-old brother more interesting?

We all went out, leaving them alone for fifteen minutes. Then they got up, dressed, and we all moved on to the bullfight and masque.

I HAD NEVER SEEN A BULLFIGHT. Needless to say, we had none in Montalto where I grew up, and during the last years of Pope Innocent's reign in Rome there had been few festivities. Rodrigo seemed determined to make up for lost time. As Vice-Chancellor his public entertainments had been famous. Now, with all the assets of the Vatican to call upon, they were simply spectacular.

The entire square in front of St. Peter's had been sanded for equestrian contests, a wooden wall nearly my height erected around the entire thing so that contests would stay in bounds, while the stands had been built behind them to quite a considerable height. Hung with bunting in the colors of all the great families who meant to compete in the events or cheer for one champion or another, it was a brave sight. Sforza blue and gold warred with Neapolitan red and blue and white and Orsini red and white, every other great family contributing, while the Borgia Bull reigned above all, red bull *passant* on a green field.

The first event was the ring joust, which I saw very little of because I was finishing preparations for the masque that night. Each champion wore full armor, as did their horses, and they flew down the marked course trying to catch suspended rings over their lance. Time mattered, but so did accuracy. I heard the cheers and gathered from them that Prince Ferrandino had gotten six out of six rings, thus carrying the day. I was still completing the arrangements when the bullfight was announced, and thus slipped into the stands late after the pageantry was completed and the fight was on in earnest.

The only bull I had known was our bull in Montalto. He was a sweet old boy named Pompey who required no more to handle or move from one pasture to another than me with an apple in my hand. Attended by our sheepdog, Fidelis, he would follow me as gently as a lamb for the promised reward and I had never had the slightest trouble with him. This bull was different. He had been bred to fight, and thus I suppose was as different from Pompey as Fidelis was from one of the mastiffs bred and trained for dogfighting. They beat the dogs to make them fierce, and I suppose the same had been done with the bull. He was enormous and angry, already smarting from a flesh wound to the back when I slid into my seat beside Rodrigo.

He glanced at me quickly. "Is everything well?"

"Yes," I said, settling my skirts. I glanced out at the three men who made a loose triangle around the bull, swords drawn. "Is that Cesare?" It was hard to mistake him. He stood loose-limbed, sword in a deceptively casual guard, his hair pulled back from his shoulders in a knot like a street fighter, only his rich red brocade doublet a nod to family and Church.

"It's a sport for a young *hidalgo* in Spain," Rodrigo said, his eyes on the bull. "To play the bull. To be *torero*...." His accent crept back when he was thinking of Spain, as it sometimes did, for all that he'd worked for decades at losing it.

"It looks like a good way to get trampled," I said as the bull made a run at one of the men who barely managed to get out of the way. However, it gave Cesare the opening he wanted, stepping in from the side graceful as a dancer, plunging the tip of his sword into the bull's flank.

It bellowed, turning on him, but Cesare backed out of the way, keeping the bull sideways to him in his pain and fury.

"Some do get trampled," Rodrigo said. He didn't sound unduly concerned. "All good sport."

So is boar hunting, I thought, *but at least that has purpose*. One can't let wild boar maraud around the countryside. They'll attack people, especially children. A bull will leave people alone and go about his own business unless you interfere with him.

"Did you do it?" I asked, and then knew from the twitch at the corner of his mouth that of course he had not. *Hidalgo*, he had said, gentlemen born of impeccable blood and considerable means. Rodrigo had been neither.

"I was for the Church," he said shortly. And then he jumped nearly to his feet, applauding as Cesare did whatever he did and managed to open another wound. The other men distracted the bull from countercharging, and Cesare bowed, straight backed, to his father and the rest of us in the Papal box, before turning back to the business at hand. The crowd shouted his name. More than one young woman threw flowers or ribbons to fall unheeded in the sand.

And yet by the time it was done I felt instead a strange detachment. The bull stumbled to his knees at last, bleeding from six wounds, and did not try to rise. Instead, he looked up at Cesare without hate or fear, just resignation in his large brown eyes beneath his gilded horns. One of the men goaded him, trying to get him to stand and make a last charge, but the bull simply waited. *A sacrifice*, I thought. It did not respond any longer to swords or pain, but just looked up at Cesare, and only closed its eyes a moment before the blow fell.

The crowd went wild with cheers as Cesare turned in triumph, yet I felt a cold horror sink over me. The bull's head flopped down in the dust, rivulets of blood pooling around it on the sand. *I had seen this*, I thought. *I saw this long ago in the tomb in Montalto, in Proserpina's pool. The bull, the sword of fine Toledo steel, the blood of the bull staining white stones....*

Ice filled me, a nameless dread. And yet all around me was sunshine, bright May morning and the celebrating crowd enjoying the spectacle.

Rodrigo was applauding. Cesare bowed, first to his father, and then to the ladies. He laughed then, turning his face up to the sun.

Lucrezia clapped wildly. "Isn't he amazing?" she gushed to her husband. "Cesare is the most gallant man in Rome."

"Very exciting," Giovanni said. He looked a little bored, though perhaps he was just tired. A bridegroom might be.

Lucrezia was all enthusiasm. "And there is a masque tonight! Isn't that wonderful? Upon a Biblical theme." She preened, as well a satisfied bride might. "I shall be Queen Esther and Giovanni will be the King of Persia. Who are you going to be, Papa?"

Rodrigo preened right back. "I am King David and Giulia is Bathsheba." I thought the costumes were a little too on the nose, but it was his idea.

Lucrezia laughed. "I thought you were going to be Methuselah!"

I saw the flash of real annoyance on Rodrigo's face. It wouldn't have been funny at dinner at home. It certainly wasn't in a public place in front of the Sforza and half the College. "Lucrezia, that is rude," I said. I took his hand and lifted it to my lips. "His Holiness will make an admirable King David."

"Does that make Laura into Solomon then?" She just would not let it go. "That seems odd."

"It is a costume for a masque, Lucrezia," I said.

"Who then shall be Absalom?" she said, glancing at her husband to see if he appreciated her wit.

I felt a sudden chill once again, a wind like a breath of cold though the sun was bright, King David rending his garments beside a corpse, shouting to a merciless God, 'Oh Absalom, my son, my son!' To say it was ill-omened was the least one could say. I could not shake this sense of dread.

"That is enough, Lucrezia," Rodrigo said. He got to his feet to depart the dais before the next bit of the festivities. A great many eyes followed him.

I caught at his wrist as he passed me. "Where are you going?" I whispered.

"The necessary," he said, shaking my hand off. "Don't cling."

I could not watch him go. It would only make his exit more conspicuous. I smiled serenely, facing forward to the boys bringing around the horses for the horse race.

"Ah, there's a fine Carthusian!" Giovanni said, pointing to a blood bay that danced, the groom holding onto its bridle. "Look at that conformation, Lucrezia. Have you ever seen such withers? He's got power in the jump, I'll warrant!"

"I suppose?" Lucrezia had no interest in horses.

"I'd like to know his bloodline," Giovanni said. "Who does he belong to?"

"I haven't the faintest," Lucrezia said.

"One of the d'Este family," I said. "Alphonso, I believe." A very handsome young man of about seventeen was gentling him now, dark head against the stallion's neck as he whispered to him. He wore d'Este blue, tall and lean, with broad shoulders that would doubtless fill out in time. As though he'd heard me speak his name, he looked up. His eyes slid from me to Lucrezia, and he bowed, hand on heart.

"He's married to my cousin, Anna," Giovanni said. "And his sister is married to Ludovico Sforza, the Duke of Milan." He gave the horse another admiring look. "He'll be Duke of Ferrara himself, after his father."

"You know bloodlines as well as horseflesh," I said.

"What's the difference?" Giovanni said. "It's true of animals and men alike. The sire is everything." Which was precisely the sentiment I expected from a legitimized bastard who held tenuous claim to a noble and powerful line.

There were two spots of color on Lucrezia's cheeks. "Does not the dam have anything to do with it?"

"She is a vessel," Giovanni said pompously. "The seed is the active principle in generation."

"I would dispute that," Lucrezia said. "Natural scientists say…."

"…not to argue with your lord and husband," I said, leaning in quietly. "In public, where it will harm him in others' opinions."

Lucrezia looked furious. "You argue with Papa!"

"I do not dispute with him in front of the court," I said, close enough to whisper. "There is ample time to tell him what I think in private. It lessens a man's stature to appear hen-pecked."

Lucrezia tossed her head. "Well, what do you think of that, then?"

Rodrigo was at the end of the row, bending down with a smile to listen to something said by a lovely blond. She was my age, petite and well-endowed, her gown showing a hint of cleavage, her hair the same reddish-gold as Vannozza's. Her lips were very pink, her teeth white, and she laughed, glancing up at him from beneath her eyelashes, tiny and pert and blushing. Rodrigo grinned, that feral, sensual smile that showed teeth.

"Her name is Emilia Vespucci," Lucrezia said. "Her husband is the Genoese ambassador. He's thirty years older. Pretty, don't you think?"

"She's a nice bird," Giovanni said, though it wasn't him who had been asked. "Blonds are the most beautiful, as everyone knows." Then he blinked. "Your pardon, Donna Giulia."

"You meant it as a gallantry to your bride," I said. Rodrigo was bending over her hand now, lingering longer than politeness required.

Lucrezia had perked up at that. "I am glad you think so," she said sweetly. "Perhaps you could tell me later how much you admire them."

"Didn't I just say it?" Giovanni asked.

Rodrigo admired blonds. He was certainly admiring this one. He offered her his hand to help her down the steps from the dais, and she took it with a simper. She bobbed a curtsy, and then turned, walking away behind the stands. He watched for a moment, until she was out of sight. I kept my face perfectly bland and agreeable as he rejoined us. "Did I miss anything?"

"The race is about to begin," I said.

Each of the riders was mounting up. Most of them carried a lady's colors, though the young d'Este did not. Someone was clearly asking him about it. He glanced around, then proclaimed loudly, "I ride for the pleasure of the bride!"

Lucrezia stood up, blushing. "Then, Sir Gallant Knight, will you wear my ribbon?" She loosed a yellow ribbon from her sleeve and held it out.

"It is my honor," he said, and rose in his stirrups to take it from her hand. He kissed it, then tied it through the gap in the buttons of his doublet, gold on blue.

Giovanni looked put out. "Lucrezia," he began.

"You are not riding," she said, and sat down. "I shall cheer for my champion."

With a flourish of trumpets, the race began.

CHAPTER 4

The masque that evening was held in the Vatican itself. I fed Laura before I dressed. At not quite eighteen months, she had many opinions, and her idea of what constituted acceptable food was changing daily. She had grown into a beautiful little girl with melting brown eyes and soft dark hair that had a distinct wave to it. In short, she looked like her father. She also had his stubbornness and his temper, something of a drawback when it came to eating appropriate meals. "No! No, no, no, no, no!" she shouted, pushing away a lovely bowl of bean soup with such force that it splashed over my hand. "Never!"

That made me laugh. "You will never eat bean soup? Never for the rest of your life?"

"Never," she said, looking me straight in the eye.

I put the bowl down where she couldn't reach it. "Then I suppose you can't watch me dress for the masque. Only girls who eat their dinner can watch me put on my costume."

Her brows knit exactly like Rodrigo's when he washed up on the shores of a conundrum. She looked up at me with enormous sincere eyes. "I eat some. Then I watch?"

"Humm," I said. "A bargain. That's a good opening to a negotiation. But you must eat at least half or it doesn't count."

"Whole costume," she said. She'd get the whole experience for half price.

"Done," I said, and inwardly shook my head. What was I going to do with her when she was Lucrezia's age?

People were used to our matching costumes by now. What had caused great comment two years ago was no longer worthy of more than a note. After all, "Giulia Farnese is still here" isn't news. Nor is "the Pope still has a concubine," and while the concept of David and Bathsheba was a bit pointed, our costumes weren't revealing at all.

Everyone wanted to talk to Rodrigo as usual, and there were a fair number who had something to say to me as well. I made certain that Rodrigo's glass came from the taster, not a serving man's tray, and got one myself before the crowd parted us.

"Bathsheba, I believe?" said a voice behind me, and I turned to greet Cardinal Orsini.

He wore his full red robes rather than a costume, and I curtsied neatly. "Your Eminence."

"Were you bathing on the roof?" he asked, the obvious Biblical reference which begged imagining me naked while I wore a costume that showed nothing.

"Alas, I fear not," I said. I smiled to soften the words. I did not dislike Cardinal Orsini, though he was part of the traditionalist faction. He had supported Rodrigo's election only because he had been well-paid to do so and because his own ambitions were clearly not going to bear fruit.

"How is our cousin, Uriah the Hittite?" he asked. This was a metaphor he just wasn't going to let go of, was it?

"Orsino is very happy at Vasanello," I said. "He enjoys the best health away from the river fevers."

"And anything else unsalutary," the Cardinal said, glancing toward the knot of people around Rodrigo.

"Indeed," I said, taking a sip of my wine. Rodrigo had certainly not threatened to kill Orsino. That would have been completely unnecessary. I had not even seen my husband since the day he'd taken the estate of Vasanello in exchange for me, Rodrigo buying my freedom with a castle. Adriana visited him at least twice a year, but I had never been there. The entire business with Orsino had resolved with nothing more violent than signing a contract. I supposed that by now, nearly four years later, there was a much more dramatic story circulating.

"I understand from my cousin, the Gonfaloniere, that he owes military service to Prince Ferrandino of Naples now," Cardinal Orsini said.

"I hadn't heard that." The last thing I wanted to talk about was Orsino. I cast about for someone to bring into the conversation. Fortunately a nearby plumed hat covered the head of someone I actually liked. I reached out, touching the man's sleeve and drawing him into the conversation. "Cardinal, have you met Maestro di Betto? He is better known as Pinturicchio, and is the master who is in charge of the new decoration of the Papal Apartments. Maestro, this is Cardinal Orsini."

Pinturicchio bowed neatly and then straightened. "I am greatly honored, Your Eminence." He was a small man, nearly a head shorter than I, with a plain face and intense dark eyes. He was a master indeed, capable of taking on a great commission like a six-room suite, with seven apprentices helping though he did all of the fine work himself. Rodrigo had hired him last summer after he'd moved his official residence out of the stuffy rooms the previous pope had used and into a new suite that had much more light and air. Pinturiccho's work was lovely.

"Maestro," the Cardinal said.

"May I say that I am so pleased to make Your Eminence's acquaintance?" Pinturicchio said.

"Very nice, yes." Clearly chatting with a painter wasn't to his taste. "Donna Giulia, another time."

"Of course, Your Eminence."

Pinturicchio put his head to the side with an ironic smile as the cardinal departed. "I'm not much of a catch at a party like this."

"You are a catch under all circumstances," I said. "Art is an aristocracy unto itself."

He laughed. "And that's why you're my favorite model. Who are you tonight?"

"Bathsheba," I said. "And please don't start."

He raised his hands in mock surrender. "One of His Holiness' less successful conceits?"

"You could say that." I was beginning to think that the costumes had been a bad idea from the start.

"I prefer you as the Madonna." He had painted me as the Virgin in the first of the six rooms, Laura on my lap with a little wizzer added, Rodrigo kneeling in full robes at my feet. It was a gorgeous Adoration of the Virgin. Laura had wiggled the entire time the maestro was sketching, trying to slide off my lap, rolling around, attempting to grab things, and generally not acting like a serene Christ Child. Rodrigo had tried to get her to behave, playing with her feet and singing counting rhymes to her toes while kneeling on a pillow. The resulting painting was beautiful, but I could not help but title it *Wiggly Holy Infant Swats Pope Playing With Toes.*

"I'm glad of that," I said.

"You have the face," he said, looking at me keenly. "Not just beauty, but something within that is imperishable. It is what His Holiness asked me to capture in you the first time I painted you. Young, and yet ancient, was how he phrased it. I knew what he meant."

I glanced away. To see the divine in a woman's face, to adore it, and to love her carnally at once was blasphemy, and yet that was something we shared. I did not love him in spite of his priesthood, but because of it. "I am glad you think so, Maestro."

The musicians struck opening notes, and we all stepped back from the center of the room to allow the sets to form for dancing. Lucrezia and Giovanni Sforza took their places to lead the set, as was appropriate since the party was in their honor, Lucrezia blushing and beautiful. Giovanni was not much of a dancer, but he could at least tread a measure. He bowed and she curtsied, the *reverence* as they began.

I looked about for Rodrigo but did not see him. We were not supposed to lead the set, but it was odd for him to not be seated and watching. There were our chairs together, but both were empty. In fact, as I glanced about the room, I did not see him anywhere. Perhaps he had been called out on business? Such things happened all too frequently. His time was never his own. I felt like a juggler sometimes, trying to keep eight balls in the air, knowing that if I dropped any of them the results would be terrible. I was certain he felt the same, only more so. Only in the peculiar domestic life at my house could he put aside the worries of being a temporal prince and the Holy Father at once, and of late that had been no refuge either. Lucrezia's marriage had taken over everything. Even the most devoted father must get tired of bride, bride, bride! I was certainly sick unto death of it. With the diplomatic crisis with France worsening, he came less often to Santa Maria in Portico than he had before.

"If you will excuse me, Maestro," I said, and Pinturicchio bowed gracefully. Where had he gone? The dancers turned, Lucrezia leading Giovanni into the next figure. They changed partners, each making *reverence* to the new one. D'Este had Lucrezia, and I wondered how he had contrived it.

I made my way through the onlookers to the side doors. A page stood there to prevent people from wandering into the private apartments. "Has His Holiness passed this way?"

The boy gaped like a fish. "Yes, Madonna," he stammered. "A few minutes ago."

"Thank you," I said, and went through, going along the corridor to the stairs up to the sala. If something important had come up, that was where he would most likely be.

There was a heavy table on the landing at the top where during the day those who had messages or packages could leave them to be carried in. I got halfway up the stairs and stopped dead. Emilia Vespucci was sitting on the table, her skirts up, her gartered legs wrapped around Rodrigo, his costume pulled aside and his face buried between her breasts. He moved against her and she moaned softly.

I suppose I caught my breath, for her eyes flew open, a sudden moue of surprise. I stood stock still, too shocked to do anything else. He lifted his face, that transported expression remaining for an instant before it was replaced by something else. "Giulia."

I turned on my heel and went back down the steps, along the corridor. All I could think of was that I needed to leave. I could not stay here one moment.

"Giulia!" I heard him call behind me.

I didn't stop. I plunged back through the door, the frightened page standing big-eyed. Somehow, I made my way through the crowd, making polite excuses, through halls and corridors and through the basilica itself. It was quiet, echoing, and it held nothing for me tonight. I ran into the Choir Chapel, fumbling with the key to the door at the back of the robing room. I locked the secret door behind me. Through the house, up the stairs.

There was a light in the nursery. I stopped in the hall. Breath. A serene face. I tiptoed to the door. The nurse looked up from her needlework. "Laura is sleeping," she whispered. "She fell asleep a little while ago."

I nodded, coming near. She was sleeping on her back, one hand open and outflung, her soft hair curling behind her ears just as Rodrigo's did. "I see," I whispered. "Good night." Kissing her would wake her. I left her sleeping and went into my room, barring the door. It was dawn before I slept.

I remember very little of the morning. There was a note for me in Rodrigo's hand which I burned without reading. There was another note two hours later. I threw it in the fire. I met with my tutor and translated Greek. I had no idea what it was.

We were finishing the lesson when Maria, the housekeeper came to the door. "Madonna, His Holiness is here."

"Who let him in?" I asked coldly.

Maria blinked. Rodrigo came and went as he wanted. I had locked the door, so he must have come around to the front street door, the Pope with a litter or at least on foot with guardsmen. "Madonna?"

"I will see him in the sala," I said, getting up from the table. "Signore, our lesson is over for the day." He rose as I swept out.

Rodrigo was standing in my sala, wearing a robe of dark red brocade rather than anything papal, his hat in his hand. I came in and closed the door behind me, making a very proper curtsy. "Holy Father, you wished to speak with me?"

He scratched the back of his neck. "Giulia, that wasn't what it seemed...."

"Wasn't what it seemed? It wasn't you fucking Emilia Vespucci on a table?" My voice sounded scathing even to me.

"Well, yes, but...."

"Do you think I am stupid?" I shouted, losing my temper at last. "Do you think I will believe some excuse? I know what I saw! You and that lightskirted little whore!"

"My darling," he began.

"Don't you darling me!" I yelled. "How dare you?"

Now the temper was rising in his face. "How dare I? How dare you! I'm the Pope!"

"Oh, you remember that now," I said. "Last night you were King David and you had me decked out as your adulteress!"

"You never said you didn't want that costume," Rodrigo snapped. "It was a bad idea."

"It was your bad idea, and the costume is not the point!" I paced around him. "Have you been doing this all along? Fucking any woman who comes on to you behind my back?"

"What if I have?" he yelled back. "It's not any of your business."

"How could I be so blind?" I said. "Everyone told me you were like this. A randy old goat who can't keep it in his clothes!"

"You're a harridan," he said. "Clinging to me in a chokehold. What do you expect?"

"I expect you to get out of my house," I shouted.

"Actually, it's my house! I paid for it!"

I stared at him. It had really come to this. "Fine," I said tightly. "Then I'll leave."

"Fine," he yelled. "You do that! You can't tell me what to do."

"Oh, I won't!" I shouted. "Except for one more thing. Rodrigo, go fuck yourself!" I stormed out of the sala and into my camera. I dropped the bar into place.

"Giulia!" he shouted from outside. "Come out here this minute!"

"Go fuck yourself!" I yelled through the door.

I heard the sound of his feet going away. And then I heard nothing. I sank down against the door, my back to it, shaking. I did not cry. It was too deep for tears.

A LITTLE WHILE later someone knocked on the door. "Who is it?" I asked.

"Lucrezia," she replied.

"Have you come to make your father's apologies?" I said through the door.

"Papa's not here. It's just me." Her voice was very small. I opened the door. Lucrezia put her arms around me. I held onto her tightly. "I'm so sorry," she said against my hair. "I am so, so sorry."

"Lucrezia, you didn't do anything," I murmured. I still could not cry. But she should not feel guilty.

"I'm sorry Papa behaved that way." She tightened her arms around me. "I've told him exactly what I think. I told him if my Giovanni ever acted like that, he'd have a knife in the chest!"

"Really, Lucrezia!" The idea of her stabbing someone was silly.

"Really," she said. Her eyes were serious. "I thought Papa had gotten over whoring since he was with you. I'm very disappointed in his behavior."

Her tone was exactly like his. I wanted to laugh and cry at once. "I don't know what to do," I said. I glanced around. "This is his house. And I don't want to see him. I suppose Laura and I could go to Montalto. Or to my other brother at Capodimonte." I felt a pang about the last.

Montalto was my childhood home held by my brother Bartolemeo, but Capodimonte was a much finer property, one of the old Farnese castles before our fortunes dwindled. Rodrigo had made it over to my other younger brother, Angelo, last year. It was ours because of his largesse. No, it was ours because I lay with him. And what would my family say? Alessandro owed Rodrigo his red hat. He was of the Borgia faction, a protégé in the College. He would be in an impossible position.

Lucrezia was watching me as though she'd already added all of this up. "You could visit me," she said.

"Visit you?" I blinked.

"You could come on my wedding journey," she said. "Giovanni and I leave for Pesaro in a few days. I am the mistress of my own house now. It doesn't belong to Papa. It's my husband's estate. There's no reason you can't visit and bring Laura. Adriana is already coming to help me get settled. You could come, too."

"Come to Pesaro?" I had been planning Lucrezia's departure for months. It never occurred to me I might go with her.

"Why not?" Lucrezia sat back at arms length. "You know I love you. You're a sister to me. Or a stepmother. Or a former stepmother. Or something."

"Former stepmother." I looked down at my lap. "I suppose that's what I am."

She shrugged. "If you want to be. Papa's in a towering fury because he knows he's wrong. But he'll get over it. And then you can decide if you want to keep him or not."

"We are done," I said. "I never want to see him again."

Lucrezia looked as though she was thinking something but deciding not to say it. "Well, you could come to Pesaro with me and then decide what you want to do. There's no hurry. You and Laura can be my guests for as long as you like. You will always, always be welcome."

"Very well," I said. "Thank you, Lucrezia. I will come to Pesaro."

· · ·

THE NEXT DAY, as I was packing, Fiammetta showed up. She wore green, a color that was beautiful with her red hair and ivory skin and rushed at me as if we'd been apart for months rather than a few days. "Darling! I heard the terrible news. I am so sorry."

I wondered what she thought was terrible – Rodrigo's behavior or me leaving town. I didn't wonder where she'd heard it, however. "Cesare told you."

"Of course." This house had no garden, so we went up to my sala to talk privately. She sat down beside me. "Men are horrible, aren't they?"

"I did not formerly think so," I said. I did not want him to be horrible. I wanted him to be what I had thought he was.

"They're all animals," Fiammetta said. "They have no more sense than stallions. They see a mare in heat, and not another thought goes through their minds."

"I think men have more self-control than stallions," I said dryly.

One of her plucked eyebrows rose. "Some might. Or perhaps they're just less virile to start with. Or prefer men, a perfect Florentine."

"Would you put up with such a thing?" I demanded. Of course I knew she would.

"Darling, all men stray."

I looked at her suspiciously. "Did Cesare ask you to talk to me?"

"Certainly not," she said. "He is of the opinion this will all blow over in a week or two. Then I heard that you were leaving town." Fiammetta took my hand. "It's all very well to make him sorry for straying as long as you don't push it too far. Leaving town is too far."

"I'm not playing some game of making him sorry," I said. "I am done with him."

She looked at me seriously. "Honey, one does not break up with the Pope."

"This one does," I said.

"He could destroy you," Fiammetta said quietly. "He could destroy your family. Your brother's career. Your sister's marriage prospects. He could take the child."

"He would not do that," I said. I couldn't quite bear to say Rodrigo's name.

"Who do you think he is?" she squeezed my hands. "Giulia, baby, we're the women of Borgias. They may be the hottest rides in town, but they're the most dangerous. You've sat on his knee like a pampered pussycat in the devil's lap. Did you not notice that when he snaps his fingers, bad things happen to people?"

"He would never hurt me," I said. And yet he had. What was this if not hurt? What if I had been wrong about him all these years?

Fiammetta shook her head. "I hope that's true. I hope you do all right."

"I'll be fine," I said, blinking. "I came to Rome five years ago wanting excitement. Well, I've had it. It's time to go." I squeezed her hands back. "Thank you for your friendship. It's meant so much to me. And please tell Cesare...." I halted, then continued. "Tell him I have valued his friendship too."

"I'll tell him," she promised. "He's more worried about France right now than about you and his father."

"What about France?"

"Cesare says that the French are using Genoa as a staging area for 22,000 troops and that Ludovico Sforza is allowing it," she said.

"The Sforza are our allies," I said. "Giovanni and Lucrezia...."

"The Sforza have no one's interests at heart but their own," Fiammetta said. "The news came yesterday that they're in Genoa. Cesare says it's the biggest army on Italian soil since the Goths or Visigoths or something. It's a problem."

"I see that it is," I said. Rodrigo would have told me about it. He would have wanted to think through his responses, lying in my bed, sketching out answers. But it was not my problem anymore. It was his. "Well, I'm sure Cesare will think of something," I said. "I'm leaving tomorrow with Lucrezia." I took my leave of Fiammetta thus. If I felt any uneasiness, I put it down to sorrow.

CHAPTER 5

We left Rome on the 29th of May. It was an utterly gorgeous day, a clear blue sky at dawn and perfect weather for a journey through the countryside. Laura was bouncing and excited. She would travel in the carriage with her nurse and Adriana while I rode Lilas with Lucrezia and Giovanni, but I held her while we formed up to go, pressing my face to her hair and inhaling the wonderful baby smell of her. Some little distance away, Rodrigo was embracing Lucrezia and saying something. He was wearing his long white brocade gown, though without a miter, as that would have made it official. I ignored him. I was not even going to look at him. If he looked at me, I didn't see it. For that matter, Lilas was a gift, my own horse. I had every right to take her.

I suppose our departure was something to see. We had fourteen wagons to carry Lucrezia's goods and those of her entire household, three maids, five cooks, and six pages, plus Adriana, me, Laura, the baby's nurse, Adriana's maid, and my maid Tina. We had twenty grooms and ostlers, twenty guards with Sforza arms, Giovanni's page and two esquires, and who knew how many horses. With banners flying in the bright May sunshine, Sforza and Borgia colors displayed against the sky, it was incredibly beautiful. I had come to Rome with little, slipping in unnoticed. I left in a grand procession, crowds gathering to watch the golden-haired bride beaming and throwing alms. I rode behind her in sober Farnese blue looking like the duenna in a play. I felt a thousand years old.

After we were through the city gates, Giovanni rode in front with his men and Lucrezia dropped back to ride with me. "Papa would have liked to say goodbye to Laura," she said.

"Ah." I supposed he would. He had doted on her.

Lucrezia was silent for a while. Her horse was a white palfrey and very gentle though pretty. Lucrezia was not a notable horsewoman. "You know, when Mama and Papa ended, they made plans together about where we would live," she said. "So that both of them would see us."

"I don't expect that made your mother happy," I said. I could not imagine going a day without seeing Laura.

"Actually, it did," Lucrezia said. "She was very glad they arranged things together. I was six and Gioffre was three and Juan was ten, so we lived with her but Papa came to see us. Cesare lived with Papa and he came to see Mama. And then when Cesare went away to school and I was nine, I went to live with Donna Adriana near Papa. Then Juan and Carlo quarreled, so Mama said that Papa could handle him so he went to live with Papa. But I've always had both of them, both in the same city. Even when I lived with Mama, I was never fatherless."

I blinked. Of course I had known her when she first came to Adriana's house. I had married Orsino at about the same time. Rodrigo had adored her. Was it cruel to take Laura from him? He hadn't tried to stop me, but Laura was a baby. I squelched down any guilt I felt. "Laura isn't fatherless," I said. "I am married, remember? She will inherit Vasanello from Orsino."

"We are stopping at Vasanello tonight," Lucrezia said.

I turned in the saddle to boggle at her. "What?"

"Vasanello is on the road north," Lucrezia said. "A day's journey from Rome on the Via Flaminia. Since Adriana is with us, we're stopping there as the first stage of the journey."

I drew a deep breath. Well I remembered how holdings along the roads were expected to host noble travelers! At Montalto we had struggled to keep up with the entourages who dropped in on us expecting a welcome. Of course we would stop at Vasanello. And why not? Adriana visited Orsino in the country often. Lucrezia had known him when she was a child. Why would they not expect hospitality from him? "Oh dear," I said.

I rode back along the column to the carriage. Adriana looked out as I came alongside. "Is something wrong?"

I pulled Lilas to a walk beside, close enough to talk. "I did not know we were stopping at Vasanello," I said.

"The plans have been made for weeks," she said. "Before you decided to join us." Adriana had scrupulously avoided any comment on my fight with Rodrigo.

"Yes, but...."

"Giulia, you cannot avoid visiting the estate you are theorctically the mistress of," she said. "She dropped her voice. "If you and Rodrigo are done, you must think of your future. And Laura's. If she is the heir to Vasanello and she will have nothing else from Rodrigo, she must be known there. She must be acknowledged as the heir."

I could see the wisdom in that. After all, Rodrigo had said four years ago that part of the point of giving Vasanello to Orsino was to safeguard the future of our hypothetical children. I was married to Orsino. Lawfully, Laura was Orsino's heir. She would be Lady of Vasanello someday. I drew a deep breath. "It's awkward."

"Of course it is," Adriana said somewhat sharply. "But unless you mean to turn around and go straight back to Rodrigo, isn't it better to see Orsino with a large party that is only staying two nights and the day between? You must speak with him at some point. When will it be easier?"

"It won't be," I said. This was not at all what I wanted, the humiliation of facing my husband having lost my lover. Well, having left my lover. When I had ended matters with Orsino, I had been so certain that I would be with Rodrigo forever! "Two nights and a day between?"

"That is all," Adriana said.

"Then so be it," I said.

WE CAME to Vasanello an hour after sunset, just as the stars were appearing in the clear sky. The last stretch of road was lined with cypress trees shaped like arrowheads, and a little village huddled at the castle's feet on the other side, as picturesque as anyone could possibly want. It was a sight out of a story – the guards all in Sforza blue, the bride on her white horse, the lanterns lighting the streets to the castle steps where the young lord waited in red and white to welcome his guests. There was quite a crowd assembled to watch us arrive.

I had not seen Orsino in four years, and I would not have recognized him. For one thing, he stood up straight. He was as tall as Cesare, fair as Cesare was dark, with blond hair and an aquiline nose. He wore Orsini red, a short doublet over white hose, and came down the steps to greet Lucrezia with some grace. She was stiff from riding all day and had been complaining for an hour, but she smiled when he bent over her hand. He greeted Giovanni Sforza in a manly way, and then turned to embrace his mother, who had gotten out of the carriage. I dismounted.

"I hope you didn't have rough travel," he said to Adriana.

"The roads were dry and it was entirely pleasant," she replied. Then she looked at me. "Orsino, will you not greet your lady wife? And your daughter?"

His mouth dropped open and he looked at me incredulously. "My what?"

The nurse was at my elbow, Laura asleep in her arms, having dozed off in the carriage. I took Laura from her. My heart was beating very fast. Best to have it done. If he was going to repudiate Laura, he would have to do it now, in front of all witnesses. If he was going to call me adulteress.

"Your wife," Adriana prompted. "Giulia."

Orsino was not a forceful person at the best of times, and Adriana had entirely blindsided him. "My wife," he said. "Er. Welcome to Vasanello."

"Thank you," I said. It wasn't precisely an acknowledgement, but it wasn't a repudiation either.

"I am so delighted to be here," Lucrezia gushed, taking his arm. "Your mother is a better traveler than I, for I fear I am sadly done by our journey and cannot wait for dinner and bed! It is so good to see you, Orsino! I almost feel you are my brother, for did we not live together as children? I have so wanted for you to meet my good husband, Giovanni. I know you will have much in common!" Lucrezia was a force of nature. It was impossible not to escort her indoors immediately, Giovanni Sforza following.

Adriana hung back with me and Laura. "I usually occupy the mistress' suite when I am here," she said quietly, "and I am sure it has been prepared for me. Will you and Laura share it?"

"That would be very kind of you," I said. I didn't want to throw Adriana out of her own rooms, and I certainly didn't want to join Orsino in his!

She gave me an encouraging smile, then turned to a servant. "Please take Donna Giulia's things and the baby's to my suite. Little Laura is very tired and I'm sure you'll want to put her to bed."

"She will need some dinner first," I said. "A tray with something simple?"

"I think we will all have a tray sent up," Adriana said. "Tomorrow night Orsino will put on a dinner of note, but I sent word ahead that we would be quite late tonight and that we would all be too tired for a banquet."

"Of course, Madonna," the servant said. She'd sent word ahead, I thought. She could just as easily have told him I was with her as when we might arrive. She'd surprised him on purpose. Well, it did prevent him from having time to think about whether to repudiate me or not. And having not, given Orsino's general lack of forcefulness, he was unlikely ever to. It was a kindness to me, though not to him. I followed the servants up.

The mistress' sala was a large, airy room with a tiled floor and tasteful dark furniture, smelling of beeswax and bay leaves. There was a fire laid against a chilly night, but it had not been lit since the day was warm, and would be lit or not at Adriana's pleasure. There was a deep embrasure with a window seat, casements open. I sat down on the rose-colored cushions, looking out into a lovely little walled garden. It was very peaceful. Vasanello was a greater fortress than Montalto, with four massive towers at the corners, but it had much of the same air about it.

"Mama!" Laura came tearing across the floor to me, awake now and in a strange place.

I picked her up. "There, sweetest," I said. "You fell asleep in the carriage. We are at Vasanello now, where we will stay for two nights before we go on to Aunt Lucrezia's house."

"Papa here?" she asked hopefully.

"No, darling," I said, and held her tightly, a wave of something suddenly crushing against me. It felt like sorrow, not anger.

"Papa coming?" She was too young to remember last autumn in Nepi, but people had told her of it, a castle in the country where Papa and Mama shared chambers.

And what was Rodrigo doing in Rome right now? Probably at some revel like Fiammetta's, with a courtesan feeding him grapes.

"No, Laura," I said. "There is only me."

IN THE MORNING I woke beside Adriana in her big bed. She was still sleeping. I should be. Laura had been up in the middle of the night, her sleep disrupted by a long nap in the carriage, and thus she'd been wild at midnight. Now, as the light grew at the window and the birds sang in the garden, she was sound asleep. I got up, leaving Adriana sleeping, and put one of my plainer cottas on over my camisa and went out into the sala. Laura and her nurse were both sleeping in the dressing room, and I cracked the door to see. All was quiet. I shut the door again and went to the window.

I stood there a long moment, looking out at the garden. There were clipped bushes and beds of herbs fragrant with dew, a bay laurel tree beneath the window. Once, I had wanted a garden like this. Once I had hoped to be mistress of a house like this, before I had come to Rome, before I had ever heard of a Borgia.

I went out and down the stairs, trying to remember how we had come up last night. Like Montalto, Vasanello had not been built all of a piece, so the layout of rooms was not logical. In the great hall, there were tables being set up, presumably for tonight's banquet, a young woman in the seventh or eighth month of pregnancy directing the boys who carried them. She glanced up at me, and for a moment I thought I saw fear and pain crossing her face in swift succession before it was schooled to professional pleasantness. "May I help you, Madonna?" she asked.

"Yes, thank you," I said, as gently as I could. "I am looking for a door to the garden."

"It's through the passage there," she said, pointing. "Then turn to the right."

"Thank you," I said. I looked about the hall. Faded Orsini banners hung from the ceiling. They must have been there decades, since before Vasanello had been a Church property. Orsino certainly hadn't had them done in the last four years. "What is your name?"

"Gentilia," she said, bobbing, her eyes casting down. She was little and buxom, pretty in an uncontrived way.

"The hall looks lovely," I said. "I am sure the banquet will be wonderful."

"Yes, Madonna." She did not look up, but I saw her hand clench. There was something here I did not understand.

"I will be in the garden if anyone asks for me," I said, and went the way she had indicated.

It was small but lovely, the dew still standing on leaves. The walls were mellow stone, three different colors where different sections had been added, a little ornamental patch and then stairs down to the larger kitchen garden. Grapevines shaded an arbor, each vine tied neatly up with twine. Everything was beautifully cared for. One could sit under this arbor reading a book while a child played, safe within the walls.

"Giulia." I turned. Orsino was standing by the bay tree. He wore patched hose and a brown doublet over his shirt, looking more like a servant than the master here.

"Orsino." I waited as he approached, taking a deep breath. "The arbor is lovely," I said. "Vasanello agrees with you."

"We need to talk," he said. His blue eyes were very direct and didn't shy from mine.

"Yes," I said. My heart was beating quickly. Whatever he had to say, I deserved to hear it.

He sat down on the bench in the arbor, and I sat down on the other end. He picked up a grape leaf that had fallen. "So you and Borgia have ended?"

"Yes," I said. "Probably."

He looked up at the vines, not at me. "Vasanello," he said. "This. It's all I've ever wanted." I waited, letting him find words in his own time. "My mother has ambitions for me. Had ambitions for me. But this is everything. I don't want to be a soldier. I don't even like slaughtering pigs for winter. I don't want to serve some prince or go to banquets. This is what I love."

I smiled, looking down at my lap. "You are a country gentleman," I said. "And obviously you are a good and well-loved master."

"This is my home," Orsino said quietly. He had a face off a Roman coin in profile, but there was nothing of the Caesars about him. "I love this place. I don't want things to change. And I don't want to go to war."

"I don't see why you should," I said.

He shrugged. "My cousin the cardinal says I owe service to Prince Ferrandino. If I'm called, I'm supposed to go. There's some reason I might be. I don't know what."

"The French," I said. "Ludovico Sforza has given them passage into Milan as part of their chess game to acquire rights to the Kingdom of Naples, though the Venetians are less than thrilled with this. Lord Bracciano, the Gonfaloniere, also holds lands from the King of Naples, and he is sworn to protect the Papal States. So there may be some trouble with the French in the north."

Orsino huffed. "See? You know these things. I have no idea. And I don't want to." He turned the leaf around in his hands. "Politics. You and the Borgias. My mother does it too, always knee-deep in something."

I should be honest, as he was. "And now I have shown up on your doorstep unexpectedly with a Borgia bastard."

He glanced at me sideways. "My heir." I said nothing. He put the leaf carefully on the ground. "I've always known what the deal was. I get Vasanello for my lifetime but it goes to Borgia's child. That was the plan. That's what he offered. And it's a good deal, right? I'm steward of a fine estate. Like a steward, I can't pass it on. No matter what."

Things fit. "Gentilia," I said.

Orsino looked at me. "You're fast." I shrugged. "She's my bailiff's daughter. She's a gentlewoman. We've been keeping company two years, married in all but name. The baby's due at Assumption."

"Ah, Orsino," I said, putting my head back. "And now unexpectedly your wife shows up. What a tangle!"

"Just don't hurt her," Orsino said. "Anything but that."

"Can you imagine I would?" I asked.

He shrugged again. "Borgia."

"Where have you been hearing this?" I asked. "You knew His Holiness when he was a cardinal and in your mother's house. Did you see him going around murdering people? Can you imagine me doing such a thing?"

"I don't know. It's just a thing you hear."

I shook my head. "Orsino, I would never harm your Gentilia. Or your child. That isn't a thing I could do." I looked up at the arbor. A pleasant place for a lady's delight, I had thought, an ideal place for a young child to play. It had been made by Orsino for his lady and the child she carried. Of course.

"Laura will get Vasanello," he said. "She's my heir on paper. What I want you to promise is that you won't contest my will leaving my personal property to Gentilia and the child." He met my eyes. "You could leave them destitute. A court would rule in my wife's favor. Please don't."

"I won't," I promised. "Orsino, I swear before God that I will not contest your will, should you die before me. I swear that I will take nothing from your woman or your children. I will grant them what you meant for them to have with dignity and good grace."

He nodded, something lightening in him. "Thank you. And I swear I will not repudiate Laura nor challenge her holding Vasanello after me."

"We will do right by each other's children," I said, "and perhaps we can be friends."

"Maybe so," Orsino said. "Where do you go next?"

"I am going to Pesaro with Lucrezia," I said. "For the summer, maybe. After that...." Truly, I had not thought that far. "I don't know." Clearly I would not be moving to Vasanello. The last thing Orsino would want right on top of his child's birth would be me and Laura!

"Back to Rome?"

I sighed. "Maybe. I could live with my brother, Alessandro." Alessandro was a cardinal now. He had a house of his own. Lucrezia had a point that it would not be good for Laura to never see her father. Vannozza and Rodrigo had managed to be friendly ex-lovers. Perhaps someday I could manage as much.

"You like Rome," Orsino said. He almost smiled. "I don't."

"Well, to each their own," I said, and smiled back.

"A favor," he said. "Don't tell my mother we've had this conversation. She doesn't think Gentilia is good enough for me. I don't want to hear her go on about it."

"Of course," I said. "This is between us. And you may assure Gentilia that tomorrow I will be gone, and that I wish her a safe delivery and a healthy child."

"Good," Orsino said. "And I wish you well, wherever you go."

We came in from the garden together.

. . .

THUS, the night's banquet was not as bad as I had feared. I sat beside Orsino in the center of the high table, introduced to all and sundry as his lady wife, and toasts were drunk to the honored guests, the Lord and Lady of Pesaro. Lucrezia had slept half the day, so she seemed ready to dance half the night after the tables were pushed back. Giovanni did one dance as was proper, then turned her over to Orsino. I saw Gentilia across the hall, watching, but her eyes were not on me.

I sat by Adriana and watched the dancers. It was very old-fashioned – the leaping fire in the huge hearth, the faded banners and local musicians, the dinner with the entire household with the high table eating in view of the servants and men at arms. There were no forks at the lower tables. In Rome, we always used forks.

"You and Orsino seem to be getting along," Adriana said to me quietly.

"Yes," I said, watching him turn round with Lucrezia. "He's grown up."

"It has been four years," Adriana said. "One should expect so." She paused, then went on. "You might make a go of the marriage now."

"I don't think so," I replied, trying to sound as though the question weren't very interesting. I had promised Orsino not to tell her about our agreement.

"If you and Rodrigo are finished, I don't know why not."

I shrugged, watching the dancers. "It's much too soon to think of such things," I said, and she let the matter drop.

CHAPTER 6

In the morning we were on the road early. Needless to say, we were incredibly slow. Such a grand procession made very poor time. It took us four days over the Apennines to Urbino, which would have taken a courier at best a day and a half.

Indeed, the post riders passed us and passed us, Lilas tossing her head as they went by at a trot, experienced men on horses who knew every bit of their usual length of road, going back and forth between two familiar posting stations, passing their saddle bags and dispatch pouches to the next rider. One could simply pay them to carry a message, though Rodrigo usually sent a Borgia courier, either alone or to be escorted at good speed by the post rider, because he often had letters that were either urgent or confidential. The weather was good and the riders made little of the road. We, however, trudged along at a walk. I was nearly as impatient as Lilas.

At Urbino we were only a day from Pesaro, and Giovanni sent a messenger ahead to tell them to prepare for our arrival. We spent a day shopping, as the Florentine merchants had houses there, and there was beautiful cloth by the bolt that had not come to Rome, both from Florence and from Venice. Laura had an early supper before we were to dine with the Duke of Urbino. It was a very refined and elegant court, and the young Duke was a loyal ally of both the Sforza and the Pope. He had been in Rome on a number of occasions, including Rodrigo's coronation, and was well known to us all. I was looking forward to the evening. I liked his wife, Elisabetta, very much.

I knocked on Lucrezia's door, having seen to Laura's meal, to see what she was planning to wear. "Come in!" she called, and I did.

Lucrezia was sitting on the edge of her bed, her lap desk open, all its little bottles of ink displayed. "I'm replying to a letter from Papa," she said. "So that he will know that we are all in good health and that the journey has been safe and pleasant. You know he will worry."

"About you," I said.

She looked at me reproachfully. "He will worry about Laura. And you." It was certainly true he would worry about Laura. He had been a devoted father to her, just as he had been to Lucrezia. "You could write too," Lucrezia said quietly. "Just a note to put in with mine."

"He didn't write to me," I said. "If you had a letter from him by messenger, I did not."

"You weren't speaking to him," she said. "And he asked after you in my letter. He asked how you were."

"Well," I said. "I suppose I could." I sat down beside her and she passed the lap desk across. It was the one Rodrigo had given her for her tenth birthday. I had thought it lovely at the time and had then never seen anything like it.

Written at Urbino, the 6th day of June, 1494

That part was easy. The next was hard. One could always take refuge in propriety.

To the Most Revered Holy Father, my greetings.

I glanced up at Lucrezia. She was considering her own letter.

I am at Urbino with Lucrezia. We are all in good health. I hope that you too are well.

The letter could not be two lines. I cast about for something to say.

Lucrezia and I have been shopping in the houses of the Florentine merchants for they get good custom here at the court of Urbino.

I had now said I was in Urbino three times, which he already knew.

We are so magnificent it seems we have ransacked Florence for brocade. Tomorrow we continue on to Pesaro.

How could one possibly end it? Was 'best wishes' too cold? I was certainly not 'obedient' or 'dutiful' anything! Nor would 'fond regards' do. I was certainly not fond. I simply signed my name.

Giulia Farnese

"There," Lucrezia said. "That wasn't so bad, was it?"

There was another lavish banquet that evening. At this rate, I would have to let out all my clothes in a month! There were certainly magnificent entertainments at the Papal Court, but not every night. In any event, I did not go to every dinner and party I was asked to. Generally, since his election, Rodrigo and I had been to something perhaps twice a week, and he attended various other dinners that were all masculine affairs. Or at least, I thought in retrospect, involved no acknowledged partners. If there were girls at those sorts of dinners, they were hired by the hour. I had given them little thought, as Rodrigo usually came to me after, looking blameless and generally hungry for my favors. I had presumed that a man his age wouldn't have one woman with dinner and then another two hours later, but maybe I was wrong. I had to doubt everything I had assumed.

I had thought he treasured those quiet, late suppers with me as much as I did. I had thought he found it balm to put aside everything, even who he was, in an elaborate play with us as performers and audience at once. We contrived such games for each other, stories spun for our mutual delight. Sometimes, in the firelight, in the intensity of the moment, I could almost feel us in another place or another time, slipping into the dream so completely that the walls faded to nothing and we loved in distant ages past. Once, it seemed we coupled at the top of a vast tower into the stars, a torchlit city beneath us, or that we lay on a terrace with the whisper of the sea beyond, odd red inverted columns holding up the portico above us. I thought he shared it, at least a breath of what I saw, of what we were.

Rodrigo had said that he had never known anyone like me. He said I was unique in his admittedly broad experience. Was that such a light thing to lose? If I searched my whole life, would I ever find another like him? Surely in all the world there was only one Rodrigo Borgia.

It was in these gloomy thoughts, watching yet another round of Lucrezia dancing and dancing, that I was occupying myself when there was a quiet tap on my shoulder. I startled, looking around at the Duke of Urbino.

"Donna Giulia?" he asked. "Will you walk with me?"

"Of course, Your Grace," I said.

Guidobaldo da Montefeltro was only a year older than I, though he had inherited the Dukedom of Urbino in childhood. He was of medium height, fair and long faced, and I had talked with him any number of times in Rome. He and his wife, Elisabetta, were one of the few couples I knew who had an affectionate arranged marriage, though they had no children. I knew Elisabetta rather better. She was one of the other ladies who hunted, and I enjoyed her company enormously though she was the better horsewoman. He led me outside onto a terrace that overlooked the moonlit countryside, a beautiful place for an assignation, but I certainly did not expect one with him. He was devoted to his wife.

He stopped by the carved stone rail. "You've just come from Rome, I understand."

"We have not hurried on the road," I said. "Not with a bridal entourage. Couriers have distanced us easily. But yes, we left eight days ago."

Giudobaldo dropped his voice. "The Holy Father knows that I

have the utmost respect for him and for the Throne of St. Peter. I am seriously alarmed at the news from Genoa."

"That the French are there?" I asked.

"That's old news," the duke said. "His Holiness had hired Prospero Colonna, that old *condottiero*, to help defend Rome should the French invade the Papal States. But Cardinal Ascanio Sforza and his brother, Ludovico of Milan, are also paying him."

"What?" I wasn't sure I'd heard correctly.

"Prospero Colonna is in the pay of the Pope and the Sforza both," he said impatiently. "Which is fine, as long as they're allies. But Ludovico isn't. He's welcomed the French into Genoa."

"The Sforza are buttering their bread on both sides," I said flatly.

He glanced back toward the doors, the music from the dance clamoring out, the voices of happy people. Through the open door I could see Lucrezia dancing in a pink gamurra. "And now I have Giovanni Sforza in my house," Guidobaldo said, "with His Holiness' daughter as his bride. I wish them well, but...."

"You are suspicious," I finished. I tapped my hand on the stone railing. "Ascanio Sforza helped arrange this match."

"Ascanio Sforza is paying Prospero Colonna." He leaned against the rail beside me. "Does His Holiness know that?"

"I don't know," I said. I should know. I would have, three weeks ago. Was this something he and Ascanio had cooked up together, or was Ascanio double-dealing? I liked Ascanio personally, but his ambition was obvious and he put his family above all. He had great good from Rodrigo at present, but I doubted he'd stay bought if there were a higher bidder. He'd made that clear in the papal election.

"Can you ask him?" Guidobaldo asked. "This needs to be confidential. You've got Borgia men as messengers. I don't want to trust it to the post, given that the Sforza own half the posting stations."

Writing to Rodrigo confidentially.... I closed my eyes. It would have to be secret even from Lucrezia. She should not be put in a position of having to keep secrets from her new husband, or worse yet deal with his kin's plots against her father. But if this wasn't something Rodrigo and Ascanio had planned together, he needed to know. Whatever else, I was still of the Borgia faction. "Of course," I said.

I left the party early claiming that I was tired. I got pen and ink and sat in the pretty guest chamber, Laura sleeping in a borrowed cradle beside me. She was such a little traveler, so daring and bright. My heart hurt with how much I loved her.

Your Holiness,

Ascanio Sforza and his brother Ludovico are paying Prospero Colonna as well, so I hear. It is possible that Your Holiness knows this and approves, in which case I do not mean to interfere. But if you do not, it is best that you know.

I did not sign it. He would know my hand. I sealed it inside the letter Lucrezia had already seen addressed for him. It would go in a courier's pouch tomorrow without further examination, and we would travel on to Pesaro.

We left Urbino the next morning under a lowering sky. By noon it was pouring rain, a drenching downpour that seemed to go on and on. Lucrezia asked Giovanni to halt so that the tents could be pitched. I heard him reply, rather testily, that we were not three hours from Pesaro and that the rain was likely to continue all evening and all night, and he intended to sleep at last in his own bed tonight. Had he married a bride who could not get wet?

Personally, I was in agreement with Giovanni Sforza. Nine days of this procession was quite enough. I didn't melt at the first drop of rain, Laura was in the carriage with Adriana and her nurse, and if Lucrezia wanted, she could be too. I urged Lilas forward, seeing Lucrezia's stubborn face and Giovanni's exasperated one. "Dear Lucrezia," I said, "wouldn't you like to keep Adriana company in the carriage? Laura is fretful and you are so good with her." Laura was not. Laura was a good campaigner and in any event she wasn't wet.

"I will do that," Lucrezia said. She looked sideways at her husband. "Someone here cares for my comfort. Thank you, Giulia."

"At least we will keep going," I said to Giovanni as Lucrezia turned back toward the carriage, and he nodded, the plume on his hat dripping.

We came into Pesaro in late afternoon, and I confess I had little impression of the place, other than that the road was steep and the carts and carriage looked precarious in the mud but came through without incident. The fortress sat on a hill, vistas beyond obscured by pouring rain. Giovanni had apparently ordered a grand welcome but the bridal garlands were sagging with wet and whatever musicians or local rustic dances were scheduled were cancelled by the weather. Instead we crossed an arched bridge over an empty moat to a very stern and well-constructed fortress. It could not have been fifty years old, so modern and neat was its design, and indeed I learned later it had been built by Giovanni's father.

My chamber was small but well appointed, high in a round tower with a tiny window that looked out over the road and the empty, muddy moat. The fire was lit, a cradle waiting for Laura, and the tiny anteroom had a bed for her nurse. The cradle could be moved back and forth between bedchamber and anteroom as wished. I shed wet clothes for dry ones with the help of my maid, Tina, who let my hair down to dry before the fire. It came well below my knees, to mid-calf, currently crimped into wet folds from soaked braids, and I sat down in a chair by the hearth to let it dry while Laura explored and ate an early dinner. It was a very nice room and there was no reason to compare it unfavorably to Nepi. At Nepi I had the lady's chamber, while here that was Lucrezia's. At Nepi everything had been intended for me. This was simply a pleasant guest room. It was not mine, and why should it be?

Dinner was another elaborate banquet, no doubt long planned to welcome the new Lady of Pesaro. Lucrezia was radiant in deep sapphire which turned her eyes the color of her dress. There was dancing, which I excused myself from on the grounds that I was tired. There was every local notable to meet her, all in their most elaborate clothes and best manners, vying for her attention. No one vied for mine. I should not have felt it. And yet I did. I made myself smile, watching the dancers. *You are growing spoiled, Giulia*, I said to myself.

You are used to flattery and being made much of, used to attention and fine clothes and every vanity. You are used to being the Lady, and now you are jealous. It is unworthy. This is Lucrezia's, and she is dear to you. Act with good grace.

So I did. I smiled and was pleasant to everyone and did nothing that would diminish Lucrezia's pleasure. She did not even notice when I excused myself, saying that I was tired from the journey, as she danced and danced. I sought my cold bed alone and lay in the dark sleepless, listening to the rain against the window. I did not cry.

In the morning the weather was perfect, everything washed bright and clean. I took Laura for a walk. Pesaro was a port and Laura had never been to the sea. I, of course, had grown up in Montalto not two miles from the ocean and had missed it. Unlike Montalto, there were no salt marshes and gentle wetlands. We were on a hill that looked far out over the blue Adriatic, so that one could almost see the Dalmatian coast in the distance. There were headlands and rocks, tumbled slopes redolent of lavender, and the town clustered about the port where a semi-circle of sandy beach marked the shallow water. It was picturesque and lovely.

Laura thought it was madness that I directed her to take her shoes off on the beach but we walked together, her hand in mine and our shoes in my other hand. The wind blew straight off the sea. The water lapped at our feet, the sand smooth and cool in the morning. I took a deep breath of salt air. How I had missed this! I did not need vanities, surely. Couldn't I be happy with this – ocean and sky and my daughter's hand in mine? I did not need the world, and surely the world did not need me. I had thought that my actions and words made a difference. I had thought my voice could matter, but would not someone else do as well as I had? What did it matter, really, if I was at Rodrigo's side or not? He would do what he would do with me or without me. Perhaps some individual clients would have to find a new patron, but the course of events would spin on without Giulia Farnese. I was free from power and responsibility alike, for power is responsibility. If I spent my days picking up shells with Laura, surely that was enough for a woman to want. I could devote myself to my child as a good mother should and think no more of courts or princes. We paddled in the little waves and then walked back to the castle.

A Borgia courier had come in while I was out, one Signore Francesc, a Catalan agent of Rodrigo's. He had brought letters for Lucrezia and Adriana and even a lengthy one for Giovanni, but nothing for me. Presumably Francesc had left Rome before my letter from Urbino had arrived. I caught him downstairs in the hall after he had delivered his letters and he made a nice bow. "Madonna Giulia."

"I was wondering," I said, "what you might tell me of the situation in Rome?"

"His Holiness has gone to Tivoli," he said, "to meet with the representatives of Milan and Naples in one place. He entertains them royally and many confidences are shared as regards the French king."

"That is good to hear," I said. "I am certain the Holy Father will contrive all."

"He has asked me to give report of you," Francesc said, "of your manner, health and state of mind."

My eyebrows rose. "And yet he conveys no letter to me."

"Indeed, Madonna."

I shook my head. "If he wishes to know my state of mind, he has but to ask."

"I believe he has asked of Madonna Adriana," he said. "But he is greatly concerned for you."

"He has no need for concern," I said. "My health is good and my mind has not changed."

"Will you give me a letter to return with?" he asked.

"I suppose." That afternoon, while Lucrezia rested to be fresh for the evening's entertainments, I composed a brief letter.

Your Holiness, I am touched by your inquiry after my health. We are all well here, and none of us has the slightest complaint. Pesaro is beautiful and ideally situated. Lucrezia is enjoying herself tremendously, and my lord Sforza seems a popular and competent lord. Laura likes the ocean. So do I. The country life is very agreeable.

I stopped. It seemed quite cold. And yet this ongoing crisis with France worried me. He would hardly put much in a letter, but…. What did I need to know it for anyway? I had renounced knowledge and power. I was in Pesaro in summer, verdant earth and my beautiful child. What did I need to know of the French or politics?

I hear that you are at Tivoli and are engaged in diplomatic matters of great import. I hope that your efforts to cultivate peace bear fruit. I have every faith in your invention and skill.

I could not but hope he succeeded. Perhaps this was simply a vote of confidence. I did trust him to manage affairs in the best possible way. That had not changed. Surely I could support him as a ruler without embracing him as a lover?

I gave Francesc the letter and watched him put it in his bag to take the next day. I could not help but notice that Lucrezia's letter was one page and Adriana's seemed quite thick. No doubt Rodrigo had asked her to report on us as well. Well, he could. I had no doubt Adriana would bore him silly with accounts of every movement of Lucrezia's. Of me and Laura there was little to say.

CHAPTER 7

A few days later I was enjoying Lucrezia's new solar. It was like something out of a fairy tale, a balcony with roses twining up from the garden below, now in brilliant bloom, pink and white. I sat staring at them. *Rosa mundi*, I thought. Rose of the world.

I had a letter from Rodrigo on my lap. It was brief and full of the Papal 'we'.

> *Giulia, dear girl, we are pleased to hear that you are in good health, as are the others. Lucrezia writes that the weather is very fine so we are glad you did not have rain for your journey and we hope your shopping in Urbino was satisfactory. It is difficult in Rome just now as the French are in Milan with an army and the situation is becoming complex. Needless to say, there is little gaiety here. We are glad you are in Pesaro in the company of our good friends the Sforza. We were glad to receive your letter. In Christ, Alexander*

He could not have gotten my second letter sent with Francesc when he wrote it, but it said nothing of the note I had enclosed about the Sforza with the letter from Urbino. Or did it? Was his line about "good friends" meant to convey that he and Ascanio had an arrangement? Or the opposite? Or did it mean to tell me to mind my business? I didn't hear Lucrezia's step until she sat down on the edge of the balcony opposite me. "You look so sad, Giulia."

"I'm not at all," I said.

She crossed her leg, little pale blue slipper beneath its matching gown. "Is it because of Papa?"

"No," I said, and then I stopped, looking at her face. She was not still ten years old. She was a woman and a wife and my dear friend. "Yes." I took a deep breath. "His letter was cordial and cool. I fear relations between us have simply run their course. Perhaps it was mutual infatuation, and the years have shown that what I thought was love was not. Four years is a long time, is it not?"

Lucrezia's face was concerned, her voice gentle. "You feel nothing for him anymore? It seemed to me you were in a rage when you found him with Emilia Vespucci and thereafter."

"And now my rage is gone and there is nothing," I said. I touched one of her roses, its petals soft and pliable. "I do not care what he does. I feel nothing." I shrugged. "Perhaps it is simply time for both of us to move on. I have money. I have my station still."

"You have my friendship," Lucrezia said. "And that will not wane." She came and hugged me, my face against her soft hair. Her goodness, her friendship, was real. She let go, sitting down on the rail again. "But I do believe my father adores you."

"And behave as he did?"

Lucrezia shrugged. "After four years."

"He said that he was constant in his affections," I said, not liking the tone of bitterness I heard in my own voice.

"In his affections, yes. But not in his person. Never in his person," Lucrezia said. "I've never known him to go four years before without straying. Perhaps he's slowed down, or perhaps he was just well-satisfied."

"Your mother put up with this?" I asked incredulously. I found that hard to imagine. Vannozza seemed to be a woman who put up with little imposition.

She shrugged again. "Of course. He loved her and she him. It is not as though she was true to him, or there wouldn't be a question about whether he's Gioffre's father! My parents had an understanding. Both of them had others, as long as they kept to their agreement. When they parted, it was about ambition, not sex. My father can be an ass. And he never keeps it to himself."

I took a deep breath. "You think I should simply tolerate this?"

"You know who he is," Lucrezia said. "It is up to you if you want it or not." She swung her little slippered foot. "He will want you back. I'm sure by now he's missing you and regretting his temper. You both have tempers. Better temper than indifference." She glanced down at her hands.

I frowned. "And is your husband indifferent?"

Lucrezia squared her shoulders. "Oh, you know. Giovanni is all right. As arranged marriages go, I suppose it's a success. We have nothing to talk about and nothing to quarrel about. I bring up a book or a piece of music, and he finds the topic boring. He brings up hunting and I find it boring. And in the bedchamber...." She rolled her eyes. "He just does the same thing, over and over and over. Hop on and ride. There's nothing wrong with that, I suppose. But truly, isn't there better?"

"Well," I said, "perhaps he's being careful with his bride and does not wish to give offense by treating you like a loose woman."

"Yes, but when I suggest something!" There were two spots of pink high on her cheeks. "I suggested that he be gallant Lancelot paying court to Queen Guinevere, forbidden love and yet irresistible! He looked at me in complete confusion. He said, 'but I'm not Lancelot!' What am I to do with that?"

"Oh dear," I said. I felt a clench in my chest. How often had I been Proserpina to his Pluto? Oriana to his Amadis? Europa, Galatea, even Messalina? How many worlds had we explored together? There was always a new story.

"I'd like a man who was gallant. Who wore my favor as a prize."

"You mean like Alfonso d'Este at the horse race?" I asked. She had seemed quite taken with the Duke of Ferrara's heir who had begged a ribbon of hers to wear.

Lucrezia tossed her head. "I don't like him anymore."

"And why not?" It was a very mutable favor.

"He said I was spoiled. I'm not talking to him anymore. Besides, he's married to my husband's cousin." She sighed. "I wonder if Giovanni has an imaginative bone in his body! He's handsome enough. But it takes more than a look at him, doesn't it? I'd like a man who talked."

"I understand that," I said. Her father was never quiet. He talked about everything and anything. I was his sounding board, his confidant, the person he spun out some dream to in the middle of the night. We could talk and talk and talk. Gossip, learning, politics, history, theology, plots – it was all one. I would lie against his shoulder or sit in the garden with him, spinning out great webs of thought for hours. It never staled.

Lucrezia looked at me keenly. "My father talks. I don't imagine Emilia Vespucci does. She's pretty but she doesn't have a thought between her ears. Imagine her trying to keep up with a Greek epigram! Or answer him with a witty and well-chosen quotation?"

"She's very blond."

Lucrezia shrugged. "That gets old." She looked down at her hands, rings glittering on seven fingers. "He probably regrets it all by now. But you know he's proud. And you did tell him to go fuck himself."

"He may regret it, but I certainly don't." I lifted my chin. "I'm well rid of him." She just looked at me, and I thrust the letter at her. "He says he is glad I am in Pesaro."

"He also says there is little gaiety in Rome," Lucrezia said, reading it. "Which doesn't sound like he's having a good time without you."

"He said he was going to do whatever he wanted and I was a harridan."

"You quarreled." Lucrezia said. "You both have tempers. You shouted at each other. And he was in the wrong, I give you that freely. That's why I think you should punish him more before you go back."

"Punish him? As though he were a bad dog?"

"Bad Pope. No treats," Lucrezia said archly, and we both laughed as she intended. "Get him to beg for you to come back. That shouldn't be hard. Papa's quite easy to manipulate if he loves you."

"If he loves you," I said. I had no doubt he adored his daughter. But if what he felt for me was simply an infatuation which had run its course….

"He loves you," she said. She paused. "The question is whether or not you want him back."

"I honestly don't know," I said. "Yes, I miss him terribly. Are you satisfied that I admit it? I miss Rome and my friends and my life and most of all I miss him." When I woke in the night, the absence of him beside me was like a hole in my heart. When I watched Laura do some new and adorable thing, I wished he might share it. I closed my eyes. I could smell the sweet fragrance of the roses. "I don't know if I can trust him again. He won't be faithful."

"No," Lucrezia said. "He won't be. You know who he is. It's all one piece, all of him. You take the bad with the good. But isn't that true of all of us?"

"I suppose," I said. She was right, of course. Rodrigo was Rodrigo, magnificent and clever and fabulous and petty, the most sincere sinner the world had ever known. I would not change him.

"I have an idea," Lucrezia said. She paused dramatically, "Paris!"

"I should go to France?" That seemed extreme.

"No, Paris!" Lucrezia waved her hands. "Golden apple. For the fairest. A beauty contest!"

"I'm not following this," I said.

She rolled her eyes. "We should have a beauty contest judged by the gentlemen here. And we should all write to Papa about it, you, me, Adriana, Giovanni, everyone." She looked inspired. "In fact, Giovanni could ask Papa his opinion. And then he will be reminded of how much he misses you and how many other admirers you might have, were you to be inconstant, which of course you are not."

It seemed a little juvenile, but then Lucrezia knew him well. He did have a jealous streak. "Really?"

"Sauce for the goose is sauce for the gander," Lucrezia said. "Let him wonder if you'll find someone else. That will put him on his good behavior. He'll be begging for you to come back to Rome and forgive him." She smiled. "And then you do, on the condition he go and sin no more."

"Well," I said.

"If he promised," Lucrezia said.

"Maybe," I said. "How much is his promise worth?"

She smiled, repeating what she'd said years ago the first time I'd asked her that. "My papa always tells the truth except when he lies."

"Fine," I said. "I'll punish him. Let's have a beauty contest."

THERE WAS QUITE a little Court of Love at Pesaro. Lucrezia roped all the ladies into her scheme, some more willing than others. She would not, herself, contend for the role of Queen of Love and Beauty, as she proclaimed that it would be ungallant for any gentleman to vote against her, as she was the hostess and the bride. She sang my praises instead.

My chief rival was to be another visitor, Caterina Gonzaga, a renowned beauty from the north. She was much more invested in this than I. There was only one gentleman whose attention I craved, and he was not here.

I suspected it was not Giovanni's arm that was twisted, but some less public part of his anatomy, to get him to write to Rodrigo asking his opinion of which lady was loveliest. Lucrezia showed me her letter describing Caterina to Rodrigo.

She is taller than Madonna Giulia. She has beautiful skin and hands and her figure is also beautiful but her mouth is ugly and her teeth are very ugly indeed, her eyes large and gray and her nose is more ugly than beautiful with a long face and the color of her hair is ugly. I wanted to see her dance and it was not a very satisfactory performance. In fact, in all things she does not measure up to the lady whom I hold as a sister.

I winced. "Lucrezia, that is very uncharitable! What has Caterina ever done to you?"

Lucrezia shrugged. "She's stuck up. Besides, she'll never see the letter. Only Papa will. What have you written to him?" I handed her my letter.

Madonna Caterina is very beautiful indeed. She has a shapely figure and lovely blond hair, and I know how you like blonds. Her nose is sculptural rather than plain like mine. She is graceful in every way and as virtuous and modest as she is beautiful. Beside her I am a little mouse next to an elegant hare.

Lucrezia burst out laughing. "A little mouse! Might as well say you're a cow beside a mare!"

"I thought of that," I said. "But then the bull would be inescapable."

We were bent over in wild laughter together when Adriana came in. "What is so amusing?" she asked.

"We are writing to Papa," Lucrezia said. "Do you want to send a letter in the packet with mine?"

"Giulia is writing?" Her brows rose. "I thought you were not on terms, Giulia."

"I am attempting to be cordial for Laura's sake," I said. I had my fill of Adriana's doom and gloom before. I was quite determined that whatever was worked out about Laura, Adriana would not have any part of it.

"Ah," she said. "I will indeed have a letter. Thank you for asking, Lucrezia."

The letters went off that afternoon by a Borgia courier, and I confess I waited on tenterhooks for the replies, as silly as it was. I was not fourteen like Lucrezia. I was a grown woman and knew better than to play at such games. Still, in Pesaro frivolity was the tone of the house. Lucrezia wanted a constant circus of entertainments, masques, and diversions. There was dancing every night. It was all very innocent, as such things went, but it was completely exhausting.

At the same time, there was very little news. Often couriers came for Giovanni Sforza, but whatever news they brought was not shared with the ladies. Lucrezia hardly noticed. I was used to hearing the most confidential reports on a daily basis. After all, Rodrigo wanted to talk them over with someone, and I had long since proved my discretion and loyalty. What in the world was happening in Genoa and Milan? Were the French advancing or simply massing to make a point? And what about Florence? If the French king really intended to march down the peninsula to Naples and make his claim on the throne there, he would first have to pass through the Florentine Republic. Would Florence refuse passage? Could they? The situation there was very unstable, the Medici all but deposed by Savonarola, who theoretically held no office at all but in truth ruled Florence. Equally theoretically, as a friar he owed his allegiance to the Pope, but he openly defied Rodrigo. What was going on? It made me itch not to know.

By the time Lucrezia came running into her solar triumphantly, waving a letter for me, I was keyed up enough to grab it eagerly.

> *Giulia, my sweet girl, we received a letter from you and the longer it was, the more pleasing it was to us because it took more time to read. In your eagerness to describe this woman who isn't fit to unlace your shoes, we see that you are very modest, and we know why you are. You know well that everyone who has written to us assures us that beside you she is like a lantern compared to the sun. Thus, we understand your perfection, of which we have never truly been in doubt.*

I felt a blush rising in my face. That was nicely put. So I was no longer a harridan but perfect?

> *We wish that you will recognize this clearly and devote yourself once again to the one who loves you more than anyone in the world. And when you have made up your mind about this, if you have not done so already, we will know that you are as wise as you are perfect.*

"Oh," I said. *The one who loves me more than anyone in the world.*
"What does Papa say?" Lucrezia asked.

We know Lucrezia is reading this letter, so we will put no further news as we
know you will read hers.

I laughed aloud. "Here," I said, and handed the letter to her.

Lucrezia read it quickly. "That's pretty," she said. "He loves you
more than anyone in the world. And says you're perfect. And wants
you to devote yourself again. How do you devote?"

I was blushing wildly. I could certainly imagine some devotions I
had not had in quite a while. "I should reply to the letter," I said.

"Oooh," said Lucrezia. "What are you going to say?"

"Something private," I said. I was probably bright red. "That is not
appropriate for your ears."

"Not appropriate for my ears!" she said prissily, but she was
smiling. "Something filthy dirty then. Are you getting back
together?"

I put my face in my hands. "Maybe. I'm thinking about it. If he
keeps asking nicely." Wanting him was like an ache. If we were in the
same room, his hands on me, wrapped in his arms with his face
against mine, I would fold my hand like a losing gambler. But he'd
said when he first offered for me that I should consider him coldly
and decide when he wasn't there. I could do that again. He wasn't
here. I could not be distracted by desire. I could decide what I wanted
my life to be. There was no hurry. I could take as long as I needed in
Pesaro to make up my mind.

"I hope you do," Lucrezia said simply. "I love you both."

She'd named me sister, but I was much more her stepmother. Of
course she wanted us to stay together. "I know, my dear," I said and
embraced her.

Alone in my room, I wrote my response carefully.

There are many diversions here in Pesaro, dances, entertainments, banquets
and the like, but Your Holiness is absent from me and since all my happiness

depends on you, I can find no joy or satisfaction in tasting such pleasures, for where my treasure is, there my heart is also.

When I had folded it, I brought it out to Lucrezia to put in the courier's bag. Lucrezia pointedly did not open it. "I thought you'd like to see Cesare's letter to me," she said. "Since it bears."

Dear sister, I am glad you are having a good time in Pesaro and that you find yourself comfortably situated. I'm glad you're there. Things are not good in Rome and are growing worse. The French invasion is not a joke. It's a catastrophe. It relieves my mind that you are far from the corridor of the advance in a town that is not near any military objective of theirs.

I am trying to be cardinal and condottiero at once. Lucrezia, I ask your favor. Please clear up this business with Giulia. Papa mopes and rants alternately, parsing every word she writes as though it were holy writ one moment, and the next certain that she will not return to him. I've told him to get another girl to no effect. I need his mind on the French, not Giulia. Adriana wrote to him saying that you had been to Vasanello together and that Giulia and Orsino were getting along famously. He spent better part of an hour pacing around demanding of me, "She wouldn't fuck monkey-boy, would she?" Lucrezia, I don't care who Giulia fucks. But I'd like Papa to concentrate. We have problems enough. Take care of this one for me. Your loving brother, Cesare

"Oh my poor Rodrigo," I murmured. "Jealous of Orsino!"

"Sauce for the gander," Lucrezia said. "You know when he had a fit at my mother about her sleeping with her husband she said, 'Rodrigo, I'd like to hear you explain how lying with my husband is a mortal sin and lying with a cardinal isn't? Or is that beyond your powers of disputation?' So I don't see how he could complain if you did sleep with Orsino."

"I did not sleep with Orsino, and neither he nor I have any interest in doing so," I said.

"Adriana hopes you'll reconcile," she said. "She says that would be the best thing for everyone." She frowned, a look of consideration on her face. "If you and Orsino had a son, he would inherit Vasanello before Laura, wouldn't he?"

I shook my head. "Lucrezia, that's not going to happen." I said nothing about Gentilia or his coming child. Orsino had trusted me and spilling his secrets to Lucrezia would ensure that everyone heard them in a matter of days, especially his mother. Adriana had always hoped that somehow this arranged marriage would work out, but we were man and woman and quite certain that we did not want to be husband and wife to one another!

"Because of Papa?" she asked a little too discerningly.

"I would not lie with Orsino if he were the last man on this earth," I said. "Is that definite enough for you?" I glanced back at Cesare's letter. "I am concerned about the French," I said. "He does not say where he fears they will go." The best route was straight down the Via Aurelia, through Montalto to Rome. The old road hugged the coast, broad and easy, though I supposed a great army would need to use more than one road, one of the inland ones. I could not quite see it without a map. The Duke of Urbino had good ones, surely. Urbino was less than a day away.

"Cesare can handle the French," Lucrezia said.

"He is a cardinal, not a *condottiero*," I replied. "And the Papal Army frankly isn't much."

She looked shocked. "They are splendid men!"

"There are very few of them," I said, "and no cannon to speak of. France has 22,000 men at Genoa."

Lucrezia blinked. "I can't even imagine how many that is."

"A third of the population of Rome," I said. "An entire city on the march. Do you think a third of the people of Rome are soldiers? That is what we would need to face them evenly."

The color drained from her face. She might be young, but Lucrezia was no fool. "That's impossible."

"Yes," I said. "And so your father plays chess with many fewer pieces on the board than his opponent. I do not say he cannot win, but it will require skill."

She nodded grimly. "Then he will need you more than ever."

"We will see," I said. I handed her my letter. He had not yet said he was sorry. "I will wait for his reply."

THAT NIGHT I tossed and turned in my bed. It was a beautiful summer evening. The windows were open and a cool breeze blowing, comfortable and quiet. The moon was waxing, silvering the stones. I lay alone. My own hands could not relieve desire without slipping into fantasy, into some shared story that we had built together. There had been so many in not quite four years, conceits at first, tricks of costume or posture to render sexual invention less revealing, sultan and houri, knight and highborn lady. We could smooth the raw edges of asking or receiving by making it part of a play.

At first he had done it for me, or so I thought. I was entirely inexperienced. A play allowed me to tell him what I wanted, what I had imagined or sought, without awkwardness. I had not realized at the time how careful he had been with me those first months not to hurt me or push me faster than I wanted. A story in which he was a knight who had to beg for my not-so-chaste favors allowed me to deny him without feeling as though I did.

Not that I denied him much. Cultivated sensuality bloomed like a rose. Having never known a rough hand, I was as sleek and willing as a young mare who loves the hunt. I wanted the hurdles higher and higher, the performance to stretch me toward virtuosity. I wanted to push as far as even the most jaded and satiated tastes could go, exploring my limits and his. And he had limits. He had limits of the mind and body. I discerned the latter soon enough. I was given to understand by Fiammetta and other women that younger men often wanted to go three or four times in a night, and that five minutes of hard play would get them there. Once was enough for Rodrigo, or maybe twice in a night and morning. He was not young. It took more to get started, relaxation and sensuality and a story to put away his cares. Taking time was not solely a condescension to me. Having learned that, I saw how to seamlessly awaken him, and if it pleased me at the same time, so much the better. He liked to bring me to the brink first, my desire the spur to his passion, and I can say I had no complaints of that. Other women said with annoyance that their lovers couldn't be bothered. Mine could be.

Thus our plays grew more and more elaborate, extending before and after. As he had made my first night with him an enchanted visit to the underworld, so when there was time we could sink into a play for hours, shutting the doors and dining in a dream, or loving, sleeping, waking, and loving all in one piece, as though a night was a visit to another realm. Usually there was not time, but when there was, such a dream could sustain the waking world for weeks.

And usually there was not time. Whether we had been at some function together or he came to me late after his obligations, we had a few hours before midnight to dawn. Thus plays had to extend over many nights, a scene or a bit of one embroidered again and again, redone to suit our tempers and tastes as often as we wished.

The story of the little succubus had begun in my pregnancy-induced insatiability, when it seemed that I was constantly in a state of desire and frustration. Surely a succubus could feel thus! Perhaps it was her nature to desire so keenly and so often that she slipped into the rooms of sleeping men to tempt them to half-dreaming follies that would be regretted in the morning, if they were even remembered. But what should happen if in slaking her lust with a priest, she found that tempting him to sin was more than satisfactory? What should happen if she became rather too attached to one source of release? What if she fell in love?

I closed my eyes in my lonely room in Pesaro. I let my hands rove, lifting my camisa, stroking across my belly. Thus, silvered in moonlight, to entrance and awaken a lover who sought to deny himself, and yet could not resist his friend. She was there, the reflection of his pent-up desires. She was his Shadow, for he had named her and thus turned her from spirit to flesh, from imagining to woman who lived and loved. My hand slipped lower, tangling in my curls and then the soft folds beneath. I imagined that Rodrigo watched, silent voyeur to my pleasure. "Shadow," he would whisper. He would say it breathlessly, as though waking to find me there.

I bent my head, a slow smile, opening and displaying to tempt. He would watch. He would lie against my side, hand covering mine, feeling what I felt. "Shadow." Not really a creature of darkness, curiously innocent and fresh-born, pure in her passion. What did she know of evil or good, desire incarnate and only just named? And yet she was herself. He had named her and in doing so given her herself. She was not his dream or imagining, but a woman with feelings and thoughts of her own. We had only just gotten to this part in the story. What jeopardy would they face? How would a spirit given flesh make her way in the world, and could this love which had given her shape survive reality?

I bit down on my lip. I wanted to know how the story came out. It was more than this sensual dipping of honey, of rhythm and release. I wanted his face against my shoulder, the feel of his knowing smile. I wanted his hand on mine. Imagining was not the same. He was the one conjured out of moonlight and memory, and it was enough to push me over the edge, gasping and releasing in my empty bed.

And yet, afterwards, sleep still eluded me. We would be talking now. What were the French doing? What were the Sforza doing? Having got the edge off, he would tell me everything he knew, satisfied and replete, my hand open on his chest. Now I had no idea. I got up and went to the window in my camisa, looking out at the night. What was happening?

Was there a way to deliberately see? I had practiced some with Dionisio Treschi in the last year and a half, sitting like a sibyl on a three-legged stool in the midst of a square, looking into a blackened mirror. Results had been mixed. Often nothing at all happened, or I could not tell what was vision and what was merely imagining. We were missing some critical element, I thought. Or else maybe I wasn't very good at it. Now, tonight, I felt the weight of events like a thrumming too low for hearing, a bass note beneath the silver notes of the moonlight. It wanted to be seen. Something wanted me to see. Someone wanted to show me.

I had no chalk, no square and no blackened mirror. But did I need those things, truly? When I was a Dove, my heart had been my compass in our wild flight across Rome by night. Did I need those things to see? I looked around the guest room for what I could do quietly that would not bother Laura or her nurse in the dressing room. There was a washstand with a big pottery basin, a pretty medium blue color by day, but dark by night. If it were filled with water, and if I put it on the windowsill so the moon could reflect in it.... I poured water from the pitcher and carried it to the window.

I stood beside it, the moon making patterns across the ripples in the surface where I did not hold it still. There was something that should go with it, some words. I searched for serviceable ones. "Holy Lady, Queen of the Heavens," I whispered. "Show me the pattern. Show me the most likely path."

For a long moment nothing happened. My eyes watered, focusing on the surface. I closed them.

Four paths diverged by night in a wood. I could almost feel the pine needles under my feet, under bright stars above.

"The most likely path," I whispered.

Ascanio Sforza stood beside another man in Sforza blue, stockier and darker, a sword with a glittering hilt at his side. Other men stood near, and one woman, tall and fair. Ascanio gestured, a smile of welcome, and Cesare stepped forward energetically, clasping hands with the man in blue. They nodded and smiled, apparently very pleased with something. And then it was day and I was outside, standing on a hillside overlooking fields green with summer. A swollen river rolled turgid at the bottom of the slope, soldiers trying to drag cannon through it though the water at the ford was more than hip deep, bogged down by the weight of the water. And then a shout, eyes looking up, a formation flying past me, men on horse, steel and leather, banners flying. The guns in the river could not move, much less fire. I saw Urbino's standard, and Giovanni Sforza's. And there was Cesare in the press, black and red, the bull lowering over a company of mounted men....

The bowl tipped, water spilling on my feet, and I gasped. I caught the bowl before it fell and broke. Carefully, I put it back on its stand, then returned to the window. It could not have been more than a few minutes. "Thank you," I whispered. The most likely path was that the

Sforza would be true. The French might invade, but it would be quickly stopped by allies.

I took a deep breath, looking out at the night. Cesare, Ascanio Sforza, and the other man who was probably his brother Ludovico, Duke of Milan. Well, if that was the most likely course, the best thing to do was continue as we were. I crossed myself, looking out at the night, and went to bed well pleased.

CHAPTER 8

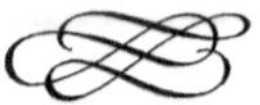

*I*f I had left for Rome the next day…. I might have. But it is useless to imagine what might have been. I did not leave. I tarried pleasantly in Pesaro in high summer for eight days, playing with Laura in the gardens, enjoying Lucrezia's company and that of her new friends. I cheerfully ceded the beauty contest to Caterina and she was crowned with roses in the garden while gentlemen pretended to be troubadours of old. I smiled from the sidelines. The only man I wanted on his knees proclaiming his unworthiness of my love was not here. Who should be on their knees to the other first? That was a diverting thought. If he begged me, would I let him into my bed again? Probably. I had little doubt of his melting charm and its effect on me. Even if I viewed it with a more jaundiced eye than formerly, I was not immune to it.

A letter came that was as fulsome and affectionate as one might wish, though still not saying that he would never stray again, delicately closing on the inquiry of what my plans might be for returning to Rome now that Lucrezia was comfortably settled. Might I return in July as the month was already upon us?

I replied by return courier that Lucrezia wished to give me a birthday fête on the 23rd, which was the following week, and that I would leave soon after. She had already ordered fireworks, I said, and so it would be rude to leave beforehand.

Two days later I was sitting in the solar with Laura playing on the floor when a maidservant came in. "Madonna Giulia, there is a messenger for you who says his letter is urgent." She held out the folded paper to me.

"Papa?" Laura asked.

"I don't know, dear," I said as I pried up the seal. It was not Rodrigo's usual imprint of the bull and keys.

My dearest Giulia, it is with a heavy heart that I write to you. Your brother Angelo is terribly ill. I fear that he will not be with us long. I beg you to come to Capodimonte so that you may say your farewell. I need you. Your loving mother

I read it twice, a cold wave descending over me. "Mama?" Laura said.

"It is from Grandmama," I said. "Uncle Angelo is very sick." Angelo was Lucrezia's age, and I doubted Laura remembered him since she had not seen him since Christmastide in Rome. He was a cheerful, boisterous young man as he had always been a carefree boy. Rodrigo had given him the old Farnese fortress of Capodimonte then and invested him as a Papal vassal holding a hereditary property from the Church. I had never been to Capodimonte. Mother had gone with him, since he wasn't really able to manage a property alone and it was a much grander place than Montalto.

"Sick?" Laura said, frowning.

"Yes, darling." I took a deep breath. "Grandmama wants me to come and help her take care of him." That would make sense to Laura. I certainly took care of her when she was sick. I would have to go, of course. I looked down at Laura. But what about her? I could hardly take her into sickness. Mother did not say what he was ill of. I expected it was the summer sickness.

For a moment my head spun. I had been younger than Lucrezia when my father and my grandmother had died of it. My baby brother

Amadeo had died. He had been Laura's age. *I need you*, she said. That was bad. She had needed me then. "Come on, sweetheart," I said, picking her up. "Let's find your sister."

Lucrezia protested, of course. "You can't go into summer sickness!"

"I can't take Laura," I said, "but I must certainly go. I've already had it, and while that doesn't mean I won't have it again, I have survived it once and it is generally less deadly the second time."

"Your brother's had it once before too," Lucrezia pointed out. "Perhaps he's better and mending as we speak. Won't you send a reply and see before you go? Surely your mother would not want you to endanger yourself, much less her only grandchild?" She had liked Angelo very much at Christmas. She didn't want it to be serious, and yet it was. I had known more sorrow in my life than Lucrezia. When I was her age, Alessandro and I were struggling to keep our family afloat, that part of it which had survived.

"If she has written to me, she has surely written to Alessandro too," I mused. Alessandro was in Rome, of course.

"And perhaps he will go and you will not need to," Lucrezia said. "And you cannot go today in any case. There must be guards and wagons and all the rest. A great lady cannot just take off on horseback."

Well I knew it. "Then those preparations must be made," I said. "Will you at least keep Laura for me? You're right that it's too dangerous for her. But she will be safe here with you, and the water here is good so there has been no sickness here." Capodimonte was beside a marshy lake, which I thought was a factor.

"Of course!" Lucrezia replied. She had been with me when Laura was born and had known her every day of her life. Laura was her baby sister. Laura would not be frightened to remain with Lucrezia. "She and her nurse can stay here and I will take good care of her."

Adriana had come in, and I explained to her what had happened. She looked dismayed. "Surely you can't go to Capodimonte."

"I must," I said. I realized that they were concerned for my health, but there was really no question. My brother was sick, my mother needed me, and I would go. "Lucrezia says that Laura can remain here. I expect you will too."

Adriana's mouth opened and shut again. "I should come with you," she said. "You may need my help. I have nursed many sick people."

"That is kind of you, Adriana," I said, and embraced her. She was stiff for a moment, then put her arms around me in return. "Truly, I appreciate it so much." It nearly moved me to tears that she would go into sickness for me to help people she did not know well.

"Papa will have a fit if you go," Lucrezia said. "He would forbid it."

"Since we are not together, he cannot forbid me anything," I said briskly. I had no doubt she was right. Rodrigo would not want me to take the chance. I would not obey him if he told me to my face, but since he was in Rome, that was a fight I did not need to have. "I will leave day after tomorrow," I said. "It's late in the day, and it will take a full day to get wagons organized and provisioned."

The next day another message came from my mother, saying that my brother had taken a turn for the worse. Was I coming? She wanted to be certain I had a letter in case the first went astray. It was not like her to send one on top of the other when I could not possibly have responded to the first one. She also made no mention of Alessandro. Was he coming? Did he know? I shook my head. He was in the opposite direction from me. Letters to him were a different courier. Just in case, I wrote out a message for him in Rome to go in the next courier bag Lucrezia sent. I also wrote to Rodrigo, telling him that I was going to Capodimonte because my brother was ill and that I would return to Pesaro afterwards, since Laura was staying with Lucrezia. He would not like it, but he didn't have to. The only thing I could do was hurry the preparations for leaving.

The carriage belonged to Giovanni Sforza, so it stayed in Pesaro. I had Lilas to ride, and Adriana took a horse of Lucrezia's, her older gelding rather than the elegant palfrey. We had a wagon for our things, our maids, ten guardsmen and four servants. We were a much smaller party than we had been on the way, and I hoped we would make better time. Giovanni even unbent enough to show me a map of our course. We would retrace our steps as far as Spoleto, but then rather than continue south to Rome on the Via Flaminia, we would turn west by lesser roads and come to Montefiascone from the east. There it was a short distance around the southern shore of Lake Bolsena to Capodimonte.

It was, as the crow flies, not twenty miles from my childhood home at Montalto. All the lands between had been Farnese feudal lands two hundred years ago. Then Capodimonte had been the jewel in the Farnese crown, the richest of the holdings. That it was restored to the family through me was something that might endure, even if I did nothing else of note. That, at least, would be remembered. *She slept with the Pope and got our castle back.*

And why was I writing my epitaph? I knew full well. There was nothing in the world I feared as much as the summer sickness. And so I tucked Laura in the last night I was there, singing to her and cuddling her until she slept, wondering if she would remember me, at least as a vague dream of early childhood. I cried when she slept, my tears falling on her as they had on Amadeo's little body. I did not want to go. Yet I would have to live with myself after if I did not.

WE WERE two and a half days on the road, going over the back of the mountains and then down into Tuscany. The last part of the journey was the hardest. We were off the Roman roads and onto roads which were less well-built, following the contours of the land rather than smoothing them. It was just before noon on the third day when we reached Montefiascone on the shores of Lake Bolsena and then followed around the southern shore of the lake to Capodimonte.

The fortress itself was a tower house on a peninsula jutting out into the lake so that two sides of it were over a steep drop to the water below. The other two sides faced the village, and the walls seemed stout and sturdy. It had all been built in pale golden stone and shone in the summer light reflected from the blue waters of the lake. We clattered through the cobbled streets to the castle, its portcullis standing open.

The first person I saw was Alessandro, and I knew before he said a word. It caught the breath from me like a fist to the stomach.

He came forward with the grooms, his plain black gown like a cassock. He reached up for me to dismount. "Giulia."

"What happened?" I said.

"Angelo died just before dawn this morning," he said, and I dismounted into his arms, Alessandro holding me tightly.

"If I had left a day earlier...." I could have, if I hadn't let Lucrezia talk me into waiting a day. I pressed my face against his, his cheek uncharacteristically unshaved.

"I'm glad you're here," he said. I felt him swallow. "Girolama is sick too." I closed my eyes and held on tight. Our baby sister, our father's posthumous child, was eight years old. Had it been eight years since that terrible summer? I had been hardly more than a child and Alessandro had been a university student. Now he was a cardinal and I was... something.

"Oh God," I said. "Where is Mother?"

"Sitting with his body," Alessandro said.

Angelo was laid out in the saletta, his hair combed neatly, his hands clasped around a cross on his breast, wearing his best doublet in Farnese blue velvet. He lay on the bier, candles at the four corners. Mother sat in a chair beside him, her head bent in prayer.

"Mother!" My voice broke, and she got up. I embraced her, Alessandro's arms around us both.

"I'm so glad you came, Giulia," she whispered. "Alessandro got here yesterday. He was here last night. He gave his brother last rites and was holding his hand when he died. I can't tell you how much it meant to have him give Angelo...." She broke down. We just held on, a knot of three, beside the bier.

THAT NIGHT ALESSANDRO and I sat vigil together. Mother hadn't slept in the last two nights nursing Angelo. Now that there was nothing more she could do for him, she slept. Girolama, fortunately, was not as bad as I had feared. She seemed to be steadily improving.

"She had it first," Alessandro said. We sat one to each side of the body, opposite his head. "The summer sickness came with the first hot days. Girolama and some friends of hers went fishing along the lakeshore and didn't come back until dusk. She was flushed the next day and then…." He shrugged.

"The fever came," I said. It often did. "Oh, Angelo." I reached out and brushed his hair off his cold brow. As his flesh had shrunk back one could see the golden hairs on his chin, the beginnings of the beard he would never grow. His skin was frigid, papery. There was still the faint glisten of the oil on his forehead.

"I know," Alessandro said. "I know you came as quickly as you could. But there wasn't anything you could have done. What's important is that we're here for mother now."

I nodded. It seemed that all the last eight years had shrunk to this, the circle of firelight, the body, and Alessandro. These were the bookends to my life. I had known a lifetime of glory between these two shadowed moments.

"It always comes down to us," Alessandro said. He reached out and took my hand in his.

"It does."

"I came as fast as I could," he said. "But it was more than a week." It took me a moment to realize he didn't mean now. He meant then, that summer eight years ago. "I got off the wagon and the streets were deserted and I went in and there was nobody in the kitchen, nobody at all. I started up the stairs and there you were, your hair under a kerchief and vomit all down the side of your dress…."

"…Bartolemeo was sick and I didn't have time so I just dried it off…"

"…looking like a waif. Your face was so thin I hardly knew you."

"I'd already been sick. I was better then," I said. "Oh God, Alessandro. You were the answer to a prayer. I've never been so glad to see someone in my life."

"You were barely out of sickbed and only thirteen," he said.

"The steward was dead. Papa was dead and Grandmother was

dead. Mama was too sick to stand. What else could I do?" His hand was tight around mine. "We managed, you and I."

"We did." We held hands over our brother's dead clasped ones.

"We always will," he said. "That I promise you."

"And I you," I said.

We sat together, sometimes silent, sometimes praying. Vigil rang two hours past midnight. The candles flickered.

"Only three hours and a bit until dawn," Alessandro said, stretching his legs out. "This close to midsummer the nights are short. I'll be up for Lauds today."

"I'm often up for Lauds," I said, and then stopped.

"His Holiness keeps it?"

"Usually," I said. I had grown accustomed to Rodrigo getting up for the dawn prayer even if he came back to bed afterwards.

"I'm glad to hear it." Alessandro sighed. "I know he's sincere. Even when…."

"…even when he's being fabulous," I said. "Well, an Andalusian isn't a draft horse. One can't expect it."

"Tactfully put," he said.

"And how is Rome? I have heard very little in Pesaro but what I have heard is alarming." I could count on Alessandro to tell me what he knew.

"Not good," he said. Alessandro let go of my hand and shifted in his chair. "Venice has decided to stay neutral. They've been France's ally, but they don't want to burn their bridges with His Holiness or Naples either. So they won't help. Meanwhile the Colonna won't do anything either."

"I thought His Holiness had hired Prospero Colonna as a *condottiero*," I said.

"Prospero's all very well, but he's not the head of the family." Alessandro shook his head. "Piero de Medici is utterly useless in Florence. He can't convince the Signoria to do anything and he has Savonarola saying that Charles is the instrument of God, so he's sitting on his ass, too. In a word, His Holiness is trying to light a fire under somebody and they're all wet tinder."

I could well imagine how frustrated Rodrigo must be. "What about Alfonso of Naples?"

"He keeps saying he'll send troops north. We'd love to see them sooner rather than later. But so far, they're still in the south."

"None of that is good news."

"No." My brother looked tired. "I'm going to stay here as long as Mother needs me. Capodimonte is a stout fortress and it's more defensible than Montalto, as well as not being right on the Via Aurelia."

"Surely you don't expect the French to come this far?" I said. The prospect was alarming.

"I can't dismiss it," Alessandro said gravely. "And neither should you."

THE FUNERAL WAS the next afternoon in the little church in Capodimonte. Alessandro officiated. I found it comforting, his voice leading the funeral Mass, a final blessing for his much-loved little brother. The church was stiflingly hot. I sat with Mother in the front, and there was not a breath of air to move the candleflames.

Afterwards, Angelo was interred in the crypt beneath, a gloomy arched space with the tombs of ancestors of ours from a hundred years ago, lords of Capodimonte when it had been a Farnese property before. I had not known any of them and did not even recognize their names, but I hoped they would watch over this latest son of their house.

The smell of incense covered the smell of death. Alessandro wore a white rochet over his red robes, and his was the last blessing before the tomb closed, making the sign of the cross amid the smoke.

I came back from the funeral almost in a dream. I had not slept the night before, and it seemed like a nightmare indeed, as though I had fallen into a terrible memory. My mother walked slowly, holding onto Alessandro's arm. I followed behind. There were many mourners, or so I thought. The young lord must have been popular, brief as his time here had been. I took a heaving breath, almost a sob. So short a time, my cheerful, delightful Angelo. I nearly stumbled on the uneven pavers.

A hand caught my elbow and I glanced over. It was a young priest, his hair cut in a tonsure, wearing the dark cassock of the Dominicans. "Allow me, Madonna."

"Thank you," I said. "Father...."

"Theoso," he said. "If there is anything I may do that is of any comfort...." His voice trailed off. He had very sincere brown eyes.

"Angelo was so very young," I said, blinking furiously.

"It is a tragedy when someone with their life ahead of them is taken," he said quietly. "We cannot understand God's purposes at such a time, only seek His peace."

"Just so," I said.

He helped me up the steps. "If I may offer my services as a chaplain to you and the family? I know you came here in haste and did not bring your own chaplain. If you would like to confess and hear Mass, I place myself at your disposal."

I blinked again. "That is very kind of you, Father. It is true I would find it comforting." I had not confessed since before I left Rome, since before Rodrigo and I ended. I was not in the habit of going several months. "If you would be able to make time tomorrow?"

"I am at your service," he said, and left me at the door of the hall.

THE NEXT DAY Father Theoso presented himself in the morning, and we sat in the little sala off my room in two chairs opposite the empty fireplace. I took a deep breath. "Father, I have sinned in the weeks since my last confession. I have been proud and obstinate. I have been vain and unkind." I was tired and heartsick.

"How have you been so?" he asked gently.

It made me squirm to speak of it, but it was true. "I have sought to punish one who loves me, to hurt him because he hurt me. I have refused to accept attempts to make amends out of pride. I have persisted in childish games when I know better, rather than discuss our differences like adults." I shook my head. "I regret my pride and sincerely repent of it."

"I'm afraid I don't understand," he said. And how would he? He must be a local priest in Capodimonte. He had no idea of the gossip of Rome or any of the rest of it. He was simply a good-hearted young man, a counselor more often accustomed to the troubles of the heart of ordinary people. And were these not ordinary troubles of the heart? How many women had quarreled with a lover and regretted it? He met my eyes guilelessly. "You may unburden yourself to me."

And so I did. He knew none of the people. He could pass on no gossip where it would harm me, even if he did not respect the sanctity of the confessional. I told him all, from the moment I had seen Rodrigo with Emilia Vespucci to the present moment. To my horror, I found myself weeping as I finished.

Father Theoso looked at me gravely. "Madonna, I see that you are indeed proud and defiant, but I put it to you that the principal blame in this situation is not yours."

"I know that he...."

He raised a hand gently. "Please, Madonna, hear me out."

"Of course, Father."

His eyes were comforting. "You are a young woman, and if I understand rightly you were a very young and innocent one, a girl really, when you began your relations with this man. He is much older, and as a vicar of Christ should not take advantage of trust placed in him. Not only did he take advantage of your trust, but he then broke your trust in him by the cause of his licentious infidelity."

"He should not have," I began. "I did trust him. I did believe that he was true to me as I was true to him."

"Madonna, despite your sin I see that you yearn for goodness," he said. "You were faithful. You lived almost as a wife. And yet unsurprisingly a man known for debauchery and carnal sin continued to indulge in it with others." He spread his hands. "Now you do not know how many other women there might have been or if he ever meant his words to you. You know that it is unlikely that he did. You recall all the warnings you were given. You know that his life has been marked with these sins for decades. You are not the first young woman to be taken advantage of, and you won't be the last."

His words were like pins sticking in my flesh, yet I could not deny them. I put my hands to my mouth.

"But now you have left," he said. "You have the opportunity to begin anew. You can seek a life of peace and virtue. Of course you are in pain. It hurts to change. To leave behind one's illusions is always difficult."

"I cannot believe I was so wrong about him," I said. "There was so much good." I closed my eyes.

"I put it to you, Madonna, that you brought much good to it. You have a sincere desire for virtue. That you presumed it existed where it did not is only naïveté, not sin. He is the one who bears the guilt of betraying your hopes." Father Theoso shook his head. "It is the same story, whether with the great or the common. Many young women fall victim to an older man's lies to their great sorrow. But Christ welcomes repentance. If you come to Him with a sorrowful and broken heart, you may lay it at His feet and be cleansed of it."

"I don't know what to do," I said. "I was going to return to Rome, but then I came here instead because Angelo was ill."

"And you must not leave immediately," he said.

"I did not plan to stay long," I said. "I am returning to Pesaro for my daughter in a day or two."

He gave me a sad smile. "Surely she will be well there a little longer. Your mother needs you."

I nodded. "I know. I should not hurry away. My poor Mama, losing him…." I choked. I could only imagine the pain she felt. I had ached when my brother Amadeo had died at Laura's age, but I had not known how it must have hurt her until I had a child of my own. And Angelo – what could I even say about Angelo?

"I absolve you of your pride," he said. "For that is truly the only sin which is yours. You have been led into grave sin, and now you waken as if from a dream. Do you have a rosary?"

"Not with me," I said.

"You may have mine," he said, and pressed a plain rosary of

wooden beads into my hands. "Pray the rosary twenty times and ask for forgiveness."

"I will, Father," I said.

THE ROSARY HAD NOT BEEN part of my usual practice, being a Dominican exercise, but I did find it comforting. And how should I not? I was heartsick. I was sad. I reached for grace and comfort, and yet found it hard to touch. Was it that my sin stood like a wall between? I missed Rodrigo. And I missed God. Surely the two were separable.

"Perhaps it has little to do with anyone else," Father Theoso said the next day when I asked for him again. "Perhaps the bridge between you and God is your contrition. You have ended these sinful relations, but still you sway on the brink of returning to them. Pray that you may be freed, and surely you will be."

I did not know that I wished to be. And yet Rodrigo had said I would never know peace with him. He was the first to admit that he was a sinner. And yet he did it again, I said to myself. If he promised that he would be true to me, could I even believe it? Or would I watch him for the next time? He had not even promised it. I sat in the solar with Father Theoso, a ray of sun across the floor, and I shivered.

"You can begin anew," he said gently. "It is never too late to live a virtuous life." He met my eyes squarely. "You have been the victim of a powerful man who made you feel important and gave you ephemeral things. But it is not your fault."

"I entered into relations with him willingly," I said. Rodrigo had been fair. He had offered for me plainly, as honestly as any marriage. "And he was good to me."

Father Theoso nodded slowly. "So you believe. But I put it to you that you may have thought that you did it willingly, but you were not able to make such a decision. Your youth, your vulnerability, and your sex speak against it. Young women are fragile. You should have been protected, and only a man who sought your ruin would have courted you when his intentions could not be other than lustful. He did you great violence, and at the same time made you believe that you chose it."

I shivered again. It was a warm summer day, and yet I felt a cold wind. "It did not seem so at the time."

"But now, in retrospect, with the scales fallen from your eyes, you see what he did," Father Theoso said. "Now you see."

I did. I saw each moment anew, all the way back to the volumes of Plutarch he had given me. And why should he? Where was the propriety in an expensive gift for the bride of his cousin's son? He should not have given me the books nor discussed them with me. We should not have sat together in the garden, laughing and talking of Alexander the Great. He should not have told me I was beautiful. He should not have asked what I thought of things or conversed with me as though I were a person of worth. If he were good, he would have ignored me and dismissed me as others did.

"I loved my books," I said. "I had been so lonely. His company was so sweet."

"And so wrong," Father Theoso said gently. "You thought it made you happy. He charmed you."

"He is charming," I said. I looked at my hands in my lap. "And funny and warm and generous."

"Or seemed to be, when he cultivated you," he said.

A tear fell on my clasped hands. "Yes."

"That part of your life is over," Father Theoso said quietly. "Like so many before you, you repent of your wayward ways and are welcome at Christ's feet. You may be cleansed of all of it and begin again, doing good work and living virtuously."

"I don't know," I said. I could see us there, in Adriana's garden. Perhaps it had been illusion. Rodrigo was skilled at such. He was my Merlin, enchanting the world until it flickered with light. How hard had it been to shape an impressionable girl into believing she loved him?

This time I shook. I did not feel right at all. Why was it so cold? And then I knew. It settled on me like a blanket of ice. "Father," I said. "Would you be so kind as to fetch my mother? I think I am ill."

CHAPTER 9

$\mathcal{I}$ had a fever, like Angelo before me. My mother put me to bed with comforting words and a face drawn with worry. "I'm sure it will pass quickly," I said. "I'm strong. A good sleep and I will be better." I saw her expression ease, and I smiled though I did not believe it. "It's just a touch of fever. You know I never get very sick."

Except when I was thirteen, when I had nearly died of the summer sickness. As my brother just had. I was rigid with terror and yet I smiled for her.

I slept. I woke. I shook with fever. I took water that a maidservant held. I slept. It was night. It was morning. I fell asleep again to dream fitfully.

I was in Adriana's garden, only it was much bigger. It seemed to stretch on infinitely. Each time I turned a corner of the bushes, there was more garden. It was dusk. There should be the lights of the house around us, but instead there was another twist, another fountain, more gardens. Or maybe it was the gardens at Nepi. I could hear the drums, the music of the Bacchanal. Figures writhed in corners, men and women and strange beasts locked in unnatural congress. A woman linked her legs around a hairy satyr's back, her red hair falling down from elaborate braids, her breasts bare. She looked at me with knowing eyes.

I dodged around a row of cedar trees. The music was louder here, dancers turning amid a knot garden, Mars and Venus and creatures too strange for fable. Ascanio Sforza smiled at me, his face transformed into a wolf's face, long canine teeth showing. Creatures paced the figures holding the hands of children. A little girl looked at me wide eyed, then grinned at me, showing her fangs. A man in a leopardskin lifted a woman shrieking in the air, pain or pleasure, and then dashed her against the edge of the fountain, the sound of her head striking it carrying over the music. I saw Lucrezia, her camisa plastered wetly to her body as she forced two men to their knees, screaming as she plied a whip against their bare backs.

And there was Rodrigo, lord of the Court Infernal, lolling on the papal throne with one leg over the arm, a golden goblet in his hand. He gave me a feral smile, lifting his robe to expose himself, empurpled and ready.

I turned and fled, dodging among the bushes. A hand grabbed at my shoulder. I screamed.

I woke. It was day, and Father Theoso and a maidservant were there, his head bent over his rosary. "Father," I whispered. My voice sounded thready. "Will you pray for me?" A dream. It was a dream. Of course it was.

"Yes," he said, "Will you give me your confession, Madonna?"

In case I died. In case I needed last rites. I closed my eyes. "Father, it has been two days since my last confession. I have been proud and resistant." I squeezed them shut. The Court Infernal. Rodrigo. My friends. My family. All monsters. We were monsters.

"You see what truly is," Father Theoso said. "The scales have fallen from your eyes."

"Scales." As though I were a lizard.

"You could come to Florence when you are well," he said. "You would be welcome. Penitent, you would be an example to others. You could lead them to truth. By your example, others could be freed from vanity and sin. You would be exalted among women for your purity and your devotion."

"Purity. Devotion."

I would be on my knees. I would be scourged clean. All would look at me and marvel. They would cherish the splatters of my blood. They would kiss my hem.

"Only at the moment of martyrdom does one truly know God," Rodrigo said. He wore the Papal tiara on his brow, silver and gold. "God glories in pain. Only in extremity does one find union."

"They will love you," Father Theoso said. "Love you."

"You yearn for love like a dove for the sky," Rodrigo said.

Like a dove taking off from his hand, spiraling up to the oculus of the Church of St. Mary and the Martyrs, the ancient Pantheon, while the tambours of Pentecost sounded, making a joyful noise unto the Lord.

I opened my eyes. "Florence."

Father Theoso nodded. "You could come to Florence, Madonna. You would be safe there. We understand how you have been ill-used. We will hold you blameless. You are a victim. You could bring down the man who has done this to you. You could avenge all wrongs visited on women. They will adore you for it. You could do penance and make amends."

"Amends," I whispered. They would hurt me and love me.

"The Borgia Magdalene," he said. "Repentant and earnest in her desire to save others. Honored and beloved."

I tasted bile in my mouth. I turned my head and heaved stomach bile onto the pillows and then lay exhausted while the maidservant exclaimed. I felt the bed tilt.

It was dark. It was so dark. Someone was pulling at me.

"Madonna, can you turn to the side?" A woman's voice.

"Giulia. Giulia, can you hear me?" My mother, her voice ragged.

"Here, Madonna. I can get the sheet this way." The first woman again.

Pulling. Yanking on my hair.

The creatures yanked on my hair and I ran, racing and stumbling through the turns of the cave. It was enormous. Or perhaps not. What looked like corridors were mirrors. There were shining sheets of glass, and when I tried to walk through them, they were solid, cold under my fingers. I could not go this way or that. I was trapped far underground. I reached for my reflection, my fingers meeting my own. Not glass, but rock. It was a crystal cave.

"Viviane," I said. I stopped, looking this way and that. Viviane trapped Merlin in a cave of crystal, its mirrored surfaces reflecting his power back upon him. She trapped him, caged him, made him hers forever and he told her all his secrets. Or was that the story? There was more than one. There was the one where she shaved her mound and inked his name upon it backwards, writing in the mirror, so that when he looked upon it he was hers forever. "Am I your mask or your mirror?"

He stood in a column of crystal, frozen like a fly in amber. Rodrigo's face was worn, lines deeply graven, bags of flesh under his chin, the night shadow of beard on his jaw. His hair was more gray than dark, eyes open and staring before him as though halted in mid-sentence. Frozen.

I walked around the column. Merlin was at my mercy, the enchanter enchanted.

"Florence," I said. "The Borgia Magdalene." I could make Rodrigo pay. I could bring him down. I knew his secrets. I had his trust. I could pour out every bedroom betrayal to Savonarola. I could testify before the College when they deposed him, tell every sin for which he could be removed. I could kneel, beautiful and penitent, desired and loved and admired as I testified against him. He would gape and gasp and hurt as I had hurt. I could hurt him worse. I could destroy everything he had ever loved, and he could do nothing to stop me. I could drive the knife between his ribs and ask him if it hurt the way he had hurt me. Chain him, depose him, throw him into a dungeon where he would never see the sun again, never touch a woman's breast, never whisper to someone meaningless words of love, never slake his lust with anyone else.

I looked at his frozen face, ugly, swollen, monstrous. He deserved it. He was nothing but an unfaithful man.

And I.... I turned, catching a glimpse of my own face in the maze of mirrors. I was beautiful and implacable, raven hair and winged eyebrows, eyes dark as night, skin pale as moonlight, lips red as blood. Bat wings rose behind the shoulders of my black gown. A Fury. An avenger of the wrongs of women. I touched my lovely face.

A succubus.

I stopped. It was as though somewhere a faint bell had sounded. "That's not the story," I whispered. "She has a name."

She had a name in the story, Shadow. The little succubus of our games had a name. He gave it to her, her clerical lover. He gave her a name and with it free will. She was no longer a demon but a woman, choosing love and life. She was not a force of destruction. She was herself.

"Shadow," I said, and touched my face. One tear marred it. Furies cannot weep. And yet I wept. I saw the tear make its solitary way down my cheek. "I am Shadow," I said. "And all the rest besides." I drew myself up, meeting my own eyes. It welled up within me. "I am Viviane. I am Oriana. I am Galatea."

I looked back at myself and I knew myself at last. "I am Proserpina." I saw the power in my face. "You cannot cage the Queen of the Underworld in the Underworld. I am the mistress here."

The mirrors shattered. They broke into a million shards, crystal crumbling into dust as though touched by sudden light.

Around me the caves stretched, vast and beautiful, fields of lilies growing in darkness, each petal limned with silver. "I am the mistress here," I said again. "I have nothing to fear." I walked through the meads, seeking the path to the sun.

IT WAS morning when I woke. The window was closed but golden light came in through the panes. There was no one with me, though a chair had been drawn up near the bed. I felt wrung out, like a damp cloth left to dry, but I wasn't shaking with fever. Not at the moment, anyway. The fever tended to break in early morning and return by night. I had nursed enough people to know.

Carefully, I swung my legs over the edge of the bed and stood up, holding onto the back of the chair. It was not far to the toilet chair, though it seemed a long way, my legs shaking. I did my business and got up. There was blood in my urine.

I took a long breath. I knew what that meant. It was a bad sign indeed.

I made my way back to the bed, the last few steps bent over with both hands on it, and lay down again, turning my head toward the window. The light streamed in, bright and pure. The pearl and gold cross Rodrigo had given me was on the night table, and I reached for it instead of the rosary, closing my hand around it and holding it to my lips. "Holy Mary, Mother of God, pray for us sinners now and at the hour of our death." I closed my eyes.

The words were a thin thread leading into the darkness. It seemed that I was spinning, lifting, as though I were no longer lying in the bed, but floating above in cool night. It was peaceful, restful as lying on the breast of the sea. I could still hear the words whispering, all the words of different prayers, as though beyond all was a vast cathedral in quiet dark, hundreds of voices in point and counterpoint, each with a different prayer, each at a different part of the litany. It was beautiful. It was like flying among the stars. My heart soared, lifting like a bird trying its wings.

And yet there was one voice. "...Hail, Holy Queen, Mother of Mercy, our life, our sweetness and our hope." I knew that voice, deep and resonant. "To you we cry, poor banished children of Eve. To you we send up our mourning and weeping in this vale of tears." I turned.

It was as though I looked down through the ceiling. Rodrigo knelt in the Lady Chapel of St. Peter's, his white vestments pooled around him, head bent over his hands. He looked so tired. Candles glowed on the altar before him. No one was there except an acolyte, silent at the back of the chapel. The fire glittered off his pearl and gold ring, his eyes squeezed shut. "Most gracious Advocate, turn your eyes of mercy toward us...."

It was like being caught in a net, as though a golden net hung above me. It was like a snood, like my golden hair net. I could not slip through. It caught me. I could not fall upward into the air.

"Mother of the Word Incarnate, Blessed Virgin, we beseech your aid and comfort for your daughter, Giulia." Rodrigo was still talking. "Bring her safe through her trials in your loving arms." It was like a net of his prayers, spinning out like thread, gold and linen wound together as though to make cloth of gold, plain and serviceable linen wound about with something precious and eternal. "We beseech you, bring her safe to her child who needs her. Hold her in your care."

Laura, I thought. *Laura needed me so much. Rodrigo needed me. It was written in every line of his body, in every line of his face.*

"Holy Mary, Mother of God, Lady of the Stars and Seas, turn your face to her...."

And yet it was fading. I could no longer see him. I could hear his voice, but it was growing dark around me. So dark.

"Mother!" I shouted.

It came out a whisper. "I'm here," she said.

I opened my eyes. It was twilight in the room, my mother sitting in the chair beside my bed, rubbing my hands and arms with a damp cloth. "Mother...."

"I'm here, Giulia," she said. "There, darling. I'm right here."

"Rodrigo," I whispered.

"You were calling him in your sleep," she said. Her voice caught. "Rest, baby. Don't try to talk."

It was so hard to stay awake. "Tell him I'm sorry," I said. "Tell him I love him."

"You will tell him yourself," she said, "when you are back in Rome."

"In Rome," I said. I closed my eyes. "Not Florence. Rome."

WHEN I WOKE AGAIN, it was night. There were candles on the side table, and Dionisio Treschi sat in the chair, a book open on his lap. "Dionisio?" I murmured. It could not be. He was in Rome.

He looked up, then put the book down on the side of the bed. "How are you? Do you need anything?"

"A drink of water." My voice sounded thready even to me.

"I can do that." I waited while he brought some in a pottery cup.

I could not take it from him. My hand shook and the water splashed over my fingers. "You'll have to help me."

"Of course," he said. He was steady and gentle, raising me up in bed so that it wouldn't go all over me, holding me with one arm and the cup with the other hand so that I could drink, then laying me back against the pillows again.

I closed my eyes and then opened them again. He was still there. "How are you here?" I whispered. "You're in Rome."

"His Holiness sent me with his own doctor," Dionisio said. "He's very worried about you."

"I know," I said. "I heard him praying."

"He's in Rome," Dionisio said gently.

"I know. In the Lady Chapel at St. Peter's." I looked up toward the ceiling. I had felt it like a net, catching me, keeping me from falling up into the stars.

"I think you were delirious," Dionisio said. "The doctor said your fever was very high."

"My mother…." My mother had been here.

"She's in your brother's room. She asked me to watch."

"My brother." Angelo was dead.

Dionisio put the cup down. "His Eminence."

"Alessandro?" I tried to raise up. "Alessandro is sick?"

"He's not as sick as you are," Dionisio said, trying to keep me from rising. "But yes, he's sick too. God willing, you will both be well soon. I certainly don't want to have to explain to His Holiness that you're not."

"Yes, that would be awkward," I said, and lay back on the pillows. "His doctor. And you."

"Yes."

I looked at him sideways. "What does he think you'll do?"

"Amuse you with witty repartee?" Dionisio smiled. Then he

sobered. "Maybe he thinks you need your own man, someone who answers to no one else. And I asked to come."

"Into sickness?" It was very brave of him.

"It's hard to break in a good patron," Dionisio said.

"Where is Father Theoso?" I asked.

"Sleeping, I suppose," Dionisio said. "Do you want me to get him?"

"No." I did not want to see him. I was not entirely certain why. "Will you read to me?"

He lifted the book. "Of course. It's Diodorus Siculus, volumes sixteen and seventeen. His Holiness thought you might enjoy it. Pretty dry going, if you ask me, but...." He shrugged, "Who am I to argue with him?"

"Who indeed?" I said. "Yes, please read." It would keep me from morbid thoughts. He had sent me Diodorus, his doctor, and Dionisio.

"When Eubulus was archon at Athens and the Romans elected as consuls Marcus Fabius and Servius Sculpius, in this year Timoleon the Corinthian made ready for his expedition to Sicily...."

I SLEPT, waking to eat a little from a bowl my mother held. I slept. I woke. I took water. I slept. I had no real sense of time passing. Sometimes I shivered with fever. Sometimes I lay in sheets soaked with sweat, a maidservant rolling me to the side to change them. Sometimes Dionisio read to me. He was reading about the reign of Philip of Macedon now. It was comforting.

I heard Father Theoso's voice. "Send him away," I whispered. "Mother, send him away." He argued. I heard that. My mother sent him away.

Another time, morning now, and my head was clearer. My hand did not shake against the blanket piled on me, and the girl who brought me water helped me sit up a little. "What day is it?" I asked.

"The Eve of Assumption, Madonna," she said. She had a broad, sweet face under a white cap.

"Assumption?" How could that be? How could it be mid-August? I had lost more than two weeks. And what about Alessandro? "How is His Eminence?" I asked.

"He got up for a few minutes yesterday," she said. "He is mending."

I took a deep breath. "Praise be to God." I had feared for him when I did not fear for myself.

She glanced at the side table. There was a stack of papers on it next to my cross. "These come by fast post for you every day or two." Her eyes were very wide. "From His Holiness."

"He must be frantic," I said. "Can you read them to me?"

"I do not read, Madonna," she said.

I didn't think I could so much as hold a paper. "Can you send Dr. Treschi to me then?"

I dozed again, but woke as Dionisio came in. "You asked for me?" He looked harried but not ill himself. "What can I do?"

"Read me the letters," I said. "Begin with the first."

"Are you sure? They may be private," he said hesitantly.

"Please." I didn't have energy to argue.

"Very well." He opened the first and unfolded it, clearing his throat.

Disobedient and reckless Giulia, how could you go to Capodimonte? You knew that I would expressly forbid it out of care for your health and your safety which is precious to me. Instead you deliberately did not ask my permission but did just as you pleased without regard for my wishes and without regard for the pain it would cause me if you were to succumb to illness and without regard for the child who needs your tender care.

Dionisio looked up at me, an alarmed expression on his face.

"Yes, he's annoyed," I said. I closed my eyes. "Read another one."

I heard the sound of parchment unfolding, and he began again.

My sweet and terrible girl, for you are both, sweet because you are the honey which sweetens my life and gives incomparable joy and terrible because you have gone into such peril and terrify me, as indeed you do nearly daily these last years. You are too bold and yet I can hardly scold you for courage or fidelity as those are admirable traits when not taken to extreme. I have heard

*of your brother Angelo's death and I will pray for him. He was a fine young
man of whom anyone would be proud....*

Dionisio stopped because I was sobbing. "Donna Giulia?"
"A moment," I said, and cried myself to sleep.

WHEN I WOKE it was late at night. There were no sounds. The
moonlight shone in through the windowpanes, a silver patch on the
floor. The household was entirely quiet. I must be out of immediate
danger if no one was sitting with me. Indeed, while the sheets were
damp with sweat, I did not shiver. I felt clean and hollow, like a wind
had blown through me. For the moment the fever had broken.

I reached for one of the letters and tried to read it in the light from
the window.

My Giulia for so I think of you still

It was hard to read in the near-dark, but the writing was his own,
even and blocky, a clerk's hand. His Giulia. Once I had wanted to be
that more than anything.

Another silver summer night, four years ago – I had been at the
Vice-Chancellor's palazzo with him, only a few days since we had
begun. I was giddy with wonder, this lovely house with gallery and
library, a seamstress who had measured me for what seemed like an
amazing array of clothes and showed me beautiful fabrics for me to
make my choice, dinners with the household sitting at the head table
with fifty people looking at me as though I were the lady, and nights
in Rodrigo's bed. I had long imagined sensual indulgence. I had
learned my own body as young women will, but I had not truly
understood pleasure at the hands of someone with years of experience and patience to match.

I remembered his hands sweeping down my spine as I lay on my
belly, gathering up my long hair and kissing the back of my neck.
Such simple things – his hand over mine, the pressure of his fingers

between mine – I had not thought such things could arouse passion as surely as his knowing smile as he bent his head to my nipples. He watched everything. He saw my breath, felt my responses as surely as he gauged my delight in books or fine cloth, the better to know what would move me. He brought me to the edge, breathlessly leaping the last hurdle, before he took me. I was still new to this. Open, relaxed, fully aroused, it wouldn't hurt. I remembered that I surprised him, pushing him down on his back so that he couldn't control depth, straddling him and taking it hard. "You're a fierce creature," he said when he could talk.

"Yes," I said, settling down against him, body to body. To have that power, to break him beneath me, prisoner of his desire, was intoxicating. "Is that bad?"

"Not to me," Rodrigo said.

I'd gone to sleep on his shoulder feeling safe and loved. Was it wrong to have been so happy? Had he simply manipulated me as Father Theoso said? Had I only thought I was happy? It had seemed to me that I was at the time. Was it wrong to be happy and feel safe and loved? Perhaps that was the true question. I looked up at the ceiling above me in the dark. Does God want us to be happy or want us to suffer?

I could not answer that. I closed my eyes. "Holy Mother," I whispered. "Show me what's right." It comforted me enough to sleep.

I SLEPT AND WOKE, then drank broth that my mother fed me with her own hands. "I am sorry to be such trouble to you," I whispered, having finished half of it. "I came to help."

There were lines of stress around her mouth where there were not before. "I should not have asked you to come," she said. "You and Alessandro. I would never forgive myself...." If we had died. She did not need to finish the sentence. "Alessandro wrote to Bartolemeo at the university in Pisa and told him to stay there. Girolama is nearly well again."

I nodded. That was a relief. My mother helped me lean forward, arranging pillows behind me. "Good. What is going on in the world? It is past Assumption and I have no idea what is happening."

Her face was grim. "Ludovico Sforza has gone over to the French."

"What?" I gasped. The most likely path, the most likely future I had seen, was that the Sforza were true. Ludovico going over to the French was a disaster.

"There was a battle. The Neapolitans were defeated and have withdrawn south toward Rome. If the King of France wishes to come himself, there is nothing to stop him north of Florence."

"What about the armies of the Papal States?" I asked. "What about Urbino? What about the Orsini?"

"I have no news of them," my mother said. She glanced at the pile of letters on the table. "Do you know nothing? He sends you letters almost every day."

"He remonstrates with me for being here," I said. "And tells me I am his sweetness in turn. What can one make of that?"

"That he is worried about you," my mother said. She shook her head, her eyes on my face. "And he is a man accustomed to his own way."

I laughed, though doing so made my chest hurt. "I think he believes that he can just talk God around most of the time if he wears out His ear."

"So his cousin says."

"How is Adriana?" I asked. I had, I am sorry to say, entirely forgotten about her.

"She has not been ill," my mother said. "She hasn't helped at sickbeds." Her voice was studiously neutral, and I heard my own tone in it. I had exactly her expression when I disapproved but did not say anything that could be quoted to my detriment.

"I see," I said. "Well, Adriana is no sicknurse, and I was frankly surprised she came with me. We are not so close as all that."

"I thought perhaps you were." My mother looked thoughtful, sitting back in the chair. "Well, maybe she needs the favor of her powerful cousin and knows His Holiness would be angry if she left you."

"Probably," I said. Rodrigo had been very upset that Adriana had decamped to the country during the Papal Election, leaving me pregnant and on my own. I had been fine, but he'd been furious with her. "In theory she is my chaperone, or rather Lucrezia's, though Lucrezia is married now and not in Rome. And I do not live in her house." I had not quite thought about it that way before. Adriana's house was rented out for her income, and she had lived with me and Lucrezia and Laura in Palazzo Santa Maria in Portico for not quite two years, but it was clear she was not the mistress of the house. Rodrigo owned it, as he'd said. The master's apartments, with sala, camera, generous bathing room and study, were mine rather than Adriana's, and done in the most expensive style and greatest comfort. Rodrigo was there often enough. He stayed with me as a man might stay in his wife's room. And there was a pang of pain again. I was used to being treated as his wife. I was used to his confidence and his children and the work of being his consort. Not that men weren't unfaithful to wives. It happened more often than not.

"Will she move back into her own house now?" my mother asked. "If the child she had charge of is grown and married?"

"I don't know," I said. "I suppose she might return to Pesaro. Or go to Vasanello." And yet Adriana loved Rome. She had professed no desire for country life. Would she have enough money to keep her house open without Rodrigo's stipend to care for Lucrezia? I had no idea what Orsino's revenues from Vasanello looked like or how much he gave Adriana. He did not have to give her anything, as he was her stepson from her husband's first marriage, rather than her own child, but she had raised him since he was three and he called her mother. Surely he provided some support now that he had an estate. The household expenses at Santa Maria in Portico had been paid entirely by Rodrigo.

Though if we were done, that would stop. I took a deep breath. Unlike Adriana, I could certainly stay here. Capodimonte was Alessandro's now and mother would need to run it. Also, Alessandro rented a small palazzo in town but did not have a mistress to be his hostess. It would be perfectly respectable for me and Laura to move in with Alessandro and I could do him much good in society. I had alternatives to Rodrigo, as surely he knew. They might not be as luxurious, but they would be perfectly comfortable, and I always prized my freedom over luxury.

"Did you quarrel with her confessor?" my mother asked. "He was much with you and then you asked me to send him away."

"Her confessor?"

"Father Theoso."

I was perplexed. "He's not Adriana's confessor. That's Father Leo. Isn't Father Theoso the local priest?"

My mother shook her head, a little line between her brows. "I've never seen him before. Adriana said he was her confessor when he arrived. You were sick and so was Alessandro. He said he came from Rome with letters and would stay if she wished."

"How very odd," I said, and lay back on the pillows. Something was not right. I could not put my finger on it. Had he said those things? Had he asked me to go to Florence, or had I dreamed it when I was terribly ill? I didn't know. "Letters from Rodrigo?"

"Letters for her, I presume," my mother said. She glanced at the stack of papers. "His Holiness's letters come by Borgia courier."

"Of course," I said. "The Sforzas own half the posting stations. He doesn't trust anything private to the regular post."

"Will you return to him?" my mother asked gently, smoothing my hair back from my forehead.

"I don't know yet," I said. His letters were passionate, angry and loving by turns, but he did not say he was sorry. "I haven't decided." My dreams were discomfiting, dreaming him a demon and then in prayer. I knew what I wanted, and yet I doubted myself. I looked at her. She had much to gain from this liaison. Her son had gotten a cardinal's hat and a castle. And yet surely she also cared for my happiness. "What do you think I should do?"

"What your heart tells you," she said, and embraced me.

I put my face against her shoulder, the familiar scent of her, the softness of her washed linen camisa. "Mama, how can you say that? It's against your self-interest."

She laughed. "My darling, you've been in Rome too long."

"Perhaps I have," I said.

She let go, sitting on the side of the bed, still smiling. "Did I ever tell you about how I met your father?"

"You told me he inherited Montalto and went to your father and asked for your hand," I said. He had been thirty-nine and she eighteen.

"There was more to it than that," she said. She smiled at me smugly. "My father was a useful nephew of the Lord of Fondi, and he held the town of Sermoneta as steward. I was seventeen, the seventh daughter of eight, with one brother. By then my father had paid six dowries, five to suitors and one to the Church, and there were two to go. Needless to say, my dowry wasn't large."

"And you were seventeen," I said. "Old to be without a betrothal."

She nodded. "There were no takers. I was as badly suited to the convent as you are. I did not want to be locked away from the world. So I made myself useful as a companion in my older sister's house, helping with her children, teaching them letters, taking them to church. It got me to Florence, which was much more exciting than Sermoneta." Her smile grew. "And I was seduced by a *condottiero*."

My mouth dropped open. "What?"

My mother laughed. "You shouldn't be so shocked! Were you not a headstrong and wayward girl? What do you think I did as an overripe virgin when a handsome, hard man on a big, black horse told me that I was a vision of heaven? Wrapped my arms around him and held on, of course!"

"I can't believe it," I said. I had never heard this story before.

"My sister was a completely inadequate chaperone, and we carried on for months under her nose, sneaking out for assignations all over town. Your father was a Farnese on the wrong side of the blanket. His father had acknowledged him and he had the Farnese name, but a younger half-brother was the legitimate heir. He had no money. He hoped he'd win some in battle, enough to buy a property. I said I didn't care. When I got pregnant, we found a priest who would marry us without permission." She squeezed my hand. "You should have seen the scene when it all came out! Tears and shouting, betrayal and weeping, and me vowing that I would be with my love no matter what and that I would bear this child in all honor. I walked out and said that if I was disowned, I would be. I walked from Florence to Pisa, four months pregnant, to where his company had been ordered, and moved into camp with him."

I boggled at her. "Like any soldier's woman."

"That is what I was, my dear. And that's where Alessandro was born, on a rainy night in a bivouac with a camp follower as midwife." She smiled as though the memory was sweet. "And three months later, your father got word his half-brother had died without issue and he had inherited Montalto. So he retired from arms and we became Lord and Lady. My parents reconciled with me when they saw I was decently settled. But that's why there are now Caetani relatives coming out of the woodwork asking you for favors! They thought my children of little enough account when they were born. Now they are your dearest friends and I their beloved aunt or cousin!"

"I wondered at that," I said. "Being cultivated by so many people of noble blood who I had never heard of before or met."

"But now Alessandro is Cardinal Farnese, and you are His Holiness' concubine," she said. "And we are worth knowing."

"But it's false," I said. "It didn't feel right."

"Fides et Amor," she said. "That is what we put on the crest we made for ourselves. Honor and love. That is what you children are heir to."

I sat forward as much as I could, putting my arms around her again. "Thank you, Mama." I sniffled. "I seem to be crying a lot of late."

"Cry all you want," my mother said. "As long as you're still with us."

"I'm strong," I said. Of course she'd been afraid of losing me too.

"I know it, baby," she said, and held me tight.

CHAPTER 10

I was able to eat some soup that evening. Dionisio read to me. A few days later I got up with help and took a few steps around the room, my hand in my mother's as though I were a toddler. It made me cry again. "I miss Laura so much."

"It was better not to bring her," my mother said. "Not with sickness here."

I nodded. We both remembered how quickly my baby brother Amadeo had succumbed to the summer sickness when he was Laura's age. "She is safer in Pesaro," I said. "She has her nurse and Lucrezia loves her."

"Her half-sister," my mother said, depositing me gently back on the side of the bed. "Complicated families."

"Always," I said. "I love Lucrezia dearly. But isn't family as much about heart as blood?"

My mother helped me to lie down again. "Of course. You've been with her since she was nine, and for all practical purposes you've been her stepmother for the last four years. Naturally you love her. Unfortunately it goes the other way too. Aren't there plenty of brothers at each other's throats?"

"A problem as old as Cain and Abel," I said.

She smoothed the covers around me. "You children have never been at each other's throats."

"A testimonial to you as our mother," I said.

"There are many good mothers with unruly children." She sat down on the edge of the bed. "We wish we could control everything so that no ill befalls you, but we can't." Her brows knit just as Alessandro's did. "You were thirteen when your father died, and your grandmother and Amadeo. I was so sick when Girolama was born."

"They said we'd lose you both," I said. "But we didn't." Even now it made my voice choke. That horrible hot summer, my mother sweating and straining to give birth, still in the throes of fever herself.... "You're the strongest woman I've ever known, Mama."

"It was too much on you, but there was no choice," she said. "I'm so sorry."

"There was nothing else to do," I said. Thirteen, and mistress of the house, half the household sick and all of us bereaved, my little brothers sick unto death. I had managed alone for a week before Alessandro arrived. "Truly, Mama. We all just did the best we could. I have never been angry."

"And then this Orsini marriage...." She shook her head. "I wish I could have spared you."

"Even that I do not mind," I said, "for it took me to Rome and to Rodrigo. All the good I have in my life, learning and friendship and love and Laura and work that matters, came from that."

"Then you should go back to it," she said.

"Is it that simple?" I lay back on the pillow.

"Yes." She brushed my hair back where it had escaped from braids in the front. "Giulia, you've always complicated things too much. You think one way and then another and consider another point of view and perhaps that's useful if you are dispensing justice or deciding who to patronize. But it's no use in matters of the heart. Other people's opinions don't matter. The only one who matters is you."

"I want to know what is right," I said.

"No one can tell you that, baby," she said. "Not even me." She smoothed my hair again. "If you want to stay here, you can. You and

Laura can live here with me and we'll hold Capodimonte for Alessandro. It's a great estate and has been neglected until this year. There's a lot of work to do. It's not a bad future."

"It's not," I said slowly. "But I miss Rome. I think that even if Rodrigo and I were done, I would want the game. I would play for someone else. Maybe I'd live with Alessandro in Rome and play for him."

"You could do that," she said. "And you could find another lover if you wanted. You're young. I don't expect you're suited to a life of celibacy any more than I was."

"I'm not," I said.

Mother put her head to the side. "So, if you were looking for a man of your choosing, what would you want?"

I hadn't seriously considered it. "Not one of those silly boys Lucrezia likes or some headstrong young man. Forty or fifty at least. Someone mature who knows themselves and who has experience of life."

She nodded. "And what else?"

"Educated, serious, driven. Someone who loves the arts. A humanist. A man who loves children. Someone intellectually curious and unafraid of new ideas." Someone who would allow me to pursue my magical studies as well as my more conventional studies, or at least would not interfere. And I could never bear someone like Orsino, to whom the tumults of the world meant nothing. "Someone who plays the game."

"And do you know any such men?" my mother asked quietly.

I considered. "Well, I do not know him, but I have heard that Prince Ferrandino's father is such. He's widowed now. He was married to Ascanio Sforza's older sister, but she died a few years ago. Certainly his children, even his illegitimate daughter Sancia, seem well-raised and he is a patron of the universities." I considered further. "And there are several cardinals. I am fond of Raffaele Riario, though he has a mistress. I can't say Ascanio is displeasing, though again he has a mistress and I am not sure I'd want to be embroiled with the Sforza. I do like Carafa, though he's so pedantic I'm not sure I could live with him." I shrugged. "The Duke of Urbino is devoted to his wife and he's too young for my taste, but Ercole of Ferrara is said to be quite charming. He invented the cat-flap, did you know? So many cats in the palace and all the guards opening and shutting doors for them all the time."

My mother laughed. "That certainly shows his mind."

"It does, doesn't it?"

She was smiling. "So kings, princes of the Church, sovereign dukes…. You don't think little of yourself!"

"Mama, I've had the Pope!"

"So you have." Now she looked like she'd laugh. "So why not set your sights high?"

"I have been the queen on the chessboard, and I like it," I said. "All false modesty required for the world aside, I'm very good at it. I'm an asset to any man who wants to play the game. Not just any woman can do what I do, as Rodrigo knows full well after the papal election. I am exceptional and I have no desire to sell myself short."

"I think there is little danger of that," my mother said, her mouth twitching. "You and Alessandro. I do have ambitious children. But you don't need to decide now. Rest and get your strength back." She fingered the braid. "I'm sorry I had to cut your hair. It was so lovely all the way to your knees. It's only to the middle of your back now. I just couldn't manage it with the fever."

"I understand," I said. "I have a lot of hair."

"There's still enough to braid."

I smiled. "I know. And I will rest and think."

THE FEVER CAME BACK, of course. It's always like that, advancing and retreating, but as one begins to mend it doesn't go as high or as often. I dreamed of war. Armies marched and buildings burned, an almond tree in bloom standing for a moment silhouetted against a wall of flame. Pieces of type lay scattered among shards of glass in the cobbled street while torn pages blew in the wind. A crenellated wall collapsed in rubble, defenders broken like puppets as they fell among the great stones. People walked the road with burdens on their backs, thin-faced children cringing as riders went by. Blood spread on stones, the black bull's head in the dust, his horns gilded and the wreath of flowers still on his brow as his blood pumped out. "The bull is wreathed for the sacrifice, and the slayer too is ready," a woman said.

I woke, my heart racing. It was day. There was no one in the room with me. All was quiet. Was it the bullfight I remembered? I had thought it ill-omened at the time. I hugged my arms to my body. I didn't feel feverish. I had heard those words somewhere before, the words from my dream. I said them aloud to the empty room. "The bull is wreathed for the sacrifice, and the slayer too is ready." I could not place them, but the inference was obvious. Who came to slay the bull?

There was a knock on the door, a man's voice. "Madonna, did you call?"

"No, I'm sorry. What?" I replied, not loudly apparently.

The door opened and Father Theoso looked in. "Madonna? I heard your voice but could not make out the words. Is there something that you need?" He looked young and concerned, a simple priest who had heard a cry from a sickroom. How had I imagined he had frightened me?

"I was calling my mother," I said.

"I believe she's in the kitchens tending to something," he replied. "Do you want me to fetch her?"

"No, it's all right." My poor mother was still trying to run the household. "It's not important."

He came inside. "Is there anything I can do, Madonna? Would you like to confess?"

"I have been too sick to sin," I said with a trace of my old tartness.

He half smiled, a little shrug. "It's my trade," he said. He glanced at the pile of letters on the table by the bed. "Donna Giulia, if I may say so, one is not cured of sin. It requires constant examination, lest one fall back into doubt or unhealthy habits. I understand you have had letters from this man," he said. He did not say His Holiness.

"I have," I said.

"May I see them?"

"No," I said shortly.

Father Theoso's eyes were filled with concern and compassion. "Madonna, I fear for the state of your soul. You are clean, and yet you professed yourself tempted to return to sin. Instead of reading these letters, which may persuade you to fall once more, I beg you to turn them over to me and I will destroy them unread."

"I cannot," I said, "in any propriety. You are my confessor, not His Holiness's. These words are his, not mine, and spoken in confidence." The idea of him reading Rodrigo's letters made me squirm. Was it simply guilt? What was true? "Father, I was so ill that my memory fails me. Did you invite me to come to Florence?"

His gaze did not shrink from mine. "Why would I do that, Madonna?"

"I don't know," I said.

He seemed guileless. "However, if you would like to go to Florence, I'm sure that could be arranged. I can see why you might feel safer outside of the Papal States if you mean to remain virtuous in the face of his wishes. Also," he said gently, "your presence puts your brother in a terrible position. He has sworn obedience to this man, and yet wishes to preserve his sister's honor. The only honest recourse for him would be to reply that you are not here and he cannot return you to Rome. If you were in Florence, there would be no difficulty."

All these words were true. I had no doubt that Rodrigo would rail at Alessandro if he were in a temper, but I doubted it would come to anything beyond an irate letter, if he were the man I thought he was. If he weren't, one could imagine Alessandro and myself brought back under guard.

"I'm certain you would find welcome in Florence," Father Theoso said.

"I will think on it," I said. I lay back in the bed. "Even a little conversation tires me. Thank you." I did not take my eyes off the pile of letters. I saw how his gaze returned to it.

"Of course, Madonna," he said courteously, going out and closing the door.

Laboriously, I got up and gathered the letters together. I put them under my pillow.

AN HOUR or two later Dionisio came in with another one. "Fresh from a Borgia courier," he said, handing it to me with the seal intact. He looked at the empty table. "What happened to the rest?"

"They're under my pillow," I said.

He smiled. "Well, that's a good place for love letters."

"It's for safekeeping."

Dionisio's face grew solemn. "Who do you fear?"

"Perhaps foolishly," I said. "It is nothing." I held the new letter in my hands. I was well enough to read now. And to wonder. "Tell me, Dionisio," I said slowly. "Does this mean anything to you? 'The bull is wreathed for the sacrifice, and the slayer too is ready?'"

He sat down on the chair beside the bed. "It's Diodorus," he said. "I read it to you a few days ago."

That was something of a relief! "I don't remember," I said.

"You asked me to read when you were feverish. You said it calmed your mind. So I read." He looked at me keenly. "Why?"

"What was the context? What did it mean?"

"It's the words of the Oracle at Delphi, the Delphic Sibyl, to King Philip of Macedon. He asked if he would conquer Persia. Instead, he was assassinated at a celebration before he embarked and his son, Alexander the Great, became King of Macedon. Philip was the bull, not Persia." Dionisio saw something in my face. "Madonna, what's wrong?"

"I dreamed it," I said. "The bull. The Borgia bull. The sacrifice."

"You've been feverish," Dionisio said. "You dreamed a lot of things. This was just something I read to you."

"You, of all people, know I'm a Dove," I said.

"I think you are worried about His Holiness," he said gently. "And you probably should be. The political situation isn't good."

"Tell me."

"The King of France has crossed the Alps in person. His army is now reported to be nearly 30,000 men. It's said he has cannon mounted on wheels so that they can be brought to bear wherever he wishes. He's in Genoa with the Sforza."

I shook my head. "That's awful news. What about Venice?"

"Staying out of it. Prince Ferrandino has retreated south to Rome."

"And Florence?" I asked.

"Piero de Medici isn't his father. Lorenzo might have held Florence against him. But I don't know." Dionisio looked off into the distance. "Savonarola rules for all practical purposes."

"Father Theoso suggested I might go to Florence."

Dionisio's eyes snapped back to me. "That would be a terrible idea," he said flatly.

"So I think." I met his gaze. "Dionisio, there is something wrong."

He gave a short laugh. "You mean other than the French are invading, Savonarola is destroying irreplaceable art and books, and there's sickness here?

"Something hidden," I said. 'And no, it's not that I'm feverish. Can you not feel it, Dionisio? You're a magus. Can't you feel it like a malaise? Like an illness, spreading from some source, transforming and blighting everything it touches."

He ducked his head, the light from the window touching his hair and the collar of his shabby black robe. "I've heard that music so long that I'm deaf."

"You know what I mean," I said.

Dionisio nodded. "When I was in Florence a couple of years ago my old maestro, Pico della Mirandola, asked me to hear Savonarola preach. He asked me as a favor to him. On my love for him, he said." There was misery in his voice. "I had loved him."

That was no surprise. "So you went," I said.

"I don't know how to explain what it was like. I was caught up, enraptured. It seemed to me that every word he said was truth, and that nothing could be greater bliss than to join the crowd in their responses, crying our guilt and pain to heaven." He glanced at me.

"Afterwards I felt sick. Like I'd eaten something that tasted good but griped my guts. But Pico…. He burned his own books. Even after His Holiness acquitted him of heresy, he wasn't the same."

"Have you ever felt anything like that?" I asked.

He shook his head. "No," he said. "And I never hope to again. Giulia, tell me you won't go to Florence."

"I won't," I said. Whatever I chose, it would not be that.

THE NEWS FROM THE NORTH, when it came, was all bad. On October 29th the French took the fortress of Fivizzano on the borders of Florence and killed the entire garrison to a man, even the servants who did not fight. Piero de Medici asked for terms in a humiliating way, promising King Charles 200,000 florins and allowing him the freedom of the city, which the Signoria of Florence had not agreed to. Nevertheless, it was clear Florence would fall.

The text of Savonarola's sermon came to us within a few days. "Oh Italy, because of your lust, your avarice, your pride, your envy, your thieving, your extortion, you will suffer! Oh clergy who are the source of these evils, you will pay the price. God's scourge is coming! The righteous may yet be spared!" If there was any heart left in the Florentine defenders, this ended it.

We heard it from Guilio de Medici, who had galloped south with three men and saddlebags full of family treasures. His cousin, the cardinal, was still in Florence but he'd sent Guilio off to Rome with precious and portable things, including the sapphire necklace belonging to the late Contessina de Bardi, Giulio's great-grandmother.

A maid helped me to go down the hall to the master's sala which Alessandro was using. He too was able to get up, and we sat beside the fire despite the warm September day. His face looked pinched and thin, and I wondered if I looked as bad as he did.

"I'm sorry to have intruded upon you when you've been ill," Giulio said, sitting down at the table to dine with us. "And when you've lost your brother. You have my most sincere condolences."

"Of course you're welcome," Alessandro said. "But what's happening in Florence? I have had no recent news."

"You know the King of France is in Milan?"

"I knew he was in Genoa. Is he as far as Milan?" Alessandro looked alarmed.

"There was a battle. The French held the field and killed all the enemy wounded. Then they sacked the town of Rapello. Ludovico Sforza immediately granted free passage to the French and his alliance." Giulio shook his head. "On the next Sunday, Savonarola preached a sermon in the cathedral. I was there. It was on the Book of Genesis, the story of Noah, the part that starts, 'Behold I will bring a flood of waters upon the earth to destroy all flesh. Everything which is on the earth will die.' Then he went on to say that the flood was upon us and it was God's punishment for the sinful among us. He said the sword had descended and that God Himself was leading the French army."

I looked at Alessandro and he looked at me. "That's utter heresy," I said.

Giulio shrugged. "That may be, Madonna. He said that it was the fulfillment of his prophecies, that God had given it to him to see the future, and now it was taking place before all our eyes. God had sent King Charles to cleanse the land with fire and sword and bring about the Kingdom of God. The righteous ride with the King and the evil oppose him."

"Cardinal della Rovere," I said.

"He rides with the French." Giulio took a sip of wine, then looked up. "Savonarola's sermon was the most terrifying thing I've ever seen. People wept and quaked and shouted out to the heavens for mercy. Some even fell to the ground writhing. Others tore their clothes and clawed at their own flesh with their nails."

I had heard about this from Dionisio, but Alessandro looked utterly shocked. "How could that be?"

"I don't know what we're going to do," Giulio said candidly. "Your Eminence, we would be hard pressed to hold the city if we tried. Now we simply can't. Anyone who tries to defend it will be stabbed in the back for opposing God's anointed. Why the King of France is anyone's deliverer is a mystery to me. At Fivizzano he killed everyone, even the kitchen boys! At Rapello he slaughtered the country people who had done nothing except seek sanctuary in the town, hundreds of innocent peasants who were not even armed! This is not how we wage war in Italy."

"Apparently it's how they wage it in France," I said.

"Meanwhile the citizens of Florence have lost their minds." Giulio applied himself to the roast duck we were having for dinner. "Anyone with any sense is getting out while they can. I saw Theoso from the monastery of San Marco in the hall."

"What?" It came out more sharply than I intended.

"Father Theoso from San Marco," Giulio said. "Another Florentine. I presumed he also sought His Eminence's protection."

"In a manner of speaking." Alessandro's eyes met mine, and I said nothing. "He's a Dominican."

"Of course. San Marco is a Dominican house. It's Savonarola's own." Giulio said. "Anyone who disagrees with him has to leave." He stopped, a bite of the roast duck enroute to his mouth. "That's not it, is it?"

"No," I said tightly. "He invited me to go to Florence."

Giulio put down his fork. "That would be bad. Very bad," he said baldly. "Donna Giulia, you must not do that. As much as I love my city, visiting now would be...." He spread his hands, apparently running out of words. "It's like an evil spell in a romance. You know. The sort where all the denizens of a castle are turned into beasts or something like that."

"Perhaps the sorcerer wears a friar's coat," I said. And yet it was disquieting. I had seen Rodrigo move a crowd to tears or to joy. What if he had tried to move them to rage or despair?

"They're angry at my cousin, Piero," he said, "and I understand that. Piero tries but he's not Lorenzo the Magnificent. Who is? We all just have to do the best we can."

"You are seventeen," I said gently. "It's hardly your fault if you're not a peerless statesman yet."

"At least I can keep faith with my family and my city, even if they've lost their minds," he said. "I can't be great but I can be good."

It was such a simple and heartfelt statement that Alessandro gripped his hand across the table. "That is all any of us can do, Giulio. God judges us not by our successes but by our efforts."

As soon as it would not be rude, I left the two of them talking and went to find Adriana. She was downstairs in the hall directing the cleaning of the big iron wheel chandeliers that hung from the ceiling. They could be let down on ropes for the candles to be changed and the wax drippings removed. I was glad to see her helping. She hadn't been at my bedside, or at least not that I remembered. She came to me with a smile. "Giulia! I'm happy to see you looking so well!"

"I am mending," I said. "I'm much better."

"Rodrigo's been frantic," she said. "He writes to me constantly. I'm so relieved to be able to tell him truthfully that you are improving."

"He writes to you?"

"Of course," Adriana said, dusting off her hands. "The Borgia couriers bring letters for us both. He asks how you are. You were too ill to write for a while, so I had a letter almost every day about you. I let him know how you were."

"Naturally," I said. I tried to phrase it casually. "I have found Father Theoso such a comfort. He is your confessor?"

Adriana frowned. "Not really. I've seen him a few times here to confess. But you know my confessor, Father Leo. Isn't Father Theoso a local priest?"

"Oh, I suppose," I said airily. "I thought he said he was your confessor."

"I suppose I've seen him two or three times in the last two months," she said. "He's not as learned as Father Leo, but he's all right for a parish priest. I'm glad he's brought comfort to you. We were all so worried about you." Her brow was furrowed.

"Dear Adriana," I said and embraced her. She was helping as best she could. Adriana was not very brave, as I had often seen. "I am much better."

I WAS tired and had to lie down for a while. It was late that night before I managed to get down the hall on my own to Alessandro's room. I knocked. "Come in," he said.

Alessandro was propped up in his bed, a book in his lap, the bed curtains half drawn. "How are you feeling?" I asked.

"Better." He winced. "Not wonderful."

I sat down on the end of the bed. "I got downstairs today. And then I had to lie down for the rest of the afternoon."

"No fever?"

I shook my head. "I asked Adriana about Father Theoso."

"Ah." Alessandro put the book down.

"He's not her confessor, except in that she's seen him a few times since she was here. That must be what was meant. I fear that he wormed his way into the household by gaining Adriana's confidence."

He sighed. "When did you first meet him?"

"On the way back from Angelo's funeral," I said, thinking back. "He implied he was the parish priest. I suppose he presented himself to Adriana the same way and then told Mother he was her confessor, since she'd know the parish priests." I leaned back against the post. "If Giulio de Medici hadn't come, we wouldn't suspect a thing."

"He must be Savonarola's agent," Alessandro said. He passed his hand over his eyes. "Now is the moment I need to be at my best and I can't seem to put two thoughts together. Going from here to the chair exhausts me. What a mess, sister."

"If we throw him out, they'll send someone else," I said. "Now we know who the spy is."

"What does he want?" Alessandro said. "There's nothing of importance in Capodimonte."

"There is me," I said. "And Rodrigo's letters." It made my chest ache. I had told Theoso so much. Not necessarily things of political importance, but all my thoughts, all my feelings. I had trusted while he told me not to trust Rodrigo. While everything twisted. "I'm sure Rodrigo's letters would be useful to Savonarola."

Loving, angry, tender, intimate in every sense, the kind of letters one would only write to a lover – a great deal could be made of them. He had not been circumspect. He trusted me. I closed my eyes. Rodrigo trusted me with his thoughts and his feelings, and he was not a trusting man. He knew I would never betray that trust, even if I did not want to be his concubine. He would never imagine that it would tempt me to suffer and be made whole. And yet it was the dark reverse of the coin, was it not? Not passion as in love, but the Passion. Torment as love. To give myself to hurt and to richly inflict damage as recompense. To be thought innocent. To have no responsibility for my own choices, even for my own mistakes – it was tempting.

No, I thought, *for good or ill my life was my own. I wanted it back. I wanted him back.* My mother said I overthought things, but that was the root of it. I wanted to go home to my lover and my friends and my work and all of the beauties and dangers of the court. I did not want to suffer. I wanted to kneel at his feet not in pain but in love, a joyful game that we played between us. I wanted his hands on my hair, to see his face transported, to know my power over him. This twisted power to break him was evil. I did not want to hurt Rodrigo, not anymore. I wanted to love as we once had. Perhaps that was possible and perhaps it wasn't, but I would not betray him.

"You'd best keep those letters close then," Alessandro said. "I'll find some harmless duties for Theoso. He can't refuse me. I'm a cardinal." His expression was grim.

"Now that we know, we can be careful," I said. "And we will be strong again soon."

Unsurprisingly, when Alessandro sent for Father Theoso, he was nowhere to be found. He was simply gone. Inquiry yielded only a townswoman who said she'd seen him on the road north, a bundle on his back.

"Good riddance," Alessandro said.

"He knew that Giulio recognized him," I said grimly. "And left the moment he knew he had been seen. There is more trouble coming from Florence."

In the morning Giulio rode south to Rome, a chubby young man with a fortune in his saddlebags. I considered asking him to take a letter to Rodrigo telling him about Theoso, but what could Rodrigo do? It would only worry him to know that I had become a target for Savonarola, and surely he had as much news from Florence as we had. Giulio would tell him what he'd seen as he'd told us.

CHAPTER 11

Three days later I went downstairs carefully, and into the study. It was a large room with old-fashioned walls enlivened with fresh paint and decoration. There was a big fireplace, the logs burning brightly to take off the chill. Alessandro sat at the desk, just handing something off to a courier who bowed. "Your Eminence," he said, and bowed again as he went past me.

I shut the door behind him. "News from Rome?" I had not had a letter from Rodrigo in four days, which was unusual.

Alessandro looked worried. "No," he said. "From the French. Florence has fallen. They are occupying the city." He held out a paper to me. "I have a letter from Cardinal della Rovere."

I didn't take it yet. "What does he offer?"

"Your safety for my vote. He seems to think you're at Vasanello." Alessandro's eyebrows twitched. "It makes me wonder why."

"What vote?" I asked tightly.

"The one that will be taken when the French army has captured Rome. The one to depose His Holiness. And to elect Cardinal della Rovere in his stead to the Throne of St. Peter." Alessandro stood up, pacing over to the fire. "In exchange for my support, he will allow you to remain at Vasanello with your husband, 'unbothered by events,' as he says."

"Alessandro," I said, "You can't think of doing this."

He rested his forehead against the mantel. "I have told him that I am too ill to travel to Rome. Which is not far off the truth. I did not say you were here."

I said nothing but sat down in one of the chairs before the fire. I was still none too steady on my feet.

"We hold this fortress by the good grace of His Holiness," Alessandro said. "And we have had it less than a year. Angelo is dead." He let out a long breath. "Bartolemeo is seventeen and holds Montalto, though I hold here. There is mother and you and Girolama in my care. I have been a cardinal for a year, and yes, I know it's by His Holiness' grace as well. We owe him everything. Only now you have left him while he sends letters like a lovesick boy! Della Rovere plots deposition and the French army advances. What would you have me do, Giulia?"

"I don't know," I said miserably. "I would be reconciled with him if I could be. Alessandro, I regret so much."

"Giulia, that's really the least of my worries at the moment."

"I know." I looked up at him, his face thinned by illness. "Della Rovere truly thinks he can depose Rodrigo?"

"With the aid of French arms, he probably can." Alessandro sat down heavily in the other chair. "His Holiness will have to flee Rome. But della Rovere won't have anything like a quorum of the College in Rome to either vote for deposition or to elect another pope. We've scattered like ants to the four winds. If he does take a vote, it won't be legitimate."

"And yet he will say it is, and France will say so."

"And others will say it is not. We will have two popes and another schism. It will split on three axes. France will support della Rovere and Spain will support Pope Alexander. The traditionalists will support della Rovere and the humanists will support Pope Alexander."

"As everyone did in the election," I said. "But what is the third axis?"

"Savonarola," Alessandro said.

"He's in Florence."

Alessandro shook his head. "There is a current…. Giulia, I don't think most of the cardinals are even aware of it. They're old men and they're Roman, sons of great families who, if they attended the universities, were there decades ago. Pico della Mirandola is just the tip of it, a discontent, a desire for greater freedoms."

"And are they not getting it under His Holiness?" I asked. "He lets the universities teach as they wish and he doesn't persecute scholars for heresy, as della Rovere would."

"They are, and they'll support him," Alessandro said. He gave me a wry smile. "If della Rovere were Pope, he would have to make common cause with Savonarola. He does not have the support of Naples, Venice, or Milan. The moment the King of France leaves, all he will have is Florence. Della Rovere would have to exalt Savonarola, perhaps even make him a cardinal."

"That would be a terrible idea," I said flatly.

"And that's not the worst. Spain will support Pope Alexander, so he'll have to counter that. The best way to do that would be to make the Grand Inquisitor a cardinal as well. Pope Alexander's clashed with Torquemada many times and they can't stand each other. This summer he appointed four 'assistant inquisitors' to take over the day-to-day work of the Inquisition due to Torquemada's 'failing health' and invited him to retire to a monastery to recuperate. Which we all know means he's pushing him out and trying to get control of the Inquisition. Making Torquemada a cardinal would drive a wedge into His Holiness's influence with King Ferdinand and Queen Isabella. And give the Inquisition reach beyond Spain."

I closed my eyes. "Savonarola and Torquemada in the College together." I couldn't imagine worse. The implications were so large I could hardly get my mind around them. "It would be the end," I said. "The end of all of this we love – learning and art and the preservation of ancient treasures. There would be a wave of persecutions and purifications like nothing we've seen in centuries."

"I would do my best," Alessandro said, "But I'm not the Grand

Inquisitor with the Spanish Inquisition behind me or a street preacher with a mob at his command. I'm a new cardinal with nothing but a single vote, and I owe that to His Holiness."

"If you didn't have to flee."

"Which I might," Alessandro said. "Which is better? To stay and try to temper della Rovere's policies or go with Pope Alexander and the humanist cardinals? Two Colleges. Two popes." He leaned forward, steepling his hands as he looked into the fire. For a moment I thought he seemed much older than his twenty-five years, something old in his face. "It is possible for this schism to split the Church."

"Permanently?" I said incredulously. "Not simply rival popes for a few years?" And yet a chill ran down my back. Was this what I had seen, armies clashing with guns and steel, shattered glass and scattered type in the street, a fruit tree in bloom standing for a moment against fire?

"Permanently," Alessandro said.

"All of Europe enveloped in war," I said quietly. The horror sat upon me like a fever chill. "All will rally to one side or another, kings and commons alike, and all will burn." I looked into the fire, into the blue heart beneath the flames. "If the spark that lights reform is Savonarola, if it is his hand that guides the course...."

"Della Rovere can't control him and he certainly can't control the Grand Inquisitor," Alessandro said. "He can't control the flood. He thinks he can, but he doesn't understand that if he does what he says he will, he will open the sluices."

"Rodrigo won't give up," I said. I knew him. "He will not acquiesce and let them depose him." I could see the shadows shifting in the fire, shades of possibility. "There has to be another way." I could see the paths in the wood, three paths rather than four now. The broadest led to schism. And yet there were still two others. *Show me*, I whispered inside, *Holy Mother, Queen of Heaven, show me, please!*

The flames shifted, whorls of smoke rising into the blackened chimney. There was darkness beneath the fire. *St. Peter's and bright day, clear cold light through the clerestory windows. Rodrigo stood before the high altar, and I saw the men he argued with, French colors and steel, one man grabbing another's arm to prevent him from drawing sword. And yet another did draw. I saw the sword rise. Rodrigo did not move, only closed his eyes before the blow fell. Red on white, blood on vestments, pouring out over the floor, like the blood at the bullfight. A sword of Toledo steel, a spatter on white stones....*

My breath caught, but I did not look away from the flames. *The procession and the torches, the commons shouting his name, della Rovere's palazzo burning.* "St. Alexander the Martyr," I whispered. *Ascanio Sforza in white, the Papal Tiara on his head, standing where Rodrigo fell, pronouncing anathema on the King of France, excommunication for murdering the pope.* "It would be the end of them," I said. My eyes over-flowed, breaking the vision. I scrubbed at them.

Alessandro's arm was around my back. He knelt beside my chair. "We promise," he said quietly, "to shed our blood for Our Mother Church."

I nodded. "It would be Thomas à Becket all over again, only worse. If the King of France killed the pope.... Could one really excommunicate a king?"

"If one had to," Alessandro said grimly.

"It's his last move," I whispered. "If they kill him, he wins." I closed my eyes. "He will be the sacrifice, St. Alexander the Martyr, revered and mourned, and there will be no schism."

"Not today," Alessandro said. "Not with Savonarola and the Inquisition." He took a deep breath. "And we will build the world that comes. I will keep my family safe. That's what I can do right now."

I bent my face against Alessandro's and sobbed.

I WAS RESTING in the solar two days later when a maidservant came hurrying upstairs. "Madonna, your mother says to tell you that a Borgia courier is arriving."

If not precisely running downstairs, I did at least walk down without losing my breath. It had now been six days since my last letter from Rodrigo, which was longer than it had ever been. I had seriously begun to wonder if they were being intercepted or if the couriers were no longer able to get through. By the time I had come down to the hall, Adriana was also waiting, and the courier handed a letter to her with a flourish. "From His Holiness," the courier said.

"Do you have one for me?" I asked.

"Of course, Madonna Giulia." He gave me my letter and I tore the seal open with delight.

And simply gaped at it in disbelief.

Ungrateful and perfidious Giulia, I have received your letter in which you say you cannot return to Rome without the permission of Orsino. And although at this moment I understand your wicked state of mind and that of those who advise you, I can't believe that you would act with such treachery and deceitfulness having promised so many times that you were true to me and that there was nothing between you and Orsino. Now you are doing the opposite and plan to go to Vasanello at the risk of your life! I can't believe that you would do so for any other reason than to reconcile with that monkey. I hope that you and treacherous Adriana will come to your senses and change your mind. Finally, by this letter, under threat of excommunication and eternal damnation, I order you not to leave Capodimonte. And still further not to go to Vasanello under any circumstances!

My hands were shaking. "What in the world? Has Rodrigo lost his mind?"

Adriana leaned over my shoulder and I handed it to her so she could read it. Her lips tightened in a straight line and she shook her head. "Giulia..."

"What is he talking about?" I said. "I'm not going to Vasanello. And Orsino?"

Adriana sighed. "Lucrezia."

"What about her?"

"You remember the beauty contest last summer? And how she was convinced that the way to reconcile you and her father was to make him jealous? It was childish but harmless. But this has gone too far."

"You think Lucrezia said I was going to Vasanello to be with Orsino?" It was all too possible. She'd been convinced that making

Rodrigo jealous was the way to get him to apologize. Telling him I meant to come to terms with Orsino would make him furious. This letter was certainly that. He sounded incensed.

Adriana handed the letter back to me. "I can think of no other explanation. We did stay at Vasanello one night, but that was months ago. He doesn't trust you. If he did, he wouldn't bite your head off like this over some foolishness of Lucrezia's."

"I can't believe he would think that!" I crumpled it in my hand. "After all that I have said, after I have assured him over and over that there was nothing between me and Orsino! I have never been unfaithful to him. Not once. Not for one moment! He's the one who deceived me!"

"I'm sorry, my dear," Adriana said. "Rodrigo has a temper and he likes to have his own way. He never stays true to one woman but he's jealous if she so much as looks at another man. That's simply who he is."

"He should trust me by now," I said.

"You're not together anymore," Adriana said. "Who could blame you if you reconciled with your husband? It's a smart move to make if you're no longer his concubine. And Lucrezia isn't helping matters by stirring up the pot."

"Maybe I should tell him I'm not going to do what he says," I said. "If we're not together, I make my own decisions about where I go and when." My blood was boiling.

"You need to be circumspect," Adriana said. "He is the pope, and…."

"I'll very sweetly tell him to go jump in Lake Bolsena," I said, and went up to my room to write out a reply for the courier to take the next day. I also enclosed a letter to be sent on to Lucrezia telling her that her help was not helpful, and to please stop. Adriana was right. It had gone too far.

MY LETTERS WENT out the next morning, so I was somewhat surprised to be sent for late in the afternoon because another courier had

arrived. Had Rodrigo thought better of his words when his temper
had cooled and sent another messenger on the heels of the first?

However, when I reached the hall, I saw that the courier was not in
Borgia livery. Alessandro handed me two letters. "From Vasanello,"
Alessandro said.

I frowned, watching him pay the messenger and send him off to
the kitchen for a meal. "What in the world?" I murmured as I opened
the first.

Madonna Giulia, if I may so address you, I write to you in urgency for love of a man's immortal soul. Your husband, the most honored and puissant Lord Orsino, is frantic with worry about you. He weeps and remonstrates that you are absent from him, and his tender concern knows no bounds. Indeed, he is ill with worry. So violent is his passion, so strong his desire to see you and to know that you are safe with him and in no danger of falling once again into sin, that we fear that he will harm himself. Indeed, that is the cause of this letter. I fear for his life should you gainsay him. If you do not return immediately to Vasanello, he may very well take his own life in despair. Please, Madonna, take the road south as soon as you may! His happiness and his life and his immortal soul rest in your hands. Friar Piero

"What?" I said sharply, and Alessandro looked around. I tore the
second letter open.

To my wife, Giulia, greetings. I require your presence here at my side at Vasanello. It is not to be borne that you return to Rome or remain at Capodimonte. You remember last summer when we spoke in the garden and you promised me that you would be an obedient and good wife to me henceforth? You promised me that you would see him no more and that you would come home and live as a chaste wife. You will remember what you promised for the sake of our children. Therefore, I command you to come directly to Vasanello with all possible haste. Do not go to Rome. Here you will be safe and I will know that you well remember your sworn word. Your husband, Orsino Orsini, Lord of Vasanello

I read it twice. Then I read it again. I swallowed the depths of the betrayal. "Of all people," I said evenly. "To think that I must rely on a clever warning from Orsino."

"What does he say?" Alessandro said. Wordlessly, I handed him the letters. He frowned as he read them. "How does this even make sense?"

Adriana had come downstairs and was getting her letter from the courier. I took Alessandro's elbow. "Walk with me on the battlements," I said.

We went up and up again, at last coming out on one of the bastions. The stones were warm in the late afternoon sun, golden in the slanting light. The lake sparkled. Away south twilight was already hiding in the folds of the hills, purple and gray with the colors of winter. The wind was brisk, but it was warm enough in the shelter of the crenellations. I sat down on one of them and Alessandro sat beside me, pulling his fur-lined robe about him. "What's going on?"

"We did indeed speak in the garden, but we said no such things as he says, and he knows that I will know he writes this under duress. What Orsino and I promised, for the sake of our children, was to do honestly by one another," I said in clipped tones. "He would not repudiate Laura and I would grant his bequests to his child if I outlived him." I took a deep breath. "He has a woman he loves and they were expecting a child in August. He has no desire to reconcile with me, no more than I do with him. We came to a cordial agreement. This would seem a reasonable letter, except that I would know that it is false."

Alessandro looked serious. "You didn't tell me that before."

"It was between me and Orsino," I said. "I told no one."

He tilted his head. "Not Adriana?"

"No." I looked at him. "He asked me not to. He said that she didn't approve of his Gentilia and I didn't wish to make trouble for him. I kept our conversation in confidence until this moment. I didn't tell anyone at all."

Alessandro steepled his fingers, leaning back against the battlement. "So Orsino writes to you under duress. Who is this Friar Piero?"

"I have no idea," I said. "I've never heard of him before."

"This friar does not know you either," Alessandro said, picking up the letter and looking at it again. "This letter might have a profound effect on a sweet young woman who readily felt guilt and unease at her conduct."

"Well, thank you for that!" I said.

"You know what I mean," Alessandro said. "Cardinal della Rovere thought you were at Vasanello. His Holiness thought you were going to Vasanello. And now Orsino and this friar beg you to come to Vasanello. Someone wants you there very badly,"

It tasted like gall in my mouth. "Not Lucrezia," I said. "Adriana." I tilted my head back against the stones. "She had a letter from Vasanello today too. And a letter from Rodrigo yesterday. What did they say?"

"That's an excellent question."

The door at the end of the guard walk opened and Adriana came out, coming toward us hurriedly. As she came close enough she said, "There you are! Giulia, I have had a very upsetting letter from Orsino."

"So have I," I said.

"Orsino is in a terrible state of mind," she said. "He thought that the two of you were reconciling, and now he is distraught at the idea that you might once again leave him. I have had the most piteous letter. In any event, it is hardly safe for you in Rome at present. It would be better to go to Vasanello and remain there until this crisis with the French is over."

I did not look at Alessandro, nor he at me. "So he says," I said. "It is most distressing."

"Giulia, my dear, I think perhaps we had best go back to Vasanello," Adriana said. "This letter has frightened me."

"Of course it has," I said. "I was just discussing it with my brother, His Eminence. He was absolutely refusing to let me travel yet. He says that my health is far too fragile for him to permit me to go."

Alessandro played his cue. "I couldn't possibly allow Giulia to leave just now, Donna Adriana. She is barely out of her sick bed."

"I tire so very easily," I said. "I do not think I can ride, Adriana."

"I won't permit it," Alessandro said. "Not until she is fully recovered. Perhaps in a few days."

"Of course," Adriana said, looking from him to me. "In a few days, then."

"I think that is best," I said. "I will write to him in the meantime. I'm sure you will want to do so as well. We can send the courier back with letters tomorrow."

Adriana professed herself satisfied with that, and in a bit went below, complaining that the wind was chilly and she needed to write the letter. The sun was setting, the light almost horizontal, touching us on the wall though the village was in shadow beneath us.

"What does she want?" Alessandro asked in a low tone.

I took a deep breath. Everything was clear to me now. "She wants me and Orsino to reconcile. That's what she's always wanted. When she thought I was Bracciano's mistress, she said that as soon as he tired of me, Orsino and I could go on with our lives together. She said at Vasanello last summer that if Rodrigo and I were done, I needed to reconcile with Orsino – the same arrangement as she had imagined with Bracciano. She will not get it through her head that neither Orsino or I want that."

Alessandro looked at me keenly. "You know Adriana can't actually believe he's mad for love of you. Which means she's lying."

"I know," I said. I stood up, walking to the embrasure and leaning on the crenellation. I wasn't sure why something hurt. "Tonight, when everyone is at dinner, can you keep Adriana at the table when I excuse myself? I'm going to see what was in the letters to her."

"Of course," my brother said.

A COLD CALM had descended on me. I was polite and quiet at dinner, seated at the long table between Adriana and my sister Girolama. Mother was at the other end, but she looked up when I stood, and I smiled at her reassuringly.

"Excuse me a moment," I said to Adriana quietly.

"Are you unwell?" she asked.

"Just a little queasy," I said. "Please don't distress yourself."

"Donna Adriana, I am wondering if you might tell me something," Alessandro began from across the table, engaging her as I slipped out.

Needless to say, I didn't seek the necessary. I went straight upstairs to the guest chamber Adriana had been staying in for weeks, opening the door quietly and slipping inside. The fire was built up and burning brightly to warm the room before bedtime, the curtains drawn over the window. No candles had been lit yet, but the firelight was enough. There were Adriana's trunks, there the writing desk by the window, there the basin and mirror.

The desk first, I thought. There was paper, pen and ink, a piece of heavy parchment for a blotter or to cover an inner sheet to send off, but nothing written on any of them. Well, if I were hiding correspondence, I wouldn't leave it sitting on my writing desk either! Beneath her pillow? Too much chance of the maidservant finding it when she made the bed. Folded into her clothing in the trunk? Carefully, I eased the lid open and started searching. There were ten gowns, all of them nice and folded neatly, a gracious number for a lady traveling. One was made of cloth Lucrezia had bought at Urbino. She must have had it made up as a gift for Adriana. And Adriana had blamed Lucrezia.... I had sent that letter telling her to mind her own business, which she'd receive with astonishment and hurt. My fingers clenched.

Nothing among the dresses. And yet the lining of the trunk was not smooth. It was not nailed down at some point. I searched along the side, then slid my hand into the slit and pulled out the letters. I sat back on my heels, then carried them over to the fire so that I could see to read.

The first was in a hand I knew very well.

Deceitful Adriana, your wicked mind is revealed and your plot in declaring that you did not wish Giulia to go to Rome against the will of Orsino. I forbid you to leave Capodimonte without my express permission. I know that you brought her to Vasanello and that now you counsel her to return to his bed. It does not escape me that it would well suit you to have her settled at Vasanello. Now you lead her into danger and although she is faithless, she is still under

*my protection. Therefore I have instructed the Gonfaloniere to order Orsino
to return Giulia and you to my care immediately, and for Orsino to cease
malingering as he has done these past months and report immediately to
Prince Ferrandino as is his honorable duty.*

It was the same date as my letter, received yesterday. I swallowed.
So the other one had come from Vasanello today, supposedly the
piteous plea from Orsino. I opened it.

*Donna Adriana, by the same courier come two letters for Farnese, one from
her husband requiring her obedience and one from a priest pleading with her
to come for fear of his health. Make certain that you bring her immediately to
Vasanello as we discussed. She must be there no later than the fifteenth day of
December. Our agreement is contingent on your success, not just your protes-
tations of effort. I expect your customary compliance. How hard can it be? B.*

I had trusted her. I had tried so hard to love her. I had tried to be a
good daughter to her. And Rodrigo…. Rodrigo had known her since
she was a child. Rodrigo's love was not a thing lightly given. We were
exactly alike that way, though he seemed genial and I seemed cool, but
our reserve was the same, the tightly-held palisades of our hearts. I
remembered now how she had been displeased when I wrote to
Rodrigo at Urbino and how she had put a letter in the same packet. I
remembered how Lucrezia had said that he asked about all my
admirers when there were none. She had been trying to prevent
reconciliation, an intrigue on her son's behalf to be sure, but it had
become more. Four and a half years ago she'd tried to juggle both
Rodrigo and Bracciano as patrons, and Rodrigo had told her she could
only serve one. He'd offered her a better bargain and gave Vasanello to
Orsino. When had she changed sides?

I heard her voice in the hall, Alessandro's voice behind her
conversing too loudly, a warning to me. I was through with warnings.
When Adriana opened the door, I was standing by the fire, the two
letters in my hand. "How long have you been in Bracciano's pay?" I
asked coldly.

She blanched. "Giulia!"

I held the letters out. "What did Lord Bracciano promise you in exchange for me?" She was speechless and I went on. "Rodrigo knows what you did. Now so do I."

"Rodrigo is being unreasonable. You know he has a temper." She took a step back, but Alessandro stood behind her in the doorway.

"That's not what Bracciano's letter says, is it? It says you'd better deliver me by December 15th with your 'customary compliance.' How many times have you spied for him? How long have you been betraying Rodrigo? And what happens December 15th?"

"I don't know!" Adriana's eyes were wide and she looked as though she might weep. "He said he would kill Orsino if I didn't do as he wished," she said. Her usual composure had entirely fled. "And it wasn't to hurt you. He said you would be safe if you stayed at Vasanello. He just didn't want you to go to Rome."

"To stay at Vasanello as a hostage," I said. My voice did not shake at all. "Bracciano would let Rodrigo know that I was in his power. And then what?"

"I don't know." Her voice trembled.

Alessandro met my eyes over her head. "There's only one way that move makes sense, Giulia. Bracciano is planning to go over to the French and take the Papal Army with him. With the Gonfaloniere defecting and you in his power, His Holiness will have no choice except to yield and be deposed."

"He promised not to hurt you," Adriana said. "Or hurt Orsino. Both of you could stay peacefully at Vasanello."

"While Rodrigo was deposed and murdered?" My voice scaled up.

Adriana avoided my eyes. "I don't know."

"You do," I said. "You know perfectly well what would happen. Did you know that Father Theoso was a Florentine agent?"

"A what?" She sounded innocent, but she did not meet my eyes.

"You let Theoso in," Alessandro said. "That wasn't an accident. We would have figured it out earlier if we hadn't been sick and Mother so upset and busy that she had no time to think about it. She let that bastard in my house! By God, if I catch him, he'll answer to

Cardinal Farnese!" There was fury in his voice I'd never heard before.

"You were told that Father Theoso would counsel me to return to my husband. You told Rodrigo I was faithless. You told him I wanted to stay with Orsino." Of course she had. Lucrezia had asked me if Orsino and I had a son, if he would inherit Vasanello before Laura. That was her plan. That was what she'd said years ago when she thought Bracciano used me – when he was done, Orsino and I would live respectably. That was what she wanted, respectability and money. That was all she'd ever wanted.

"What happens on December 15th?" Alessandro demanded.

There was only one way this made sense. "December 15th is when Bracciano intends to betray Rodrigo. And today is November 29th. Two weeks." I looked at my brother. "I am leaving for Rome tomorrow."

He stared at me. "Giulia, the French are holding the Via Aurelia! Also, in case you forgot, the other road runs directly past Bracciano Castle! And even if you went all the way east to the Via Flaminia, it goes past Vasanello, which you know is a trap."

"Of course it's a trap," I said. "I am certainly not going anywhere near Vasanello."

"His Holiness said to say here," Alessandro said. "This is the safest place for you."

"I can't," I said. Bracciano was planning to turn. Rodrigo had never trusted him, but he needed to know the day and that Bracciano would take the Papal Army with him. He would die thinking I had deserted him for Orsino. I could not live with that.

"Giulia, he said on pain of excommunication not to leave Capodimonte. It's not a request." Alessandro was serious. "You must stay here."

"Are you going to lock me up? Because if you're not, I'm leaving." I handed him Adriana's letters. "I have stayed too long. It may be impossible to get back to Rome now, but I have to try."

"Giulia...."

"I have to try!" I shouted. "Alessandro, I can't let him die thinking that I settled for Orsino to save my own skin!"

He sighed. "You are the worst and most stubborn and willful sister in the world."

"Yes," I said. "I'm a monster and I don't care who thinks so. I am going back to Rome and back to Rodrigo tomorrow! There is not going to be a better time. There may never be another time. I pray that I'm not too late."

CHAPTER 12

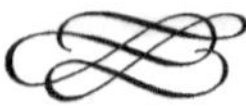

They say a lady cannot travel without two days' notice. Well, I can. It was not quite noon the next day when we assembled in the courtyard, me, my maid Tina, Dionisio, and the four Borgia men at arms who had accompanied us to Capodimonte from Pesaro. And Adriana.

"What is she doing here?" I demanded. She was standing by her saddled horse looking pale.

"Giulia, I do not know what this foolishness is," she began.

My mother came around from where she had been petting Lilas. "Don't you think you've done enough to my daughter?"

Alessandro looked down at her, drawn up to his full height. "Madonna, let me make this clear. You are no longer welcome under this roof. You are leaving today. You may return to Rome with Giulia or you may take yourself off where you wish, but you will not stay in Capodimonte one more hour."

"You are throwing me out? A woman alone in the midst of a war?"

"You can return to Rome with Giulia. Or not as you choose," Alessandro said coldly. "You may not stay here. You have abused the hospitality of my family. If Giulia will have you, you may travel to Rome with Borgia men at arms. If I were you, I'd ask her nicely."

Adriana could not have looked more shocked if the cardinal had slapped her. "Giulia...."

"Of course you can travel with me," I said. "Now, let us discuss the route." I turned to the men at arms. "We're going to backtrack the route taken by the last courier. We'll go east to Montefiascone, then take the road south from there. We'll turn east again and cross the Tiber by the old bridge far upstream, then go all the way around and come in from the Via Appia rather than straight down the Via Flaminia. If any road to Rome is secure, it's the one that connects Rome and Naples."

"Spoken like a *condottiero*," my mother said. She embraced me. "Your father would be so proud of you," she whispered in my ear.

"I have to stay here," Alessandro said.

"I know." I hugged him in turn. "Someone must hold Capodimonte. That must be you. Who knows what the French will do?"

"Godspeed, sister," he said.

I kissed him and then he held his hands for me to mount up. Lilas tossed her head, clearly ready to go. At noon on the 30th day of November we rode for Rome.

WE CUT DIRECTLY east across the fields, then followed the curve of Lake Bolsena around its southern shore. The day was beautiful, a breeze off the lake cool but not cold, and the sky was a rich autumn blue. My heart lifted despite everything. I was no longer an invalid, no longer cooped up behind walls. I was on my way home. I could not lift my wings and fly, but I had Lilas and she was the next best thing. Sixty miles to Rome as the crow flies, it was probably more like twice that as far around as we would have to go, but even so, I was at last homeward bound.

Adriana pushed her horse forward to ride beside me, her skirts flowing down its flanks in a cascade of dark russet and red. "Giulia, I had no choice."

I looked at her sideways. "Because of Orsino? This goes back months. This was not something that just happened. Rodrigo knows that you have been telling him things to mislead him since we left Rome."

"He said that?" She looked astonished.

"He knows, Adriana. And I know that you told Rodrigo I had slept with Orsino at Vasanello last summer when you knew it was a lie. Orsino did not agree to this either."

"Orsino doesn't know what is good for him," Adriana snapped. "If things were left to him, he'd sit like a mushroom until he became inconvenient to someone."

"And so you play for him? Or for yourself?"

"What other choice is there?" The color was high in her face. "We are women and have no power except what we contrive. We are blown about by every wind. If we do not take care of ourselves, we will simply be destroyed."

"You had no choice," I said flatly. "It seems to me that in the last six months you have had many, many choices." I put my heels to Lilas, trotting forward away from her. I was so angry that I feared I would say something I would regret. I have a temper and I knew myself.

Wisely, she did not follow me. It was Dionisio who came forward to ride with me. He didn't say anything for a time, just waited until I could speak without snapping. I looked across at him. "Not that I don't love a good jaunt," Dionisio said, "and not that I'm not eager to get back to Rome, but what happened today to make it imperative?"

I explained, and he shook his head. "Well, that's a bad business. So now we warn His Holiness that the Gonfaloniere intends to betray him?"

"That's the size of it," I said. "And hope that we are in time." I would have said more, but Dionisio suddenly stiffened.

"Giulia? Who are those men?"

A bend in the road around the lake now showed the village of Montefiascone, and on the road from the village was a group of about twenty men on horseback. They had sword and shield, though their horses did not wear barding or caparisons, and beneath their steel breastplates they wore blue and white. The leader had a blue plume on his steel helm, a fleur-de-lys on his shield.

"A French cavalry patrol." As I said it, they put spurs to their horses, moving to a brisk trot to intercept us.

I looked at Dionisio and he looked at me, the same thought in both our minds. "If they've got heavy war horses and steel, you might outrun them," he said.

Lilas was an Andalusian. I might. But there was not a moment longer. I turned her head abruptly away, back the way we'd come and a little south, toward the woods on the higher ground away from the lake, and then I put my heels to her. "Go!"

We broke into a flat gallop across the fallow fields, our shadow stretching out beside us, mare and woman bent low in the saddle. "Come on, Lilas. Go, sweetheart." Her hooves were a drum. My heart beat in time, pounding with her. Behind, I heard shouts. The wind tore them away.

Where the land began to rise away from the lakeshore there was a wood, dark green cedars among the golden leaves of other trees. If we could reach the wood....

I heard voices, dared a glance behind, my head ducked. There were five or six men in pursuit, blue pennant streaming from a lance. Not warhorses. It was a light cavalry troop. They were spread out in a fan so that whichever way I turned it would be closer to one of them.

A bird started from among the stubbled fields, and Lilas veered to the left. She didn't shy. She was too well-trained for that, but we were closer to the leader, a lean man on a brown horse, a steel cap on his head.

If we could just reach the wood.... Above, a hawk screamed in the autumn sky.

And then we were at the verge, Lilas taking a little ditch in a flying leap as though the hounds were before her. We were in among the trees, and I ducked low on her neck to avoid the branches which whipped at me. I let her have her head. She was a breakneck hunter, and the best thing to do was let her pick her own way.

She turned abruptly, jumping a fallen tree and dodging between two cedars, and I leaned with her, my breath harsh in my throat. Someone was shouting but I couldn't make out the words.

A gap in the trees ahead, a little slope and then we were out the other side of the woods, pounding across open fields. They were coming in from the left, and I turned her head to the right. And there was the leader, still behind, his plume gone. He stuck directly on me. The others were coming up to both sides, trying to get ahead of me, a cage from which there was no escaping. There were six of them and one of me. Ahead, the ground was very broken and there was a stone wall along the edge of a field. I might take it. And I might not. Lilas was game. She would try it if I wanted. I could hear her breath. I wouldn't risk her. It was as high as I was tall, and she was all heart but she'd only been ridden lightly for months.

With a sob in my throat, I pulled back gently, slowing her to a trot.

The leader came along side me, reaching over and grabbing my bridle, pulling us to a walk. "A good run, Madame, but it is done," he said in Italian. There was admiration in his eyes. "Your name?"

"I am Giulia Farnese," I said.

I WAS LED BACK to the road and the village of Montefiascone. The rest of the party was waiting, a group of French cavalry around them. Dionisio's face fell when he saw me. I shook my head. Lilas was sweated. Truly, she'd done her best and so had I.

"Fall in," the French captain said, and followed it with orders in French I did not understand. I had just enough to understand "fall in." Fortunately, it seemed he spoke Italian.

Each of us had a trooper assigned to us, and boxed as I was between horsemen I could not have bolted again if I'd tried. And there was no point in trying. Lilas was tired and there were horsemen who were fresh. If they'd caught me before, they'd catch me again. Perhaps they wouldn't have a year ago, when I had spent weeks hunting at Nepi, but they would now. Was Nepi only a year ago? It seemed like a lifetime.

We headed east and south, away from Lake Bolsena and Capodimonte, more or less in the direction I'd intended to go. Twenty men or so was not a large group. They must be scouts ranging far ahead of the rest of the army. Perhaps when we stopped for the night there would be an opportunity. I watched where we went very carefully.

Shortly before dusk I saw cooksmoke ahead. Along a stream at the bottom of the hill was a camp, tents pitched everywhere, horses on picket lines. My breath caught. I looked at the horseman beside me and thought I could try my very limited French. "C'est l'armee Français?"

"Non, Madame. Seulement un regiment."

That was clear enough. It seemed like an army to me but was merely a single light cavalry regiment. Hundreds and hundreds of them.

Adriana, my maid Tina and I were herded into a tent. Dionisio was hustled off separately with the men at arms. I looked around. There were four pallets on camp beds, a little folding table and a lamp. Our bags had been piled haphazardly in the middle of the floor. Tina started crying. Adriana ignored her, sitting down on one of the beds. Outside, a sentry stood at the door.

Adriana looked up at me, eyes blazing. "This is your fault. We could be safe in Capodimonte if you hadn't decided you had to go to Rome today. Every last bit of this is because of you!"

I slapped her across the face. "I have had enough of you!" I snapped. Tina sobbed. I slapped her again. "You're not going to fight back, are you? Leaves in the stream! Blown about by the wind! You have no will and no responsibility and everything you do, every treacherous and vile choice you make, is someone else's fault!" I raised my hand again. "I am the bitch, then! Just try me!" A fighting fury was on me, and if I'd had so much as an eating knife, I would have stabbed her.

Of course she didn't fight. She simply put her face in her hands and began to wail.

A man cleared his throat at the door, and I looked around. His Italian was halting. "The Captain requires Giulia Farnese to be his guest at dinner, alone."

I would need this fury. I would need this heat. "Of course," I said to him. I looked down at Adriana, who was weeping into her hands. "I go to face my fate now. You'll be next." With my head high, I followed him out.

The French soldiers were making camp. It was after dusk, growing dark. Each neat circle of tents had a fire before it, men cooking their dinners. They looked up curiously as I was escorted past, but none yelled or called. They were disciplined. I was escorted by three men. I lifted my skirts over the mud, keeping my chin high. This captain would see no weakness from me, I vowed. I would not weep or beg. I would endure. Surely pride and temper would armor me. Nothing else would.

The captain's tent was like the others, save the front was drawn back and a table set within, two chairs at it. A servant held a bottle of wine.

The captain had divested himself of his steel breastplate, wearing a doublet of good blue cloth. He was the man I'd seen before, perhaps forty, with dark hair and keen, intelligent eyes. He stepped out and bowed over my hand very properly. "Madame, I am honored," he said in good Italian.

"Captain," I said, with a nod. "I am afraid I do not know your name."

"Yves d'Allegre, Chevalier," he said with another bow, precise and formal. "If you will join me, Madame?"

"I am your prisoner, so I must," I said, and let him seat me. With the front tent flaps open we were in full view of all passers by. Was that good or bad?

The servant poured, then disappeared, presumably to find the meal. I lifted my glass and took a sip. If he wished to kill me, poison would be entirely superfluous.

He seated himself opposite. "I regret that you are discommoded," he said.

It seemed a very villainous thing to say, like a cat toying with a mouse. "If that is what you call it," I said. I put my glass down. "You have arrested an innocent party of travelers on the road, and I am in your power, which you have demonstrated with this show of politeness. Shall we save us both some trouble and simply move to the endgame?"

D'Allegre blinked at me. "I believe you have taken us for ogres."

"What else should I take you for?" I lifted my chin.

He looked a little bemused. "Madame, we are chivalrous knights. We are the heroes of this tale. You are the villains."

"Is that how you see it? Invading our land with fire and sword, bathed in the blood of those who resist you, so that you may sack the Holy City of Rome and kill God's anointed?" I looked at him over the rim of the wineglass.

"Forgive me for my bluntness, my lady, but you serve a Borgia. He is no true pope, but a marrano schemer who has bought the Throne of St. Peter through simony, and whose name is rightfully a synonym for corruption." His brow furrowed. "I do not mean to be indelicate, but does not your own position testify to his unworthiness?"

"And you are the best judge of who is worthy in God's sight?" I asked mildly. "I do not mean to be indelicate either, Captain, but surely the College of Cardinals are best suited to determine who shall occupy the Throne of St. Peter, not a chevalier of France." I lifted my glass. "Do you look into men's hearts, captain? Are you so pure that you may judge? And did not Christ Himself say that he who is without sin should cast the first stone?"

D'Allegre frowned. "The judgment of the woman taken in adultery."

"Just so," I said with a serene smile, and took a sip of my wine.

The servant returned with the meal, a rabbit nicely braised with fresh onions, and the serving occupied us for some moments. Once the food was on our plates and the man withdrawn, I looked up at d'Allegre again. "If Christ dined with courtesans and tax collectors, how may the Holy Father be corrupted by doing so? Unless you would prefer he only dine with Dominican friars."

That struck something. D'Allegre looked troubled. "I think we need no more Dominicans."

"You have been to Florence, then," I guessed. Savonarola had perhaps not made a good impression on the captain.

"Yes," he said shortly.

"And you did not like what you saw there?"

"No." His dark eyes were very frank. "I did not like it."

"Your allies do not touch on your honor, of course," I said. "If Savonarola has paved the road before the King of France with prophecies that he is the New Cyrus, come to free the faithful from the chains of the earth by sword and pestilence, that does not reflect on you."

"The King of France is a sovereign, no more than that," d'Allegre said. "He is no part of any prophecy of apocalypse."

"Of course not," I said. "I have heard no ill of King Charles. Indeed, the Holy Father has no quarrel with him. He speaks of him as a well-meaning young man who shoulders a great responsibility, and who he fears has been led astray by Cardinal della Rovere." I was guessing now, stabbing in the dark. D'Allegre was the king's man. I thought I could see how to do it, to speak to the man he tried to be. I took another sip, letting my eyes meet his over the glass. "Della Rovere wanted to be Pope, and he begged 200,000 ducats of your lord to buy the election. It did not avail him. The other cardinals knew him and their votes were not bought. They thought my lord the better man. And what else can I say of that, other than that His Holiness knows full well that he is unworthy of the honor and that he must rise to the occasion? And yet he will not hand power to a deranged prophet who welcomes the end of the world."

D'Allegre's frown deepened. "Cardinal della Rovere will do that?"

"He must, mustn't he?" I asked, cutting a sliver of rabbit with my knife. "Who else will support him? He needs Florence, for he has nothing else. I tell you, captain, that while he blames my dear lord for his loss, he did not have more than eight votes in consistory. If His Holiness had not been elected, it would not have been della Rovere! His peers know him and have known him for long years, which His Majesty of France has not. It is true he is fair-spoken, and no doubt he promised much to King Charles. But he is a viper, and those who have long acquaintance know it. He lost the election, as he had lost the one before, for this reason. But like a loser in the lists who will not accept defeat, he seeks to overturn the judging."

D'Allegre applied himself to his meal, his manners as graceful as any courtier. Perhaps he was a courtier in Paris. Or perhaps he imagined himself the perfect, gentle knight, a Lancelot or Amadis. "I had not heard that," he said. He did not look at me. "You speak well of the Borgia pope."

How to answer that? "Captain, my lord is a man like any other. He has his flaws and his moral weaknesses, as all men do. He has been raised by the vote of his peers to unimaginable glory, to be Christ's Earthly Habitation. He is no saint or prophet. He strives to be worthy. Nay, struggles to be worthy, as would not any man uncertain of his own sanctity who occupied the Throne of St. Peter? To my mind, humility is becoming. A man who thinks Christ gets a good bargain in him thinks well of himself indeed."

D'Allegre snorted. "True."

I put my knife down, looking at him over the dinner. "Captain, you have heard of me. You knew my name, and you know my station."

"I do," he said. "Forgive me, Madame, but I understand that you are his concubine."

I thought I guessed him rightly. I lifted my chin. "I am his love. I am his Oriana. And if the love of a woman is forbidden him, it is nonetheless inexorable. I am no harlot, captain. I have been with no other man in my life, and he is my dear lord, he and none other." I did not need to make my voice shake. "You may take my virtue, for I am your prisoner, but he will receive me polluted and hold me blameless, should I live to see him again."

"I would not do such a thing, Madame," he said, and I saw in his eyes that I had hit home. "I am an honorable man."

"Honorable men are rare in this world," I said. "I am fortunate to have fallen to such." That was absolutely no less than the truth. Truly, some saint had interceded for me! "What will you do with me, then?" I looked away. "All that I ask is that you not hand me to Friar Savonarola, for he will see me stoned."

D'Allegre looked shocked, as I meant him to. "We are France,

Madame. We do not answer to the Florentine Dominican, nor hand over prisoners to him."

"Then what will you do?" I asked. How was I going to keep him from handing me to Bracciano? Bracciano would seem an honest go-between, and I could hardly accuse him of future treachery.

"What would you have me do?" he asked.

"Ransom me to His Holiness. Surely he will pay a fair ransom." Of all outcomes, that was best. "The other lady is Donna Adriana de Mila, the Holy Father's cousin. He will assuredly ransom her too. And our retainers. He is responsible for them as well." That was a good touch.

"Of course," d'Allegre said. He nodded slowly, and I held my breath until his next words. "There is no need to ransom retainers. The gentleman says he is your secretary?"

"Dr. Treschi is my secretary," I said. "Tina is my maid, and there are four guards."

He nodded. "In the morning I will send an envoy. Will you write a note so that the Holy Father will believe that it is really you?"

"Naturally, Captain," I said, inclining my head. Holy Father now, not that Borgia. I had achieved something as well as my own salvation, though that was enough.

CHAPTER 13

I was escorted back to the tent after dinner. Tina jumped up when she saw me. Adriana did not move. She sat expressionless on one of the camp beds. I let the tent flap fall shut behind me. "I have not been raped," I said to her. "I'm sure you're disappointed."

"What happened, Madonna?" Tina asked.

I took a deep breath. Of course Tina was worried, and nothing of this was her fault. "We are the prisoners of Captain Yves d'Allegre," I said. "He is a gallant gentleman and offered me no offense. He intends to ransom us to His Holiness."

Tina closed her eyes, her hand going to the saint's medal at her throat. "Praise upon praise," she said. "Thank you."

"Tomorrow I will write a letter in his presence, and he will have it carried to Rome under a flag of truce," I said.

"Why not a letter to Cardinal Farnese at Capodimonte?" Adriana demanded. "He would surely ransom us and it is much closer."

"And you would love that," I retorted. "To go back to Capodimonte and not to face Rodrigo!"

Adriana got to her feet, her hands clenched. "Do you not understand, you stupid girl, that Rodrigo is falling? He cannot help us! He cannot help himself! It's over, Giulia. He's done." I said nothing and she continued. "It was always a foolish gamble. He knew they hated him and would bring him down. The great families were never going to let a Borgia, a Spanish interloper, hold the papacy! If he'd been contented as a cardinal – but no! Rodrigo had to try for it." Her face was pale with anger. "If he ransoms us, which is not certain given the state of your relations with him, and if we go to Rome, we will then be on the wrong side of the French attack! We will be helpless in a city about to be sacked. If we were in Capodimonte, we might survive this." Her voice dropped. "You did well for yourself, no doubt about it, getting Capodimonte for your family. You have had all the good from the Borgias you will have. It's time to leave the table while you still have some winnings. Laura will be hard to put aside, and even so your brother is a cardinal and has a great estate. Rodrigo will be a prisoner or dead before December is out."

I did not shout. I was beyond anger. I simply looked at her. "After all these years, you understand me less than that man I broke bread with tonight."

"I don't know what you mean."

"It doesn't matter whether Rodrigo is losing or not. It doesn't matter if every power arrays against him or if he can continue to be of use to my family. I have my honor."

"Your honor was forfeit when you lay with him," Adriana said.

I shook my head. "My honor is not in my chastity. My honor is in my conduct. My father was an honest mercenary, and I am an honest whore. I have given my word and I will not break it."

"You are a naïve fool."

"Perhaps," I said tightly.

"Rodrigo has no honor. And you can wager any money that no Borgia would be so lenient as this d'Allegre," Adriana said. "It is foolish to keep faith with the faithless."

"It doesn't matter what Rodrigo does," I said, "or whether he keeps faith with me. Or whether he even welcomes me back. This is upon my soul. At the end, I will answer to God, not Rodrigo."

A tear rolled down her cheek. "Do you think God cares what we do? If He did, and if He was not a cruel master, how would He allow all this suffering?" Her voice shook. "What did I ever do to deserve four dead babies? Four! All of them born before their time, not one of them living a day! What did we do, Ludovico and I, to deserve that? No matter how we prayed, no matter what we did… I was a good woman. I was a good wife. And that whore Vannozza had healthy child after healthy child!" She turned her back. "Go away. I am sick of you."

I took a deep breath. My anger had fled, and in its place I felt a curious emptiness. Of course she hated me. Of course she hated Vannozza, mother of the little girl who lived with her when she had no daughter of her own. Of course she hated Rodrigo and at the same time owed him everything. Always Adriana in the background, expected to care for the children of others, to watch over his concubine. But without him what was she except Orsino's stepmother, widow of a man who left her nothing? Did Orsino even want her at Vasanello, or was he enjoying being his own man without her to tell him what to do? Did anyone want her? She was young enough to marry again but had no desire to make herself pleasant to another man. What was left to her except bitterness?

And that was the cruelty, I thought. *Bracciano knew. He took advantage of misery to make more misery. Or was it Typhon who knew hearts so well?*

"As you wish, Adriana," I said quietly. I turned instead to Tina. "Tomorrow we will travel with the French column. I am certain His Holiness will ransom us as quickly as he can." She would have to face Rodrigo in due time, and I did not know what he would say. I thought he would be more hurt than angry.

Tina looked relieved. "It will be good to be home," she said. She glanced at Adriana's back. "I will be glad of it, Madonna."

WE RODE east and south to Rome by the road I had intended, then turned south onto the Via Flaminia. Each day, scouts ranged far and wide over the countryside, returning to report. Needless to say, I did not know what they said. Still, it was clear that they were not resisted. I heard enough to know that.

We lived off the land, which is to say that the French looted whatever they wanted. Farmsteads and villages, the harvest just in, were stripped bare in a day. What would happen to the people with the entire winter before them was not d'Allegre's problem. I said so acerbically the third day, that for heroes and paladins they left misery behind.

"It is war, Madame," he said.

"You have made this war, not we," I said, my temper barely in check as we left behind another village, chickens and ducks taken, slung by their feet over the saddlebows to be cooked for dinner.

"We didn't kill the children," he said. "They can replace their animals."

I bit down on my lip, looking off into the distance. "And now you speak like my lord," I said, "in that you do not do as much evil as you might, and thus excuse what you do."

D'Allegre looked startled. "Madame?"

"You come with fire and sword to trouble people who have done nothing to you, and for what?" I asked. "Why are you here, Captain?"

"To keep faith with my king," he replied.

"And why is your king here?" I waited for an answer, but he gave none. "To do the bidding of Cardinal della Rovere is not a deed befitting a great captain."

I said no more. At least I was allowed to ride with Dionisio. I had no desire to ride with Adriana, who I treated with a frosty politeness. I would not think about how I had tried to please her and win her affection, and indeed believed that she cared about me, when she'd thought me a stupid girl the entire time, her cousin's whore that she had to put up with. If my temper was hot, the coldness that followed it was final.

That night a messenger came in, and d'Allegre informed me that His Holiness had agreed to the ransom. My price was set at 3,000 ducats. I nearly laughed. It was the amount of my original dowry when I'd married Orsino, and Rodrigo would have paid ten times that amount. D'Allegre had only set Adriana's price at 1,500 ducats, so at least I was not so discounted!

I thanked d'Allegre gravely. "I am very glad to hear it, Captain."

His eyes searched my face. "I am told he agreed instantly without questioning the ransom at all."

"I am his Oriana," I said. "I am worth more than gold to him." I lifted my head with a sad, sweet smile. "Is there someone who waits at home for you? I will pray that you see her again."

He hesitated. "My Jeanne," he said. "We have a little boy four years old. He's our only surviving child."

"What is his name?" I asked.

"Gabriel," he said. "He is the happiest child." D'Allegre swallowed.

"May God bring you safe home to them," I said, "as you bring me safe home."

THE MORNING we were to reach Rome we passed Vasanello. Four hundred strong, we rode with tight discipline. I heard one of the men riding escort complaining to another that there was no pillage. "Orders. These are the lands of allied lords."

I kept my eyes straight ahead. I did not look at Adriana. Perhaps she had not heard. The Orsini were the allies of the French, and even a regular soldier knew it.

And yet if Orsino knew we were there, and at least he knew there were French troops, he did nothing. He did not help nor hinder. He did not come to Adriana's aid, nor repel the French, nor welcome them. Perhaps, as I had thought, he was all but a prisoner himself. In any event, we did not follow the road to the castle or village a mile away across the fields.

I put my heels to Lilas and went forward along the column to ride with Captain d'Allegre. "We are moving fast," I said.

He nodded. There was tension in his face. "We will be at our meeting point outside the walls later this afternoon. I've sent a man ahead to give terms for the exchange." He glanced at me. "The Pope is to send the ransom money and an escort of no more than a hundred men. We will meet at a distance and the ransom will be conveyed to us and I will check it personally. If all is in order, you and your party may proceed under our eyes to the escort and return to Rome with them."

"That sounds eminently reasonable, Captain," I said tranquilly. If Rodrigo did it. Four hundred on a hundred? He might well think it was a trap. Still, he had men he could send, and if they were set upon it would not be so many or such a grave loss that they were captured. And was it a trap? Would the captain keep his word? There must be some way to guess. "I will tell His Holiness of the King of France's gallantry."

D'Allegre's brow twitched. "That is not necessary, Madame."

"Of your gallantry, then," I said, and fell back. Did the King of France even know this exchange was intended? Was this d'Allegre's own gambit? Did he hope someone of note would come to the exchange? Most likely Rodrigo would send Captain Rizzoli or another who knew me. There was the off chance he might send Cesare, dressed not as a cardinal but as a bravo. Unless Adriana told him, d'Allegre would not know him on sight.

Dionisio came up beside me as I fell back. "What are we doing?" he asked in a low voice.

"There is to be an exchange some distance from the city walls. They are to send the ransom, d'Allegre will check it to be sure there is no subterfuge, and then he will send us across." I met his eyes. "I know, Dionisio. It could be a trap for them."

"Your play, Madonna," he said.

I had Lilas and Dionisio was a decent rider. "If it comes to it," I said, "we will break loose and ride for our walls as hard as we can. Stay low and angle away from the center to confuse archers. They won't have more than one or two shots before we are out of range. If we need to break, don't be right on my heels. We'll each have a better chance if we give separate targets."

"His Holiness must be told the Orsini are traitors."

"Yes," I said, "if d'Allegre plays us false, one of us must get through. If they recapture the other...." I shrugged. Likely they'd try to recapture me. I could be used as a hostage. Dionisio was expendable. There could not be any hanging back to cover me. "You go ahead. If they lose you and keep me, we've succeeded."

He nodded and we rode along serenely together past the cedars that marked the edge of the estate belonging to my husband.

THREE HOURS AFTER NOON, the sun westering in the December sky, and we came in sight of the walls of Rome, of the Flaminian Gate. We stopped well out of cannon or bow shot from the walls. At this season, the fields were fallow, stubble sticking up out of turned earth, though in some fields the stubble had been burned to ash to fertilize the land for spring. A murder of crows took flight, black wings against the cool sky.

A man in French colors, a white pennant on his lance, came spurring back to our lines and conferred with d'Allegre.

Adriana dismounted, walking around her horse and stretching. A number of the French did as well. I supposed d'Allegre had given the order. And why not? They could remount easily at any threat. If the gates opened, they would see a sortie far across the fields.

D'Allegre beckoned to me, and I rode over to him, Dionisio just behind me. "Our terms are acceptable for the exchange," he said. "Madame, you and your party will wait while the ransom is brought."

"Gladly, Captain," I said. I stepped out of the line beside him, turning Lilas broadside to the walls, my head high and visible. Even now, someone would be looking to see if it was truly me. Lilas was very identifiable. Hopefully I was too. I did not dare raise my hand or signal.

It seemed like a very long time that we waited. Perhaps they were uncertain. Perhaps Rizzoli or whomever had to send a message to the Vatican and wait for a reply. At this distance I could occasionally see figures moving on the wall, just heads really, above the parapet. Of course I could not distinguish anyone, just see that the defenses were manned.

At last the gates began to open. I stepped Lilas back so that d'Allegre could not reach across and take my rein. Adriana walked her horse up beside me, still dismounted. "Thank God," she said. I did not reply.

There were ten men of the Papal Army and ten Borgia guards leading out four mules, each carrying two small chests. We waited.

"Fair enough," d'Allegre said. Twenty men on foot were hardly going to attack four hundred horse!

The senior Borgia guard looked familiar, though he was not Rizzoli. I must have seen him, though he was usually part of someone else's bodyguard. He bowed politely. "Captain d'Allegre, I am Gianni di Marcelo."

"Di Marcelo," Allegre said, with an equally polite bow from the saddle.

"I have brought the requested ransom. I would like to see the ladies."

"You see them before you," d'Allegre said.

"I am Giulia Farnese," I said to him. "As you see, I am well, as is Donna Adriana de Mila and our party. I hope you will convey this."

He searched my face, no doubt remembering my face as I remembered his, vaguely. I wondered why they hadn't sent a man who knew me. "I will, Madonna."

"When we have inspected the ransom and assured ourselves it is complete, we will send the ladies," d'Allegre said.

There were more bows all around. Everyone was being exceedingly polite! Then our party turned, heading back to the walls minus the mules, which were led behind French lines.

"I hope Rodrigo has not tried to cheat him," Adriana said. I did not answer. I simply stepped Lilas out to be a little more visible.

The sun dipped behind a cloud, its shadow skating across the fallow fields. Above, high and far, a hawk cried. We waited. The afternoon was wearing on. What were they doing? D'Allegre had left the front line, going back to oversee the inspection of the chests. There were movements on the walls but I could see nothing that told me anything. Did we have archers? Who was there? Someone had to authorize this. Perhaps that's where Rizzoli was. He was the logical person to arrange it. He would be watching now to see that the French intended to comply with the agreement. I had tried to convey my earnestness, but I did not know the man he sent. Another cloud crossed the sun, a cold breeze from the west, and I shivered. It was turning cold.

At last d'Allegre returned. "The ransom is in order, Madonna," he said. "You and your party will step out. You will proceed a third of the distance with our escort and we will await the other party."

"As you say, Captain." I attempted cool serenity. I think I succeeded. Meanwhile I was thinking, a third of the way across? We are going forward with fifty mounted men, a third of the way across a field the other three hundred and fifty could cross quickly. It did not take a military genius to realize that crossing a third of the distance rather than two thirds of the distance was much faster! Was I bait? I glanced at Dionisio and he nodded fractionally. If I had to run for it, I would.

D'Allegre halted us with a raised hand a third of the way. We waited. Lilas stomped, then raised her head and nickered. The gates opened. A party of forty came out on horseback, Borgia guards in red and steel, the bull on their breastplates, and my heart stopped. The wind was from Rome. Lilas had known before I did. There was Rodrigo on Memnon.

He wore black velvet embroidered with gold, a velvet cap with a feather on his head. He wore a sword, which I had never seen him do before. Rizzoli was ahead and to his left, and they came on, forty on fifty, or forty on four hundred. If it was a trap, Rodrigo had walked straight into it himself. I could not swear it was not, just that I was no part of it.

I wanted to scream at him. How could he risk himself this way? Did he not know how badly this could go? Of course he did. And yet there he was. There he was, my Lord of the Underworld in his black velvet. He looked so aged. His hair was more gray than I remembered, the lines of his face more deeply carved.

I supposed I caught my breath, for d'Allegre looked at me. "Madame?"

"Yes?" My voice was cool.

"You may start forward."

"Thank you, captain," I said. "I will not forget your chivalry." It seemed as though it all passed in a dream, or some play on stage where we each knew the lines. I thought he must be able to hear the pounding of my heart. I put my heels to Lilas. She jumped forward. She knew her home. I did not watch to see if Dionisio and Adriana and the rest followed. I let her have her head and we flew across the burned, stubbled field, my eyes stinging with tears.

The escort opened ahead of me, a man running to catch my bridle, and I dismounted in a rush, practically flinging myself out of the saddle. And there was Rodrigo, on foot as well, and I ran the last few steps into his arms. Solid and warm, smelling of sweated velvet and himself, incense and cedar, and I buried my face in his shoulder as he clasped me tight, spinning me around so that my feet left the ground.

"My Giulia," he said. "My Giulia."

I was laughing and crying at once. "I don't care if you have a thousand women," I said caught against his chest, "as long as I am one of them."

His words were lost against the side of my head, my hair, my ear. "Never. No one but you. My heart, my Giulia." He kissed me in front of all, and I hung on tight, as though it had been a year. I am sure we looked both scandalous and ridiculous, and I didn't care at all.

Rizzoli cleared his throat. "Your Holiness, we need to get behind the walls."

We broke apart. "Of course, captain," Rodrigo said. I held to his left side as one of the men brought up Lilas for me. With a swagger, Rodrigo cupped his hands for me to mount, his own holy hands. He wore sword and dagger on crossed belts like a bravo.

I dipped my head against his shoulder. "Are those Cesare's?"

"Shhh," he said, and kissed my cheek. He'd let the belts out quite a few notches. "Cesare is having a fit on the walls."

I put my toe in his hands and swung up. "I should think," I said. I looked back toward French lines. Not a horse moved. Captain d'Allegre saw me and bowed in the saddle, his hand on his breast. I returned his courtesy.

Rodrigo mounted up on Memnon. "We need to go," Rizzoli said. He was carefully keeping his body between Rodrigo and any archer's line of sight.

We trotted the rest of the way across the field, Dionisio and the others behind with the escort. Cesare was just inside the gate, on foot and wearing leather and steel. "Come on, Papa. Hurry." The gates closed the moment the last of our party were within. "Giulia."

"It's good to see you, Cesare," I said. I couldn't stop smiling. I could readily imagine how it had gone: he'd intended to ride out, but Rodrigo had insisted on doing it himself while Cesare twitched. If it had been a trap....

Adriana. I needed to tell Rodrigo. She was sitting on her horse at the back of the line, behind even Tina, looking drawn and pale. She looked up and met my eyes.

I urged Lilas forward, next to Memnon as we came out of the shadow of the gate. "Where do we go?" I asked Rodrigo. I did not reach across and clasp his hand, though I wanted to. I settled for devouring him with my eyes, every inch of him.

"Back to the Vatican," he said. "We hold the walls. Barely. Prince Ferrandino of Naples still has enough men." He did not take his eyes from me either. "And we hold the Castel Sant'Angelo."

I nodded, coming closer so that our stirrups nearly touched. There were things that came before endearments. "Rodrigo, you must put Adriana under house arrest."

He did not look shocked. "What else?"

"The Orsini are planning to betray you," I said. "Bracciano will lead the Papal Army over to the French on December 15th. He intended me to be a hostage to secure your resignation. Adriana tried to deliver me to Bracciano at Vasanello."

"That is precisely why I told you to stay at Capodimonte," Rodrigo said, but there was no heat in it. "And yet here you are."

"You knew?"

"I guessed. I didn't know for certain until now, and I did not know the date. When I heard that you intended to return to Vasanello, I thought it was a trap." Memnon twitched and he sidled closer. "I told you to stay where it was safe."

"It was not safe anymore. Adriana introduced Savonarola's spy into Capodimonte. She promised Bracciano she would bring me to Vasanello. She said you were falling and that I had had all the good I would have of you." There was a bitter sound in my voice.

Rodrigo took a deep breath. He had known her since she was a child. "I see." He turned his horse. "So be it."

CHAPTER 14

The sun was setting as we crossed the bridge. The city had been quiet. So too was the river traffic. Only a few small boats moved. The parapets of the Castel Sant'Angelo gleamed in the last rays of the descending sun. Beyond, the square before St. Peter's was in darkness. We dismounted. I walked Lilas in circles. We had been riding all day, not even a pause for First Meal, just a little bread and wine in the morning. I was tired, and I was certain Lilas was too.

Rodrigo was talking quietly with Captain Rizzoli and Cesare. Tina turned to me. "Madonna, are we going home?" She meant Palazzo Santa Maria in Portico, of course.

"I don't know," I said.

Adriana had also dismounted. I did not know what to say to her that would neither be conciliatory nor gloating.

Rodrigo spoke to her first, striding across the stones still wearing Cesare's blades. "Captain Rizzoli will escort you to Palazzo Santa Maria in Portico," he said. "You will remain there under guard in your rooms. Doctor Treschi, if you will accept our hospitality, will you also go there and watch over Donna Adriana?"

"It would be my pleasure, Your Holiness," Dionisio said, bowing from the waist. He had lodgings, but what his plans had been when he left for Capodimonte months ago I had no idea. There were certainly comfortable guest rooms in the house. Tina would go with them, of course. She'd lived at Santa Maria in Portico for years.

"Rodrigo," Adriana began.

"That would be Holy Father," he said coldly.

Adriana stopped as if she'd been slapped. She went to her knees on the cobblestones, clearly prepared for a scene of supplication, but he turned and walked away, leaving her kneeling to nothing.

"Get up," I said in a low voice. "You are lucky that you are simply under guard in your own rooms, not in the dungeons of the Castel Sant'Angelo. If I were you, I would not try his temper."

She got to her feet, her eyes searching my face. "You think you've won."

"I think you have lost," I said evenly. "Whoever wins, no one will trust you."

"I had no choice!"

"You say that a lot," I said. I could not say anymore. Anger had fled. It was simply sadness. Five years ago I had wanted so much for us to be close. I had been prepared to trust her and love her. And now there was nothing to do but walk away.

I joined Rodrigo and Cesare, who were finishing the orders for the guard at Santa Maria in Portico. Rodrigo had taken off the crossed belts and given them back to Cesare, who was buckling them on. "Am I going with them?"

Rodrigo looked at me a little sheepishly. "I thought you might stay in the Vatican. If you wanted."

"As Your Holiness wishes," I said. There was a flash of uncertainty in his face. "Nothing would please me more."

Cesare looked heavenward. "Papa, we have Prince Ferrandino and the captains in the morning. We've lost the whole day to this. They'll be here for the meeting at prime. Please be on time."

"I'll be on time." Rodrigo was looking at me, not Cesare.

"He will be on time," I assured Cesare. "Fed, watered and appropriately dressed."

Cesare started laughing, eyes meeting mine. "It's good to have you home, Giulia."

"It's good to be home," I said.

WE WENT in through the main entrances. The Vatican, like the city, was curiously deserted. I didn't think I'd ever seen it when it wasn't a beehive, teeming with clerks, priests, prelates, ambassadors, guards, servants, and an assortment of others. Now there were a few people here and there. The guards on the doors stood alert as Rodrigo approached, but there were not the usual crowds trying to get his attention when he passed through a public space in the Vatican. "Where is everyone?" I murmured.

"Gone like rats deserting a sinking ship," he said in a low voice. "Like the College of Cardinals, except for Carafa, Cybo, Riario and Piccolomini."

The noted humanists. "And why are they still here?"

He looked at me sideways. "My dear, some men actually believe what they profess. And then there's Ascanio Sforza. He's still here because he wagers he can turn it to his advantage somehow. I've had to arrest him, though. It's all very congenial. He's locked in a guest chamber upstairs."

"That doesn't sound too taxing," I said. The Vatican's guest chambers were very nice indeed.

"He and his nephew, Sanseverino, are sharing." Sanseverino was all of nineteen, though he had the Sforza maturity. They learned intrigue in the cradle.

"And the other nephew?" I asked.

"Which one?" Rodrigo turned the last corner into his apartments. "There are so many. Sforzas under every bush. I understand Ascanio has thirty-four siblings, if you count the acknowledged bastards."

"Prince Ferrandino," I said. "The heir to the throne of Naples who presumably wouldn't like France to conquer Naples?"

"He's doing well," Rodrigo said. "Though a little annoyed that his uncles have intrigued at giving away his kingdom. He certainly wouldn't like me to do anything dire to Ascanio, but he has no objection to me locking him up."

"Thirty-four brothers and sisters?" That seemed excessive.

"So he says." Rodrigo shrugged as we went down the gallery. "I don't know how Ascanio's father found time for anything else. I've only sired eight that I know about and that seems a gracious plenty."

We went into the first sala, closing the door behind us. I heard the guard come to rest outside. The golden ornaments on the walls and ceiling glittered in the candlelight, breathtaking and wonderful. Pinturicchio's work in here was completed. Above the door was the Adoration he had painted, Rodrigo in his golden cope on his knees to the Virgin and Child. I held Laura on my lap and he reached for Laura's foot, playing with her toes while she laughed. My eyes were downcast, my face serene and lovely, while Rodrigo smiled at us.

"You see that every time you come in," I said.

"Not that it caused me to miss you," he said. Everyone else had stopped at the last door. It was just we two.

"No," I said. I had no idea what to say or do next.

He hesitated too. He took one step forward and stopped. "Giulia, are you…. Were you mistreated?"

Of course he thought of that. Of course he had worried. "No," I said. "Captain d'Allegre was gallant in all respects. Neither he nor his men did me any harm."

"I…." He stopped again.

"You worried," I said, taking a step forward. We did not quite touch. There had been miles between us, and now there was this awkwardness at a step.

"Naturally." His eyes roved over my face.

"And you'd have had me back anyway."

"I would never blame you for that. Or for anything you had to do." His brow twitched.

"To my great good fortune, I have met the only honorable man in this entire business," I said. "I would have done what I needed to if it would buy my freedom. But I didn't have to." It may have been that my voice shook, the weight of the last week making itself felt. It had been a very long week.

"Giulia. Are you ill?"

"I'm hungry," I said. "I never had First Meal at all and it is now past Vespers." I really was famished.

"Of course. I'll have dinner sent up. You should have said so." He went back into the hall, calling for one of the pages.

I strolled through the next room, which was clearly being used for receiving visitors formally, with Rodrigo's great chair under a white canopy with hanging gold bullion beneath Pinturicchio's beautiful Annunciation and Nativity. None of the candles had been lit in here, though there was a glow through the door beyond, and I followed it.

This room hadn't been finished when I left, and there were still blank spaces on the walls where more paintings had not yet been begun. I went in, turning about in the haze of candlelight which reflected from the gilding on the ceiling. I tilted my head back, reading the story that went from panel to panel above my head, the story of Isis and Osiris from Plutarch's Moralia, ending with Serapis as the Apis bull. It was lovely beyond belief, and also a bit strange, as though in firelight I had walked into some door out of the past and seen this story glittering on the ceiling. So engrossed was I that I walked into a couch. It was furnished as an informal sala, though the table was back against the wall and the plate on the credenza was dulled by the glory above.

There was a step, Rodrigo coming in. He smiled when he saw me craning my neck at the ceiling. "It came out well, I think."

"It's wonderful," I said. The wall paintings shone like jewels, Lucrezia as St. Catherine of Alexandria disputing with the elders. That one had been finished just before we left. She had posed for it amid all the wedding celebrations, her likeness to stay with Rodrigo when she was far away.

He put his arm around my waist. "It will be a little while until dinner. Unless you'd just like something cold."

"I'll wait for dinner," I said. I leaned against him sideways. "I haven't seen the other rooms yet."

"Well, then." The next room was his study, a generous room with his two-sided desk, the right side flat for writing and the left at an angle to hold a book or manuscript. There were enormous bookcases, most of his personal three hundred and more volumes easy to hand. Above one, the allegorical lady Geometry presented wisdom to Euclid, while Astrology measured the stars. Some of the paintings were begun but not finished.

"I take it Maestro di Betto is gone," I said with some disappointment.

"Absence is the better part of valor," Rodrigo said dryly. "I'm not paying him enough to die."

I turned from my perusal of Geometry. He was usually an unbridled optimist. "Is it that bad?"

He didn't evade my eyes. "The situation is very bad."

I took a deep breath. "How bad?"

He walked around the desk, one hand caressing the wood. "Abysmal. Prince Ferrandino has fifteen hundred men. Bracciano is the Gonfaloniere, and he will defect to the French, as you have told me. There are two hundred and fifty-one Borgia guards. There are a few of the Gonfaloniere's men who may stay loyal, probably fewer than two hundred. So, with Ferrandino, two thousand men against twenty-two thousand." I closed my eyes. "So you see, my love, it's impossible. I told you to stay in Capodimonte to save your life."

A thousand things ran through my mind in that moment. All the paths I had seen came down to this. There were three left, one to ruin, one to death, and only a slim path that was neither. It was unlikely, and yet rendered more probable by my presence. That was reason enough to be here.

I opened my eyes. In the flickering candlelight, Rodrigo was neither the monster of fever dreams nor my King of the Underworld. He looked tired. He'd gained weight these six months, his hair grayer and his black velvet too tight to be flattering. He did not look like the hero of a chivalric romance any more than he looked papal. And yet. There was something about his eyes, this stubborn, venal, sincere, indomitable schemer – my Rodrigo.

I took a step closer, raising my hand to rest against the side of his face. He turned his head and kissed my palm, face in profile against my skin, his nose against my fingers, closing his eyes as though he tasted the merest morsel of heaven.

Perhaps at last I saw clearly. "I love you with all my heart, and I will never desert you."

"Sweetness...." The last few inches were not so far.

"Don't talk," I said, and kissed him. Quiet, shadowed, like moving underwater, we moved together. My body remembered. I knew his touch, the feel of his lips on mine, the way we fit together. I could melt into him, draw him down like a siren into my depths. We went into his camera, closing the door and leaving the candles lit. The firelight flickered across my skin, undressing together, slowly, wordlessly. What was there to say? What could there be except this? We had bruised one another. What could we do except kiss the bruises?

After, we lay face to face among the tumbled pillows in disarrayed clothes, forehead to forehead, breathing together. The room was in shadow now, the fire sunk to coals, the light through the shutters faded. Far and high, the bells were ringing Compline.

I just held to him as though he were a rock in the sea, the tide dragging at me. "I have missed you," I whispered.

"My Giulia." His eyes were closed. I raised my hand to the back of his neck, feeling the familiar shape of his shoulders, the way his hair was too long over his collar in the back, soft and curling just a little.

I closed my eyes too, remembering. "In black velvet with sword and dagger." No doubt we had looked ridiculous. And yet what could one do but play the scene, running at each other through fallow fields as though I sought the underworld belatedly? "I wasn't sure you'd ransom me."

"How could you doubt that?" I opened my eyes to see him looking at me, half bemused and half disapproving.

"Well," I said, "the last thing you said to me before was that if I left Capodimonte without your permission you'd excommunicate me and sentence me to eternal damnation."

Rodrigo winced. "Um," he said. "That was intemperate." I waited. "I should not have said that."

I slid down, putting my head on his shoulder in our usual position. His skin was warm, a faint sheen of sweat drying on his flesh. "The College wouldn't have done it anyway."

And there was a chuckle. "No, probably not. Excommunicating my concubine for disobedience…." His left hand stroked my hair. He took a deep breath, as if steeling himself. "I am sorry."

"For threatening to excommunicate me? You should be," I said, but there was no heat in it. It had worried me more than frightened me.

"Yes, for that but…." He halted, then went on. "For the other. I should not…."

He couldn't quite manage to say it. Six months ago I would have been livid. Now it was just Rodrigo. "Have been unfaithful?" I prompted.

"That." He looked up at the ceiling. I wasn't certain which of us he was addressing, me or God. "I will try not to do it again. I will try to be true to you."

A bargain with both of us, of sorts. Celibacy was beyond him, but perhaps he could stick at one concubine. At least he would try. I opened my hand against his chest. And sooner or later he would fail. He would fall into bed with some woman or other. He would feel guilty. But he'd do it anyway. Probably he'd make sure I didn't know because the thing that compounded the sin was hurting me. But I would know, of course. Someone would always enjoy telling me. "How many times since we began?" I asked evenly. I wasn't furious. I just wanted to know.

He huffed as though that were not the question he expected. "A few," he said. "I don't know. Two or three. But after you left and said you never wanted to see me again…."

"I know," I said. "There were a dozen before I hit the city gates."

"Not a dozen. Some. You said we were done and every courtesan in Rome was trying to catch my attention…." His voice trailed off.

"And how could you disappoint them?" I shook my head ruefully. I had left him and said I never wanted to see him again.

"There were some, Giulia. Not a dozen. And none of them were you."

I knew him. I knew what he liked and I liked him. It wasn't for money or jewels but because I wanted him, charming or cranky, generous and feral, imaginative and brilliant. I could easily imagine how little Rodrigo liked being someone's job, an ageing patron whose passions must be desperately raised lest they fail to please. I never had to pretend. "There is no one like you either," I said, my cheek against his shoulder. "I did not bed Orsino. Why would I do that?"

I felt him sigh. "Why wouldn't you? He's your husband. If you never wanted to see me again, it would be sensible to reconcile with him. You were at Vasanello. Adriana said…."

"Adriana lied," I said. "Yes, Orsino and I talked. It was congenial. He has a woman he loves and a baby of his own. He asked me to not contest his will leaving his personal property to his woman and his child if he were killed. He promised not to repudiate Laura. We made an agreement. Adriana didn't know about it or have anything to do with it. He has as much interest in sleeping with me as I do with him, which is none." I craned my neck to see his face. "You know there is nothing between us. Why would you believe that?"

Rodrigo looked up at the ceiling. "When Vannozza and I…. When we were ending, I suppose…. Her marriage was intended to be a marriage of convenience. I'd lived with her for years, more or less. But then I had the Vice-Chancellor's Palazzo and my work was becoming more consuming. I needed to stay on this side of the city and there was a lot of official and unofficial entertaining. Vannozza hated that sort of thing. And there were three children. Lucrezia was Laura's age and Juan and Cesare were six and eight. She stayed at her house and I stayed at mine more and more. And yes, before you ask, there were women. There had always been women. We had an understanding. Sport that meant nothing was fair, but we belonged to each other first. Casual encounters didn't count, not for either of us."

"So Lucrezia said," I said. I didn't think I could manage such a thing, but it was fair.

"In any event, she slept with her husband. Not once, but a number of times. He was there when I wasn't, in and out of her house. And then Gioffre was born. I acknowledged him and legitimized him."

"But," I said.

He shrugged. "Who's to know? He's my son. But things were never right after. Vannozza wanted a man who made a home with her. I needed…I wanted a woman who loved the game as I did. Who wanted to play politics at this level and who didn't find official entertaining a chore and who was as ambitious as I was. We stumbled along for a few years. I truly did love her."

That had always been clear to me. "I know," I said.

"Eventually it was obvious that she wanted to have a real marriage with Carlo and that I was the third wheel on that cart. And I intended to be pope, which she hated. It was the last blow, that I was determined to be pope after Innocent. So we called it off respectfully and gently. No shouting. We were done with shouting. We were kind to one another." Rodrigo took a deep breath. "Which isn't to say we never argue, but not so much now that we stopped trying to stay together. She has Carlo and I have you." His arm tightened around me. "But you see why the idea that you might reconcile with Orsino smarted."

"Adriana knew that," I said. "Lucrezia has no discretion."

He was quiet for a long moment. "She probably did." And had deliberately chosen something that would hurt him, a deeper wedge to drive between us.

I didn't let go. I wanted to know the things I hadn't asked six months ago, too hurt to let him explain. "The woman at the masque – why, Rodrigo?"

He sighed. "I don't know. It was an impulse. It was a terrible party. The costumes were a bad idea and Lucrezia was married and Gioffre was getting married and I felt so old and sick to death of bride, bride, bride. I suppose I wanted to feel like it was a different time, when I was younger and everything was simpler." He met my eyes. "I should not have done it. And I certainly should not have done it where you would see and be hurt. I didn't mean that. I will try not to do it again."

"When you fail," I began. He winced. "…and bed some other

woman, I would like for you to tell me yourself, rather than have me find out or hear it from vicious gossips." He had not thought of that. I saw it in his face, that he had not imagined the pleasure some would take in telling me of his recreations to humiliate me in some public place.

"If I should ever stray again, am I to confess to you then?"

"Yes," I said. "You must be used to confessing carnal sins. You shall make your confession to me."

"And you will?"

"Forgive you," I said. "I forgive you, Rodrigo." I felt as though an enormous weight I had been carrying had dropped to the ground. I was light again, open to joy. I did forgive him, truly and with my heart. "My dear," I said. "It seemed so terribly important. And now it does not at all."

Rodrigo's brows knit. It was a rather sudden about face. "You told me to go fuck myself."

"I did," I said. "And I should not have said that. I should have let you apologize. I have a temper, as you know."

"I do."

I took his right hand in mine, lacing our fingers together. "I was angry. I was hurt. I thought you were tired of me and preferred someone else."

"Never. That's not…."

"You did call me a harridan and say you'd do as you pleased," I pointed out.

"After you called me a randy old goat and then you told me to fuck myself," he said. "I have a temper too."

"And so we screamed at each other and I think we have both regretted it," I said, my cheek against his shoulder.

"I have regretted it." He looked at our hands. "I missed you."

No one else could ever be this, my Pluto, my Amadis, my Merlin. I knew what I wanted, just as I always had. "And so the courtesans will be disappointed that I am back," I said. "Shall I get a broom and sweep them out? Or perhaps a bow and require them to bend it and shoot through the rings?"

The corner of Rodrigo's mouth twitched. "Are you Odysseus now, here to clear out the suitors?"

"And are you my sweet Penelope, weaving and waiting?"

He laughed, "And unraveling every night. That seems right."

"It seems ten years since I left," I said too truthfully. I closed my eyes.

We were both drifting on the edge of sleep when a page knocked on the door. "Your Holiness? Second Meal has been brought up."

Rodrigo pulled a robe on and went to the door. "Bring it in," he said. "That's right. Bring it in and put it on the table there." Two pages stumbled under trays, trying not to look at me in the bed, though I was blanketed to the chin, not an inch of flesh visible. Clearly His Holiness barefooted and in disarray was less interesting.

"Do we need to wait for a taster?" I asked. That was one of my least favorite things about dining at the Vatican.

"I expect we can chance it," Rodrigo said, looking at the dishes under covers. "There are easier ways to kill me these days."

One of the pages' eyes got very round. "Your Holiness, would you like me to taste for you?"

"No, Michele," Rodrigo said gently. "That won't be necessary. You may go." The pages left, and Rodrigo locked the door behind them. I sat up as he pulled the little table near the bed. "I've dismissed some of the pages, the ones who could get home. Michele is an orphan. He has nowhere else to go." Rodrigo sat down on the side of the bed and I cuddled up to lean on his shoulder. No father but the Holy Father, I thought. Rodrigo always treated his pages well. No wonder he volunteered to taste, a good boy, a dutiful son, a page who loved his lord. I hoped he didn't die for his fidelity. But if he were sent away from this service, what would he do, nine or ten years old with no kin who would care for him? It was better for him to put his trust in Rodrigo.

We ate in bed and then settled down to sleep, the curtains drawn tight against the cold.

CHAPTER 15

I woke to Lauds ringing. I stirred. "Those are the bells of St. Peter's," I said, half asleep.

"They are indeed, sweet," Rodrigo said, kissing the top of my head. I lay curled in his arms, my face against his breast. It was still entirely dark inside the heavy bed curtains, though outside it must be dawn.

"I'm home," I said. For a long, quiet while I just lay there, his arms around me, the room still. Then a thought occurred. "You have a meeting with the captains in less than an hour."

"It's three rooms away," Rodrigo said.

I lifted my head, running my finger down his cheek. "And you must be shaved and dressed. And you should eat something, at least some of last night's bread, so that you're not cranky."

"Cranky?" He lay back laughing. "Am I Laura now?"

"Sometimes you are just alike." My voice caught. "I miss her so much."

Rodrigo's arm tightened around me. "She's safer in Pesaro now."

"I know." I took a deep breath. "But you need to get up."

"I am," he said, and didn't move.

I was loath to move either. "Do you know what I'd like to do today? I'd like a bath. I haven't had one since I left Capodimonte."

"You could have a bath," he said. "I'll tell someone to bring water up."

"Tina is coming back later," I said. "I asked her to bring clothes. I only brought one gown from Capodimonte since I wanted to make good time and expected to be three days on the road, not ten. My winter clothes are still at Palazzo Santa Maria in Portico. I didn't take them with me to Pesaro in May, so I'll have my clothes back." The ones suitable for the Vatican, I thought, the modest ones and the formal ones and also the warmest ones. Tina would know what to bring.

Rodrigo sat up, scratching his chin. "Will you stay here with me?"

And not be under the same roof with Adriana under arrest. "Of course," I said. Once, he wouldn't have asked. He would just have assumed I would. "I think gossip is the least of our problems at the moment."

"Certainly the least. My enemies already think I'm the devil and my friends don't care if I have you for breakfast." He leaned over and kissed me hard, pinning me to the bed.

Tempting as it was…. "But Cesare will," I said, pushing him off gently. "If you're late."

"The captains." He got up. "There's no need for you to get out of bed until you want to. You can rest all you like and have a bath and do whatever you wish."

A day of quiet did sound wonderful. "Am I to be invisible?" I asked. "Can I pass through rooms or should I use the servants' stair if I go anywhere?"

Rodrigo shrugged. "I don't see that it matters if anyone knows you're here. Come in if you like."

"I will," I said, and rolled over and went back to sleep.

SEXT HAD RUNG and we were in the seventh hour after dawn before I emerged into the study, soaked and scrubbed, my hair washed and braided. It was so short, only halfway to my waist, that there wasn't much that could be done with it except two braids on the side and the rest bundled into a snood. It did take less time to dry in front of the fire, though. As short as it was, clean and brushed while it was drying, it tended to poof in all directions.

In a dark blue gamurra of expensive but not ostentatious cloth, I went through the study to the informal sala. I could hear voices on the other side, and the door was cracked into the formal sala. The meeting had just broken for First Meal, the participants milling around conversing while an aide rolled up maps and the servants laid trays of savories and heartier fare on the long table. It made my mouth water. Surely I could get a plate as well.

I tried to slip in, but Rodrigo saw me as soon as the door opened. "And here is La Bella Farnese! Giulia, darling, do you remember Prince Ferrandino?" He beckoned, and I came to his side.

Ferrandino was twenty-six years old, with the Sforza nose from his mother's family, but the good looks of the royal family of Naples came through. He looked something like Sancia, which was hardly surprising since she was his younger half-sister. I had last seen him at the wedding festivities last spring. He bent over my hand courteously. "Of course I remember Madonna Giulia. Where would this court be without your light? I am glad you have returned to us." Naturally everyone had heard about yesterday's display before the walls.

"Thank you, Your Highness," I said with a curtsy. "I had been in the country at my family's estate because of my younger brother's death. Unfortunately, the French advanced more swiftly than expected."

"My condolences on your brother's passing," Ferrandino said. "Is Cardinal Farnese also returned?"

"His Eminence was also ill," I said. "He was not yet well enough to travel when I left."

"Ah. I hope he is soon improved." Ferrandino's brow twitched. He thought we were hedging our bets, like all the rest of the families who could. I would cleave to Pope Alexander and my brother would remain neutral, or perhaps even go over to the French outright.

"He holds Capodimonte against the French," I said. I didn't want Alessandro to be thought an opportunist, rather than just not fool-hardy as I was.

"A notable endeavor," he replied.

I ventured a question. "Where is my lord Bracciano, the Gonfaloniere? Surely he should be here."

"With his men," Ferrandino said. "Or so we hear. On the Via Aurelia."

Between Montalto and Rome. I had been right to try the northern route. It had been better to be captured by the French than Bracciano.

Cesare joined us. He was wearing a black doublet, sleeves slashed with Borgia red. Did he ever wear his cardinal's robes unless absolutely necessary? It didn't seem so. Rodrigo was properly dressed in papal white, the full floor length cassock and the short stole in matching white brocade, a gold pectoral cross ornamented with rubies. "I still don't think it's much of a plan," Cesare said to Ferrandino without preamble, presumably continuing a discussion from earlier.

"I know it's not," the prince said candidly, "but keeping one gate open is all I can do with what I have. In order to repel an assault, I have to have a great enough concentration of troops. If I spread them out to all the gates, there won't be enough to hold any of them. It's best to block up all the others except the Porta San Sebastiano."

The road south to Naples, I thought. His own line of retreat, and our last tie with the world. "The Via Appia," Rodrigo said. "It's best to keep that open."

"I shall endeavor to, Your Holiness," Ferrandino said. "You know that my father's offer remains. Should events progress undesirably, he would welcome the Papal Court to the fortress of Gaeta which you may use as long as you wish and will also put 50,000 ducats at your disposal for the maintenance of the court."

Exile, I thought. *If Rodrigo abandoned Rome, he would be welcome in Naples.* This was the schism I had seen. Two popes, Rodrigo in Naples and della Rovere crowned in Rome. This was how it would begin. This was the door that led to fire. I said nothing, my face neutral.

"Can Naples hold against the French?" Cesare asked bluntly.

"We must." Ferrandino shrugged. "My father has loaned me a

company of his men, 1,500 good soldiers, but the bulk of our army remains in the south to guard Naples itself."

Rodrigo put his hand on Ferrandino's shoulder in an avuncular way. "Your father is a fine man, and his offer is greatly appreciated." I drew a quick breath. "But we will not abandon Rome without a fight. Come, gentlemen. Let us enjoy First Meal and return to our conference."

That was my dismissal and calling the meeting back to order. I got a plate and took it back into the study, leaning against the closed door for a moment. I could feel my heart pounding. It could have happened in that moment. Rodrigo could have said yes. And yet he did not. The world shifted, that path becoming a little less likely. When I closed my eyes I could see the paths beneath the trees, that one less broad, a little more overgrown. The path straight ahead led to death.

THINGS DID NOT GET BETTER, or at least the political situation did not improve. For myself, I thought it was much better. I had missed Rome, not just Rodrigo. True, many of my friends had left. Fiammetta had decamped to Spoleto, of all places, and she was hardly enamored of small towns in the winter! I wondered if Cesare had suggested or arranged it. There was a Borgia fortress at Spoleto.

The season of Christmas was usually full of cheer, but this year everything was hushed. It didn't help that it rained incessantly. Letters came from Lucrezia on the fifteenth, written nine days earlier rather than three, since they had gone the long way around via Porta San Sebastiano rather than from the north. The road past Vasanello was held by the French. I shared my letter with Rodrigo and he shared his with me.

Dearest Giulia, I miss you so dreadfully! It is cold and cheerless here and there is no society. All the guests of last summer are gone, as is Giovanni. He has been called to arms by his kinsmen, and though I begged him not to go and take up arms against Papa he said that he was a Sforza and I a Sforza wife, and I had better remember it. That is why I am writing when he is gone and there is no one here who will forbid it. Honestly, I did not think him such a tyrant! He raised his voice to me and told me to grow up.

"Oh dear," I said. I hadn't thought it was a wonderful match, but the strain of being on opposite sides of a war was a lot for any marriage to bear.

Laura is my delight and my consolation. Her second birthday was lovely. I wish you could have seen her smiles at her presents. She is so warm and happy that everyone adores her, and I am her devoted servant. I am probably spoiling her, but is that not a sister's privilege? I cannot wait to have one of my own. I will be the best mother in the world, and I am lucky to practice on Laura!

I sniffled, and Rodrigo put his arm around me as I perched on the arm of his chair to show him the letter. "I'm glad Laura is happy," I said. Missing her was like a pain in my chest. And yet she was far safer with Lucrezia than she would be in Rome right now. Here, she would be a hostage or a victim if we failed. There, Lucrezia would care for her with love and tenderness.

"I am, too," he said. "Lucrezia can be frivolous, but she loves her so much." His voice shook a little. He missed them both, of course. As I did.

I don't know if this letter will get through. The last two couriers had to turn around and I haven't had a letter from you or Papa in two weeks. I fear that your letters to me have been captured. So please be careful what you say!

"Yes, Lucrezia," I murmured. "We got that far."

So I won't ask what Cesare is doing because you shouldn't tell me. But tell him I'm praying for his safety. And Gioffre and Sancia and everybody. Please give Donna Adriana my love.

Rodrigo sighed. "She is very fond of Adriana."

"I know," I said.

Mama writes that she is safe and will stay there until this is over. She also told me that I needed to get with child and how does she think I'm going to do that when Giovanni isn't here? Well, I know how I could, but I won't. Besides there is nobody here who would do. Everyone interesting is gone. But Mama says I need to conceive to maintain my position and really I don't think the Sforza are nearly as desirable as she does. They may put on airs but three generations ago they were nothing but mercenary soldiers who made good so I'm not in the least intimidated by their blood or money because we have money and what is blood anyway?

"I doubt Lucrezia is intimidated by anything," Rodrigo said. "You should have seen her reply to me when I upbraided her for letting you leave Pesaro for Capodimonte! She practically told me to mind my own business."

"Told off the Pope, did she?" I said with a smile. "Perish the thought!"

"If Lucrezia were a boy, Italy would tremble."

"And she knows it, too," I said.

In any event, I am well and so is Laura. We will pass Christmastide together and make our own cheer. Perhaps in the spring this will all be done and the French will be vanquished and we can all be together. All my love, Lucrezia

"I pray you're right, my darling," I said.

Rodrigo scratched his ear. "Would she really take a lover? She's not but fourteen. And her husband is young and vigorous."

I turned, his arm still around my waist, sitting half in his lap. "Nearly fifteen," I said. "And Giovanni Sforza may be young and vigorous, but he's not at all romantic."

"Romantic? He's a Sforza!"

I kissed his nose. "True, but she's a Borgia. Passionate, demonstrative, and possessed of a dramatic imagination."

"I fail to see...."

Of course he did. "Let me tell you a story of last summer. We went to the seashore, Lucrezia, Laura, and I, with a bunch of ladies and visitors and her little Court of Love. Laura and I paddled along the shore and played in the sand. I heard a shriek, and Lucrezia had fallen into the waves. She'd taken off her gown and was wading in her camisa and was swept off her feet by a wave."

Rodrigo pulled his head back to see me better. "Did you go after her?" I had grown up near the shore and Lucrezia had not. I could swim.

"I had no need to. Eight gentlemen were ahead of me."

"Eight?"

"Plunging into the sea like dolphins in velvet and leather. I could swear one of them was holding another's head underwater. At last the victor emerged, Lucrezia cradled in his arms, wet camisa plastered to her body, her long golden hair unbound, one arm wrapped about the neck of her rescuer as she clung to him." Rodrigo's eyes were wide and horrified. "He strode out of the sea, followed by her entourage of gentlemen, while she professed herself forever indebted to her savior. None of the gentlemen, it's worth noting, were Giovanni Sforza. She'll have a lover by Easter."

"That's...." Rodrigo seemed rendered speechless.

"My darling, she's just like you," I said. I slid the rest of the way into his lap, his arm around me. "Lucrezia is as likely to be chaste as you are."

"The world sees it differently."

"Of course it does," I said. "A man is vigorous and virile, and a woman is a harlot. But we are who we are. She is a Borgia. You can't expect her to be different. I hope that after she's provided Giovanni Sforza an heir, they may each quietly pursue their own interests. Perhaps they can reach an understanding, as you and her mother did."

"That would be best." Rodrigo frowned. "I don't want anything bad to happen to her. She's never known cruelty."

"I know," I said. He had protected her all her life. I twined my arm around his neck, ruffling his hair. "But right now Lucrezia is the safest of all of us. So let us try to put aside worry for what she may do in the future. Giovanni Sforza may be killed and the entire question moot."

That it was a cheering thought said a great deal.

THE NEXT MORNING, I sent a guardsman to ask Dionisio to join me for First Meal. Rodrigo was busy, and we ate in the Pope's study as though it were my own house, which I asked about.

"Everything is as you left it," Dionisio said. "Except that Beneo left for the country months ago to join his daughter at Vasanello. Donna Adriana complains about it mightily, but Captain Rizzoli says that it is up to you to hire someone."

"Does she have the run of the house?" I asked with some alarm. Bracciano did not know that Rodrigo knew of his treachery, one tiny advantage. Adriana must not be able to tell him.

He shook his head. "She's confined to her rooms, sala, camera, and bath. Her meals are brought up."

"Hardly durance vile," I said tartly. "Have you talked to her?"

"Yes. But I'm not about to carry letters for her, if that's what you mean."

"I know you have more sense," I said. "You were at Capodimonte."

"Giulia, I hope you know I will never cooperate with anything that gives Savonarola more power," he said, putting his fork down beside his plate.

"I do know," I said. I took a sip of my wine. "Dionisio, I have been wondering if there is a way to ward the city."

"The city of Rome?"

"No, some other city! Yes, the city of Rome," I said. "As we warded the house during the papal election."

He considered. "If you remember, it didn't keep assassins out. A working ward like that is intended to stop incorporeal entities, not physical human beings. The French army wouldn't be affected. Also," he paused, "the amount of power to ward something the size of the city of Rome would be enormous. Normally you ward a room. We warded a house. To ward something the size of the city? Where would you get the power? And thirdly, generally you can only ward something you have sovereignty over."

"Explain that," I said.

Dionisio picked up his fork. "When we've done wards for your sibylline researches, we warded the room we were in. Your room. In your house. There is no question of sovereignty because it's yours and you permit it. If you wanted to go ward – I don't know – a room in Capodimonte, you'd need Alessandro's permission probably. It's not yours. The place doesn't recognize you as having the right, if that makes sense."

"But if Alessandro said it was fine?"

He shrugged. "Then you could do it. But who has sovereignty over the city of Rome?"

"Rodrigo," I said evenly.

He shook his head, smiling. "I suppose if you had the Pope's permission, why not? Or if he did it."

"That won't happen," I said. Rodrigo turned a blind eye to my more heretical explorations, but he drew the line at actually participating. "But it might be possible to get his permission, if the other problems were solved."

"Giulia, let me reiterate, a ward won't keep out physical humans," he said. "You'd know when they crossed it, but you'll know that already because they're a giant army! I do not know any way to ward out physical people. And before you say so, yes, it can make people uncomfortable, but as we saw with Bracciano's assassin that time, if they have orders they'll go through it. And then there's the issue of power. It's simply too big. I can't imagine where you'd get the energy to ward an entire city."

I sighed. "I will keep thinking on it." I could almost see where to get the power, but the lack of a physical barrier didn't seem surmountable.

"I wish I could be more help," Dionisio said.

"There is something I need you to do," I said, "Something dangerous." His brows rose. "Alessandro has had no word since we left and he has no way of knowing what is happening in Rome. Can you return to Capodimonte and tell him?"

Dionisio lifted his wine glass and took a sip. "Through French lines."

"Lots of people are fleeing Rome. There's no reason to stop you in particular. You're a Florentine. You're returning to Florence. They're allied with Florence. You can say you're exactly who you are – a scholar who has been employed in Rome and is now returning home. If you don't go all the way to Florence but stop at Capodimonte, that's well past the French advance."

"Unless they're feeling randomly murderous." He took another sip. "But probably not. As you say, I'm a subject of the Florentine Republic."

"I know you can explain that convincingly. And then you'll be in Capodimonte." With Alessandro, who would understand that he had an obligation to take care of my client if I was no longer able to. Dionisio had come into danger for me twice, first when he came into plague at Capodimonte and then into the French advance. I needed to get my client free of the sack of Rome if I could. He had pledged himself to me. I saw him hesitating. "Alessandro needs to know what's happening. I don't dare put anything to paper. You can tell him. And I know you will use your discretion and tell no other."

"Of course I won't," he said. Dionisio met my eyes. "A Borgia agent."

"My agent," I said. "I trust you completely."

"Then I'll go," Dionisio said.

I told him what to tell Alessandro and saw him off with a purse and a hug. Five years ago, he had seemed spineless to me, but now he had found his courage and become a man I greatly respected, a true friend. If he could reach Capodimonte, he would be safe.

AND YET IN the afternoon the thought continued to nag at me. There must be something that would help the situation! I simply couldn't see the shape of it. The shape…. Perhaps what I needed was a map. There had been one in Rodrigo's study for the captain's meeting. I looked, but after half an hour of frustration realized that the captains must have taken it away with them. Well, no doubt it was a copy. There must be one in the Vatican library.

Thus, I went downstairs and made my way through the curiously silent corridors. For the last four and a half years I had gloried in the run of the Vatican library. I do not know that it was the best in the world. Perhaps there were better in distant lands, but it was the finest library in Italy and indeed in most of Europe. Normally reserved only for priests and clerks, open only by special invitation, to use it by the Vice-Chancellor and then the Pope's express permission was not a privilege to be taken lightly. Indeed, in our early days Rodrigo had joked that I only loved him for his library! It was not true, but I remembered warmly how much he had enjoyed showing it to me and explaining where different things were under the eyes of disapproving clerks who certainly did not think a young woman should be in a library but didn't dare argue with Cardinal Borgia! They were used to me now. I had clean hands, was quiet, and did not pester the clerks or damage the books. I had become unremarkable by use.

The library, like the halls, was extremely quiet. I heard voices only from the far end, the rooms where the oldest and most valuable books were kept. Modern maps were in an entirely separate place, but curiosity led me to see what was going on.

There was Burchard, the chronicler, directing two men who were carefully packing linen-wrapped scrolls in crates full of sawdust. "What in the world?" I asked.

"Donna Giulia!" he exclaimed. "You startled me."

"I'm sorry," I said. "I came in to find a map and heard your voice. What is happening?"

"Given the delicacy of our circumstances, it seems prudent to move the oldest and most valuable books to the Castel Sant'Angelo," he said. I must have looked nonplussed, for he went on. "Libraries are very flammable, Madonna."

"Indeed," I said. I looked around at the shelves, the desks and the cubbies for scrolls. I could all too easily imagine how a fire would ravage this place. Like temples of old, it would be so easy for this all to be lost. That was how the great library of Alexandria had been destroyed. Savonarola would see many of these books on the fire with great pleasure. In Florence he was burning books and artworks in the name of God. True, della Rovere would do no such thing, but if a city is sacked many things happen which are not in the control of a cardinal who would be pope. I shivered. Had we discovered these scrolls, preserved for centuries or brought up from the earth, only to see them destroyed? "That is very prudent."

"His Holiness thought so," Burchard said. The corner of his mouth twitched. "I am always prudent."

"Indeed," I said. "Then I will leave you to your work. I came in to find a map of the city."

"If there are any remaining, they are in the map room," Burchard said. "But I believe that they were wanted for the captains."

I sighed. "Of course." And truly, I did not need a map so much. I knew the shape of the city.

"There is an old one in a frame on the wall," Burchard said. "But it's a hundred years old and of little utility."

"Thank you," I said, and went to look for it. It would have the walls and gates, which was what interested me. Those were ancient. It was where Burchard said, and I stared at it, somewhat confused at first for it had south at the top of the page and north at the bottom, thus making the entire city look unfamiliar until I recognized the drawings of various places and the entire picture snapped into place. Well, it did not matter whether a circle began at the north or south; it was a circle all the same. If the circle of the walls were a working circle…. If the ancient walls could be used….

I didn't have it. There were gaps in the walls, modern repairs, places where the old patterns were broken. And in any event, I had no idea how to transform a ward into a barrier, if such could even be done. The concept was there, tantalizingly out of reach. Something I could do with the city itself, something with the circuit of the walls…. And yet nothing.

· · ·

I RETURNED to the Borgia Apartments in a serious frame of mind. Burchard was unflappable. If he felt such preparations were necessary, the situation was dire indeed. Not that I didn't know that, but that he should seriously fear for the survival of priceless manuscripts resident at the Vatican for hundreds of years made the stakes quite clear. Therefore, I made dinner delightful. I had Rodrigo to myself, a private dinner in his camera beneath the half-finished wall paintings, and was as cheerful and witty as possible. I did not know how many times I would have the opportunity. There was that prickle at my back.

He was also expansive and generous, telling amusing anecdotes and laughing at my jokes. We retired immediately, propping up on a pile of pillows, the fire warm, shadows dancing on the red velvet bed curtains. I came to his side, resting on his left shoulder with his arm around me. The walls on either side of the fireplace were bare, only the sketches of figures on smooth plaster. Pinturicchio had just begun this room. I could not quite tell what the pictures were supposed to be, and I asked Rodrigo.

"The Apostles," he said, "Each holding a scroll that narrates a verse of the Apostles Creed."

"That's very conventional," I said.

"It can't all be controversial," he said. "Maybe I should have you and Laura over the door just there. Another Madonna and Child."

"When Pinturicchio is back and Laura is home," I said, and my voice did not shake at all.

"Yes, duckling," he said.

I laughed. "Duckling?" Rodrigo shrugged with a sideways smile. "I have gone from angel to duckling?"

"An angelic duckling. An angel with duck's wings."

"You could have Pinturicchio paint me as an angel with duck wings," I said. "It would be pretty."

"I think swan's wings are traditional."

"But why?" I asked, snuggling against his side. "Why not duck wings?"

Rodrigo was smiling, as I meant him to. "I suppose when people ask, I could say wisely, 'of course the theological reference is obvious.'"

"He sees when a duck falls?" I misquoted.

"Consider the ducks of the field, they do not toil or spin."

"How would a duck spin?" I said, and we both laughed.

"I suppose I could open a window of the Castel Sant'Angelo and throw out a duck to return with an olive branch when the French are gone."

"And a duck went sailing down to land neatly on the river," I said, "and was last seen paddling contemplatively downstream."

"Like a duck to water." We both fell apart again, laughing, and I kissed his nose. "While shepherds watched their ducks by night," Rodrigo began again.

"Inappropriate ducks in scripture," I said. "Just add a duck. You could release a duck instead of a dove in the Pentecost Mass."

"My darling, ducks don't soar upward in beautiful spirals," he said, demonstrating with his right hand the path of an ideal duck.

"Instead, they flutter squawking into the parishioners and then waddle about admonishing them." We clung to each other in helpless laughter, imagining the very noble and beautiful service with the addition of a fat barnyard duck. I laughed until my sides hurt. And then I caught him looking at me, and I knew that expression. I knew what he was thinking. He was wondering if this was the last time we would laugh together. "Are you scared?"

"How can I possibly answer that?" he said.

"Truthfully."

"Yes."

I laid my head on his shoulder. Once, I had thought him infallible. Once, I had believed him the master of his world. He was my protector, my sanctuary, all-powerful and perfect. Now he was just Rodrigo. And Christ's Earthly Habitation. He needed me. He needed me to believe in him. "You will find a way," I said. "You always do."

"Ah my Giulia. You steady me," he said.

CHAPTER 16

*I*n the morning Rodrigo was to visit the defenders on the wall to give them his blessing and put heart into them. He intended to begin at Porta Flaminia, where the road ran north past Vasanello, and then proceed clockwise around to the southeast, to Porta San Sebastiano where the old Via Appia left the city walls on the first leg of the journey to Naples. Half a circle...

It was cold. I wore dark blue velvet and a black cloak that came down to my boot tops. Lilas' breath came in great clouds in the air. Rodrigo wore white brocade, though a short version that came just below the knee with boots beneath rather than slippers for riding in the cold. It was a hybrid sort of outfit, but it was unmistakably papal. His black horse and my light gray horse made us look as though we'd mixed and matched a set.

He began the inspection of the defenders early, at the Church of Santa Maria del Populo, just inside the gates, and I joined him for the first morning Mass. It was a favorite church of Rodrigo's. Indeed, he had commissioned the new high altar and the icon of the Madonna twenty years ago. He heard Mass in the church, and then we went out to the gates. It was quite cold, but there was a gratifying cheer as His Holiness arrived. He chatted with the captain and then went up on the wall to have things pointed out. I stayed with the horses and the grooms, Rizzoli having gone with him to the wall. I felt a frisson and looked up. He was indeed blessing the gate, making the sign of the cross over the arch.

One begins a square at the northernmost point. Did he do it by accident or purpose? No, knowing Rodrigo, it simply felt right so he did it. He always followed the compass of his heart. And what harm indeed in blessing the gate and its defenders?

In that moment, I knew how to do it. The circle of the city walls, Rodrigo's authority and power…. It was like warding the house two years ago during the election when I'd asked Alessandro to walk the circuit of the walls blessing them with holy water, only a thousand times more potent. The Pope's blessing, the ancient stones of Rome…. It all came together in a flash. Dionisio had made it clear that a ward wouldn't keep out physical people, but what we'd done with the house was aversion. We made it uncomfortable. We made it seem difficult and unpleasant to cross the line. Aversion was what we needed now. Not to prevent the French from entering Rome – that was impossible – but to make them reluctant. To make men like Captain d'Allegre feel the wrongness of entering the Holy City under arms. To make Charles hesitate at the brink.

In a few minutes Rodrigo came down chafing his hands together. I could feel the stones still echoing from his touch. A page was bringing Memnon up for him to mount.

"Rodrigo," I said, "Don't you think it would be nice to come around and inspect the western gates too?"

"I've been to the western gates near the Vatican lately," he said. "And Prince Ferrandino is at Porta San Sebastiano."

"Yes, but I'm sure it would be appreciated." It would take hours more, rather than simply cutting through the city home. "I would love to ride with you."

His eyebrows rose. It was unusual for me to request to participate in something official when he didn't invite me. For a moment he hesitated on the edge of asking me why, but I saw him decide he didn't really want to know. Or perhaps he did know, but if it was some heretical reason, best not to. "If you like, my dear," he said mildly.

The sun was watery behind thin clouds as we rode on. We stopped at the Porta Collina, where once again Rodrigo blessed everyone and everything, then on to Porta Salaria, Porta Sant'Agnese, and Porta San Lorenzo. I could feel it like the faint thrum of rising music, the hum of viols beginning softly. I put my hand on the stones while he blessed them, like touching trees with deep roots, sap stirring far underground, rising at his touch.

It was nearly noon when we came to Porta San Sebastiano. Prince Ferrandino's men made a fine show, the Neapolitan army in red and white striped hose and red caps with white plumes. Prince Ferrandino himself welcomed His Holiness to their garrison, wearing full shining plate mail with horse trappings in yellow and scarlet, his lance painted in spirals of red and white and blue. He dismounted while a beautifully dressed squire held his rein, then went to one knee at Rodrigo's side. His men cheered.

Rodrigo dismounted, laying his hand on Ferrandino's head in blessing, then making the wide sign of the cross over him. There was another cheer. I followed as the whole party went into the garrison, Ferrandino presenting various officers to His Holiness. There was a light meal laid out, and Ferrandino was divested of plate mail to sit with the Pope on camp stools in a very theatrical fashion. They dined on plain soup and bread as though it were Lent. Captain Rizzoli had wine and bread and cheese and dried figs, and I ate with him outside, as my presence was superfluous to this drama being staged.

"Are you well, Madonna Giulia?" Rizzoli asked.

"Yes," I said. "And very glad to be home."

"You might have been safer in Capodimonte," he said.

"I expect so," I said. "But my duty is here."

He paused for a moment, then nodded. "He needs you," Rizzoli said.

"I know." We ate in companionable silence.

I could tell the moment Rodrigo blessed the gate. I could feel it like a tremor beneath the earth. We were halfway around the circuit, a circle that could not keep the French out. And yet. The stones of Rome itself answered to his hand, to his words, to the blessing laid upon them. I looked up. The banner that flew over our little party was the Keys of St. Peter.

His voice came clear to us in the frosty air. "…in the name of St. Peter, the first Steward of Christ, I bless this gate and those who defend it." I thought that he glanced at me, feeling my hand upon the wall as well, as though we both touched the same restive horse between us. "As the Steward defends his master's house against brigands and looters, so we defend our Master's house, this Holy City of Rome, against those who would do her harm. This is Christ's sacred charge, laid upon His Steward and all who defend her. As the guardsmen of a great house answer the call to push back brigands from the gate, so you do the same. In the name of the Father, Son and Holy Spirit." He made wide the sign of the cross over the gate and over the soldiers.

Rising like a flood, this unstoppable power…. Rome itself, immeasurably old and slow and strong, awakening to his touch. *There*, I whispered to it. *You hear the Steward's voice, Christ's Earthly Representative. Waken. Do not let them in. Send them from this place. Hold strong. Hold firm.* The physical walls of Rome might be crumbling in places, but I could see them as they had been built, the Aurelian Walls of which Porta San Sebastiano was part, strong and ruddy. The towers still rose, five stories in height, crenelations and flanking walkways for archers. A thousand years old, unyielding and purposeful. They had been built to resist barbarians from the north. They knew their purpose. *The Gauls come*, I whispered to it, *stand as you were meant to.*

The Prince's men looked cheerful despite the cold as they escorted the Holy Father to his horse and gave a cheer as we went on.

Porta Latina, Porta Trigeminia that led to Ostia, and then Porta San Pancrazio. The sun declined, and with each stop the power grew until I wondered that no one could hear it, music rising each time Rodrigo brought another instrument into harmony, another gate, another section of wall.

Dusk was falling. The bells of St. Peter's were ringing Vespers.

Porta Fabrica was almost in the shadow of the Vatican, torches streaming as Rodrigo blessed the guards and the gate itself. Though he had been doing this since early morning, he didn't look tired. He looked as though he gained strength at each station, a pilgrimage designed for him. And perhaps that was what it was, I thought. Perhaps he gained strength from the city as she gained strength and purpose from him.

The last gate was Porta Sant'Angelo. I brought Lilas up beside Rodrigo as he mounted up after he had blessed it. It was full dark, midwinter's night. "Can we go on to Porta Flaminia?" He looked at me sharply. We were no more than ten minutes from the Vatican and I suggested we go back to where we had started, completing the circle. "Would it not be appropriate to end the day with Compline at Santa Maria del Populo?"

The corner of his mouth twitched. Whatever he might say would not be said before the escort. "It would indeed," Rodrigo said.

We went to the gate before the church. Rodrigo dismounted beneath it, the captain on duty hurrying out to greet him. He was smiling as he stepped up to it, and as he touched it the rising notes ceased. All was still. The circuit was complete. The power rested easily, contained and stable, ready if it was needed, but for the moment placid, like a vast reservoir that waits for someone to open a floodgate.

"In the name of the Father, Son, and Holy Spirit," he said, and then turned. "We will hear Mass at Santa Maria del Populo."

They were surprised to see us, and the church was quite crowded, but obviously no one was going to tell the Pope he wasn't welcome for the evening service! To my surprise, Rodrigo took the heart of the Mass himself. Kneeling, my head bent over my hands, his voice rolling over me, I felt a bone-deep peace. Outside the storm might rage, but we were in God's hands. I had no words, but I did not need any. I simply closed my eyes and let the words of the Mass carry me.

"An entirely perfect day," Rodrigo said as we went out into the cold street, torchlight glittering off the gold on his robes.

"Without a doubt," I said.

. . .

THE NEXT DAY at mid-morning I was reading in the camera while Rodrigo worked in the informal sala when a footman apologetically knocked on the door from the bathing room and servants' stair. "Your pardon, Madonna, but we're here to disassemble and move His Holiness' bed."

"Ah!" I got up from my chair, putting the book on the little table. "The bed."

Two other footmen followed the first in. "To move it to the Castel Sant'Angelo, Madonna."

"Of course," I said. So that's where we were. If we were taking refuge in the Castel Sant'Angelo, Rodrigo was bringing his comfortable bed! "I will get out of your way, then." I went into the study and looked around, from the fireplace on one end to the window on the other. It was very full. I'd better pack the books.

I went back in and asked the footmen to bring me some crates, then came back. I felt a pang for my own books, but mine were in Palazzo Santa Maria in Portico which would not be a target for looters as the Vatican would be. Also my books were not hand copied or old except for the partial manuscript of the *Moralia*, but were modern printed copies – expensive and precious to me, but not irreplaceable. Rodrigo had many books that were old and valuable and some he had copied out himself as a boy. I would pack those first.

I was carefully putting them in crates with wood shavings to cushion them when I heard a familiar voice through the door from the informal sala next door. "What a surprise, Your Holiness." It was Ascanio Sforza. I got to my feet and went to the door, cracking it enough to peek through. Ascanio stood between two guards in his gorgeous scarlet robes, his hat slightly askew as was his smile. "Imagine meeting you here."

Rodrigo got up from his carved chair. "You may leave us," he said to the guards. They turned neatly and did so, closing the opposite door behind them. "Wine?"

"Yes. To what do I owe such congeniality?" Ascanio asked. He came around the couch as Rodrigo poured from a carafe into two Venetian glass goblets. "Prisoner, guest, how fortune's wheel turns!"

"You can say that again," Rodrigo said, handing him one of the glasses.

"You first," Ascanio said. "Or should I insist we trade glasses?"

"If you'd like." Rodrigo was smiling. "Surely you're not buying all that Borgia poisoner business?"

"Ah, but you're nefarious." Ascanio raised his glass and looked at the wine.

"Then surely I would guess that a canny Sforza would suspect that I had poisoned his glass and insist on trading, so therefore I would poison my own glass instead and then give it to him," Rodrigo said.

"But a canny Sforza would know that you would think that," Ascanio said. "And therefore would know that the only glass safe to drink from would be the one he'd been given."

"And I would know that you would know that, so perhaps I'd poison them both and let you drink first."

Ascanio chuckled. "So neither of us can drink, rendering the entire exercise pointless."

"Except of course if I wanted to poison you, I could have had you poisoned anytime in the last week since I control all food and drink in your chamber," Rodrigo said. "So why would I wait until you were here?"

"Because your Borgia cruelty requires that I die before you?" Ascanio asked.

"And yet your Sforza cleverness thwarts me?" Rodrigo replied.

"Touché," Ascanio said. "To your very good health." They touched glasses and both drank at once.

Behind the door I rolled my eyes. Rodrigo just could not resist playing scenes!

"You're probably wondering why I've sent for you," Rodrigo said.

"The thought did cross my mind." Ascanio sat down in one of the chairs. "I presume you're in a lot of trouble. Unsurprising, since I can hear the wolves howling from my room."

"I thought that was your nephew weeping," Rodrigo said, sitting down in his own chair.

Ascanio shrugged. "He's actually doing quite well. Sanseverino's a good boy. We bear up patiently."

Rodrigo took another sip of his wine. "He won't have to bear up much longer. I'm releasing both of you."

His brows rose. "And to what do we owe this reprieve? My brother Ludovico on your doorstep with an army?"

"Not yet," Rodrigo said. "As far as I know, Ludovico is in Milan filled with remorse for having let the French in. Unsurprisingly, it turns out that Charles of France has his own best interests at heart, not Milan's."

Ascanio shrugged to concede the point. "Unsurprisingly, as you say."

"But I do have Charles of France on my doorstep preparing to sack the city. Therefore, I have no further use for you or your nephew and you may go free."

"Just like that?" Ascanio was facing me. Rodrigo had his back to me and I could not see his expressions.

"I presume you'll take yourselves off to French lines at the first opportunity, thus being a thorn in Charles' side." Rodrigo sounded amused. "And Cardinal della Rovere will greet you with great enthusiasm. He needs your two votes to depose me."

Ascanio looked at his jeweled hands. "Unless I have greatly miscounted, there's nothing like a quorum for a vote."

"Does that matter?" Rodrigo raised his goblet. "I understand that the articles have already been drawn up. They'll be voted pro forma and if there are later objections that the vote was improper, it will be too late."

"In order for that to work, you'd need to be in Naples. Or Spain." Ascanio's gaze was keen. "The Spanish Crown would back you and call the vote into question. Two popes, you and della Rovere, with the College divided."

There was no amusement in Rodrigo's voice now. "There will be one pope. The question is who it will be – della Rovere or you."

Ascanio leaned forward. "What are you doing?"

"I will not break our Mother Church. I will not surrender Rome. The French will attack and I will be killed." His voice was perfectly even. "Let us see if French guns will open up on the Pope and the Host. If they do…" He spread his hands.

"It would be an outrage that would echo throughout Christendom. Every land would rise against them." Ascanio took a deep breath.

"And who could more loudly decry such an atrocity than Cardinal Sforza, the Vice-Chancellor?" Rodrigo asked mildly.

"You are talking about being shredded by shot."

"Yes," Rodrigo said. I closed my eyes for a moment.

"Della Rovere would be a French tool, a heretic who raised his hand to God's anointed," Ascanio said. "I would rightly oppose him and his works. How could I not?"

"You would be pope," Rodrigo said.

"And you'd be dead."

I opened my eyes. "Unfortunately." Rodrigo's tone was regretful. "But the Church would survive. We would not go back to the days of the Avignon Captivity or worse yet, face another Great Schism. You'd be an able pope." He shifted in his chair, and I could see his profile. "But for that, you need to be with the French army when it happens. Hence my generous release."

"Unless, and forgive me if I sound opportunistic about your demise," Ascanio began.

"Of course," Rodrigo said.

"…the French do not in fact kill you? What if King Charles has enough sense not to fire on the Pope and the Host? What if he negotiates?"

"He's not likely to do that with Cardinal della Rovere giving him counsel, is he?" Rodrigo said.

Ascanio leaned back in his chair, lifting his glass. "But he might if Cardinal Sforza gave him counsel, mightn't he?"

"It's possible," Rodrigo said. "Unlikely but possible. Della Rovere has wormed his way deep in the king's confidence and has embraced Savonarola's idea that Charles is the savior of Italy. He's dear to the king, or so I hear, whereas Charles has never even met you. Even such a distinguished Borgia prisoner as you will have little influence."

"I win either way," Ascanio said. "You're dead, I'm Pope. You're alive, I'm Vice-Chancellor and trusted by everyone."

"Aren't you a clever man," Rodrigo murmured, taking a sip of his wine. "Almost as though you set it up that way when you didn't flee Rome and were instead taken prisoner."

"Almost as though," Ascanio said. He leaned forward, raising his goblet. "To better days, my friend."

"To better days," Rodrigo said, and touched his glass to Ascanio's.

I had to back up from the door lest I make a sound. I went over to the fire and sat on the hearth, staring into the flames, trying to take the picture from my mind of Rodrigo blown to pieces by French guns. There must be something I could do. I had no idea what.

THE PAGES BROUGHT in First Meal a little later, the taster trailing along and sampling before Rodrigo came in from the sala. By then I had composed myself. "Shall we have a pleasant luncheon, Rodrigo? I've been packing your books."

"Thank you, my dear." He sat down opposite, the little page Michele lifting the covers on the dishes. Michele seemed to have gotten used to me remarkably quickly. He glanced at the spinach and onion timbale. "Delicious."

"It does look beautiful," I said.

There was a stir in the sala, and one of the guards came to the door. "Your Holiness, Prince Ferrandino insists on speaking with you immediately."

Rodrigo didn't even have time to answer before Ferrandino pushed the door open and strode in. "Holy Father, what is the meaning of this?" He waved a sheet of paper.

"The meaning of what, Ferrandino? Would you care to join us for First Meal?" Rodrigo asked mildly. "Donna Giulia would be happy if you would join us."

"Thank you, Donna Giulia, not just now," he said quickly. He had not forgotten his manners. "Your Holiness, my father understood that you were firm in your opposition to the French and that by no account would you recognize their claim to Naples! Now you release Cardinal Sforza and you send me this letter saying to retreat! What am I to think other than you have made terms or seek to do so?"

"Ferrandino." Rodrigo stood up, putting his hand on the prince's shoulder. "Calmly, my son. I have no intention of surrendering to the French, nor of betraying your father's trust."

"You would not trade the sovereignty of Naples for French agreement not to sack Rome?" Ferrandino demanded. "I find that hard to believe. You would not trade the safety of our realm for the safety of yours?"

"Our realm is not of this earth," Rodrigo said, and there was that timbre in his voice. "We are the Pope. But if you are asking if we would trade the safety of the Holy City of Rome for recognition of Charles as ruler of Naples, if we were going to do that, would not we have done it months ago?"

"Months ago there was not an overwhelming French army on your doorstep," Ferrandino said.

"And now there is," Rodrigo said. His hand shook when he reached for Ferrandino's arm. "My dear son, do you think I do not know how fortunate I am to have your friendship and your father's? Do you think that I would repay your father's trust by causing the death of his only son and heir? Ferrandino, I know you are bold – too bold – and that you and my son Cesare would take on the French army together with courage. However, the fact remains that we have, with your generous aid, 2,000 men against their 22,000. We will not prevail by force of arms. Should we try, we will sacrifice the flower of manhood to no avail." He leaned on Ferrandino's arm. "You will die. Cesare will die. And you will not win."

I sat frozen in my chair. Rodrigo looked so old, so broken. He had not seemed so with Ascanio.

Ferrandino's voice was gentle. "Holy Father, I do not fear death beside you. Will you not say as Christ said, 'Today you will be with me in paradise?'"

"Our Lord said that to a thief," Rodrigo said. "Not to a prince who has his realm and his people to think of. I will not rob your father of his son or your people of their young lord in a doomed last stand. You must live. You must fight another day. When I am gone, nothing will stand against Charles of France except you."

"And Spain," Ferrandino said. "My father writes that King Ferdinand is sending troops to Sicily to aid us, and he has sent a fast ship to Naples for you. You have but to say the word and it is at your disposal to sail to Sicily or Spain as you prefer."

I took a shuddering breath. I could not help it.

"Then I must delay Charles of France until Spanish help can arrive," Rodrigo said. "My son, I know Ferdinand. I was Papal Legate to Spain for decades. He will help, but he will take his time. It will be spring before any notable force comes, and you and your father cannot hold Charles off for three or four months. If I can buy a month or perhaps two, Naples may yet stand. If I can stall and talk and negotiate, you have time for reinforcements to arrive."

"That is true," Ferrandino said. He looked worried. "Your Holiness, it is you I fear for."

"I do not fear," Rodrigo said. "What happens is God's will." There were tears in his eyes. "Moses sacrificed a bull to atone for the sins of the people of Israel. Sometimes the bull must be sacrificed."

Ferrandino clasped him in his arms. "Holy Father, I do not know what to say."

Rodrigo was weeping openly now. "Say that you will go. Take your men and retreat south to Naples to guard your kingdom. If you stay, you will only throw away their lives in a hopeless battle. Tell your father that I send my thanks and my blessing."

"Your Holiness," Ferrandino said, and he wept as well. "I will go if you wish. I will never forget your words or your nobility of spirit." In the end he agreed to retreat. His troops would begin their march down the Via Appia in the next few days. When they went, we would essentially be defenseless.

Cesare came in as Ferrandino left, clasping hands like brothers who never expected to see one another again. When the door closed, Cesare came around the table. "Papa, we need those men."

Rodrigo paced over to the fireplace, kicking his skirts out of the way. "We won't win by force of arms, Cesare."

"Then how?" Cesare looked at me. "Giulia, tell him what danger he's in!"

"He knows," I said. "But sometimes the only way to win is to lose."

"That's ridiculous."

"Cesare, if you saw your enemy kneeling in the dust before you, would you behead him?" Rodrigo asked.

"Of course."

Rodrigo threw up his hands. "You would. But that's you."

"Anyone with any sense would," Cesare said. "Papa, this is not *Amadis de Gaula*! In real life people don't grant their enemies quarter or raise them up and restore them to their throne."

"Alexander the Great did with King Poros," I pointed out. "It's in Diodorus."

Cesare shot me a look. "You're not helping."

Rodrigo put his hand on Cesare's shoulder. "We can't win by fighting. Count the troops, Cesare! If we fight this battle now, on King Charles' terms, we will lose. You and I will both be dead. There are no more moves after that. We will be dead and the fortunes of our family extinguished. In order to win, we have to live. Understand?"

"Yes, Papa."

"Then grant that I know what I'm doing. We negotiate. We play nicely. We promise and swear and pull the fangs of the Sforza snake." He steered Cesare over to the fire. "I've got Ascanio where I want him. I don't have Ludovico yet. I need time, Cesare."

"What about Naples?" he demanded.

"Charles may take Naples but he can't hold it," Rodrigo said.

"So we smile and take it like a whore?" Cesare said.

"We let Charles have us fore and aft," Rodrigo said. "And then we stab him."

Cesare started laughing. "All right, Papa. What do you need me to do?"

Rodrigo clapped him on the shoulder. "I need you to be Cardinal Borgia – cardinal, not *condottiero*. I need you to smile."

"And murder while I smile?"

"Hold off on the murder until I tell you to," Rodrigo said. "First we negotiate. Now get out there and see Prince Ferrandino off on the road south."

"It's a pity there's no way to withdraw to Spain," Cesare said. "We could regroup and return with Spanish troops."

"Too late for that," Rodrigo said. "Now get going. Once Ferrandino leaves, we're stretched thin. Make it look good. We need to appear ready to defend ourselves."

"Yes, Papa." Cesare embraced him. "You can rely on me."

"I know it," Rodrigo said and kissed him.

Once the door had closed, I lifted my glass and took a sip of my wine. Rodrigo sat back down at the table. "You know, at this point I have no idea what you're doing," I said.

He gave me a sideways smile. "Don't you?"

"Every time I think I do, you twist around again. I have no idea what is real."

"This lovely timbale," he said. "Which has gotten cold. No matter. It will still be tasty." He picked up his fork.

I shook my head. "Rodrigo."

He met my eyes over the timbale. "Trust me."

"I do," I said.

He sighed. "You always want to see behind the curtain. Very well. The King of France has gotten himself into a terrible situation and I intend to help him out of it."

"He's in a terrible situation?" I said incredulously. "He's besieging you! He outnumbers you ten to one and most of your troops are going to defect to him."

"A stroke of fortune for me," Rodrigo said. "If I had the troops to put up a pitched battle…. But no. And that's why it's best for Ferrandino to leave. We are essentially defenseless."

My voice may have been a little clipped. "And why is this good?"

"Because, sweet, it is not at all what he expected. Charles of France can simply roll over us if he wishes. But I am still here." He paused, a little smile playing around his mouth. "Cardinal della Rovere promised him that if he approached Rome with an army I would flee to Spain. Charles would march into abandoned Rome and restore order while the College elected a new pope."

"Della Rovere," I said. "But surely he knows you might not leave."

"I don't think that crossed his mind." Rodrigo took a bite of the timbale. "Men who are for sale believe everyone is for sale."

"Aren't you for sale?" I asked. Rodrigo had never balked at bribery.

"Darling, I'm a buyer, not a seller." He reached for the wine glass. "You've seen me offer many a bribe, but have you ever seen me take one?"

"Point," I said.

"Charles paid 200,000 ducats for della Rovere's allegiance. The traditionalists in the College have always been suspicious of him because he seemed insufficiently sincere. They believe, truly and immutably, that the world can be returned to the way it was a hundred years ago. Impossible, but their belief is sincere. They know della Rovere is using them. They're not stupid men. They know he's for sale and that he will espouse their theological positions if it will bring him power. But now he's promised Charles something he can't deliver – a bloodless victory. He promised Charles he would be a hero, not the author of a massacre that will resound throughout the world."

"And now, instead of fleeing for Spain and leaving the field clear, you're still here," I said.

"It's unfathomable to della Rovere. Of course I would leave and save my fortune and my life. He's never understood actions based on genuine belief, not self-interest. Why would I be willing to die for this?" He gestured around the walls of the Vatican.

I felt a prickle behind my eyes. "Because this is our Holy Mother Church."

Rodrigo smiled ruefully. "Something you have always understood, Giulia."

"Yes," I said, and there was no waiver in my voice. "I have always known that you were God's man." As though God were his liege lord.

"I will not break the Church," he said quietly. "And so the King of France has a dilemma. He can sack Rome and kill the pope or slink away defeated by nothing. The latter is impossible for a warrior king. The former will set every nation in Christendom against him. And della Rovere is realizing that even if Charles kills me, he won't be pope." Rodrigo took another sip. "If he calls for a vote to depose me, he doesn't have the votes to be elected in my stead. He would still have to win a 2/3 majority of those present. Given most of the College has scattered to the four winds, most of those he could buy aren't here. But who is here are...."

"...Carafa, Riario and Cybo," I said. "The staunch humanists who will never vote for della Rovere. Even with Orsini and those cardinals who are with the King of France...."

"And Cesare is here. So four solid votes against. Della Rovere would need eight votes to win," Rodrigo said. "Even if he pays Ascanio and Sanseverino he could not get to more than six given who's actually present."

"There would have to be a compromise candidate," I said. "Someone Carafa, Riario and Cybo would vote for. Ascanio Sforza."

Rodrigo spread his hands. "Ascanio Sforza indeed. And Ascanio is not about to sell his vote to della Rovere when he could actually win. So unless della Rovere would like to make Ascanio pope, he can't call a conclave to depose me."

"And if Charles kills you, every hand is raised against him." I said it dispassionately.

"I would rather not die, sweet. But if I must."

"If you must." I understood.

"So I will try to give Charles a way out of his bind, if he has the wit to take it," Rodrigo said.

CHAPTER 17

That night we moved to the Castel Sant'Angelo. Word came that there had been French troops seen in the edges of the city near Monte Mario, and that their scouts had come as far as the church of San Lazzaro. This was the other side of the city from Prince Ferrandino's forces. It was true he could not possibly defend more than one gate, and we certainly could not. A letter was sent to Bracciano ordering the Gonfaloniere to fall back to defend Rome.

"Not that he will," Rodrigo said. "But he has the orders. Now he will have to directly disobey them and break his sworn oaths." He shrugged, looking around the half-packed study. "Such a lovely room. It's a pity the paintings aren't finished."

He sounded as though he were saying goodbye, and it sent a chill up my spine. "Pinturicchio will finish them when he gets back," I said.

"Of course, my sweet." He paced around, admiring Geometry measuring the world. "It's to be the Sibyls in the next room. Each paired with a Biblical prophet, woman and man, pagan and Jew, all speaking truth. I hope Pinturicchio will have a chance to finish."

"Come on, darling," I said. "It's just for a little while." I linked my arm with his. "What else are secret passages for?"

The passeto to the Castel Sant'Angelo wasn't actually secret because dozens of people knew about it. It was private. The entire household went through, including footmen with some of Rodrigo's clothes. We went in the middle accompanied by the two little pages who were left.

Though it was an ancient building, originally the tomb of the Roman Emperor Hadrian, the Castel Sant'Angelo had been modernized in the last century. There were windows that looked in every direction; small and barred but nevertheless providing an amazing view of the city. The Roman stonework of the battlements was not in good condition, but the walls were sound. Above, the roof had four gun emplacements around the perimeter which Pope Innocent had installed fifteen years ago. Below, there were layers of guest chambers, the rooms for the garrison and the kitchen, and below that storerooms and dungeon. It was a very complete fortress, and its position on the river meant that at least on one side there could be no sappers. In short, it was as safe as one could be without abandoning Rome.

Needless to say, on December 15 Bracciano disobeyed his orders. The next evening, we had word that he had turned over the fortress of Bracciano itself to the French and now rode at King Charles' side. Some eighty men of the Papal Army returned to Rome, having refused to take part. The rest of our forces were with their general.

"Mercenaries," Rodrigo said, shaking his head.

"Orsini," I said. It was in my opinion less about money than the traditional power of the great families. Bracciano had stuffed the ranks with adherents of his own house.

"They'll pay for this," Cesare said, though his threat was empty. Our reach extended no further than the blocks around the Castel Sant'Angelo and the Vatican, plus some of the nearer neighborhoods directly across the river.

"Patience, my son," Rodrigo said ponderously.

Cesare looked at me as if to say, *can you get him out of this mood and into another role?*

I shrugged. I would try.

Cesare went out to inspect the defenders and attempt to rally their spirits. Rodrigo had said he was to be cardinal rather than *condottiere,* but you wouldn't have guessed it from his leather and steel. Cesare certainly intended to put up a fight.

Rodrigo watched him go and I knew what he was thinking: his eldest son was a fine warrior, but even the best may be overwhelmed by sheer numbers. He had not been dissembling when he told Ferrandino that he and Cesare would fall together if they attempted to fight. Now Ferrandino was withdrawing. Would anything save Cesare?

He returned two hours later with a printed sheet which he brandished at his father. "I got this from our men on the wall. It's from Cardinal Peraudi who is with della Rovere and Charles of France. Look at this drivel! He's swearing that the French won't loot and burn and that they only come to right undefined sins."

Rodrigo took the paper from him. "God has turned His face from us because He is deeply offended by our sins and wickedness, and unless He is placated by the prayers of devout persons, peace between the Princes of Christendom cannot be achieved." His voice was dry. "Clear enough. No peace unless devout persons placate God by deposing the Borgia pope. And Good King Charles is here to cleanse the land with fire and sword. I fear Cardinal Peraudi has been listening to Friar Savonarola."

"What are we going to do?" Cesare demanded, pacing around the neat little sala. "Kill Peraudi?"

Rodrigo looked theatrically heavenward. "We are going to talk. Do you understand that our effective force is now only 500 men?"

"Yes, I know, Papa! I told you that!" Cesare paced back again.

Rodrigo caught him by the shoulders. "Then stop. We will not win this with arms. Put on your robes and act like a cardinal! Cesare, you must learn wile. What we are going to do is celebrate Mass. In the Sistine Chapel. On Christmas Day, which is tomorrow in case you've forgotten. We are inviting the French to send envoys. Let us show them a different story."

"The full beauty and power," I said. "Not darkness, but light. You fight story with story." I understood. It just might work.

Rodrigo smiled. "Exactly. We are very beautiful. There are no shadows without a prodigious light to cast them."

"What is God's grace for if not to protect His flock?" I said. "The people of Rome. And all those who have everything to lose. The scholars, the poor, the sodomites, the Jews...."

Cesare looked worried. "I don't understand, Papa."

"You don't have to," Rodrigo said. "I need you to go to put on your red robes and take a message to the King of France inviting envoys to join us for Christmas Mass. I am certain that Cardinal Sforza will receive your embassy gently and publicly."

Cesare snorted. "So that seizing an ambassador, one churchman visiting another under a flag of truce, is impossible."

"You take a very nice letter. Ascanio receives it and relays its invitation to the worthies of the French court." He clapped Cesare on the arm. "Go dress. I'll draw up the letter." He watched his son leave, then sat down at his desk, the two-sided one that had been moved from the apartments at the Vatican.

I came behind him, my hand on his shoulder. "Do you think it will work?"

Rodrigo looked up at me. "Will they come? Oh yes. Will that be enough? Probably not, but it's a beginning."

For now that was what we had.

EVEN THE KING of France could see that it would look bad to sack the Vatican on Christmas Day. He sent envoys. One was the Lord Marshal of France, while the other two were worthy gentlemen, one the President of the Paris Parlement and the other the Seigneur de Rohan. In short, he did not stint on their importance, nor their entourage.

We went over via the pasetto, and I slipped in the back of the Sistine Chapel with some of the staff while Cardinal Cybo and Cardinal Carafa prepared for the Mass. Noted humanists, they had not fled to della Rovere and would not. There were some who stood with Rodrigo out of principle rather than self-interest. Their courage was worth noting.

Beneath the star-studded ceiling the chapel was filled with light. Every candlestand was aglow, additional candles placed behind and around the altar. There was greenery. There were baskets of fruits on the steps, great mounds of oranges and lemons and pomegranates, some of the oranges pierced with cloves so that a sweet fragrance rose. It mingled with the clouds of incense, costly frankincense and myrrh like the Magi had brought to the Christ Child.

The Christmas Mass is a beautiful thing, a celebration, a victory, and every bit of light and glory is present. A Son is born to us all, and we rejoice. Though the choir was somewhat short, their voices soared.

Rodrigo sat in his chair to the side beneath the canopy with its bullion fringe, his white robes spotless, his face grave and kind, baskets of fruit and greenery at his feet. I saw the envoys in the front row watching him, but of course he gave no sign. Did they wonder if he was the Great Beast and waited for him to do something dreadful? If so, they were disappointed.

Burchard was buzzing around seating the latecomers. He had put the Lord Marshal nearest to Rodrigo with the other two envoys in the first row, but many of the entourage had sat whatever they wanted. Even as the Mass began, Burchard was trying to remove them to places he deemed more appropriate, arguing in hissed whispers in the rows. One of the gentlemen argued and Burchard remonstrated with him, making shooing motions.

Rodrigo actually got up from his throne and came over, his white gown glittering in the candlelight. "In the name of God, Burchard," he said furiously, "let the French sit wherever they want! Are you trying to destroy all my work?"

"Your Holiness," Burchard began.

"Wherever they want," Rodrigo said. "This is a papal order."

"Very well, Your Holiness," Burchard said stiffly. Rodrigo gave the Frenchmen a smile and proceeded back to his throne. I drew a breath. Burchard sat down next to me. "Sit wherever you want. As though there were no rules."

He was scared, of course, and he showed his courage through pedantry. "I am not in a correctly assigned seat either," I whispered.

"Madonna Giulia, since you are not anyone who is here, you cannot possibly be assigned a seat by precedence, so therefore you cannot possibly either be in it or not in it." He looked at me primly.

It actually took me a moment to parse that. "So I'm not here," I said.

"Certainly not." He lifted his chin.

"So I am not talking to you."

"Absolutely not." There was the ghost of a smile on Burchard's face.

"Then I shall not squeeze your hand reassuringly and tell you that His Holiness knows what he's doing," I said.

"That shall certainly not have happened," Burchard said as I did so, but his shoulders relaxed. "We may live through this yet," he said contemplatively.

Voices soared, the Mass beginning. Cardinal Cybo began in his red robes, tall and imposing and majestic. He had a very deep voice and the bearing of a leading man and looked every bit the part of a cardinal. Needless to say, every flourish was employed. The music was lovely and clouds of incense rolled across the envoys where they sat, at intimate quarters with the Pope. When Rodrigo stood to take the heart of the Mass himself he all but glowed, white against scarlet, his hands upraised in blessing, I felt the familiar frisson. He lifted his eyes, his face filled with serene peace. He was the Pope. It was that simple. Each movement was grace. Each word had weight. It was as though all Masses before were shadows of this Holy Eucharist. It was indeed the blood and body of Christ, present and real. When his eyes closed for a moment, the chalice in his hands, it was like silent thunder.

When the Lord Marshal knelt to receive communion, the cynical watchfulness that had marked his face was gone. In its place was reverence.

I bent my head over my hands. *Thank you for this*, I prayed. *Thank you for your grace upon us in this beautiful and flawed garden.*

· · ·

THAT NIGHT the stars were very bright over Rome, clear in the December sky. At the heart of the Castel Sant'Angelo was a garden, though in winter nothing was green except clipped ornamental shrubs standing like sentinels in their enormous pots. I wrapped my cloak around me more tightly. Even the light breeze off the river was cold though the battlements above sheltered the garden. Away to the north, beyond the girdle of the city walls, a hundred stars had come to earth – the campfires of the French army which now almost encircled us. Only Porta San Sebastiano on the Via Appia was still open.

Rodrigo came and stood behind me, and I leaned back against his shoulder. "You can't stay here," he said quietly.

I closed my eyes. "I know." At least there was this moment.

"You'll be a hostage against me."

"I know that, too." D'Allegre had known it and still let me go. I would not meet a man of honor more than once. Della Rovere would use me, knowing what Rodrigo might do for my safety. And Ascanio Sforza – I did not think he would ill-treat me, but he would certainly know my worth as a bargaining chip. "At least Laura is safe with Lucrezia in Pesaro."

He put his arm around my waist, my fingers lacing with his. "Yes. Lucrezia will take good care of her." He did not add, *if she is left an orphan.* I felt him take a breath. "You must leave, sweet. It's not that I don't want you here...."

"I know." My voice was completely even. "Porta San Sebastiano is still open. There is Naples." I didn't quite ask. We could go together. We could retreat with Ferrandino ahead of the French. If need be, there were Spanish ships at Naples. The sea was not closed.

"Giulia, you know I can't. But you can and you must."

I squeezed my eyes shut. I had known he would say that. His decision was made. When I looked for the junction of paths in the woods, there were only two paths now. The one that led to ruin and fire was gone, the one to schism and the destruction of everything Rodrigo had ever cared about. The ones that remained.... I could see the path under the branches so clearly, laid before his feet. "I know, my dear," I said.

"Do you?" His voice was dry. Rodrigo hesitated. "Will you see for me?" He had never asked me to see anything for him. He never asked me what I saw.

"Yes," I said. His fingers were warm in mine, his ring heavy against my hand.

He dropped his face against my hair. "What do you need to do?"

"Stop trying not to." I closed my eyes. It was easy to stop resisting it. It crowded in so close around me, like currents in the ocean while I stood waist deep in the waves. "That path is closed," I said. My voice was dreaming, inexorable. "You will not flee. You will not go to Naples and hence to Sicily where the Spanish forces wait. You will not be deposed *in absentia*, della Rovere elected by a truncated College, one pope backed by France and another by Spain. It will not break on this, all the dissatisfaction and anger overflowing into channels wrought of grievance and fire. If you are steadfast, the Church will not split today in brimstone and Messianic prophecy. Rain will quench the fires." I could see it coming down, rain on city streets, lit pyres steaming. A fire literally quenched....

His hand tightened on mine. I held tight, an anchor in a storm as the words poured out. "If they kill you in St. Peter's before witnesses, the world will rise against them. Ascanio Sforza will excommunicate the King of France and his power will be broken. Della Rovere will be scorned, expelled from the College. And you...." I could see the statue, standing where he fell on the marble floor, life size and stern, one hand raised in blessing, see it as I knelt before it, my skirts a puddle around me. "St. Alexander the Martyr. You will be canonized. All your sins will be washed out, bought by the blood of the bull. The sacrifice dies, and in him all things are reborn." I tilted my head up, tears leaking beneath my closed lashes. I looked up at the statue, cold marble face so unlike him. "I will be erased from the story. St. Alexander was a very holy man whose enemies said things to his discredit, now forgotten. Or perhaps I will be your Magdelene."

He turned round me, hand on my waist, and I opened my eyes. His were urgent. "Say you won't repent of me."

"Never," I said. "I will never repent of you. I will never be sorry." I held to his sleeve, and for a moment before the paths closed, I saw the other one. I knelt again, this time beside a little wall tomb, the little church quiet and smelling of beeswax, a modest church like so many. My hand was old and worn where it reached to touch his carved face. I would be buried beneath the floor a few feet away, unmarked and unregarded, invisible by his side....

Rodrigo caught me against him, a kiss desperate with all unsaid. "You won't regret."

"No," I said, and clung to him as though it were the last time. Flesh had words where we did not. *I need you. I love you. I will mourn you even as I live with grace and courage. I will never regret. I will never repent. I will live as we have lived, defiant in our pride and grace.*

At last we broke apart, and I rested my face against his shoulder. "I wonder what I'll be patron saint of," he said. His voice was almost normal.

"Alum miners," I said.

"What?"

"In St. Alexander's day, the Vatican opened alum mines," I said, as though I quoted from some tome centuries hence.

"I know absolutely nothing about alum mining." Rodrigo sounded bemused.

"You will after a few centuries of being called on by alum miners," I said. "Surely you'll learn the business on the job."

"What a fate," Rodrigo said. "At the beck and call of alum miners forever! Still, I suppose all the good things to be patron saint of are already taken."

"Wayward women." I smiled against him. He was irrepressible.

"I consider myself something of an expert on wayward women, and I am decidedly not an expert on alum mines." His arms were tight and warm. Of course we looked scandalous. Every guard on the battlements above could see the Pope embracing his mistress in the garden of the Castel Sant'Angelo.

"We could go inside," I said. "And you could instruct me further." I wanted him, living and real.

The other future hovered too, less likely but not closed, the path choked with bushes but still leading away through the forest. He would be hated rather than venerated, but he would live. We would soar like birds of prey over this city which stood unsacked, and in the end no one would thank him. And still that was the best path. I shook my head, trying to banish the strangeness. I did not want to see more.

His camera was warm and tight against the night, his own bed from the Vatican neatly assembled, scarlet curtains and soft linens. I bent my head and he undid my hair, scant as it was. "Shadow?" he asked.

I turned to him, hands against his shoulders. "Shadow saved me when I was ill," I said. "Or rather our game did." Rodrigo put his head to the side quizzically. "I was in some terrible dream where we were all monsters. And I was Shadow. But she's not a monster."

"Just a sweet little succubus," he said, running his hand down my back as though petting invisible wings.

"Not a monster," I said. "Just created this way. For are we all not imperfect creations and imperfect instruments?"

"An ideal theological basis for a bedroom game," Rodrigo said, bending his head to kiss my throat, which I raised to him, head back. "There is no one in the world like you." He said it fondly, and it was true.

"I am your Shadow," I said, and meant all the ways that could be taken. We lay down together to love in rooms between garden and dungeon.

In the morning of the day after Christmas, I prepared to leave the Castel Sant'Angelo. There was a *condottiero* that Cesare knew, Mariano Savelli, who had been in the pay of the Colonnas and at least could be trusted to hate the Orsini. He had been given a purse to take me to Ferrandino with a letter saying that he would be paid as much again by Ferrandino when we arrived. It seemed risky, but I could think of no better plan.

I did not cry. I was cold and composed, much as the day was, overcast but with the scent of snow. I took only a small bundle that I could carry and wore a plain gown beneath an unremarkable cloak, none of my jewels with me, not even Rodrigo's cross. I looked like a maidservant in her mistress's cast-off clothes.

It was hard to go. It was more than likely this farewell was forever. At least, I thought, kissing him goodbye in his rooms for the last time, we had this two weeks. Two weeks. That was what my return to Rome had bought me, and it was worth every moment of it.

"One more kiss," he said, "then you must go."

"I know," I said. "One, ten, a hundred would not be enough." I put my hand to the side of his face, worn and handsome and mine.

"If you are here when they take the city, you will be used against me." He folded my hand in his. "I need to know that you are away and safe." So that he could act freely. I understood that and more besides.

"You cannot be Rodrigo now," I said. "Only Alexander." He nodded, that strangeness at the back of his eyes. "You must put on the armor of light."

"That's the First Sunday of Advent," he said, "not St. Stephen's Day."

"You know what I mean," I said, and he nodded.

"Goodbye, Giulia." This time he took a step back so that we did not touch, though his eyes did not leave me.

"Goodbye, love," I said, and walked out into the hallway to where Savelli waited.

"Ready, Madonna?" Savelli asked. He was a sturdy man of some thirty years wearing plain leather, a sword at his side, with no badge or token at all.

"Yes," I said. I was proud that my voice didn't shake at all. I put on my cloak and pulled the hood up, picking up my little bundle that contained nothing but a change of clothes and a few small provisions for the road.

"Then we go now," he said. "Stealth and quiet are best. We do not want attention."

"No." I followed him downstairs and we went out like a pair of servants, a girl sent to do the shopping and a bravo to escort her. He walked at my elbow.

The bridge was deserted. There were no watchmen. There was no one at all. I felt oddly exposed as we crossed. At the far end I looked back. Perhaps there was a flash of white at one of the upper windows. I raised my arm in farewell. A duck, I thought. Throw a duck out the window of the Castel Sant'Angelo and have it return with an olive branch when the French are gone. I smiled through my tears, and then turned and followed Savelli into the streets I knew well.

They too were empty. It was a cold morning with the threat of snow, but no one was about at all. Everyone was locked in tight. Now and then, as we crossed the city, I wondered how many had fled and how many simply hid.

Porta San Sebastiano was all the way on the other side of town, at the south-eastern corner. In fact, much of the land inside the gate was for the most part deserted, ruins overgrown with grass and orchards showing where the ancient city had been much greater than the modern one. One of Rodrigo's scholarly friends had said at dinner once that in the time of Marcus Aurelius Rome might have had two million residents rather than the 60,000 or so who lived there now! I could not even imagine two million people. However, I could certainly see how many streets had fallen into ruin and how far out the walls were on this side from the places where people actually lived. Even the Lateran was bordered by fields.

It took us until late afternoon to reach the gates, stopping to rest more than once. Savelli was courteous. "I understand you were recently ill, Madonna Giulia," he said. "There is no hurry. It may be best to pass the gates after dark in any event."

In case the French were close, I thought. "Of course as you think best, Signore," I said. It would not be long until sunset. The days were short at this time of year.

The old road led toward the gates entirely devoid of any traffic, cutting straight through ruins and an olive grove to the walls. Here and there in the fields there were farmhouses, but for the most part it seemed a desolate landscape beneath the lowering winter sky. As we came closer, I slowed my steps. "Signore Savelli? Those do not look like our men."

The condottiero swore. "No, Madonna," he said grimly. The men guarding the gate were unmistakably French. Ferrandino had withdrawn. We had lost the last gate.

I stood quite still, thinking. "I cannot be captured by the French," I said. "Signore, do you know of any place we might go at some distance from the gates to consider what to do?" The last thing we should do was stand conspicuously in the open in full view of the French.

He nodded, looking about. There was a farmhouse a little distance away. "I know the people who live there. Let us go there."

We hurried across the empty field in the gathering dusk. A friendly light gleamed at a window and smoke rose from the chimney. I was chilled. "It seems as though your friends are home," I said as Savelli knocked and then opened the door, motioning for me to precede him.

"Assuredly, Madonna," he said.

I knew the man who rose from a chair by the fire and inclined his head in a courtly bow. "Giulia Farnese."

My voice was even. "My Lord Bracciano. What a surprise."

CHAPTER 18

"My Lord," Savelli said. "Here is Farnese as we discussed."

Bracciano reached for a purse on the table and threw it to Savelli, who caught it with a satisfied clink. "Close the door behind you," he said. Savelli backed out and shut the door. "Will you join me by the fire?" Bracciano asked. "You must be cold."

"Thank you," I said. There was little point in standing by the door and less in trying to bolt back out it. No doubt Savelli was standing on the other side. Assuredly there were Orsini retainers about. Bracciano had not come alone with not so much as a groom. I would have to wait for a better chance. Besides, Bracciano wore sword and dagger and he was nearly twice my weight, a big man if a little past his prime.

"I would offer you wine but ..." He spread his hands.

"I thank you for your kind offer, but I cannot accept," I said. Drugging me insensible would definitely remove my options.

"Well then."

"I presume you intend to use me to pressure His Holiness into surrender," I said.

Bracciano smiled, and I saw the teeth behind it. "No, I intend to kill you."

I froze. That was not Bracciano. Or rather, it was more than Bracciano. "Typhon." I met Bracciano's eyes. "What did you promise him, my lord?"

"He promised me nothing new," he replied. "A lifetime of service in exchange for my help."

"And you will make him great and an exalted ruler," I said. I took a deep breath. *Isis*, I thought, *he is your enemy as he is mine. Help me.*

"Why be Gonfaloniere when you can be a prince?" Bracciano shrugged. "If the pope were in his proper spiritual sphere, a temporal ruler would guide Rome. Should that not naturally be an Orsini, the oldest and noblest of the great families? The world is changing. States require princes. This is an age of kings."

"And you think della Rovere will let you decide temporal matters?" I raised an eyebrow skeptically. "He would be a warrior pope and he has no love for you or the Orsini. Of all the men unlikely to be your puppet, he is the most unlikely."

"He won't be pope, will he?" Bracciano said, pacing to the window. "Not after he's bloodied his hands with the Borgia pope. And since Cardinal Sforza will be dead, it will go to a compromise candidate. With all factions in disarray, it will be someone who offends no one and does little."

"Your cousin Cardinal Orsini," I said. I shook my head. I felt a whisper, as though there were someone standing behind me, just a kindly presence.

"Which makes you an untidy loose end. Still, there is a use for you." Bracciano turned back to the door.

I could guess. "Whatever you intend, you need blood to fuel your fires." A sacrifice was the most potent fuel imaginable, and it did not have to be willing.

"If your body is ever found, you were set upon by thieves trying to leave the city. If it is ever found." He gave me a narrow smile. "I don't imagine Borgia will ever know what happened to you. Or," he paused thoughtfully, "I suppose we could find your body and return it to him when we occupy the Vatican. It would certainly strip him of his dignity to make a ridiculous scene about it. Not a regal figure at all.

Just a foolish old man sexually obsessed with a woman young enough to be his granddaughter. Weeping and blathering, not a noble martyr at all."

A coldness descended on me. That was Typhon's plan, to be the ruin of Rodrigo's attempt to stop the schism. If Rodrigo died a martyr, he still won. If he died ridiculed and laughable, he lost. He was steeled for the blow, the bull prepared for sacrifice. What could shake him now? My death. My mutilated body brought before him, "returned" so civilly. I must deny Typhon that, by my life or the manner of my death.

"So you think," I said. "You will find that His Holiness is made of sterner stuff." But he wasn't. There was nothing cold in Rodrigo. He was not stoic. His strength was in his love.

The love of the world, someone whispered behind me. *Is not the love of the world the love of God?*

"You won't be there to find out," Bracciano said. "Savelli!"

The condottiere opened the door. "My Lord?"

"Take Donna Giulia to the storage room. I will join you before the sixth hour of the night." Bracciano inclined his head. "Madonna."

"My Lord," I followed Savelli out proudly.

There were three men in the farmyard now, two of them with horses that they were rubbing down, having just arrived in December cold. If I could steal a horse…. It was an idea, but there were four men and me, and I could not get mounted before I was grabbed. No, best to wait and watch for the opportunity. I would try it if it seemed I could get up faster.

Savelli and a guard marched me across a long field shining with frost toward massive ruins ahead, arches against the sky huge as the basilica, and I knew where I was. These were the Baths of Caracalla. The entire Papal Court had come here to picnic once, last spring when Laura was one and a bit. I had walked around the ruins with Alessandro while Laura played with Lucrezia and Rodrigo held court in a tent hung with lamps and filled with pillows. Turkish was all the fashion last spring. Alessandro and I had guessed what the rooms might be and he had enthused about how much must still lie beneath the surface awaiting excavation. But of course Savelli had no idea I had ever been here. "What is this place?" I asked in a shaky voice. "Some evil temple?"

He snorted. "No idea."

"It's getting very cold," I said, chafing my arms under my cloak. That was no more than truth. It was getting dark. The sixth hour of the night, Bracciano had said, so I had five hours or thereabouts to come up with something.

Savelli didn't respond. We came closer. Unfortunately, as I remembered, most of the ruins would be like trying to hide in the basilica. The walls stood well above ground, some three or four stories in places, massive arches showing where the vaulted ceiling had once been. There was no cover except a few spindly bushes that might have hidden a cat. The chamber that Alessandro and I had concluded was a bathing chamber was open to the sky. Two other men seemed to be clearing an area in the center, and they had a fire lit in a brazier for warmth. *Wonderful,* I thought. *Bracciano's whole group. More hunters to evade if I had the chance.*

We passed a wagon, the horses unhitched, things laid out in the bed like a peddler's goods for sale, tongs and knives. I was not going to give that any further thought. It could not help me escape.

I was led toward the side of the chamber, to a bunch of roofless cubicles that might once have been changing rooms or private rooms for massage. One of them had been fitted with a door and a bar on the outside. I stepped inside and Savelli closed it behind me. I heard the bar fall into place.

I took a deep breath. No panic. I must think this through. I could still feel that whisper of presence. I was not alone. Logic. What was in the room?

There was no furniture. In one corner were two sacks which held charcoal for the brazier. There was also a box with three unlit torches propped up in it. That was all very well, except there was no fire and nothing to make it with. The room was not completely dark; there was no ceiling, and the overcast night sky gave a little light. It was not pitch black.

The walls were crumbling stone, but they seemed sturdy in their courses to my height and half again. I might, with some difficulty, attempt to climb a wall, but where would that put me? To the side I might get into some adjacent chamber, though if they all opened into the bathing room, I'd have to sneak through it with men in it. Not impossible in the dark, but difficult. And that was assuming I could climb the wall. I had never been a great climber and I was not as strong as I had been before I was sick. Cesare would go up it like a spider, but I was not Cesare.

I paced around the room. Every step might hold an opportunity. Were there places where the wall might be easier? There was some refuse on the floor, drifts of leaves in the corners where the wind had blown them in. Bracciano's men had not swept. What use were piles of leaves to a prisoner? Except....

Holy Lady, I thought, *let this room be like the ones Alessandro and I saw last spring.* I started pulling handfuls of leaves away. Not a massage room or a changing room. A steam room.

There was the hole. It must have once been covered by an ornamental grate long since rusted away. Now it was choked with fallen leaves, a square hole a little wider than my hips. I let out a breath.

Alessandro and I had speculated on one like this. "It's so tiny," I'd said.

"Child slaves," he'd replied, "to clean out the hypocaust."

These rooms were heated by ducts beneath the floor, steam from vast boilers pouring into them to keep them toasty at all seasons and heating water for the hot baths at the same time. If I could get into the hypocaust, I could theoretically crawl to another room and find an exit. Presuming the tunnels weren't blocked. In any event, there was no way that any of the men I'd seen could get down the hole. It was going to be a tight fit for me. That decided it. The hypocaust it was, and the sooner I got started, the better. They wouldn't necessarily check on me for a while, perhaps not until the sixth hour of the night. The more of a head start I had, the better.

Carefully, I sat on the edge of the hole, lowering my feet down. It shouldn't be deep, but of course I couldn't see the bottom in the dark.

I couldn't dangle from my arms. I'd have to find the bottom with my foot or just drop into the dark.

My toe touched. A little less than waist deep. Excellent. I slid into the hole, standing up with my arms above the floor. My hips just fit through. I raked the leaves back around as best I could. If I knelt straight down with my arms above my head... My shoulders went through and then I folded forward onto all fours. It was utterly black below, the square to the room above slightly lighter, kneeling in a crawling position in a space perhaps three feet high.

Fortunately, there was plenty of air. I could feel the movement of it. I reached forward with one hand, touching a stone pillar. A hypocaust wasn't truly a tunnel. It was a maze. Floors were supported by galleries of pillars beneath, open space between each one. The warm air was supposed to circulate. Even if one pillar fell, the others should support the stones above. Of course unlike a tunnel, one could move in any direction and there was no way to see which way was best.

I strained, trying to see in the dark. Pointless. Once away from the hole, there would be no light at all. I had to simply guess. My heart pounded loudly in my ears. Any direction was better than staying where I was, waiting to be killed. I started crawling.

I had no idea how long I crawled in the dark. I tried at first to choose a direction away from the men in the main room, but I could not maintain a straight line. Some spaces between pillars were blocked with the fallen original flooring and were too small to get through. In other places, foundation walls obscured the regular plan and I had to turn and follow along them. I stuck to the wall when this happened, thinking that I might find where the hypocaust originally opened into a boiler room and I could get out. It was a good idea, but I did not find such a place.

Had it been an hour? Two hours? I heard no hue and cry above, but then I might not. There was air. I was not entirely blocked in.

I did at last find one hole that opened above, looking up through a rectangle the length of my two hands and as wide. Now, at last, I felt crushing panic. If I died down here in the dark, unable to fit through any exit….

I made myself take deep breaths of fresh air from above. If all else failed, I would stay here until morning like a fox in her hole and then rays of light would show me where to find the surface. I was in no danger here. There was nothing worse than small animals. There were not even rats, for there was nothing particularly to eat, unlike in the sewers below inhabited parts of the city. No one could get to me here. If I needed to, I would simply wait until morning. The thought steadied me.

I heard noise above and stopped. "What was that?" a man said. "It sounded like it was under the floor."

I held absolutely still.

"I don't hear anything," another man said. They were looking for me.

"Maybe it came from over there. What's that?"

I didn't move.

"A cat," the other man said. "Come on." Their footsteps moved away.

Thank you, Mother, I whispered in my mind. Did I thank Isis or the Virgin? Did it matter? *Prisca theologia*, Rodrigo would have said, the golden thread of truth that runs through all belief in all ages, leading hearts to the divine whatever face it wears.

Perhaps it was best to just stay where I was. If I emerged in some chamber while they looked for me, I might be worse off than I was here. It was chilly but I was out of the wind and they could not possibly find me. Yes, I would just wait a while. I wrapped up in my cloak and stretched out not far from the little air vent.

I had not slept much the night before. I confess it freely. We had stayed up together long after our bodies were satisfied, talking and cuddling, my head on Rodrigo's shoulder. If this was to be our last night, I could not spend it sleeping. There was a play of Shadow and her priest, a long talk about Laura's future, and a great deal of silliness, the kind of jokes that were well beneath Rodrigo's dignity. I had heard the bells for Vigil before we slept.

And so I fell asleep in the hypocaust like a rabbit in a warren, exhausted and relieved at being safe below ground. When I woke, light was pouring through the air hole. It was bright daylight.

I sat up, nearly bumping my head on the ceiling. All of yesterday's trouble came rushing back at once. I was cramped and thirsty. I did have my little bundle with me, some bread still in it, but I had no water. I crawled to the hole and listened. There was no sound except the wind, the autumn's leaves rustling. Above, the sky was piercingly blue. It must be two hours after dawn at least. Surely Bracciano's men had not searched for me all night! He was not a patient man. Since they had not found me, he would have broadened the search, and in daylight there was the danger that others would see them where they weren't supposed to be. The Orsini were allies of the French, but Savelli had not seemed keen on attracting their attention. Perhaps Bracciano and his men had gained access to the city from the French, but the French did not know what they intended? Likely, I thought. Bracciano was playing his own game as usual. I had certainly ruined his plan last night. The sacrifice had gone missing, so whatever evil he intended was averted temporarily. Well, he would not be sitting in a ruin for twelve hours! Even if his men had been left to look for me, he had more important things to do. It was in this frame of mind that I began crawling again, looking for an entrance wide enough to get through.

At last I found a place where much of the floor had collapsed above, making a hole in the pavement perhaps six feet wide. There was something buried beneath it, and I dug in the loose dirt enough to see, unearthing what seemed to be a snout and nostril carved in fine marble. A large statue had stood there. Its weight must have eventually caused the floor to collapse. I caressed it, then smiled. It was a bull's head. It lifted its nose like a swimmer in deep water, the tip of the statue beneath. What better sign could I want? I clambered up on the fallen floor, creeping out into the room above.

It was another huge chamber, arches almost meeting above as high as the ceiling in St. Peter's. Between the gaps, the sky was clear. Everything was quiet. I looked about. It did seem familiar. This was one of the places Alessandro and I had walked. The sun was rising well south of east at this season, so I needed to go away from the sun to go north. Carefully, in case Bracciano's men were still about, I made my way through the ruin. I saw no one. Reaching the edge and looking north, the road ran among the trees and low tussocks of stones beneath earth. The hills were bright in the morning, crowned with church towers.

I could not leave Rome. Porta San Sebastiano was held by the French; that much was plain. I could try to return to the Vatican, but surely that would be where Bracciano would expect me to go. Even if I did get there, Rodrigo would be in the same bind he'd been in before, with me as a potential hostage. My own house at Santa Maria in Portico was no better. Anyone with any sense would seek me there, and the French would surely fully occupy the city in the next few days. Dionisio had a lodging, but he had gone to Capodimonte, and likewise my other friends had fled or been sent away for safekeeping, unless their men were on the fence between Rodrigo and della Rovere's faction, in which case I could not trust them. Who could I trust who had no other allegiance of family or fortune, and where I would never be sought?

Chaya Sarfati. Two years ago, I had helped her and her brother and sister when they came to Rome as Jewish refugees from Grenada. Thanks to Rodrigo's policies as Pope, they'd been allowed to become permanent residents of Rome. Her brother, Mois, had rented a house and his mother, older sister, and her husband and children had joined them. He and his brother-in-law had set up as bookbinders with Chaya to mind the shop. I'd been there several times to buy books or to have a damaged book of Rodrigo's rebound. They would not turn me out, no more than I had turned them out into the chaos in the streets during the papal election, and nobody would ever think to find me in the house of a Jewish bookbinder.

I turned my face to Rome and started walking.

. . .

IT WAS early afternoon before I reached their house. It was near the river in a narrow street of lodging houses and little shops with rooms to let above, or the houses of Jewish families that had shop below and homes above. There were people in the streets here. It wasn't busy, but there were enough people abroad that I was not unusual. My skirts were dusty from crawling, my cloak dirty and torn, and I expect I looked like an impoverished woman who sought alms. Certainly nobody paid me the slightest attention.

I knocked, and after a moment Mois Sarfati answered it himself, only opening it a crack. "What do you want?" he asked.

"It's me," I said, lifting my hood so he could see my face. "May I come in?"

His eyes widened. "Of course." He shot the bolt and opened the door, beckoning me into the shop. Then he closed the door behind. "Donna Giula! What brings you here!"

"May I have some water?" I asked. "I have not had any since yesterday. Please?"

"Come into the kitchen." He led me into the kitchen behind the shop, Chaya and Sincha looking up from breadmaking. "Donna Giulia is here."

"And in terrible straits!" Chaya said, leaping up from her stool and coming to take my cloak. "Sit down! What has happened to you?"

"It's a very long story," I said, and sank down gratefully at the table before the kitchen fire. "I would not have come here if it had not been urgent."

"You are always welcome in our house," Mois said. "As we were welcome in yours."

I had hoped so, but my eyes filled unexpectedly with tears. "Thank you."

Chaya brought me a bowl of delicious bean soup and well-watered wine, and I told them all that had happened since I had left the Vatican. Had it been only yesterday morning? It had been a very long day.

"Bracciano," Mois said grimly. "The one whose men attacked your house before."

"The same," I said. Mois had fought side by side with Cesare when

Bracciano's men had attacked just after Rodrigo had been elected. No doubt he still carried the scar on his arm from that fight.

"We can't let him win," Chaya said. Mois looked at her incredulously and she went on. "Our safety depends on the pope! Pope Alexander granted us asylum. This della Rovere backed the Inquisition in Spain! If he rules, we can't stay here." She looked around their little house. "Mois, we'll lose everything again!"

"Do not even think of resisting the French," I said. "It cannot be done and many people will be killed. The best thing to do is to keep your heads down and trust in His Holiness."

"And yet if he is killed...." Chaya began.

"Then we will see what to do," I said. "If the French kill him, all is not lost. His death can be a symbol to bring them down. If that is the case, we must consider what will help Ascanio Sforza, but I do not yet know what that will be."

"You say that so calmly," Mois said.

"I must," I replied. He would expect no less of me.

I SPENT the afternoon in their kitchen. I was not much of a breadmaker, but as a child I'd done my share of chopping root vegetables, so I gladly helped Chaya's sister, Sincha, at the trestle table. Her shyness vanished when everyone else went out, and before long she was asking me for every detail of Lucrezia's wedding clothes and trousseau. I had forgotten that she knew Lucrezia, but of course she did. She'd "taken lessons" with Lucrezia and Dionisio when we had all been locked in because of the election. Sincha had a taste for fashion. She said that she drew illustrations of clothes she wished she could make, but she demurred when I said that I would love to see them. When we finished and set everything to roast, Sincha went out and I sat by the fire wondering what was happening. It was going toward evening.

I jumped when Chaya came in, and she smiled reassuringly. "It is only me."

"I see," I said. "It's just...."

"You expect the worst, of course." She sat down on the bench at the other side of the table, stretching her hands to the kitchen fire. "I came to tell you that Mois has been out. There are many rumors but no news. The Pope holds the Castel Sant'Angelo, and the King of France holds the city gates. Messengers go back and forth. It is said that there is a cardinal with the king who advises him."

"Della Rovere," I said tightly.

"I don't know. The man Mois talked to didn't know," Chaya said. "Will the Pope surrender?"

I shook my head. I was certain of that at least. "Never. He will die first. He will not be deposed."

"Does della Rovere know that?" she asked.

"Probably not," I said reluctantly. "He said – His Holiness said – that men who are for sale think everyone is for sale. If he believes that Rodrigo would rather be deposed or go into exile, he will keep pushing so that it will happen." Bracciano had no such illusions. He had wanted to make Rodrigo ridiculous and his death laughable. He knew that he would not surrender.

"I don't understand how they can do that," Chaya said. "How can they expect to depose the Pope?"

"He is elected and can be deposed for crimes or sins. The Pope is not above the law of the Church, and there are many who believe – who know – of his sins. And there are those who disagree with his policies, which is more important. It is they who wish to depose him so that they can change the direction of the Church."

"Savonarola," she said. "Cardinal della Rovere. He is the one who talked the old pope into canceling the right of appeal for people convicted by the Inquisition."

"Yes." I nodded. "And there are those who believe they are right and that they do God's will."

"Obviously they don't," Chaya said tartly.

I looked at her. "Why do you say that?"

Chaya turned her hands, warming them. The firelight flickered along her fingers. "I do not know a great deal of your doctrine, but I know this: the people who want to burn me at the stake are bad people. They would see my bones broken on the rack because of who I am. And there is Pope Alexander. He welcomed us to Rome and allows a synagogue. He talks with our scholars and respects our law. And you, personally, his concubine, sheltered my family when we came to Rome and kept us from harm. You took in strangers of another faith, fed us by your fire, and helped us make our home here. I know who is good and who isn't."

I hardly knew what to say. "Chaya...."

"You make it very complicated but it's simple. People say lots of things and make all kinds of justifications, but what they do is real. I have seen the Inquisition in Spain and I've seen the armies of the Reconquista. I don't care what justification someone gives for stealing my family's house or killing my neighbors." Her eyes were as bright and furious as Cesare's. "They are my enemies."

I bent my head. Strangely, there were tears creeping beneath my eyelids. "It's that easy."

"Yes." She came around the table, sitting down on the bench next to me and putting her arms around me. "It's that easy, Giulia."

I turned and cried on her shoulder, big hiccoughing sobs that certainly weren't restrained or polite.

Chaya patted me on the back. "There now," she said. "You've had a terrible year. You are parted from your baby, though it's best for her, and now you may lose him because he is brave and will stand for what is right rather than save himself. Of course you are overcome."

"He could," I said. "He could have taken the road south when it was open. We could be sitting in Spain now, drinking wine in Valencia, safe and free. He could show me Valencia." I couldn't stop crying.

"If he abandoned his flock," Chaya said. "And made a mockery of his office."

"He won't do it," I said. "And I cannot ask him to. I couldn't. I could never ask him to be less."

"You love his honor as your own," she said, stroking my hair.

I gulped. "He has no honor. So he says. So others say of him. But he won't do that."

"To go before the swords of the enemy, armored only in faith, requires both courage and honor," Chaya said. "And we, the people of Rome who have no ships waiting and no estates in Spain to flee to, know that he will do his best to turn the swords of the French from us. If they pillage and destroy the city, it will not be because he betrayed us. It will be because the first man to fall was Pope Alexander."

I squeezed my eyes shut. "He stands before us all."

"Of course you love him," Chaya said gently. "Is it easy to go before God and say, 'I am the sacrifice? I am the bull upon the altar of the Lord my God?'"

I held her tight, her thin shoulders so strong. "You understand."

"Yes." She did not shake. "I do. And you are righteous in the sight of the Lord, whatever happens. I know what you have done, and what he does this moment. God knows, for nothing is hidden from His sight."

I cried myself out on her shoulder.

That night I shared Chaya's bed, curled on a straw mattress with a good blanket and Chaya snoring softly. The window shutters were mostly closed, and curtains too, but I could see a strip of bestarred sky. The bells were ringing Vigil at some nearby church I did not know. *Holy Mother,* I prayed, *please keep Rodrigo safe. If he is dear to you, please guard him and console him, for I cannot.*

CHAPTER 19

For five days we waited thus. I presumed negotiations were in progress. I had no idea what messengers came and went from the Castel Sant'Angelo. Rumors spread, but no one really knew anything. By day people clustered in the streets talking. Cardinals and courtesans might have fled the city, but in the poorer neighborhoods near the river no one had left. No one could afford to. If there was a slaughter, it would happen here among the people who had the least to lose.

I did not go out. I might be recognized. I had lived in Rome for years and my face was widely known, even in this neighborhood. I remained cloistered in the Sarfatis' house.

On the last night in December we heard the noise. Mois and his brother-in-law went out, and it was several hours before they returned, the entire family plus me waiting breathlessly. Mois came in, stomping and rubbing his hands together. It was cold. "The French are here," he said. "There was no resistance."

"Did you see them?" Sincha asked. "What happened?"

"I was near the Palazzo San Marco," Mois said. "It was like a parade. There was no thought of anyone fighting them. People came to watch."

I drew a sharp breath. "How many?"

Mois almost laughed. "Would you like troop numbers and dispositions, Donna Giulia? I had nothing to take notes with."

"A general account will do," I said. He had made me smile.

"First there were Swiss halberdiers, perhaps a thousand, and then more with arquebuses."

"Arquebuses?" I had never seen them, but then Captain d'Allegre's men were cavalry.

"Like unto cannon in that they fire a ball propelled by gunpowder, but instead of being enormous and mounted upon a carriage, they are only a man's height and much lighter, carried by one man and then fired from a stand that he also carries." Mois shook his head. "I saw them in Grenada. It is said they were invented by the Turks, but now men of all nations have adopted them. They are deadly, Donna Giulia, but they take a long time to load and cannot be easily moved once deployed."

"Lovely," I said. It wasn't as though the Castel Sant'Angelo was a moving target.

"Then there were crossbowmen, perhaps 5,000 of them. Then cavalry, perhaps another 5,000." Mois sat down by the fire. "Then the king and his royal guard."

"Did you see him?" I asked.

"He's an ugly little man," Mois said with a grin. "Not imposing at all. But he rode with lance in hand to show that he came as a conqueror, not a guest. He had a cardinal riding on each side of him in their red robes."

"Let me guess," I said, "della Rovere."

"With people shouting his name in the crowd," Mois said. "Or his title, rather."

"And I'll wager the other was Cardinal Sforza."

"A perfect score," Mois said. "It was indeed. And they were followed by a huge number of cannons on caissons. Twenty or thirty? A lot. They took over the Palazzo San Marco, though there's a garrison at the Vice-Chancellor's palazzo too."

"Della Rovere doesn't trust Sforza," I said. "And clearly della Rovere has the French king's confidence."

"Maybe?" Mois said doubtfully. "He seemed friendly to Sforza when I saw him, leaning over and talking with him as they rode."

"Ascanio can be charming," I said.

"Those guns will blow down the walls of the Castel Sant'Angelo," Mois said, "even from across the river. Thirty cannons?"

"I know." I took a deep breath. Rodrigo had told Ascanio he would be on the walls, daring the French to fire on Pope and Host alike. Tomorrow.

"Is there any hope?" Chaya asked.

Mois shook his head. "There's a rumor that Cardinal Sforza wants a parley. That he says they can always talk and then shoot later, but not the other way around. He wants the king to meet with the Pope."

"And cut della Rovere out." It made sense. Ascanio acting in his own self-interest wanted to minimize della Rovere. Being the maestro in a negotiation fed his power. Simply blowing down the walls gave him nothing unless he'd made it clear beforehand that he was not party to it. If he was going to avenge St. Alexander the Martyr, he had to oppose della Rovere's plan, and if Rodrigo lived, he needed to limit della Rovere's influence on the king. It cost him nothing to urge negotiation.

As Rodrigo had known.

"And what does the Lord Marshal want?" I asked. He had seemed impressed on Christmas Day. And where was Captain d'Allegre in these councils?

"I don't know," Mois said, "but the French haven't started looting yet. In theory they're here to remove the Borgia Pope while on their way to Naples."

"Let's hope it stays that way," I said grimly.

THE FIRST DAY of January dawned cold. There was ice on the surface of the water barrel when I went to get water for washing, and I washed my face with cold water. The sky was slate gray. Even now were guns moving into position facing the Castel Sant'Angelo? Even now was Rodrigo dressing for the last time, white vestments and golden pectoral cross? He would look as perfect as possible. If he were going to die, he'd not do it badly dressed.

I couldn't do it. I couldn't sit in the kitchen another day. I had to find out what was happening. I had to see, even if it burned scars into me forever.

Walking up to the Castel Sant'Angelo was out of the question. Surely this side of the river facing the fortress was the French front lines. I'd have to get around another way. Perhaps cross the river as far south as this area? There were lots of small boats that ferried people across all the time. I looked like a servant. No one would question a cloak and hood on such a day. If I got across the river, I could approach the Vatican from the direction of the pilgrim way and to my house at Santa Maria in Portico. Maria or one of the guards would let me in. I could go through the secret passage into St. Peter's and the Vatican. That would work. It was better than simply sitting here.

Mois and Chaya tried to talk me out of it. "I must know," I said, and promised I would return.

The trip across the river was uneventful, paying my passage with a single coin, then scrambling up the docks on the other side and making my way through the pilgrim quarter. It was quiet, nearly deserted. Who would want to be about at a time like this? The only people around looked like me, women in old clothing who hurried from house to house with baskets.

The bells of St. Peter's were ringing Sext when I reached the kitchen door of my house, almost in the shadow of the tower. It looked the same. Nothing was different at all. It seemed that it should be. It seemed that I had been gone for years rather than months.

Of course the back door was locked. I did not have the key. Why would I? I had never intended to return. I knocked, my hood pulled up to shade my face, conscious that everyone in the neighborhood knew me well.

Except the man who answered it. He wore the colors of a Borgia guard, but I had never seen him before. "Yes?" he said, still chewing on a piece of bread. "What do you want?"

In my bedraggled gown and old cloak I did not look like anyone of importance, and I was at the kitchen door. "Is Captain Rizzoli here? I have a message for him," I said in a small voice.

"Yeah, wait here." He let me into the storeroom and locked the door behind me. "What's your name?"

"Chaya Sarfati," I said. Rizzoli knew the name. He'd been here when the Sarfatis first came to Rome, though he'd wonder why in the world Chaya was seeking him out. I stood alone in the storeroom while he went through the kitchen to find Rizzoli. Other than being a few barrels emptier than I remembered, it was the same. My house, Rodrigo's house. I had left in such anger. Now I wished I could be in my own bed. There was noise in the kitchen and I looked through the door. Eight or nine children were underfoot, the little ones no older than Laura. Who were all these children? One of the young maids glanced toward the door and I stepped back. That was Agnesa. She'd recognize me if she saw my face.

Rizzoli took his time. It seemed I waited forever before he appeared. "What's all this?" he asked. I lifted my head and he abruptly closed the door to the kitchen behind him, shutting away the din. "Madonna Giulia?" he said incredulously.

"Yes. And I am not supposed to be here."

"You're not supposed to be in Rome," he said. "We heard you were spirited out of the city by a *condottiero* in Colonna pay or that you've gone over to the French."

"Obviously I haven't," I said. "Where is Donna Adriana?"

"His Holiness sent word four days ago that she was to be allowed to go to Vasanello." I must have looked skeptical. "Or rather that she was to go to Vasanello whether she wanted to or not. You'd think that three weeks under house arrest was durance vile."

I sighed. Three weeks. Well, at least she wasn't here. And Rodrigo was right that there was nothing she could tell Bracciano now that he didn't already know. "It's probably for the best," I said. "Who are all these children?"

"His Holiness said that we could bring our families here while we guarded Donna Adriana." Now he looked sheepish. "He didn't say they had to leave when she did."

"They certainly don't have to," I said. "If the French loot the city, at least they are all together here in a stout house you can guard."

"And on this side of the river. Our men still hold this side."

"I know." I took a deep breath. *And that's about all* went without saying. "I'm hoping to get into the Vatican without being seen."

"The passage."

I nodded. "I can tell you where the key is. It's in my dressing room in the cabinet by the window, in the second drawer down with a bundle of letters and other papers." With Rodrigo's letters. I had left him the key when I went. I had not taken the letters either. "I don't dare go up to my own room."

"Your rooms are closed and left undisturbed, Madonna," Rizzoli said. "Maria said you'd be back."

I blinked. Of course she had. "I will be," I said. "I will be home soon. Can you get the key and escort me into the chapel?"

"Yes, Madonna."

I waited again. It seemed forever. The storeroom smelled right, like my own kitchen, my own house. How I loved this house! It was home. How futile to love a place. Faithful Rizzoli. Dear Maria. I did not want to endanger her or anyone else by speaking to her. It was better if no one else knew I was here. A secret shared by many does not remain secret.

Rizzoli returned after a bit. "Maria caught me coming out and wanted to know what I was doing in your room. I had to tell her." I shook my head. "She says she'll go in the chapel in an hour or so and wait for you to come back. Or whenever you need her to. So that she can let you out."

"That is wonderful," I said. I hadn't quite worked out how I was going to get back from the passage to the storeroom door without Rizzoli with the house full of people. "Let's go then." I pulled my hood up and we went through the kitchen briskly, interrupted only by one little girl who seemed to be Rizzoli's own daughter who wanted him to play with her, but was put off with "Papa's on duty." From there it was easy to cross the hall and go through the saletta to the chapel.

"Good fortune, Madonna," Rizzoli said. "Tell His Holiness we await his orders." He stood very straight.

"I will tell him," I said, "if I am able to speak with him."

Rizzoli nodded, backing out, and closing the chapel door behind him. I took a deep breath, then fit the key into the lock. The panel swung open silently and I slipped through.

As usual, the robing room of the Choir Chapel was dark. It wasn't occupied frequently since it was mainly used to store spare vestments. I stopped and closed the door and relocked it, putting the key in my bosom. Then I went to the door that led into the Choir Chapel and listened. It was very quiet. I ventured opening the door a crack.

The candles were lit, not just the altar candles but the big floor candlestands, but no one was there. I could hear voices in the nave, but there did not seem to be anything happening in the chapel. I slipped out of the robing room and crossed the floor quietly to the entrance to the nave. If there were enough people, perhaps people of Rome who had taken refuge in St. Peter's, I could simply blend in with the crowd. If not, I would have to be more cautious. I looked out.

The nave was not empty. Instead, there was a group of men coming up the nave from the main doors, four richly dressed men with steel and sword, followed by ten French soldiers in full arms. Their boot heels rang on the floor. The one in the center was short and unattractive, with a pockmarked face not improved by a short beard, the Valois lilies displayed on his steel breastplate.

In front of the baldacchino before the high altar, Rodrigo waited. Two young pages stood at the back, but there was no one else with him, no guards, no priests. He was entirely alone. I caught my breath. He wore his white vestments, but not the cope elaborately embroidered with gold or the high miter. Bareheaded, he simply waited, a sunbeam through the clerestory windows illuminating the floor at his feet, his hands clasped.

My heart stopped in my breast. I had seen this. I had seen this moment. He stood like a bull for the sacrifice. And there were the men I had seen. The one in the center was Charles, the King of France. The others – it was the man in red who had struck in my vision, tall and dark haired, the fatal sword at his side. They walked quickly, two of the nobles ahead of their master.

Rodrigo spread his arms, taking one step forward. The light struck the cross on his breast where it lay on white brocade. "My son," he said. His palms were open, fingers parted, graceful as a dancer. "You have come at last." The white walls echoed, soaring arches throwing back his voice as a whisper. The light struck his ring as he moved his arm, glittering on pearl and gold. He was the Pope. He was Christ's Earthly Habitation.

The King of France looked as though he'd walked into a wall. If he'd smacked his face into stone, he would have looked less dazed. "Holy Father," he said. Rodrigo stretched out his hand, and the king took it, bending to kiss his ring.

"No, no," Rodrigo said, stopping him, his other hand coming up to clasp the king's shoulder. "My dear son, do not make obeisance to me, a mortal man. A king should only kneel before the Lord Our God." His voice was warm, resonant. There was that strangeness behind it, that presence. I suppose I was used to it. It did not bring me to my knees unless it was turned on me. Clearly King Charles had never heard such before.

"Holy Father," he managed, "you are not what I expected."

"And you are exactly what I expected," Rodrigo said warmly. "A bold and brave young warrior, faithful as Charlemagne." He knew the king had named his only son Orlande, after Roland of the tale. And this was that tale, was it not? Charles the Great came to Rome and the Pope set the crown of France upon his head again, peerless defender of Christendom, most noble of paladins. "My dear son, I have long waited to meet you face to face."

"And I you, Holy Father," the king said. He looked somewhat breathless. "My gentlemen...."

"Let us speak as men should, heart to heart without intermediaries who may complicate matters with their ignorance," Rodrigo said. "We, who know both the burden and the reward, will understand one another." His voice was tender, a loving father who wished to counsel a grown son of whom he was proud. "Here. Walk with me so that we may talk undisturbed." He turned the king to stand beside him.

"Of course," Charles said. "We have much to discuss."

Rodrigo patted him on the back. "There is the chapel there."

One of the men spoke quickly. "Your Majesty, you should not go somewhere alone with…."

"With an old man?" Rodrigo said gently. He spread his hands again, stout and gray in his vestment with no cope. "You see that I am unarmed. Do you think I can best a young knight in steel with my bare hands?"

"Enough, de Rohan," the king said. "Obviously I will come to no harm." Rodrigo turned him toward the Choir Chapel. I scurried back out of the way. Rodrigo meant to bring him in here! Where could I go except back in the robing room? There were no other doors. I scampered into the robing room and closed the door in time. I put my eye to the crack.

I had missed some of what was said. Rodrigo crossed himself to the altar, and the king somewhat awkwardly followed. There were three steps up, and Rodrigo sat down heavily on the top one, like a man in his own house. "Now, my son," he said, "sit beside me and unburden yourself."

Charles looked like a man who wasn't used to sitting on the floor, even if it was on carpeted steps, but he could hardly call for a chair when the Pope did not. He sat down on the other end of the step, his sword clanking loudly. He unfastened it and put it aside. "Your pardon," he said.

Rodrigo smiled expansively, as though bearing a sword in the presence of the Pope was nothing. "You are a warrior. Indeed, one of the greatest France has produced." *Here comes Charlemagne,* I thought, and I was right. "You know, it was in 773 that Charles the Great came to our fair Italy to conquer the Lombards. Pope Leo greeted him here, right here in this very chapel where we sit now." Rodrigo glanced around as though Charlemagne and Leo could be lurking somewhere around the ceiling. "Could they have imagined, do you think, that their successors should sit here today as they did?"

"I don't know," Charles said.

Rodrigo rested his hand on his own knee like a genial uncle. "It was a few years later that Charles the Great conquered Southern Italy – what we would call Naples today – and prevented the Byzantines from their plots. Just as you, my son, will keep the Turks out." He smiled at Charles. "I am fortunate indeed to live in the era of another Charles, for there is no end to the perfidy of the Turks or their ambitions."

"None," Charles said. "When I have taken Naples, you will know it is strongly held." As though King Alfonso of Naples had anything to do with the Turks! A small fact both of them seemed to have forgotten.

"It does my heart good to know that," Rodrigo said. "I shall rely on you to guard against the Turks when I am gone."

"Surely your health is not so frail, Holy Father," Charles said.

Rodrigo looked surprised. "Am I not to be deposed? Do you think I will live long after? A man of my years thrown into prison?" He gave Charles a rueful smile. "Come, Your Majesty. You know those men who call for my deposition. Do you think I will not meet with some accident rather than live to be a thorn in the side of the man who follows me?" A flush rose in Charles' face and he continued. "You are wise enough to have heard such words spoken about your throne, whether they were intended for your ears or not."

"You may rest assured, Your Holiness, that I have never agreed to any such thing," he said quickly. "Assassination is not the way things are done in France. I will cut off the hand of any man who raises it to you!"

"You are a good man," Rodrigo said, putting his hand to the king's shoulder. "And yet good men may be taken advantage of by those who counsel them with a viper's tongue. I'm sure you are no stranger to men who hope to use the power of France for personal advancement."

"No." The King looked troubled. "That happens often enough."

"A hazard of being king. But I'm sure you see through their wiles."

In the robing room, I shook my head. He was a master player, and I blessed him for every moment of it, for he played with our lives.

"Cardinal della Rovere wants…."

Rodrigo laughed tolerantly. "I'm sure he wants many things, my son. He'd like you to give him wealth and station and a prancing unicorn! But if he thinks that you will abuse your power to ensure his election to the Throne of St. Peter, he's wrong. His peers have soundly refused to elect him more than once. He knows the only way he'll be pope is at swords' point. But you will decline to provide the sword." Rodrigo tapped his temple. "You're much too canny to be his tool. You'll choose your own candidate."

The king's frown deepened. "Holy Father, I have no intention of deposing you. The Cardinal may have mistaken ambitions, but I am no part of them."

"I'm very glad to hear that," Rodrigo said. "I was prepared to die for the faith, but I would rather not."

He meant it, I thought. And that was the base of it all. There was truth beneath every lie.

"Holy Father…" the king began.

"But now we must plan your triumph," Rodrigo said. "Obviously we must welcome you appropriately. I do warn you that the people of Rome are terrified of your puissant arms."

"Obviously we could make assurances," Charles said. "And I give my word that we shall pay for our billeting and that we will not tolerate looting."

Rodrigo gave him a sideways smile. "I expected no less. You are the model of chivalry. I gathered such from your Captain d'Allegre. If that is a captain's honor, the king he serves must inspire greatness. So I will welcome you personally and do reverence…."

Charles interrupted. "Of course not, Your Holiness! That would reduce the dignity of your holy office! I will be presented to you properly and come as a good Christian son. I have no desire to stand before you like some pagan conqueror."

"If it is your wish," Rodrigo said mildly. "I do not need such things for myself. But if you wish to honor God…."

"I do," Charles said, "and I will arrange matters with those cardinals now with my army. Not della Rovere, of course. Perhaps Sforza?"

"Ah, Ascanio." Rodrigo looked grieved, tilting his head back to examine the ceiling again. "My dear Ascanio. We have been friends for many years. I can't tell you how his defection saddened me. It is always thus, is it not? You cherish a man as your bosom friend, and then discover it is your station that he loves." Charles' face fell. Of course this had happened to him. How not? "Still, I would be reconciled with him, and he is an honest man."

I nearly choked. Describing Ascanio Sforza as an honest man was really more than one could take!

"Cardinal Sforza, then," the king said. "It would be my pleasure to reconcile you with your friend."

Rodrigo patted his knee. "You are a good son to think of it. Your dear father, King Louis, was taken from us too soon. I remember him well. A fine man and a brave soldier. You were thirteen when he died, were you not?"

"I was," Charles said.

"So young to have the burden placed upon you," Rodrigo said, "and yet you have borne it well. Consider me a loving kinsman who hopes to ease your pain out of respect for the giant of a man who sired you! Of course your welcome must be appropriate. And it would be my great honor if you would allow me to crown you once again, here in St. Peter's Basilica, as Charlemagne himself was crowned."

"Holy Father, I would not have dared to ask," Charles said. Or would never have intended to, I thought. Della Rovere would shit himself when he heard all of this. Rodrigo to re-crown the King of France? What more public acknowledgement of his authority could France make?

Rodrigo's head dipped, and he smiled. There was something behind it, a gentle and inexorable force. *Pacis Cultor*, I thought. His motto was the bringer of peace. If I could have kissed his hand, I would have.

"Then we will leave the arrangements to our people," Rodrigo said. "And you and I understand one another, true hearts joined in the love of God."

"Will you pray with me, Holy Father?"

"Of course," Rodrigo said, and the king turned to kneel on the step. Rodrigo turned rather more slowly, and the king reached to steady him as a son for an elderly father. "Thank you, my son."

When they bent their heads, I stepped away from the door and slipped away through the hidden door.

MARIA WAS WAITING for me in the chapel, and I embraced her warmly, if quietly. I did not want anyone to hear voices from the robing room. I locked the door firmly again and gave her the key. "Will you keep this for me?" I whispered.

"Of course, Madonna." She drew me away from the wall, holding me at arms' length. "You look terrible," she said. "Thin and pale and a mess. And what happened to your hair?"

"My mother had to cut it when I was ill," I said. "It will grow back. And I'm afraid I'm the worse for wear. I'm hiding in the city so as not to be a hostage against His Holiness. Is everything all right here? How have you been?"

"We've got the guardsmen's families all over," she said, "but it does keep the place safe. I've not let anyone in your rooms or at your things, Madonna. How is little Laura?"

"Safe in Pesaro with Donna Lucrezia," I said. "I couldn't bring her into this."

"Of course." Maria had a soft spot for both of them. "How is His Holiness?"

"Not dead," I said. My voice choked suddenly. A wave of dizziness took me. The paths through the wood had closed. We had taken one, the other lost forever. "He will not die," I whispered. "The pyre will not be his."

Maria crossed herself to the altar in the little chapel. "I've asked Our Lady to watch over him. Every single day."

My eyes filled, imagining Maria on her knees asking for grace for Rodrigo. "Dearest Maria, that would mean a great deal to him."

"It's a fine thing to have the Pope in your house at your table," she said. "So let's get on with it then. He'll clear these pesky Frenchmen out of here in no time at all. I can't say I approve of the French."

It was all I could do not to laugh out loud. "I hope he does indeed," I said.

CHAPTER 20

Needless to say, I did not see the King of France invested in St. Peter's. It was an investiture, not a coronation, since he was already king, but the difference was technical. I did not dare slip in when it was so crowded with so many people who knew me, but I could well imagine the pomp and ceremony. The French were quartered in parts of the city, and for the most part they'd not marauded widely. We heard that a house near the northern gates had been invaded and three people killed, but that was less than feared. A number of the grand palazzos belonging to absent cardinals had been looted, and I wondered how Alessandro's rented house was. He did not have a great deal there since he was not rich, but it was his. I thought Rizzoli and company would show off anyone who tried Santa Maria in Portico, and in any event it was in the shadow of the Vatican, not near where the French were quartered.

People began to venture out in the streets again. How not? We could not all stay shut in our houses for a month at a time. There had to be food and people had to ply their trades. Not that there were customers at the bookbinder, but Mois and his brother-in-law did make a point of being open for whatever business there might be.

On a bright and sunny but cold afternoon I went with Sincha and

Chaya to the market stalls further south along the river. Some farmers had started bringing in produce by little boats, thus avoiding the gates and the possible confiscation of their crops. If you went down along the shore, they'd popped up awnings and you could buy directly from the boats. With my cloak up, my face was shadowed, and in any event there were far fewer people who would recognize me on the Tiber foreshore than in St. Peter's! I carried a market basket, and since I had a small purse, meant to spend it for the family. They had shared generously of their food and wouldn't take my money, but they could hardly argue if I bought vegetables for the pot.

It was a beautiful day, the wind brisk off the river but not too cold in the sun. Chaya was dickering for eggs and Sincha and I walked a little further along, to a man who had artichokes, apples, and winter greens in his boat. I was paying him for ten apples when there was a stir. A party of Frenchmen were making their way along the shore and shouts erupted. Apparently, they were trying to requisition the food from the boats, and the farmers were resisting. More shouts. A punch was thrown. One young woman was trying to shove a boat off the shore, wading ankle deep in the water. A Frenchman grabbed her, knocking her down as the boat rocked.

"We need to leave," I said to Sincha, who was standing wide-eyed.

The crowd was pushing and shoving, half the people trying to get away from the fight and the other half wanting to join it. We were more or less stuck. Someone screamed. At the far end a group of Frenchmen on horseback were wading into the fray. A cuff from a gauntlet, and a man went down under the horses' hooves.

Screams turned to fury. People had had enough of this. A burly man grabbed the bridle of the horse. The rider plied his whip, but someone grabbed his arm on the downstroke. The horse, panicked, tried to back away, and backed into crates of vegetables displayed before a boat. They fell with a crash, produce rolling in all directions. The man still had the bridle, the rider fighting with two men who pulled him sideways, half out of the saddle. The horse showed the whites of his eyes, backing madly. His hooves slipped on the mud and stone of the foreshore and the horse fell, pinning the rider beneath in the shallow water. With a shout, the three other French horsemen piled in.

They were yelling for reinforcements. The crowd swarmed in. "Run," I said to Sincha, dragging her through the crowd toward the nearest side street.

"Chaya!" she said.

I couldn't see her anywhere. She had been further back from where the fight had started. "She's safer than we are," I said, pulling her into the nearest narrow street, a cobbled alley between buildings. "Come on."

There was a flurry of hooves and I pressed Sincha back against the wall as three men on horses flew past, iron-shod hooves striking sparks from the cobbles. There were more shouts, louder now. This was turning into a riot.

"We have to get off the street," I said. Sincha and I hurried along the wall to a cross-street. There were more Frenchmen, this time footsoldiers with pikes. Sincha looked like she was going to panic, her face pale and her breath heaving. *Grenada*, I thought. She had been in a sacking before. "This way," I said, pulling her along in the opposite direction from the French. The shops and houses were all closed. Any business that had opened had slammed doors and shutters closed.

More shouts, the sounds of heavy thumps. Rome was tinder. A match had been put to it. The street was empty except for us. How had people disappeared so quickly? Presumably they'd either run to join in or were hiding in their houses. And where were we? I'd gotten turned around and I didn't know this part of the city well, further downstream from the neighborhood where Chaya's family lived, away from the Vatican and from the houses I'd lived in. "Sincha, where are we?"

Her look of panic answered all. This reminded her of her most terrifying memories. "I can't breathe," she said.

I was going to have to get her out of here. "Yes, you can." I held both her hands in mine. "Take my hand. We're going this way."

Almost to the next corner, and there were the sounds of hooves. That couldn't be good. Any mounted party moving quickly would be

French. There was a church across the street, the sort of ordinary parish church common in poor neighborhoods. Surely the doors wouldn't be locked! I all but dragged Sincha to them. One opened.

"I can't go in there!" she gasped.

'Yes, you can." I pulled her in and dragged the door shut behind us. It was quite dark. Only the Presence was lit, and not much light came in the high, old-fashioned windows. The walls above didn't look like they'd been scrubbed of soot in a hundred years. "This way." I pulled her down the side aisle to the right, away from the door and behind the heavy Romanesque columns. The side chapels were not really more than alcoves, the floor bumpy with different memorial stones where people had been buried beneath the floor, a patchwork of names and dates that commemorated the life of the city. As soon as we were far enough along not to be seen from the door, I pulled her down to sit with our backs to one of the columns facing the wall. "There," I said.

"I'm not supposed to be here," Sincha whispered.

"God will understand. Yours and mine both," I replied. I glanced around the column toward the high altar, seeing the stiff old wall painting behind it. "Besides, this is the Virgin's house. She is a refuge. We'll be safe here." Sincha took a deep breath.

We sat for a very long time. The walls were thick. Whatever was going on outside, the sound didn't penetrate. It was an old church, shabby and comfortable, smelling of beeswax and the lingering hint of incense, and yet I felt Her presence here more strongly than in the Lady Chapel in St. Peter's. *Holy Mother*, I thought, *please protect and preserve the poor people of Rome. Please hold each and every one in your care.* I closed my eyes. Sincha leaned on me, almost lying down. I stroked her hair as I would Laura's. "There, sweetheart," I said.

I simply let Her peace enfold me, feeling Sincha's breathing slow to normal. *Prisca theologia*, I thought, the golden thread of truth that runs through all belief. Rodrigo had introduced me to the concept years ago, and there was nothing I believed more. Did it matter whether I addressed her as Holy Mother or Blessed Virgin or Lady of Peace or some other name older still, old as Rodrigo's statues? She was the same, eternal and absolute.

I put my hand flat on the floor, feeling the stone beneath me. *I will lie here beneath this floor.* The thought came with a deep sense of peace. We had taken this path. I would follow it to its ending. Why I would be laid to rest here, in this quiet old church, didn't matter. What mattered were all the steps between that day and this. *Thank you, Mother,* I prayed. *Thank you for the glorious days of my life, and for all before me, long or short.*

I don't know how long we sat there. Sincha went to sleep. I prayed. Perhaps I dozed. When I opened my eyes, the light coming in through the high windows was dim, the Presence seeming brighter in the dark. No one had come to ring the bells here, probably because of the tumult in the streets, but far away Vespers was ringing.

I shook Sincha gently. "Wake up, dear. It's safe, but your family will be worrying. We need to go back to your house."

She sat up, rubbing the sleep out of her eyes. "I'm so sorry."

"There's nothing to be sorry for," I said. "We have just waited here until whatever happened was over. Now we will go home." I got to my feet stiffly. I still had the market basket and apples. I took one out and handed the basket to Sincha. "Would you like an apple?"

She almost laughed. "Are you always so calm?"

"Lately," I said. Truly I felt a little lightheaded. We slipped out the door and I carefully pulled it shut behind me. The street was deserted. From the direction we'd came, toward the river, there was a light like a fire. A bonfire? A building alight? I looked at Sincha. "Does this street look familiar to you? Do you know where we are?"

She glanced in both directions. "I think? I think if we go left, we'll be going the right way!"

"Then let's try it," I said. "I'm sure your family will be worried by now." Frantic, most likely. Perhaps we should have gone sooner. Still, it was quiet now.

We had gotten two blocks when we heard hooves. We were in the middle of a block. "Run," I said. "The alley there." There was an alley that cut between buildings, probably not wide enough for a horseman to feel comfortable. "Down the alley like a mouse down a hole." I let Sincha get ahead of me.

"Halt!" a man yelled, the words in Italian rather than French. "Woman! Halt!"

I looked behind. There were a dozen men on foot and a horseman in red and white, his steel breastplate and helm not covering his face. I knew his colors. I knew him. And he knew me.

"Run," I said to Sincha in a low voice. "Go. I'll take care of this." She scampered down the alley quickly. I took a deep breath and then stepped out into the street, into the light of the flaring torches. "My Lord Bracciano."

He stopped, his horse stamping. The guardsmen halted too. "Donna Giulia."

I was as calm as clear water. Perhaps it was that I'd spent the afternoon in prayer, or perhaps I was simply beyond fear. Or perhaps She stood with me, his long adversary. Isis faced Typhon in the empty street. "I believe we have matters to settle."

"Take that woman into custody," he directed. One of the guardsmen stepped forward.

"Halt," I said. I did not raise my voice, just lifted my hand. He stopped, looking at his lord uncertainly. "Sorrow will come to you, oathbreaker. You swore to defend this city and instead you surrendered it to the enemy. You are foresworn before God and man. Your bonds with all who serve you are dissolved, enemy of truth."

His mouth set in a tight line. "You've bothered me one time too many."

"And yet one time more." I could feel it, a wind beneath me, a surety, a power. I held out my hand to him.

"What's that?" he asked sharply.

"An apple," I said.

He looked nervous. "Seize her!"

I reached down. Beneath my feet was the cobbled street and beneath that layer upon layer of Rome, a thousand years and a thousand more. Bones and stones, marble and lost things and broken pots and refuse and saints' medals and ancient bronzes, soaked with prayers and dreams like a cake soaked in milk. It was mine. It was hers. My heritage, her love, my body, her strength. I was her and she was me. "I think not," I said. "Lady of Night," I said, "Mother of the Heavens, wrap us in your veil."

I pulled it up, a wave of darkness. It was impenetrable, a night without stars, the night of the deep places beneath the earth. It rolled up from the streets. It quenched the torches, guttering and going out. One of the men yelled. They were blind. The darkness pulled the light from the sky. It was cool, comforting, like sleeping in a cradle. It was absolute.

I heard Bracciano shout. His horse whinnied. And yet he could see nothing. The darkness clung to him. "Giulia Farnese!" Bracciano yelled. "What witchery is this? I will have your life for this."

"I will have yours," I said calmly. "You have made your infernal bargain. Typhon promised you power, and you will pay for it with your life and your soul. Be accursed, knowing that night will bring you no peace. Oathbreaker I name you. The Furies will pursue you and when they have run you to ground, I will be there."

He snarled, unable to see the street beneath his horse's hooves. I could still see, or rather I knew where things were. I simply stepped away. I left him and his men entangled in the middle of the street, blind and frantic, and walked away. It would dissipate in time, but by then I would be long gone. My arms shook with the power that had passed through, but nothing hurt. I held an apple in my hand.

SINCHA HAD GOTTEN home before I did, and I met Mois and his brother-in-law at the end of their street where they were coming to look for me. "Sincha said you were in trouble," Mois said. "And Chaya's been home for hours."

"I lost those men in the streets," I said. "It's getting dark." There must have been something odd in my voice, for Mois looked at me sideways, and then visibly decided to let it drop. "What happened?" I said. "We hid from the riot and I know no more."

"There was a fight along the river," he said. "A boat was set on fire and several people were killed. At least one French soldier was killed too. His Holiness implored the King of France to stop it, and the French withdrew." I let out a long breath. "It's the Papal Army patrolling the streets tonight."

"Under Bracciano," I said. That explained much. Well, he certainly had not followed me nor had any idea where I might be in the city. This was not a place he'd think to look.

"I'll go out tomorrow and see what I can find out," Mois promised.

He was as good as his word. He came back just short of noon, doffing his hat and hanging it up. "The word is that the French plan to march south to Naples in a few days," Mois said.

"That's a relief," I said.

"Just like that," Mois said incredulously. "It's said the King spent two hours in conversation with His Holiness the other day. They seem the best of friends and he kissed the Pope's ring when he departed. And now he's released the Papal Army to the Pope's command!"

"My goodness," I murmured. "That does put the Gonfaloniere in a predicament. Poor Lord Bracciano."

"They say the Gonfaloniere tried to talk to the king and King Charles turned his back on him."

"Well," I said cheerfully, "the thing about selling out one master is that the next one is fairly certain you can't be trusted."

"What about the papal army?"

I shrugged. "It's a few thousand men. Most of them are Roman. Why would they want to help the King of France attack Naples? Some of the Orsini may have to go with the head of their family, though."

"Why?"

I might have smiled. It might not have been a very nice smile. "Bracciano can't stay here. He's bet everything on His Holiness being deposed. If he doesn't go with the French, he'll be locked up an hour after they leave. His Holiness will execute him for treason. Don't doubt that. He can run but he can't escape."

Mois' eyebrows rose. "God's vengeance?"

"Borgia vengeance," I said.

THE FRENCH ARMY took an entire day marching out. It was too large for it to be otherwise. While the king and his nobles, including the new Papal Legate Cardinal Cesare Borgia, were gone by midmorning, dusk was fast approaching before the last units cleared the city gates. I had no illusions that Cesare was an honored guest. He was a hostage. On the other hand, anyone who thought holding Cesare was a good idea would learn better.

The gates were shut. The entire city breathed a sigh of relief. I slept deeply and profoundly beside Chaya.

In the morning, everyone was out and about despite the cold. I embraced Chaya and each of her family warmly. "I will never forget what you have done for me," I said. My eyes misted. "If there is ever anything I can do on your behalf, you have only to ask."

"Consider us even," Chaya said. "And there is no debt between us. Just friendship."

"You could order some books," Mois said with a smile.

"I will certainly do that," I promised. It was little enough.

By noon I was in my own house, Maria making much of me. She had already begun opening and airing my room first thing in the morning, and the little maids were making the bed with fresh linens. "So it will be ready for you tonight," Maria said.

"I do not plan to be here tonight," I said, "though for a far nicer reason."

"Then you'll need a bath brought up," Maria said, and started ordering the maids about again to bring in the tub and put it before the fireplace, to heat water and drape the bathing sheets and fetch oils and soap. I'd not had a bath since I'd left the Vatican. It was far too much trouble to ask of Chaya's family and I could hardly go to a public bath while hiding.

An hour later, soaking in warm water scented with rose oil while Agnesa washed my hair, I felt like I was home again. Peace. Quiet.

Luxury. I leaned my head back on the edge of the tub padded with the bath sheets, closing my eyes while Agnesa lathered. I almost went to sleep.

I spent the afternoon writing letters while my hair dried by the fire. Alessandro and my mother were foremost, though I had to be careful what I said. I could use a Borgia courier, but it was far from certain that the road between Rome and Capodimonte was open. The main route went straight through Bracciano and was surely Orsini held. I would need to send the letters up the Via Aurelia to Montalto and hope that worked. I also wrote to Fiammetta at Spoleto, though that letter was even more circumspect. I wrote to Lucrezia, though I knew I couldn't send it today. Rodrigo would have a packet for her I could put my letter in, and he'd know the best way to get it to Pesaro. Where exactly troops were, and which lords would let a Borgia courier through, was in motion.

I sent Laura a thousand kisses. I hoped she remembered me. I had meant to be gone two or three weeks when I went to Angelo's sickbed. Instead it had been six months, which seemed forever at her age. Surely soon I could fetch her! As soon as we knew which roads were open, I knew Rodrigo would give me an armed escort. It was the dead of winter, though. It might be safer for her to wait a month, hard as that would be for me. While it rarely snowed heavily in Rome, the weather in the mountains could be very bad indeed, and we would have to cross the spine of the Apennines to Pesaro. The beginning of February was probably not the time to bring a toddler on such a journey. March would be better.

Rodrigo would hear Compline tonight I was certain, as it would be a service of thanksgiving. Then I expected he had a dinner. He would be making a point that he was in charge. Thus, I had a light dinner by myself and then dressed elegantly, Borgia red with gold, and let myself into St. Peter's through the secret door.

The basilica was quiet. There were guards in steel on the doors from the basilica into the papal apartments. I walked straight up to them. They recognized me. "Giulia Farnese," I said, and they let me through. I went up the stairs. There was the table on the landing, and I did not even flinch. Eyes followed me, and I walked straight-backed to the captain on duty. The doors to the reception room were closed.

"His Holiness is not in," the guard said. "He dines with Cardinal Sforza and Cardinal Carafa."

"Of course," I said. "I will wait."

"Madonna." He let me in. Giulia Farnese was back.

There were candles lit, and I walked through, my feet loud on the tiled floor. The sala beyond was full of light as well, Lucrezia and her brothers painted on the walls in glowing colors. I went all the way through to the study, from which I heard voices. I pushed the door open.

Burchard and a young priest were unpacking Rodrigo's books. "…there. Careful," Burchard said.

My smile as I went in was entirely genuine. "I am so glad to see you!"

Burchard stood up, a volume in one hand. "Donna Giulia. I don't see you at all."

"In His Holiness's study. No, of course not." It had become a joke between us, the places the official chronicler didn't see me. Of course I hadn't seen him at Gioffre's wedding masque either, because he certainly hadn't been there! Whoever that man dressed as St. Jerome had been, it was absolutely not Burchard!

"I'm delighted you're well," he said. "We feared the worst."

"I was simply staying discreetly in the city," I said.

Burchard nodded. "Wise. The situation was…fluid."

And yet he'd stayed. "It was," I said. "And your fidelity is notable. You risked your life to stay with His Holiness when few did."

His mouth pursed primly, as though he hid his real expression. "History is written by witnesses. The story is all, Madonna. If there are no good primary sources, all analysis is flawed."

"I know," I said. "It is times like these that show who we really are. You are a scholar. And a very brave man." I leaned in and kissed his cheek. "Thank you."

I passed through into the camera, where the fire had been lit and all was warm. Rodrigo's bed had been moved back from the Castel

Sant'Angelo, though some of the other furniture was still missing. Tomorrow, I thought. I settled down to wait.

It was longer than I thought. The room was toasty and the familiar bed comfortable. I meant to stay awake, but I fell asleep against the bolsters. I woke when the door opened. The fire had died down, leaving the room nearly dark, but I knew Rodrigo's step. I sat up.

"Who's there?" he asked sharply.

"It's me."

His voice changed entirely. "Giulia!" He made a lunge for me in the dark, not quite connecting, and we nearly bumped heads, but that gave me my bearings and I kissed the top of his head as he got my shoulder.

"What other woman were you expecting?" I asked teasingly.

"You are not supposed to be in Rome! Have you ever, ever, ever obeyed me in anything?" Each ever was punctuated with a kiss.

"It's not actually my fault this time," I said, trying to pull him closer without crushing me. "Savelli sold me to Bracciano."

He stopped, trying to see my face in the dark. "Giulia."

"So I had to escape," I said matter-of-factly. "I spent the night hiding in the hypocaust of the Baths of Caracalla, which is not comfortable. Did you know that Bracciano won't fit in a hypocaust?"

"I certainly wouldn't." He held me tight, and I could feel his heartbeat. "Cesare said Savelli was honest."

"Cesare was wrong," I said. "But the gates were closed. I had to hide in the city, so I did. You remember the Sarfati family?" He nodded. "I've been with them the whole time."

"You terrify me," he said.

"I terrify you? I was terrified for you!" I said. "I thought you would be killed." I kissed his ear, which was what seemed to be handy.

"It did look bad for a while."

I sat up, holding him at arms' length, my hands on his forearms. "That path is closed," I said, all amusement leaving my voice. "You will not be killed by the French. You will not be canonized. There will be no St. Alexander the Martyr."

"I suppose the poor alum miners will have to do without me," he said ruefully. "I'd much rather live."

"I would rather you did, too," I said. "And moreover, so would everyone who would have been killed if the city had been sacked, or they had been deported back to Spain or given over to Savonarola when della Rovere exalted him. They will never know how close we came to that abyss, or if they do, they will forget in a few short years."

"Posterity won't thank me," Rodrigo said. He shrugged. "Well, I suppose God would rather have a live pope than a dead martyr. I'll take this as a vote of confidence from God. There is still Savonarola and Bracciano, and the little problem of the huge French army which just marched south against Naples. I've fended Charles off, not defeated him." He turned round on the bed, propping up against the headboard and the bolsters and held out an arm for me. I came and curled into his left side as I usually did.

"And Bracciano?"

"Went with them, of course." He put his arm around me, ducking his face against my hair. "He's certainly no longer Gonfaloniere, though Bracciano and the other estates are still his, at least until I confiscate them for treason against his sworn overlord. He bet everything on my deposition. Imagine his chagrin that I'm still here."

"I can imagine it very well," I said. The Furies would pursue him, and it was because of his own actions. I was merely her voice. "I understand Charles of France doesn't trust him."

"Would you?" Rodrigo asked. "Della Rovere's gone too, his papers still unserved. Oddly enough, nobody seems to want to take a vote. He bet everything on my deposition too. If I were him, I'd not set foot in Rome anytime soon."

I laughed. "And I expect Ascanio Sforza is here, loyal and steadfast, at your right hand."

"Of course he is. My good Vice-Chancellor. But let me tell you it was expensive to get rid of the King of France. Nineteen mule loads of treasure to 'assist' in his expedition. Tribute, really. And Cesare to accompany them."

I shook my head. "It's a lot of money. With Cesare as a French hostage."

Rodrigo snorted. "Cesare will be loose by this time tomorrow. And the first two mules have already made their way home. They got lost, apparently."

"So seventeen mule loads of treasure. A hundred thousand ducats or thereabouts out of the Vatican treasury?"

"None," Rodrigo said smugly. "The chests are full of rocks." I craned my head to boggle at him. "Only the first two had valuables in them, the ones that somehow unfortunately got lost. The other boxes are literally boxes of rocks. Cesare opened the first two to show them fabulous gold and plate. They didn't check all the rest."

I started laughing and couldn't stop. "Imagine the French king when he sees them...."

"He won't be happy," Rodrigo said. "But kings are supposed to pay tribute to the Church, not the other way around. He extorted me. I cheated him. Fair's fair."

"You are the worst, most awful, most clever and brilliant man." I kissed him soundly. Truly there was no one in the world like Rodrigo Borgia.

"I like to think so," he said modestly.

"I don't know how you did it," I said. "I saw you with the King of France and I still don't know."

"How did you see that?"

"The robing room of the Choir Chapel," I said. "I was trying to slip into the Vatican, but then you were in the nave, so I ran back into the robing room when you came that way, and I heard the whole thing."

"Well." Rodrigo was oddly still, as though I had admitted to spying on lovemaking.

"I could see a little of it. I knew you were going to bring in Charlemagne before you said it. But the rest...." I couldn't quite put it into words. "It wasn't just being a player. It was...."

"...grace?" he said. "My sweet, I had nothing else to give, except to say, 'make me Your instrument' and then play as best I could."

I nodded slowly. Of course I had seen that luminescence in him, but I was used to it. "You were exactly what he wanted to see but it wasn't an act. It wasn't a mask. It was a mirror."

He huffed as though he would laugh. "Everyone tells themselves stories about themselves. Some of them are truer than others, but everyone imagines the narrative they're part of. That can be bad or good. What you're calling being a mirror is showing someone the best self that they imagine themselves to be. Ascanio imagines himself a canny, sophisticated antagonist, an Odysseus. Ferrandino is the hero of the piece, the role for the leading man, a bold young swordsman who will defend those he loves and respects, true to the end. Charles of France wants to be Charlemagne, peerless paladin and warrior king. In short, he wants to conquer people and be loved for it, which is something of a contradiction!"

I stroked his wrist, the back of his hand. "And so you play the scene they imagine. You are Pope Leo for Charles and Priam for Ferrandino and the sophisticated fellow antagonist for Ascanio."

"And each of them is who they want to be, their best selves. That's the only way I can explain it." He relaxed against me like a cat gentled by a touch.

I thought I understood. "When I was captured by the French, I was the prisoner of Captain Yves d'Allegre. He sent for me to speak with me alone, and I feared what would happen or what I would need to do. I knew I was playing for my life – for all our lives, really. Dionisio and Tina and Adriana and everyone with me. I knew that somehow I had to keep us from being turned over to Bracciano or from being used against you." He started to speak but I forestalled him. "He had a dinner prepared for us, but not privately. The tent flaps were open so that everyone could see that it was decent. I could see what he meant, what he wanted to be. He wants to be the perfect knight, to be Galahad or Lancelot. The *prieux chevalier*. And so I had to be Oriana." Rodrigo smiled. "The gallant lady captured by the enemy, steadfast and virtuous, honest and honorable. And once I started being Oriana, it was easy. We were dancing. We were moving to the same music. We understood each other. Is that what it feels like for you?"

"Exactly that," Rodrigo said.

"I wasn't lying. I wasn't deceiving him, except that I wasn't sure you'd ransom me. Every word I said was true. But they were the right words. He could only answer them by being the man I presumed he was." I kept stroking his hand. "That man would treat me honorably and ransom me to you. I gave him the opportunity to be the noble man he wished to be."

Rodrigo nodded. "Yes. People want to be better. Well, many of them anyway. The Church's job isn't to stamp out flaws, but for everyone to be a little better than their worst. Not perfect. Just better."

"The eyes of love," I said. "People want to be seen with love." He saw me with love, each and every part of me I wanted to explore, angel or succubus. "And that is the difference," I said slowly. "Evil twists everything to the eyes of hate. There are always two stories you can tell, the best one and the worst one. Everyone can play their best or worst self. The brave young hero can be bloody-sworded Achilles full of wrath, dishonoring the bodies of his enemies. The wise king can be the presumptuous tyrant. The loving wife can be the harpy and the bold maiden the stupid child."

"I don't use it that way," Rodrigo said, and then added more honestly, "at least I try not to."

"Because you belong to God," I said. "And you use it in His service, a consecration." It was clear now. "You try to build. Pacis Cultor – you try to make peace. You're imperfect and selfish and always luxurious and sensual, but you want the world to be a beautiful place, not a hellscape to punish the unworthy."

"Who would want to live in a hellscape, my darling?" Rodrigo asked, but his tone wasn't light. "I live here. I'd rather the world was a happy place."

"A beautiful masque, a place of joy, full of paintings and nice meals and happy people having happy babies to bless." I smiled, ducking my face to kiss the back of his hand. He must have been a sunny child like Lucrezia. His father's death had broken his world, so he tried to put it back together, to mend every shattered thing more beautiful than it had been before. 'Everybody happy' was a thing he said at the end of one of his elaborate machinations, but it truly was the goal. A successful scheme ended with everyone better off than they started. Only sometimes it couldn't work. "Savonarola hates the world. He does the same thing you do, only in reverse."

"Savonarola isn't my biggest problem at the moment," Rodrigo said. "But yes, we are unalterably opposed. Hatred of beauty has always been a strain of belief and cannot be allowed to thrive. It is heresy, pure and simple. It is opposed to Christ, that man who embraced all who came to Him and feasted with His friends and made His mother happy by making wine at a wedding when they ran out. Christ loved the world. That's the point. That He loved people enough to die for them. Not that He made them suffer for being less than perfect. The eyes of hate indeed."

"And Bracciano has made a bargain with Typhon," I said. "Destruction for the love of destruction."

"I will have to deal with Savonarola later." He shrugged. "Bracciano...."

"I will take care of Bracciano," I said. I pulled back enough to look up at him, and perhaps he heard the shadow in my voice, the timbre that was not entirely me. "Bracciano is mine."

He hesitated as though he meant to say something else, then bent his head with a smile. "Then Bracciano is yours, my sweet."

"Thank you, Rodrigo." I had no idea how I would do it, but I was determined I would bring Bracciano down. He had underestimated me one time too many.

He kissed the top of my head. "When everything was darkest, you came back to me."

"This is where I want to be," I said. "Besides, I miss Shadow. I want to know how the story ends. Do you think they live happily ever after?"

"Probably. With enough vicissitudes to provide plot." There was a smile in his voice.

"We will have to find out," I said. "I anticipate that it will take many nights' play." I rested against him, breathing him in.

"You are one of a very few people who can weave the story as I do," he said quietly. "It's intoxicating to receive it." Rodrigo stroked the back of my hand absently. "When we were first together, you thought me wholly admirable, but I knew someday I'd fall from your grace. You thought me perfect, and of course I'm not. But how I enjoyed being the man you imagined me to be!" He leaned his head sideways against mine.

I laced my fingers with his, leaning against his shoulder. I had thought of how to say this during the weeks I hid in the city. "I loved you as a young woman loves her first love – unreservedly, idealistically, consumingly. And yes, I thought you were perfect. Of course I would find out you're not." I held his hand tight. "But now I love you with a more mature love, the love of a woman for a man who shares her life, the father of her child, her dear companion. I love you no less passionately than I did. But I love you more wholly, more fully, and more truthfully. You are exactly the man I imagine you to be, and I will love you for the rest of my life and beyond." I turned my face up to his. "I am not your first love, but I will be your last."

"My Giulia." I felt him smile against me. "I need you."

I put my hand to the side of his face. Of course he did. It was a weakness to need a woman, to give anyone such power over him. I could be trusted with this power. I knew how to say it in that moment, how to knit all the strands together. "My dear, let me create an enchantment for you. In a day or two, when I have my house in order, I will plan an evening. Let me be your mirror."

"All right," he said, and I heard both curiosity and anticipation in his voice. "Is there anything you want me to do?"

"Wear black velvet," I said. "I will arrange everything else."

MONDAY NIGHT, the second day of February, seemed an ideal time. Sunset was five and a half hours after noon, so Compline would ring six and a half hours after noon and be over by the end of the seventh hour. It would be full dark but not late. I sent word that I would expect him after Compline, and Rodrigo sent a note back that he would have nothing on his schedule from then until Terce the next morning, giving us two hours after sunrise before he needed to be back in the Vatican and dressing for the day. In short, we would have almost fourteen hours together, an amazing luxury.

I sent a note in reply: *come to the door and knock*. He would know I meant the secret door, and he could easily change out of vestments into black velvet in the robing room. It was a changing room. That's what it was for.

Needless to say, my preparations involved half the household. Captain Rizzoli would have additional guards on duty since His Holiness would be here, and he had his own part to play, which bemused and pleased him both. Our cook had to plan, and Maria was in charge of the necessary household arrangements. She was utterly delighted when I told her what I wanted. "It's been a long year, Madonna Giulia. I'm glad to see it getting back to normal."

"I am too," I said. "And I am very particular about the lighting. Please make certain that Agnesa only lights one candle on the stairs and that none of the servants are visible. Things should seem to appear out of thin air."

"I understand," Maria said. "Like a fairy tale."

"Exactly," I said. We smiled at each other. "I will not be able to see what is happening once it begins, so you must orchestrate."

"Don't worry, Madonna," Maria said. "It's some fun for me to have something to do that's out of the ordinary, and don't we all need fun after this year?"

I embraced her. "Dear Maria. You knew I'd return."

"If God spared you, Madonna," she said. "But He spared us all, through the intervention of His Holiness with the French king, and this is the best way we can thank him. His Holiness, not God. Or...."

"It is quite confusing," I agreed.

Maria frowned, then shook her head, returning from the question of whether Rodrigo and Pope Alexander were exactly the same person. I agreed it was a difficult question. "I've put the big pots of bare branches in the hall and on the stairs," she said. "You're sure that's what you want? They look gloomy."

"Quite sure." I reached up and caressed one of the apple branches in the big pot in my sala. It had been cut three days earlier than the ones on the stairs, the morning after I had the idea, and had now burst into luxuriant, fragrant bloom indoors. "It's the contrast."

"Indeed," she said. "Like you, Madonna, all in white with your hair crowned with gold."

"Yes," I said, "now hurry because it's nearly time."

Maria went downstairs and I looked around my sala. Unlike the hall and stairs, it was well-lit. There were candles on the mantel above the fire and hanging lamps in rose and yellow hung from stands. The window was covered in a big tapestry brought up from downstairs so that it looked like part of the wall. There was a little table with a green cloth set with a golden plate, pitcher, goblet, and knife. On the plate rested one perfect pomegranate. I moved the dishes around a little, arranging them better.

Agnesa, the little maid, came flying in the door. "Madonna," she whispered. "He's here! Only he's in the chapel with Captain Rizzoli because he needed help to change."

Bother, I thought. *Of course he did. His vestments were very compli-cated.* "Tell the flutist to start," I whispered back. She hurried out again, silent in her slippers.

I heard a door open downstairs, then shut again. They were leaving the chapel for the hall. Rodrigo would be standing in the dark-ened hall, every door shut, his eyes adjusting to the dim light from one candle at the foot of the stairs and one on the landing.

Rizzoli cleared his throat and delivered his sole line. "The path through the darkness lies before you, signore." There was the sound of a door, Rizzoli stepping back and going into the foyer to the guard-room. Somewhere above, on the third floor at the top of the stairwell, high and sweet, the notes of the flute began.

Rodrigo would be looking about with bemusement and possibly delight. The hall was bare except for the table with a single candle and the big pots of bare branches, the green walls reflecting little light. It did not look at all as it usually did, welcoming and comfortable. The effect was as though a man had walked into his own house and found it changed.

I heard his step on the stairs, slowly coming up the first flight. A sudden intake of breath, a word. From the third floor landing above Agnesa must have thrown a handful of the apple blossom petals, as though the wind that carried the flute song had wafted them down to land on the empty treads, the dark steps with a single light.

There was his step on the stairs again. Now he could see the light coming from my sala. I stood very straight beside the table, my hands open at my waist like a dancer.

He came to the door. He wore a knee-length black velvet robe over black hose and doublet, and his face changed when he saw me, shifting with wonder as though it was not what he had expected. I stood in a golden bubble of light, a wreath of golden leaves on my hair.

"Welcome, my lord, to your own realm where you have made me queen. You have sought me in the world above, which even now is dark and rainy, sought me lest I slip away from you, but I am here waiting. And here, while all the world grows cold, here the flowers bloom." I stretched out my hand, touching the forced apple blossoms. "Will you not come into my house, my dear lord?"

"With great good will," he said, and his eyes did not leave my face. I thought he looked like the painting in the old Etruscan tomb near Montalto, Pluto with eyes only for his bride, a pomegranate in his hand. Behind, the soft notes of the flute fell like water.

I smiled, myself and not myself, feeling the whisper of power through this like warm wind on my skin. I was not afraid. I was not overwhelmed. I was prepared for this, safe and filled with light. "I have returned to you, sure as the seasons change. I always have, and I always will."

He spoke extemporaneously, but he hardly needed a script. "I am waiting for you. As I always have and always will."

"Then you know what we need." I gestured to the pomegranate on the plate.

He was beaming as he cut it carefully, and I looked at his profile to remember it forever, the lines of his face, his still-fine hands. He pulled it in two, not quite cut through, ruby seeds spilling from their chambers. "For you or for me?"

"For us both." I took half the pomegranate while he held the other. We each ate three seeds. I took a step forward, my eyes never leaving his. The music of the unseen flute still rippled down the stairs. "Like travelers overtaken by a trance," I said. When we touched it was slow and deliberate, as though we moved through the figures in a dance, folding together, the taste of pomegranate on his lips. Familiar, warm, sensual, the brightness of the lamps on my eyelids eclipsed by his head, his arm going around me as I bent like a willow into him.

"Dazzling brightness," he whispered.

"My own dear lord." There were no more words. There was no need for any.

It was a very long kiss. When at last we rested, forehead to forehead, almost of a height, I could not help a little, breathless laugh. "I have always thought you were a very good kisser."

"I'm glad of that." There was that smile, that boyish, insouciant smile that I'd seen too little lately, worn down by worry and strife. Rodrigo lifted his hand to the side of my face. "You are my treasure."

I turned my head and kissed his palm. "As though I were gold in darkness."

"Just so."

I covered his hand with mine. He had not taken off his papal ring, pearls in an ornate setting. Of course. He might put aside his office for a little while, but it was always there. "Come into my room."

I led him into my camera and closed the door. The window was covered with tapestries, lamps of colored glass everywhere, pale gold walls and dark green velvet, an oasis of light and beauty. Outside, it was a cold and rainy night at the beginning of February. In here it was warm. "Summer comes to the lands beneath," I said.

"And lilies spring where you tread." He smiled.

"Actually, apple blossoms," I said, glancing at the pot nearest the bed. "I'm afraid I don't have lilies."

"A minor point." I drew him down beside me. So sweet, so tender, as though we walked in a dream, meeting him in each pause, in each breath, in each movement. He had once created this enchantment for me, Proserpina spirited away. Now she returned, Queen of the

Underworld to her rightful place, not abducted but seeking the path in joy, running into the caves that opened before her. Eyes closed, his body moving on mine, I felt again what I had felt leaping from my horse before the walls and running into his arms, the rightness of it, the sense of the world knit whole. Not his initiate, but his lady. I knew the shape of his broad shoulders, the way his breath caught, the rhythms of his hands.

"My own," I whispered. I do not know what he answered.

Afterwards, we lay together sprawled amid the sheets. Outside, a gust of rain blew against the window. He laid his head on my shoulder. We simply lay still for a while.

There was a rattle of dishes in the sala, and he tensed. "It is just my little goblins making dinner appear," I said. "Dishes that will keep, if we don't want them immediately."

I felt him smile against me. "You create quite an enchantment."

"I learned from you," I said, and closed my eyes.

ACKNOWLEDGMENTS

I would like to thank so many people for their support of this book, including my long-time readers who have encouraged me at every step. I would particularly like to thank my pre-readers Joss Davis, Victoria Francis, Eric Jungst and Lena Strid for their feedback as I worked.

I am also indebted to Samantha Morris, who has kindly shared her original research on the Borgias with me and steered me to various sources. Her work on Lucrezia Borgia was particularly helpful. I am also appreciative of Dr. Katharine Fellows, who shared with me her doctoral thesis on Rodrigo Borgia in his years as vice-chancellor, and her work on the Papal Election of 1492. All mistakes are of course my own.

I would also like to thank both my editors. Many thanks to Athena Andreadis for her faith in this series, The Memoirs of the Borgia Sibyl, and her timely insights. I would also like to thank my second editor for this book, Melissa Scott, whose thoughts and comments have been invaluable to shaping it, and who has contributed at every stage of the work.

Most of all, I would like to thank Amy Griswold, my amazing partner, without whom this would never be. From concept to finish, this book would not exist without her.

COMING SOON: A GOLDEN BRANCH

THE FOURTH BOOK OF THE MEMOIRS OF THE BORGIA SIBYL

A Captured City, an Exiled Prince, and the Pope's Own Sibyl

1495: Rome has survived the French invasion by grace and the wiles of the Borgia Pope Alexander VI, Giulia's beloved Rodrigo. Giulia stands once again at his side, having reclaimed her power as a sibyl and a wielder of heretical magic. But this fragile reprieve cannot last. Naples has fallen to the French assault. To save Italy from ruin, Rodrigo's only hope is to forge an alliance between all the powers that oppose France: Spain, Venice, the Papal States, and the treacherous Sforza family.

The fragile alliance cannot succeed unless they retake the captured city of Naples. Acting as Rodrigo's agent in Naples, Giulia hopes to find a way to win the city back. But the armies of the exiled prince of Naples are vastly outnumbered. The few Spanish troops at his command cannot hope to assault the city walls. And Lord Bracciano, Giulia's old enemy, holds Naples for the French with magical allies that are both powerful and cruel.

And yet there are other powers in Naples, older and stronger than Bracciano's demonic magic. Beneath Mt. Vesuvius lies the ancient home of the Sibyl of Cumae, the guardian of the underworld. Only

Giulia can walk the Sibyl's path and claim her ancient power—but one wrong step on that deadly path might be her last.